THE BUCKSKINS

by

Albert R. Booky

REAL WEST

FICTION SERIES

Sunstone Press • Santa Fe • New Mexico

Dedicated to my wife, Jessa'Lee in appreciation for her unfailing support and encouragement.

Library of Congress Cataloging in Publication Data:

Booky, Albert R., 1925-
    The buckskins / by Albert R. Booky. – 1st. ed.
       p.   cm.
    ISBN 0-86534-125-7   : $10.95
    I. Title.
PS3552.06436B83   1991
813'.54–dc20   90-33902
                                                                           CIP

Published in 1991 by SUNSTONE PRESS
                Post Office Box 2321
                Santa Fe, NM 87504-2321 / USA

INTRODUCTION

The author has been unable to find any historical data which would indicate that French trapers lent assistance in the relocation of the Wyandot tribe, but there were many events which transpired in the West which were never recorded. The fact that they were not recorded doesn't mean that they couldn't have happened. What we do know, however, is that the French trappers had many dealings with the various tribes while pursuing their search for pelts. Many of them married Indian women and became indistinguishable from the Indians themselves in their daily lives.

It is also true that the battle described between the Tonkawas and the Comanche nation is entirely the invention of the author's imagination, although, these two peoples must have had many encounters with one another which were not recorded by the white man, leaving one to imagine how fierce and destructive some of these encounters could have been. Before the arrival of the white man, there must have been many major encounters as well as minor ones upon the plains which will remain forever unrecorded, proving that history does repeats itself and that there is nothing new under the sun.

CHAPTER I

"**P**ittsburgh, 'the gateway of the West', it's called, and that's where I'm headed, and points beyond! You coming with me?" The young man's eyes danced with excitement and intense interest as he waited for an answer from his friend.

"Are you crazy? That's unmapped territory and it is mostly unexplored and uninhabited, except by Indians and some crazy loonies like you! You're not talking me into this latest scheme of yours, Nat Cochran, not by a long shot." His friend grinned as he remembered other schemes he had been talked into over the years. "Besides, that country around Pittsburgh is full of Germans, and if that's not bad enough, those barbaric Scotch-Irish are almost as plentiful."

His friend stared at him in disgust. "You've been listening to Cyrus Thumpskin again, letting him fog your mind with his inaccurate and prejudiced theories about the country west of here and the people stouthearted enough to live there. The West is for men of decision, courage, and imagination. It is there that young men like you and I can make our mark just as Patrick Henry, Thomas Jefferson, George Washington, and all of the other pioneers of our country have done. This area is getting crowded though, and while those men were born to be Englishmen, we're American born and bred — in this new country. It is for us to make our new way of life come alive with strength and confidence, and that shouldn't be so hard for us, right?"

Nat readjusted his back against the huge maple which towered over them and tossed a small pebble into the smooth water of Stem's Pond.

His friend leaned against the same tree as he stood looking down at his friend of fifteen years. "I'm sorry, Nat," Garry spoke in an apologetic tone, "you're going to have to go this one alone." His arm dropped to his side and he turned slowly to look at the pond. He continued to stare into the sparkling water as he continued, "I'm all my folks have; if I were to go with you who would care for them? Who would be here to help them when they grow old? No, Nat, I can't leave them. I'll have to stay here."

"I understand, Garry." Nat rose to his feet and threw his last stone into the water.

Garry turned his head slowly toward the western mountains which were covered with the cool forests of various shades of green. From this distance they appeared impenetrable and forbidding, a distant fortress which only men such as his friend could storm. Garry turned back to his friend and said, "You belong out there, Nat." He motioned with a jerk of his head to the distant mountains. "Your grandfather was one of the first Americans to set foot in that hostile land. He and those others who were with George Rogers Clark and his Rangers.

Nat placed his hand on his friend's shoulder comfortingly as he told him, "If I were in your place, I'd do the same. If my parents were still alive, I'd have no choice but to join you in raising tobacco and cotton. My family never did know too much about the part my granfather played in the George Rogers Clark expedition into the northern part of Ohio." He looked sober now as he continued. "All we really know is that he was wounded in the attack on Vincennes and that he later died from those wounds. We only know that a French family by the name of Marquette cared for grandpa until he died and that he'd have died much sooner if it had not been for their care.

"We know even less about how my father died in the War of 1812, and I never did know my mother for she died giving birth to me. Thanks be to God that I had an older brother who cared for me; otherwise I could have ended up in one of those slave dens called an orphanage."

"You don't suppose," Garry asked his friend, "that you will go as far as Pittsburgh and try to establish yourself there and go no farther? I understand that it's a thriving city of over two thousand people, and growing rapidly. It has grown more rapidly than Steubenville, Wheeling, or Marietta, and I also understand that it has become a shipbuilding center, among other things. There should be plenty of opportunity for an ambitious fellow such as you."

"No, Garry," his friend grinned ruefully, "Pittsburgh is not for me. I'm aiming for the unknown and unconquered country west of the Mississippi River. I can't settle for less than that."

"But," Garry interrupted, "that used to be Spanish territory and besides they're Papists. They may still have the Inquisition out there. No, I forgot that Jefferson purchased the Louisiana Territory back in 1803, didn't he?"

6

"Sounds similar to some of the conditions in the east, doesn't it?" Nat grinned at his friend grimly, "When we do it, it's supposed to be all right. We've not always been the most tolerant of people about religion and we can't see the similarities to what went on in the Spanish colonies. Jefferson was right, you know; people should have freedom of religion. A person should be judged as an individual and not because of his religious beliefs or his race, for that matter."

Garry returned Nat's grin with a sober expression. "I agree, Nat, when you put it that way. Sometimes I don't think things out to a logical conclusion."

"Be careful, my friend," Nat said with a smile, "you're beginning to use reason; you're beginning to think. If we were in Europe, that could be dangerous, but thank God we're not in the old country, but in America. And thank God that many, but not nearly enough of us, are beginning to think for ourselves."

"Too few, I'm afraid," Garry answered.

"It takes time," Nat told him, "anything worth its salt does not come easily; if it did, it wouldn't be worth much. I once heard that Benjamin Franklin, using a quote from an ancient Greek, said that what is good does not come easily. Of course the ancient Greek and Benjamin Franklin had a better way of saying it than I do," he chuckled.

"I certainly hope so," Garry grinned back.

"I guess that's the main reason why I want to go west," Nat continued, "I want to think for myself and I don't want to have to justify my thinking to anyone else. I don't want to hear people criticize other people's customs and think that their way are the only ways. I want to live my life as I see fit and I want to let others do the same. I cannot understand how or why some people can be so intolerant of others, especially after they themselves experienced so much intolerance before they came to this country. At least that's why they were supposed to have come, but I guess people have short memories.

"I guess that's why you and I are friends," Garry remarked, "we think alike on most things and have respect for one another's opinions. I enjoy these talks, but this isn't getting my chores done, so I guess I'd better head for home. When do you plan to leave, Nat?"

"At sunup tomorrow; I'm packed and itching to move," Nat told his friend with a grin.

Nat reached the Monongahela River at three o'clock in the afternoon. It had been nearly nine hours since he had said his goodbyes to his brother and his brother's family.

He was riding along an old Indian trail which wasn't much wider than his horse. It was so infrequently used that the underbrush was beginning to reclaim it. Small limbs seemed to extend their thin growth outward in a continuing effort to reach a similiar growth on the opposite side of the trail, and Nat had to push back the encroaching limbs repeatedly as he rode. Eventually the narrow way tied into a trail which seemed to be more heavily traveled as it paralleled the Monongahela River. Tree stumps in the wider trail had to be avoided frequently and Nat carefully guided his horse around them.

Nat's clothing was entirely of homespun. He cradled in his left arm a rifle which had been a gift from the storekeeper, Mr. Parmerton, who had given it to him as a going away present. Nat's name and the year of his birth were burned into the stock. Nat had a feeling that Mr. Parmerton for whom he had worked, shared his longing to go west, a dream that his many responsibilities made impossible.

"What do you say we rest a spell, Cricket?" His horse was a young black gelding, not quite four, and the only white hairs on him consisted of a white snip on his nose. Cricket showed some Morgan in him, was short and powerful, with a lot of staying power. As Nat reined in and loosened the reins, the gelding quickly lowered his head to graze on the lush grass at his feet.

Nat dismounted and loosening his cinch, unsaddled as his horse grazed and then led him to the river's edge where he could drink. He looked around as the horse drank, searching for anything unusual. Off to his right, he spotted the remains of what was apparently a deer; only some hide and a few bones remained.

"Cricket," Nat told his partner, "I think you'll like this." He picked up the best rib bone he could find and taking his tin cup from his pack, he dipped water from the river and let it run over the sweaty back of his horse and used the rib to wipe the water and sweat from the animal's hide. Nat repeated this procedure and then moved to the other side, all the while talking softly.

"That is the mark of a good man," a voice said behind Nat. Nat turned quickly in that direction as the voice continued, "but it also shows his ignorance of the frontier. One of the laws of survival out here is that one should never be out of reach of his rifle, which you clearly are, laddie!"

The stranger saw before him a stockily built young man of not much over five feet eight inches but large boned and powerful. His grey eyes were separated by a straight nose which was extremely sensitive to odor, a good trait to have for one who was headed for the frontier. That, the stranger couldn't know, but he did see that the young man's eyes were quick and penetrating. His hands were not large, but on the small side, with long, thin fingers. He wore his brown hair cut just below his ears.

In his turn, Nat saw a frontiersman sitting on his horse about thirty or forty feet down the trail behind him. He looked to be of medium height and from his head to his toes, he wore buckskin. He held the barrel of his rifle in his right hand with the stock resting on his shoulder. Saddlebags were tied behind his saddle and over them was draped a colorful blanket, also tied down. High Indian moccasins extended almost to his knees and a rawhide thong wrapped around his upper leg held the moccasins in place. His long buckskin jacket would have reached to the tops of his moccasins if it had been fastened. A tomahawk was slipped through the left side of the red sash which he wore instead of a belt, and Nat could see the handle of a pistol stuck under the right side of the sash. A powder horn hung under his right arm. His fur hat was decorated with an eagle's feather and a hunting knife in its sheath hung from his saddle horn. All this Nat took in as he stood with an arm thrown over Cricket's back.

"It's a good thing that I'm not a hostile Indian or even worse, a white highwayman. If I were, you'd be dead by now, your carcass left for the vultures or whatever varmint came across it."

Nat gave a quick glance at his rifle which leaned against a tree some twenty feet back from the river. His eyes turned quickly once more to stare at the stranger. He may still kill me, thought Nat. Maybe he's playing with me as a cat with a mouse. If he intends to kill me, I'd better develop a plan in an attempt to foil his. Anything would be better than not making some sort of struggle. I've got it, I'll use Cricket as a shield and try to rush him, but I'd better try to draw him a little closer first.

"Have you developed a plan, yet, laddie?" The stranger grinned as he spoke. "You show promise, that you do, but your horse can be spooked pretty easy you know, and then you would be completely exposed. What would you do then? Or do you have a backup plan? If you haven't, you're as good as dead right now."

"How did you know what I was thinking?" Nat peered over the back of his horse in astonishment.

"If I did not think this way, I would not be alive today. Outguessing a potential enemy is essential to a frontiersman's survival and as you can see, I have survived, at least up until now."

The stranger lifted his right leg over the horn of his saddle and slid to the ground. "The time to analyze me is over; either you have come to the conclusion that I am a friend or an enemy, and I know that you have not come to the second conclusion. Am I right, laddie?"

"How do you do that?" Nat added, "You're right; I had decided that you mean me no harm."

"The name is Maurees Marquette," he said as he slid his bridle reins over his horse's head and led him toward Nat. "My friends call me Rees, and what might be your name?"

"Nat Cochran," Nat replied, "and my friends call me Nat." He could not repress a grin as he realized he was trying to impress Rees with an answer similar to his.

Rees shot a friendly smile toward Nat and said, "You sound just like an echo."

Nat returned the smile and said nothing, but his eyes studied the man's manner and particularly his dress.

"Do you approve?" Reese asked as he reached the young man.

Nat smiled and shook his head ruefully, "How do you do that? You read my mind as though I were talking out loud."

"First things first, laddie," Reese said as he started to lead his horse into the underbrush east of the trail. Without looking back after he had walked perhaps a dozen yards, he said, "Well, don't just stand there like a frightened deer; get your belongings and follow me."

Nat stared at Reese with a dazed expression and his voice brought him back to reality. He threw his saddle blanket and then his saddle over his horse's back and quickly cinched up his saddle. He led Cricket to the tree where his rifle rested and then mounted and followed in the direction which Rees had taken. When he caught up with his new companion, Rees had his horse unsaddled, and his saddle, blanket, and saddlebags rested against the trunk of a large tree.

"You fetch some dry firewood and I'll get us something to eat, and don't build a large fire; we don't need any visitors."

"Right." Nat's reply sounded as though he were a soldier answering an officer's commands.

Rees smiled to himself and disappeared into the underbrush and when he returned, he carried a turkey over his shoulder.

"I didn't hear any shots," Nat said.

Rees just smiled and dropped the turkey on the ground near Nat. "You do know how to clean a turkey, I hope." Rees looked over his shoulder at Nat as he removed his pipe from a catch-all leather pouch which hung from his neck. He looked around for a good place to sit down.

"Aren't you going to lend me a hand?" Nat asked as he began to pluck the turkey.

"I'm nearly forty years old, laddie, and I've done my apprenticeship. If you intend to be the like of me, your schoolin' has just begun."

"How do you know I want to be like you, and why do you call me laddie? Are you a Scotsman? They call young men and boys, laddie."

"The first question deserves no answer, because we both know the answer to that one. But you do deserve an answer to the second question, but before I answer it, I need an answer from you."

"What might that be?" Nat looked up from his job with a handful of feathers in his hand.

"Your name, laddie; I knew a Cochran once."

"Oh," Nat replied without looking at Rees, "I have a brother living in Virginia. Perhaps you had dealings with him."

"I've never been in Virginia but once," Reese answered as he puffed on his pipe. "Have any of your family been north of the Ohio.?" He studied the young man as he spoke.

"My father was in the War of 1812, and my grandfather was with George Rogers Clark." Nat was through with the plucking and cleaning of the turkey and was now placing it on a spit over the small fire.

"That's it . . . I should have figured it out earlier. Let the turkey roast and sit down over here. I've something to tell you that I know will interest you."

As the two men rested their backs against the huge oak, Reese began his story. "I was born in Vincennes, on the Wabash River, in Quebec Territory. You see, at that time all of the land north of the Ohio River was made part of Quebec by an English law before you Americans gained your independence from the British. My father was a trapper and a good one, too, maybe the best. He had made friends with the Indians in the area; he did not cheat, steal from them, or insult them the way some did. He was known and trusted by the Shawnee, Delware, Miami, Wyandot, Winnebago, Chippewa and Ottawa, and in a few cases by the Chickasaw and Cherokees. You see, laddie, the Chickasaws and the Cherokees lived way south of the other tribes that I have just mentioned and the territory between the two was left vacant of all Indian settlements. It was agreed upon by all concerned that it was to be a hunting ground for all tribes.

"Anyway, getting to the point I wanted to make, during the war with the British, the English stirred up the Indians against the Americans who had begun to settle on land which the Indians considered their own. The Americans suffered many losses at the hands of the Indians until a young man by the name of George Rogers Clark, the son of the Virginia planter, decided to do something about the Indian menace, of course with General Washington's permission and encouragement. They defeated the Hair Buyer, which is what Clark and his men called Lieutenant Colonel Hamilton. He had been paying the Indians for American scalps.

"To make a long story short, the twenty-six year old Clark, with only one-hundred and seventy-five men was able to outsmart and out-maneuver Hamilton, defeating him and sending him back to Virginia a prisoner. One of Clark's men was your grandfather and I can confirm that because he lived in my home under my mothers' care for quite a while. He was almost dead from the loss of blood when my mother undertook to nurse him, volunteered in fact, but he soon recovered and left us to rejoin Major Clark. We never saw or heard from him after that."

"You mean to tell me that your parents saved my grandfather's life?" Nat rose in excitement.

"I wasn't even born, laddie, at the time, so I cannot remember as much about your grandfather as you and I both wish that I could.

"Thank you for telling me this, Rees, I appreciate it, and I want to thank you on behalf of my family for the kindness which your folks gave to my grandfather."

Rees looked at Nat, smiled and nodded.

"Could you tell me more about George Rogers Clark and his rangers from what you remember hearing your folks say?"

Rees rose and walked over to prod the turkey and turn it on the spit, then resumed his seat and once more filled his pipe. "Well, I'll tell you as much as I can remember hearing. At Vincennes, the people hated the oppressive rule of Hamilton and his British garrison, but the young Virginian and his one hundred and seventy-five men dressed in their buckskins were on the last leg of their journey to liberate the fort and put an end to Hamilton's scheming with the Indians.

"From what I've always heard, the French inhabitants of the village near the fort knew well in advance of the British that the Americans were coming. They whispered among themselves the news of the approaching Americans as they passed one another on the streets of the village. Pride in their heritage and hatred of the British assured that the secret would be well guarded.

"A trapper, newly arrived at the village was pressed for news of the Americans, and as he kept a weather eye open for the British, he told them what he knew of the Americans. 'Ah, these Americans, they're a new breed all right, they live, breathe, and sleep thinking of freedom. They seem to be obsessed with it. You can't seem to stop them, you shoot them but they won't die; they just rise up again and march on with that radiant look of a free man on their faces. They'll suffer any hardship, fight any number to protect and spread their belief as stated in their Declaration of Independence.

"The leader of this force which is approaching is young Clark and he is something else. He's young as are most of them, and he is a natural born leader; his men seem to trust him completely. He has the knack of requiring and getting more from his men than anyone else in his position might do. He sets a good example for his men and he's always cheerful and shares everything with them. If a man appears hungry, he will give him his

12

food and if a man is cold, he will share his blanket. Ah, they're a good bunch of men! Each one seems to have the feeling that it is his personal responsibility to protect his country as if it were his little sister or mother. Heaven help Hamilton when they arrive!"

Rees paused to relight his pipe once more and after taking several puffs, continued, "You understand that what I've just told you was what my father told me. The news which the trapper brought the village was encouraging but the people were well aware of the obstacles which the Americans faced. The winter had been hard and the melting snow and then the heavy rains had caused flooding everywhere. Fields were under water and the rivers overflowed and the countryside was one vast swamp. How the Americans could cope with such overwhelming odds over such terrain troubled the villagers, but the trapper seemed confident that they would prevail and the settlers returned to their homes feeling hopeful.

"Your grandfather later told us of some of the hardships they had faced as they waded in water from ankle deep to having to swim the rivers. They were constantly wet and then when the weather worsened, ice formed on their clothes and why they didn't die of exposure is a miracle. They tried to keep each others' morale up by joking and talking about how history would record their victory over the British when they reached Vincennes. The support which the French were giving them was not merely passive, for they kept them informed as to the British strengths and weaknesses. Also, luckily, the Indians were beginning to back away from their friendship with Hamilton.

"As the Americans approached Vincennes, among their ranks were French volunteers who had joined them. Jokes were exchanged between the two nationalities and a feeling of camaraderie prevailed as they encountered new hardships together in the form of ice blocks in the rivers which they pushed out of the way as they held their rifles and gunpowder high over their heads. Exposure and fatigue began to take a toll and Clark ordered that canoes be made to carry the sick. When they reached some high ground, he sent out hunting parties to try to find game. And when the men had dried out and had food in their bellies, they pushed toward Vincennes once more.

"When Clark and his force finally reached Vincennes, he sent a small group to secure a position east of the fort, another to the southwest, and still another to the north. Some of the French volunteers were sent to get all the munitions that they could, for they were badly needed. Clark expected, and he was proven to be right, that the British would have attempted to seize any such stores which the villagers might have, but the villagers had anticipated such a move on the part of the British and had hidden their arms.

"While this was going on, Clark didn't have to prepare his men for the attack, but if anything had to calm their intense feelings against Hamilton. They had not come this far, under unspeakable conditions, to look upon Hamilton with anything less than deadly intent. The job they'd set themselves was about to be done and neither hell or high water was going to stop them. They itched to settle the score and their hearts were warmed as they saw the settlers run to swell their ranks. They shook hands eagerly and thanked them for their support for they realized they would need it.

"Well, Clark positioned his men so close to the fort that the British cannon could only fire over them and then gave the order to attack. After two days of intense fighting. Hamilton finally surrendered to the American Rangers and the British flag was lowered and the American flag hoisted, never to be lowered again."

Nat was silent after Rees stopped talking. Finally he spoke, "Thank you for telling me about them, Rees, it's inspiring to learn about the success of fellow Americans."

Reese glanced over at Nat, smiled and nodded and asked, "Now where did that 'laddie' bit come from? You know as well as I do that it is not a French expression, but I used to called that by some of the British who remained at Vincennes and I liked it. And to answer your last question, why am I headed for Pittsburgh? Well, my trading partner, an American, died from an Indian arrow and just before he died, he asked me to see that his share of the profits from our trapping be given to his sister who lived in Richmond. I learned after I got to Richmond that she and her husband had moved to Pittsburgh."

Nat turned and looked at the saddlebags which lay across Rees' saddle.

"It's all there, laddie, nine thousand dollars in gold, and half of it for Mrs. Hartman. Now all I have to do is locate the lady and then be on my way." Reese watched Nat closely after finishing his last sentence to see if Nat's reaction would be what he expected.

Nat was silent for a few moments and then asked, "Where will you go after you find Mrs. Hartman?"

"Back to where everything and everybody answers to no one except themselves. Where you come and go as free as you please and when you please. Where everything is yours and the air is so fresh and clear and free that every breath of it gives you strength. Where you must stand tall or be cut short by a stronger, more alert, and more cunning adversary. The weak and the timid last but a short time out there west of the Mississippi River."

When will he ask me, thought Nat. I know he is going to ask me. He must be studying me to see if he thinks I have what it takes.

"Well, laddie, what will it be?" Reese removed his pipe from his mouth and blew the smoke upward. "I know that you have it in you if you put your mind to it. As for me, my mind's made up, what will your answer be?"

"You know my answer as well as I do," grinned Nat. "I'm beginning to learn how you think already. You've been studying me and I have met with your approval. Or was it my grandfather who met with your approval?"

"Right on the first count, laddie, though you know how I feel about Clark and the men who followed him.

"I'm a French Canadian mountain man, laddie, and no one can match a French Canadian mountain man. We Marquettes go way back, and we know nothing but trapping and Indian ways. It would be my pleasure to have you along, but I want you to understand from the beginning that my life, and yours, too, if you throw in with me, will be completely alien to anything you've known before, read about, or experienced. As for those people who write about my way of life, well, let's be polite to them and just call them fools. I don't know what they think with, but I know it's not with their brains, but be that as it may, all I know and want is to live and let live. At our first opportunity, we'll have to make you some suitable and practical clothes, like what I'm wearing, but for the time being, what you're wearing will do all right."

Suddenly Rees froze and became as a statue in a seated position.

"What's wrong?"

"Shhh," Rees answered in a whisper, "we've got company and they do not come as friends."

Nat stood up quickly and grabbed his rifle which was leaning against the tree beside him. His eyes searched the forest and underbrush around the camp "Where?" He looked at Reese inquiringly.

"Out there, maybe a hundred and fifty yards," Rees whispered.

"How do you know there's someone out there?" Nat persisted.

"Look around you, laddie, and listen; can you hear or see any birds?"

Nat's eyes and ears searched for any sign of the birds who had flitted from tree to tree earlier, but now he saw and heard none. It was as quiet as if he were deaf and the trees and brush were almost motionless in the still air. The occasional crackle of the fire seemed much louder in the stillness. What little breeze remained seemed to come from the south, the direction in which Reese was looking. Nat could hear Rees inhale slowly and then exhale with his mouth closed. He was attempting to determine with his sense of smell what was out there. His eyes didn't blink, but displayed complete alertness, in fact he reminded Nat of a pointer he'd had back in Virginia.

"They're not Indians and they're not peaceable travelers. I'd guess they're river pirates," Rees finally whispered. "They're aiming to do us no good and they aren't Colonel Fluger's ruffians, either, because he operates only out of Cairo, a small town downriver where the Mississippi and the Ohio rivers join. We're too far from Fluger's stomping grounds, but it could be James Girty, the notorious Pennsylvanian bandit, who is a nephew of the Simon Gerty who has brought shame and disrespect to the rest of the mountain men. No one, they say, has ever whipped him in a fight, he's a tough one, is James Girty."

Rees slowly rose to his feet, whispering, "Laddie, here's your chance to prove yourself and if you fail, you'll never see the mountains west of here. There are three of them; one has the distinct odor of fish about him, one other has a lesser degree of the same odor, but the third, gives off a slight smell of wool, from his clothes, no doubt. He's the cleanest of the three, maybe a new recruit. Laddie, lay down in the middle of that brush over there." Rees pointed to a vigorously growing bush which boasted thick vegetation, leaves growing so close together that they were impenetrable to the eye.

Nat did as he had been told without question and Rees examined the bush to see if Nat were well concealed, meanwhile whispering, "Lay your pistol on the ground handy like and aim your rifle south of camp."

"Where will you be?" Nat asked softly.

"Where I'll have to be," Rees whispered with a grin. He threw more wood on the fire and the fire began to smoke as the wood tossed on it began to smother the flames, but in a short time, the flames shot up as the wood caught fire. Rees had disappeared into the underbrush and Nat lay motionless, hardly breathing, as the tension became almost unbearable and the seconds dragged by, seeming like hours.

Then he heard a voice say, "There's no one here." A man stepped into the clearing about the camp and repeated his earlier observation more softly as his eyes searched the campsite and surrounding area. Now a second man stepped into the clearing and then a third. All carried their rifles at the ready.

"No one here," the second stranger commented as he, too, searched the campsite with his eyes. As he did so, he spotted the saddles and saddle bags. "Well, looka there." He lowered his rifle and started toward the saddle bags. "I'll bet that gold is in those bags!"

The other two men lowered their rifles and ran to join their companion in his eager search. As he unstrapped the saddlebag and reached in, his face lit up with greed as he pulled out a leather pouch and tore it open. His hands slipped through the gold coins as they fell in a heap on the forest floor. Frantically, he emptied the other saddle bag on the ground and other leather pouches spilled out.

"We're rich, we're rich!" The other men fell to their knees and exclaimed excitedly. "How much is here, do you suppose?" One of them looked up at the leader eagerly.

"Enough for me!" He drew two pistols and fired point blank at his companions. From their kneeling positions, they slumped lifeless to the ground with expressions of disbelief still on their faces.

Their killer then holstered his pistols and turned again to the pouches as he muttered to himself in satisfaction, "Girty will think that we all got killed by Injuns. He'll never see this gold!"

"You'll never live to spend it, either," Rees's voice cut into the fevered calculations of the leader as he walked into the clearing at the opposite end of the camp. His rifle lay in the crook of his left arm.

The bandit whirled quickly from his kneeling position and gave Rees the same old stare which Rees had seen a wolf assume when challenged for its freshly killed prey.

"Laddie, be ready to send this varmint under." Rees called in a loud voice as he braced his legs apart and returned the cold stare.

"Who you callin' laddie?" The bandit looked confused and looked quickly around the camp.

"He's talking to me, renegade," Nat said as he readied himself to kill the bandit. The bandit whirled once more, but still saw no one. Suddenly, Nat stood up and the bandit quickly drew his knife and had his hand cocked to release it when Nat fired. The knife clattered to the ground fully ten feet in front of the fallen bandit.

"They must have followed you all of the way from Richmond," Nat said, "but why? How could they have known you carried gold?"

"That's a good question, laddie, for I told no one. We do know one thing for sure, though, and that's if they knew, someone else could know, and so we'd better get to Pittsburgh with all speed for Mrs. Hartman's sake."

A few hours later the two rode through a still, starry night, intent upon delivering the gold to Mrs. Hartman.

"The sooner I rid himself of this gold, the sooner I can rid myself of civilization and the like of those three varmints back there, but believe me, there are plenty more where they came from," Rees commented grimly.

For the most part, they rode silently, watchful. Rees cautioned Nat to watch his horse's ears, for his horse could sense danger before they could, but not to depend upon him completely, and be constantly on the lookout. "Only a fool or a potential dead man leaves things to chance, and I think you're neither."

As the trail narrowed, the older man said, "I'll ride on ahead and you keep a steady fifteen or twenty paces behind me. Remember, take nothing for granted and suspect everything."

Just before sunup, Rees pulled his horse to a stop and pointed to a number of camp fires just west of the road. About a hundred yards ahead they could see a number of people moving about and the clanking of pots and pants could be heard over the murmur of voices. Some of the men could be seen harnessing their teams in preparation for their departure. Nat urged his horse forward to join Rees.

"Quite a large party," he commented softly.

"There's safety in numbers and it's obvious they believe that. Large number also make for a bigger take. Large or small numbers, there's always a chance of danger," Rees replied soberly.

"Which do you believe is the safest?"

"It depends on the circumstances," Rees studied the camp, "This camp is made up of many individuals who probably happened to meet on the road and they have decided that any new addition to their number will add to their safety."

"Sounds like a good think," Nat rose in his stirrups to give his backside a rest.

"Not if one of the new additions has joined the encampment to do harm." Ree turned to Nat and said, "When we reach the camp, do not presuppose that all of those folks are innocent, law-abiding people; they may very well be, but the reverse could also be true."

As the two rode on into the encampment, most of the people looked from their chores briefly and nodded at Nat and Rees, or gave them a quick smile before returning to their duties. Some just glanced up and then returned to their work, displaying neither friendless or hostility.

To one side of the camp and hovering over a small camp fire, sat a lone figure drinking from a tin coffee cup. As he took frequent sips, his eyes stared over the rim of the cup, surveying the encampment. His rifle captured the interest of Rees, for it was different from any which Rees had ever seen. Rees abruptly reined his mount in the man's direction, full of curiosity as to the make of the rifle. As he and Nat approached the stranger, Rees called, "Good morning . . . nice morning." Rees leaned forward, resting his hands on the horn of his saddle, "That's an unusual looking rifle you have there, friend."

The stranger did not answer, but his eyes met those of Rees; they were the kind of eyes which Rees had seen many times before, they were the eyes of a man who studied each man carefully. The stranger raised his cup once more to his lips, but did not take his eyes from those of Rees.

They both sat motionless staring at each other until Nat broke the silence. "My name is Nat Cochran. I'm from Virginia and heading to Pittsburgh and points west. Who might you be?"

The stranger turned toward Nat and placed his cup in the ashes near the fire. "Who's your buckskin friend?" He spoke with a strong German accent.

"I'm sorry, please forgive my bad manners; this is Rees Marquette."

The stranger rose and said, "Sit down. Can I get you some breakfast or at least a cup of coffee? My name is Muller, Otto Muller."

Rees glanced at Nat and said, "We're not going to be impolite and refuse this good man's hospitality, are we?"

"Of course not." Nat dismounted as he spoke, dropping his reins on the ground. Their horses immediately began to graze as their riders moved closer to the fire.

"Please excuse my bad manners, Mr. Rees. I do not usually make a practice of staring at strangers as I did you. I realized from the moment I set eyes on you that you were no ordinary man, and I was trying to determine what kind of man you were."

Rees nodded at Muller, giving him a friendly smile which expressed his understanding. "Well, what conclusions did you come to, Mr. Muller?"

"Please, my friends call me Otto, and I'd be happy if you would drop the Mister."

"The same applies to us." Rees extended his hand toward Otto and at the same time eyed the rifle once more.

Otto smiled as he noticed again the interest which his rifle had aroused. "I'm a gunsmith and father back in Prussia was a gunsmith before me, before that his father and his father's father. This rifle which has caught your eye is a new invention of mine. It is what I call a breech loader. While others have had similar ideas, I believe I have some features which other rifles so far do not have." He went on to explain the working of the rifle, to the great interest of both Rees and Nat.

"Some day I hope to open a gun shop here in America," Otto told them as he finished with his explanation. "I hope to make rifles to sell."

"I'll be one of your first customers," Rees replied.

The three men rapidly developed a friendship which was destined to become deep and lasting. Otto accompanied Rees and Nat on their visit to Mrs. Hartman. She insisted that the three men accept her hospitality as her guests until they were rested and had the proper food, clothing, and transporation to continue with their journey westward.

The three used this respite wisely. Rees made arrangements with a local gunsmith to let Otto make two more rifles such as the one he carried, plus all of the equipment needed to manufacture cartridges for the guns. During that waiting period, Rees purchased some cured skins and made three beautiful scabbards for the rifles. Otto and Nat became the happy owners of two complete wardrobes of buckskins and had many compliments to bestow on Rees concerning his skilled workmanship.

Trade items such as tobacco, kettles, cloth, beads, knives, hatchets, and guns were also purchased and carefully packaged for their trip westward.

"Now listen up, you two colts, and listen closely and believe what I say, because your lives will depend on it, and I emphasize the word, 'will'." Rees faced the two younger men as they stood on the dock where their trade goods were stacked. Three canoes bobbed in the water beside the dock.

Rees continued, "Tomorrow morning, just before sunup, we will load our goods in the canoes and head downstream. I will take the lead and Nat, you will follow, and Otto, you bring up the rear. We do not want to be too far apart, not more than thirty or forty feet. Keep your rifles near and at the ready always, because somewhere down this river, we will run into bandits, river pirates, or Indians, all of whom will want our cargo. Make no mistake about it, they'll kill for it without hesitation. We will be going into the great land pirate's territory, none other than John Al Murrell. He has men stationed everywhere. Nothing escapes their eyes, and it's said that his agents can be found anywhere from here to New Orleans, even in Indian country. He himself hobnobs with the rich, powerful, and influential. He takes what he wants and when he wants, and he'll use any means to gain those ends. He does not hesitate to kill, maim, or torture, and he has his own lawyers standing by to defend his men, to prevent his men from having to serve prison terms or hanging, which is what they deserve. If you're ever unfortunate enough to meet up with him, you'll never forget how easy it is for him to sway you into thinking that he is an honest and respectable businessman. He is especially successful in persuading the ladies with his charm, good looks, and natural leadership abilities. And, if those qualities don't mislead you, he has the added quality of being a tall, physically strong man. There isn't a single crime that he and his secret organization haven't committed. This organization is highly skilled, and within it, he has trained specialized groups of men in many fields.

"From what I've heard, he has well over a thousand agents who can readily recognize one another by their organizational symbols, and passwords. Now let me ask you both a simple question. Do you think it is possible that one of his agents, or even Murrell, himself has been watching us and perhaps has already sent out word that we are on our way?"

Nat and Otto looked at each other and then Nat answered, "I guess, Rees, that we have to go under the assumption that they'll be waiting for us somewhere down the river, right?"

"Right! So what do you two young buckskins think we ought to do about it?"

"There isn't a heck of a lot we can do about it, is there? Except to be ready to fight when and where we meet up with them?" Otto looked at Reese inquiringly.

"Do you agree, laddie?" Rees turned to Nat.

"I guess," Nat hesitated and stammered before giving his answer, but he quickly added, "You have other plans, don't you?"

"I'm not a greenhorn, and I'm not about to get us killed by the likes of Murrell and his people. We can think and plan, too, only not under the rules he uses; we'll use our own rules."

Rees chuckled as he lowered himself to the dock and motioned to his friends to do likewise. "Now here is what I want you to do; you'll visit the taverns tonight and hit the ones along the riverfront. Talk up the trip down the Ohio while I stay and keep an eye on the goods. If I should talk loosely, they'd be suspicious."

"Why?" asked Otto.

"Buckskins don't talk much about where they're going and everyone knows that, so if I talked too much they'd wonder why."

"What do you mean by Buckskins?" asked Otto.

"Buckskins is the Indian term for white men out here east of the Mississippi River," Rees answered, "and everyone in Pittsburgh knows by now that you are not experienced frontiersmen, therefore they are more apt to take you at your word, at least there's a better chance that they will put your talking down to being greenhorns and knowing no better."

"How do you plan to get by Murrell?" asked Nat.

"We will leave here in the morning as planned and down the river some fifty miles, we will go ashore. I've made arrangements with Joe Hartman to have some of his trusted friends meet us there with our horses and six pack horses. We'll transfer our supplies to the horses and continue downriver on horseback until we come to Barnes' cave on the banks of the Ohio. Barnes operates the cave as a resting place for travelers who are on their way westward. He furnishes overnight accommodations as well as food and liquor. I strongly suspect that Barnes is one of Murrell's agents. We will stop there overnight and the next morning we will leave the cave and head downstream on horseback. Barnes will then send a message to his contact downriver and tell them that we have changed our plans and are traveling by land instead of by water. What do you think the pirates will do then?" Rees paused to look from one to the other of his young friends.

"They'll not be waiting for our canoes, but instead they will be on the lookout for us as we parallel the river," Nat volunteered.

"Right." Rees looked at Otto. "What do you think we should do then?"

"Go back to traveling by canoe?" Otto answered with skepticism.

"Now, we're all thinking alike," Rees said with satisfaction, "but there is one more thing and that is we must travel by land at the right time so that we bypass the Great Rapid when it is again time to travel by water."

"Where will we get the canoes?" Nat queried.

"The same place the Indians get them; we'll make them," Rees told them, "from elm bark."

"I thought the woodland Indians made their canoes out of birch bark. Why don't we do the same? I understand they are much lighter in weight."

"If they did grow this far south, it would make our construction of the canoes a lot easier. The birch tree grows several layers of bark, some as many as eight or nine sheets. The outside layer is white, but the other layers are a brownish color. It is much easier to peel the birch bark from that tree than it is from the elm, but we will not have the luxury of working with birch." He looked at his two companions and continued, "This plan may not work, you know, we could outsmart ourselves; remember the pirates can think too, so as I have said before, let us leave nothing to chance; let us be prepared for anything and hope for the best, yet suspect everyone and everything. Then, too, they may not think that what trade goods we carry is worth the effort or the risk, or they may give up the chase after we give them the slip once or twice."

Rees stopped talking while he lit his pipe and drew on it several times before he went on, "Our last stop before we leave the Ohio River and head north to Vincennes will be Cave-in-the-Rock, which is in Illinois and Miami Indian country. I know these Indians well so I don't expect any trouble with them, but we could have a run-in with the Clarks who occupy the Cave-in-the-Rock, that is, if they still run the tavern there. They are cutthroats of the worst kind, so when we reach the large cave, we will have to be double alert for their shenanigans. Two of Clark's associates, I am told, are the Harper brothers, Micajah and Wiley. I guess I should say the Harpers were associates of the Clarks because I was also told that they are no longer on this earth, but in hell."

"How do you know that they are dead?" Nat asked.

"Well, laddie, the story of the Harpers goes something like this. It was told to me that Micajah and Wiley had planned to rob a family by the name of Stigall so they both passed themselves off as preachers to Moses Stigal, the man of the house, his wife and child and a visitor there by the name of Love. I guest the Stigalls were hoodwinked by the imposters because the next morning Stigall left to tend to some business and when he returned, he found his family and their visitor dead. A posse was put together to hunt down the Harper brothers and when they found Micajah, the posse shot him, and then Stigall proceeded to cut off Micajah's head and nail it to a tree. That's how the village of Harper's Head, Kentucky got its name. This is according to what a fellow named James Hall wrote down. What happened to the other Harper, I never heard."

Rees now rose and tucked his pipe back into its pouch after tapping it against the palm of his hand. "Enough of my storytelling, maybe you'd better visit the taverns and do your gabbing and make sure that the occupants of the taverns know where you've come from and where you're going and above all, make sure they know that our canoes will be filled with trade goods."

A little later as Nat and Otto entered one of the taverns which fronted on the river front, they could see that the establishment boasted a thriving business; smoke filled the large room and the smell of ale and rum clung to the smoke as if they were one. Visibility was hampered by the dense smoke, but men of every age could be seen lounging at the tables or leaning at the long bar. The tables were placed so that they provided the maximum of seating capacity.

"What will it be, gents?" The voice came from behind the bar. Nat and Otto walked past a group a shipyard workers who were seated at a table arguing politics, and reached the bar. There was room for only one person at the bar, so Otto said, "Two ales, please."

Two tankards were handed to the newcomers and as Otto took them from the barkeep, Nat paid the burly looking fellow.

Otto gestured with his tankard, "There's two chairs at that table by the window. At least we can see the clear air if we can't breathe it."

When they reached the table, Nat asked, "Mind if we sit here?" He looked at the largest man who, with his companion, occupied two of the four chairs around the table.

"It's a free country." The fellow turned from his associate and gave Nat and Otto an inspecting glance and then turned back again to his companion, and resumed their conversation.

Nat and Otto began to talk together about their forthcoming trip downriver in voices loud enough for the other two to hear, and one of them finally turned to them and asked, "Are you Indian traders?"

"We hope to be, farther west. We're just passing through and plan to leave tomorrow, by canoe," Nat told them.

The large fellow extended his hand to each of them in turn, "This here is my friend, Timothy Shannon, and my name is Arthur Ross."

Otto and Nat introduced themselves and Tim asked, "Do you live hereabouts?"

"No, farther east." Nat told them.

"Trading with the Indians could be dangerous," Tim commented, "Indians hereabouts are treacherous, and I understand that once you cross the Mississippi River, they are extremely hostile. Not too many people who venture west of the river make it back alive, and the few that do bring some horror stories back with them!"

The four men talked for some time until Tim said, "I have better get home or my wife will flay me alive." He stood up and in a loud voice he continued, "Friends and neighbors, I want to give a toast to these two young gentlemen here who have been sitting with Art and me. To a new breed of frontiersmen who plan to carry our civilization west of the big river into the heart of the unknown, may they find what they seek and may God Almighty watch over them." He raised his tankard high above his head and then lowered it to his lips as the men in the tavern yelled, "Here, here!"

"That should do it," Nat whispered to Otto.

"Right!" Otto grinned broadly.

Nat stood up and yelled, "And here's to our success, may our canoes which are laden with trade goods, reap us rewards unimaginable." Nat downed his drink in one gulp and then men in the tavern repeated, "Here, here," as they drank down their ale.

The next morning as the sun rose over the pointed tops of the evergreens in the east, three men pushed their canoes away from the long wharf and began their journey down the Ohio River, leaving Pittsburgh behind them. All three quickly developed a smooth, seemingly effortless rhythm to their strokes. The river that morning appeared as glass, so calm was the water. The dipping of their paddles into the water caused ripples and the splashing which resulted was almost nonexistent, so quietly did they move. The three canoes glided easily over the water as the wisps of fog which were in the inlets along the shore began to lift as the sun rose. Birds of every color and size chirped and sang as they greeted the morning. Now and then the underbrush moved suddenly as some creature startled by the canoes withdrew into the forest, the branches springing back into place behind it. The forest seemed endless, secretive, and devoid of any human presence. The trees towered over them. Some appeared to reach the heavens and beneath them lay fallen limbs, trees and dead leaves.

The humidity brought sweat to the brows of the three intruders, for the men felt their presence as an alien intrusion and so said nothing as they moved along. Finally Rees pointed to Culver's Cave on the upper side of the river. He skillfully used his paddle to change the course of his lead canoe and Otto and Nat followed his example. In a few moments, all three men were pulling the canoes up onto the dry land and into the underbrush which grew close beside it. When they had their canoes safe enough from the sight of anyone else coming down the river, they sat down to rest.

"Where are we?" Nat asked Rees.

"At Culver's Cave," replied Rees. "It is here that we are supposed to rendevous with Hartman's men. Even as he answered Nat's query, his eyes constantly searched the surrounding area. "You both stay here and look after things while I scout around a little to see if I can find Hartman's men." He disappeared almost noiselessly into the undergrowth.

Nat and Otto unloaded their trade goods after Rees disappeared and stacked the waterproof bundles under a huge hickory tree. A campfire was started by Otto and Nat brought back some venison after being gone only a short time. "Didn't intend to get a deer, but ran into this one right away," he explained. They were roasting a haunch over their small fire when Rees and three men came into the little clearing with the horses. After stretching a rope between two large trees, they tied the horses to it and joined the others around the campfire. When the venison was ready, they all hunched down and enjoyed the tender meat while Reese questioned the men, whom he introduced to Nat and Otto as Sam Bartlett, Henry Wiley, and a circuit rider Methodist minister named Robert Perkins.

Rees suddenly rose to his feet, removed his pipe from his mouth, and tapped it on his palm. He looked up the river intently. "Indians," he whispered to Nat and Otto. "Smother the fire and warn the others."

Nat and Otto obeyed their instructor without hesitation while Rees stiffened and stared upstream into the wind. "Cayugas," he muttered to himself. It took his frontiersman's instincts only a few seconds for him to fathom more; it seemed to be a large party, maybe fifteen or twenty. He joined the others and gave orders softly. Within seconds, all was quiet and the men lay motionless in their defensive positions behind a large fallen tree. Otto turned to whisper, but Rees cut him off with a scolding look as he placed his finger to his lips. At least fifteen minutes elapes, and during this time not an Indian was spotted or a sound heard which they could have made.

"I think you're crazy," Bartlett said as he rose to his feet. "There are no Indians out there; you're just trying to intimidate us."

The sound of an arrow as it sped through the air could be heard just a split second before it struck Sam Bartlett in the chest. Sam clutched at his chest where the arrow had penetrated deep inside him and his eyes opened wide as they stared into the thick underbrush in front of him and then he fell forward, face first, the arrow which had penetrated his chest being pushed through his body by the force of his fall.

25

"Dammn fool! The rest of you stay down; keep your heads down," Rees whispered.

"What are they waiting for?" Nat whispered as he checked his rifle once more.

"To see if any more of us are stupid enough to stand up . . . to see see how many of us there are." Rees spoke softly as his eyes and ears did their work. "They have us surrounded except for the river, and we can't escape by water. If we try, they'll pick us off like fish in a barrel."

Apparently Henry Wiley did not think so, because he crawled rapidly on his stomach toward the canoes, pushed one into the water, jumped into it, but as he sat up to begin to paddle, an arrow struck him in the middle of his back. He released a deadly scream as he rose and fell into the water; the canoe slowly drifted downstream, carried along by the current.

Night came and went without the sighting of a single Indian, and as the sun rose slowly in the east, Rees turned to Nat and warned him in a sober voice, "Laddie, this it it; enjoy the sunrise for it may be the last one you will ever see. Check your weapons, all of you," Rees said in a loud, clear voice, "and be prepared to take as many of those red devils as you can with you, and you, Parson Perkins, say a prayer for our souls. This could be the last day we'll spend on God's earth."

Otto checked his rifle for the tenth time and laid out some cartridges on a piece of bark near his right hand. He then slid his knife in and out of its sheath. He spoke, but to no one in particular, "I'm as ready as I'll ever be . . . let's get it over with."

Nat turned to looked at him and said, "It was a short friendship, but a good one; I'll see you up there." He motioned upward with his head and smiled, "That goes for you, too, Rees," he said as he turned to his Canadian friend. Rees turned toward his two young students and said nothing he just smiled and nodded and then turned to watch for any sign of the anticipated attack.

"There, across the river," Otto said as he rolled on to his side and pointed to the south side of the river. "I thought I saw Indians."

"Could be," Rees answered as his eyes turned to look in the direction Otto had pointed. "Laddie, you and Otto face toward the river and I'll keep a lookout for movement in front of us. Perkins, you do as I do. It just might work," Rees thought aloud.

"What might just work?" Nat asked.

Rees was quiet, but the other could see from his expression that he was plotting. "We have nothing to lose," he finally muttered.

"Otto, you and Laddie crawl over to the pack horse and get the factory and when you get back, show Perkins here how to make cartridges."

This was accomplished, and the preacher was beginning to fill the cartridges when Rees said, "Now you two open fire at everything and anything that moves across the river. We want to show the Cayugas what kind of firepower they're up against. Indians respect what they call 'big medicine', meaning the power that is given to people by Manitou or other spirits. They may think that Manitou has granted us his favor and protection, and maybe, just maybe, they'll buy that notion and back off. That's the only hope we have, so let's begin to play our hand."

Nat and Otto fired round after round at the Indians who tried to conceal themselves in the brush and behind the trees. Some of them were hit, while others escaped with near misses. The accuracy and continuous fire of the two men astonished the Indians, so astonished had they become that about noon, a loud voice could be heard coming from the dense forest in front of Rees. The voice chanted, "Talk!, Talk, We talk you!"

Rees replied with the words that the Indian had used, "Talk! Talk! We talk you!"

At that moment, some brush directly ahead of Rees began to move and from behind it an unarmed Indian stepped out. He place both hands in front of his chest and then turned his left hand so that the palm faced upward.

"He wants peace," Rees said. "He's giving the sign of peace."

Rees placed his rifle on the ground and stood up, facing the Indian, and repeated the words of the Indian in sign language.

The brave then raised his hand to his chest and extended his middle and index fingers. He then moved his hand upward until it reached his face.

"He's saying 'friend', Rees told them.

The Indian then placed one of his hands into the other and raised them to his chest and squeezed them.

"He wants to shake our hands," Rees continued.

As Rees said this, he stepped forward to meet the Indian. Upon seeing this friendly gesture by Rees, the young brave walked to meet the white man. Rees estimated that the brave was no more than twenty-five years old. He was perhaps five feet eight inches tall, and wore only a breech cloth, moccasins, and split turkey feather on the back of his head, which indicated that he had been wounded several times.

"You big medicine," the brave said, "you help fight enemy?"

"Come, sit by my camp fire." Rees led him toward the hastily smothered fire and gestured for Otto to rebuild it.

The Indian turned and called to his followers and from every direction more young warriors emerged to join their leader. With the exception of a few as old as Rees, most of them were young men.

When they were all assembled, near the now blazing fire there were thirteen. Three of the warriors had been killed by Nat's and Otto's markmanship and the wound of another was being attended to by one of his fellow braves. As they placed themselves around the fire, the young Indian leader spoke to one of his war party, who shortly returned and presented to his leader a calumet pipe.

Rees quickly took the opportunity to explain to Otto, Nat and Perkins the history and significance of the pipe. "It is often used to ratify a treaty which puts an end to a war, that is why many people mistakenly call it a peace pipe, but its importance in the Indian society does not end there, for it also is used to assure safety for those who carry it. Whenever and wherever you carry the calumet, you are guaranteed safe passage. In our our case, here today, these Indians use it as a symbol of greeting, friendship, and their assurance of peace and safety, and if I am not mistaken, they also use it here in hopes of cementing an alliance of some kind. And often individual Indians use it as a medium to contact their gods."

"Before we smoke, we talk," the Indians leader said with dignity. "I am Yellow Knife."

Rees introduced those who traveled with him, and when he had finished, Yellow Knife told how a party of Miami warriors had made a raid on his village, killing three of his people, one of them his older brother, and stealing eight women and children. He and his followers, most of whom were related to those who were killed or taken captive, were on the war path, seeking revenge on the Miamis. They had unexpectedly run across Rees and his party as they were on their way to Serpent Mound, where they believed that their enemy might have made camp to rest.

"When we came across you Buckskins, it was our thought that we could overpower you and take your trade goods. We believed that our numbers would easily destroy you with little or no loss to ourselves, if we planned our attack well. We planned well, but your medicine is stronger, than we anticipated. It was our council that Manitou is protecting you and therefore we could not go against his wishes. So instead we asked him to help us to convince you to give us aid against the Miami." Yellow Knife now turned to Rees, waiting for his answer.

"My father," Rees answered after a short pause, "was taken prisoner many years ago by the Miamis and was being prepared for torture when a war party of Seneca braves made a raid on the Miami village in which he was being held captive. During the confusion, my father was able to escape, but if it were not for the Seneca, my father would have been killed, and because the Senecas are your brothers in the Iroquois Confederation, I feel it is my duty to accompany you on your raid, both to avenge my father's treatment, and show to you and your people my appreciation. However, I speak only for myself and my friends will speak for themselves."

Nat and Otto looked at one another and immediately answered, "Where Rees goes, we go."

Yellow Knife then turned to Perkins who answered, "I will accompany you only if you will guarantee my safe return to Pittsburgh after the battle."

"Agreed," Yellow Knife answered. He then turned to take the sacred calumet pipe from one of his braves. Six red feathers which were attached to a small leather bracelet around the upper part of the pipe, hung downward. The six red feathers signified war, whereas white feathers would have signified peace. The bowl of the pipe was made of pipestone, a red clay which was easily bored into, but after being exposed to the elements became much harder. The bowl, as well as the stem of the pipe was handsomely carved and painted with bright colors. On the center of the stem was carved the head of an eagle, with buffalo heads to either side of the eagle.

"Before we consummate our agreement," Rees said, "I want you to know that we do not want to take part in the attack on the Miami in their camp. We will help you with our firepower by picking off some of their warriors before you charge into the camp, and will help you in your retreat. Our firepower, the big medicine, should be able to send the pursuing Miamis reeling back into their camp if they should attempt to follow you."

"That is acceptable to us," Yellow Knife answered. He then took up the calumet pipe, stood, and extended his arms upward to the sky, offering the pipe to the heavenly spirits. He repeated the same gesture to Grandmother Earth. He then sat down once more and took four puffs from the pipe and blew the smoke in the four directions of the compass. Upon the completion of this solemn ritual, he passed the pipe clockwise to the others seated around the fire. They, in turn, puffed on the pipe. When all had participated in this ceremony, Rees turned to this friends and said, "We have smoked the calumet with the Cayugas and that means that we have taken a sacred oath to do what we have promised Yellow Knife and his braves. This oath cannot and must not be broken, for, to do so would insult the great spirit, Manitou, and to insult the Manitou would be the same thing as signing our death warrants. We have pledged our word and so have the Cayugas. The alliance has been consummated, Yellow Knife," Rees said as he turned from Nat and Otto and looked at the Cayuga. "Before we leave the campfire, I ask a favor of you. Would your braves help us to hunt a deer, an elk, or any other animal that would provide us with the hides with which to better protect our trade goods? We have one hide all ready. My friends and I will make our cache near here and at a later time we will come back for it."

Yellow Knife turned his head as he sat cross-legged in front of the fire and spoke to a young Cayuga who stood behind him. The brave turned and left the campsite.

"Is it the first war party for that young brave you spoke to, Yellow

Knife?'' Rees asked.

"You know our ways, Buckskin.'' Yellow Knife smiled, "Yes, it is his first raid. His behavior on this raid will be reported to the council of braves when we return and if the council believes that his behavior has been acceptable, he will receive his name and become a full-fledged warrior.''

Yellow Knife prepared to rise and as he did so, he continued, "My braves will furnish you with as many animal hides as you need.'' Rees nodded his approval and Yellow Knife gave the sign language symbol for "friend" as he turned and left the campfire to join his braves.

"That was sign language for friend, right?'' Nat asked Rees. "He used that sign when he first joined us.''

Rees smiled as he said, "Yes, but it could also mean brother.'' He glanced at Perkins, "You stay here by the fire and keep an eye on things while Nat, Otto, and I cache our goods.''

A safe hiding place was found and the green hides, fur side in, were wrapped around the bundles. Within a few minutes of the goods, the war party of Cayugas and their buckskin allies were on the move southward toward the probable Miami camp. Otto, Nat, Rees, and Perkins rode horseback and a fifth horse carried the 'factory'. Yellow Knife rode the sixth horse. The Cayuga leader had sent three of his braves on ahead on the other three horses; the rest of the braves traveled on foot.

"Do you know where this Serpent Mound place is?'' Nat reined in beside Rees.

"It should be no more than twenty miles or so north of here; we should be there in a few hours,'' Rees replied.

Within two hours, Yellow Knife rode back to join the main body with his three scouts and reported that the camp had been spotted about two miles ahead. The camp appeared to be guarded by three lookouts and the captives were tied to a tree close to the center of their camp. The area around the camp was rolling and covered by trees of every size and height. Brush grew everywhere. Yellow Knife dismounted after he had reported what they had found, and beckoned to his warriors and the buckskins to circle around him. He knelt on one knee and cleared the ground of debris. "Here are the locations of the guards who guard the Miami camp,'' he said as he made three crosses on the ground with a finger. "Grey Hawk, you will kill this guard.'' He designated with his finger the guard on the south side of the camp. "The guard on the west is your man, Straight Stick, and the other guard is yours, Silent Foot. I will give you ten minutes to do your work after we are in place. Then the rest of us will move in as close as we can after the lookouts have been killed. We will conceal ourselves among the trees and bushes and on my command, we will move forward until we are spotted by the Miami. At that time, you buckskins should be able to kill four of the Miami with your first rounds. The three of you who have the finest rifles can reload within a short time and prepare to fire again. Remember, after you have fired your first rounds, watch for the captives, for the Miamis may try to kill them. Choose as your targets anyone who threatens the captives. If they do not attempt to kill the captives, use your best judgement. As you have said, Rees, you and your men do not need to enter the camp and engage in hand to hand combat. That privilege will be ours, but if we have to retreat, then you can give us cover. Do you agree with my plan of attack, Rees?"

Rees nodded and said, "We'll be ready; you can depend on us to hold up our end of the plan."

"Good." Yellow Knife rose to his feet and looked at his warriors, saying, "I want as many male prisoners as possible taken alive so that we can take them back to our village. Grey Hawk, Straight Stick, and Silent Foot, be on your way."

As the small force of Indians and men dressed in buckskins moved quietly through the forest, Rees motioned for his followers to join him as they moved along.

"When we reach the Miami camp, I want you three to hold your fire until after I have fired my first shot." Rees continued to walk and pushed a small limb to one side, "Then, Nat, you will fire the second shot, Otto, the third, and Perkins the fourth. In this way, we won't be shooting at the same target. When Perkins has fired his shot, I'll be ready to fire my second, and so on. Because Perkins' long rifle will take longer to reload, he will not be able to get off as many rounds as we will, so we'll allow for that. Also, if the Miamis scatter, we can fire at will.

As Rees finished his instructions, Yellow Knife gave the signal to halt. In front of the Cayuga warrior stood Silent Foot. He held up one finger, signifying that they were nearing the camp and that the lookouts had been disposed of. The Cayugas immediately took warpaint from their pouches. When Yellow Knife had finished applying his warpaint, his chin and under his nose were blackened as though he wore a mustache and beard. Extending upward on each cheek, toward his eyes, were painted black fingers; Rees knew that meant that Yellow Knife had killed an enemy with his bare hands. The young boy who was to see battle for the first time had painted a yellow lightning symbol across his chest with short lines following it, which was the sign of hope. He hoped that he could stike like lightning. Similarly, the other warriors' warpaint told of their aspirations as well as their beginning exploits, which as yet were meager, with the exception of the few older ones.

Yellow Knife now gave the signal to spread out and approach cautiously.

Everyone obeyed and moved forward in crouched positions. They could smell the Miami campfires now, and when they had reached a distance of within perhaps three hundred yards, they fell to their knees and crawled at a much slower pace. When Rees and his men were within one hundred feet or so of the camp, they selected large trees to stand behind. All were concealed completely from the enemy as they checked their firearms one last time. Rees untied the leather pouch which hung under his arm and reached into the cartridge pouch as his eyes peered around the tree toward the Miami camp. He wet his lips as he pulled his head back behind the tree trunk. The Cayugas were on their stomachs now, slowly moving foward. Rees signaled to the others that the attack was imminent. Otto had never fired at a person before and he was nervous as he watched Rees for a signal, waiting for his lead. Rees was watching Yellow Knife, waiting for his signal. The signal came, Rees braced his rifle against the tree trunk and selected his target; the others followed his lead and did the same. Four shots rang out in rapid succession, echoing through the forest, and four Miamis fell to the ground. Their companions sprang to their feet from where they had been crouched around the campfire and looked in the direction from which the shots had come. Then automatically, they bent low as they ran for their weapons. Three more shots rang out, and three more of their number fell. The Cayuga battle cry now came from all directions as the Cayugas rose to their feet and rushed the camp. Yellow Knife reached the enemy first, flourishing his tomahawk, the white man's iron axe. The Miami who took up his challenge was a large man, wearing green, thigh-high stockings held in place by leather straps, a two inch wide beaded cloth strap below his right knee, and a short red skirt held in place by a wide decorated belt. Imbedded in the front of his headband were three feathers, one white, one red, and one green.

When Yellow Knife reached the Miami, he was running at full speed thereby giving him the advantage over the motionless Miami. As Yellow Knife's body struck the enemy brave, he thrust his knees into the other's groin at the same time grabbing his hand which brandished a hunting knife. The Miami fell to the ground with an agonized cry. As the Miami struggled to regain his feet, Yellow Knive drove his tomahawk into his enemy's forehead. Then quick as a bantam rooster, the Cayuga leader sprang into the air as if shot from a canon, looking for the next target. Before he even landed, his body seemed to turn in midair. By now the remaining Miamis made a dash for the safety of the forest, but not before Yellow Knife, with the help of Silent Foot, was able to wrestle one of them to the ground, and bind him hand and foot.

The Buckskins left the concealment of the trees and walked to join the Cayuga warriors, as Yellow Knife tied his captive to a tree, the Cayuga captives were untied amidst cries of happiness as the warriors, who were members of their families, realized that they were alive. After a short period devoted to thanksgiving and renuion, the warriors turned to take their war trophies. Otto, Nat and Perkins were unprepared for the casual way in which scalps were taken from the dead. Most of the Cayugas placed a foot on the throat of a dead warrior, took a firm hold of the scalp lock with their right hand and with their left, made quick incisions across the forehead and part way around the head with a knife; then, with a sudden jerk, followed by a popping sound, the scalp was taken.

The war screams of the victors could be heard as they dangled the bloody scalps above their heads. Some of the Cayugas demonstrated their enthusiasm for the taking of their trophies with short war dances. The proudest of the warriors was the young brave who had just completed his first successful raid against an enemy tribe. The scalplock which he removed from his victim would bring him stature and a tribal name. His fellow Cayugas had already begun to call him Tangle Legs because, as he struggled with his Miami enemy, a knife pointed at his chest he forced his right leg between those of his enemy, twisting it so rapidly that the Miami fell to the ground, giving Tangle Legs the precious seconds necessary to drive his knife home.

Rees walked over to Yellow Knife and said, "You will be highly honored when you return to your people; your war party has killed eighteen warriors, captured one brave and freed the women and children captives, and your loss is just one dead warrior. The gods travel with you and bring you good fortune. Many braves will want to join your next war party."

"Remember, I lost some braves to you and your party before this, but you fought honorably and it was no disgrace. Without you and your Buckskins this raid might have had different results. I owe much to you and your companions. I hope that some day I can repay you," Yellow Knife told him. "Will you travel with us to our village? It will honor me and my braves if you will do this."

Rees turned to look at Nat, Otto, and Perkins who had brought up the horses and then looked back at the Cayuga and said, "I will talk to the others about your invitation, but I'm sure than the medicine man with us will want to return to Pittsburgh as soon as possible. He does not travel with us."

"Yes," replied Yellow Knife, "I will assign two warriors to escort him to Pittsburgh in the morning as I have promised to do. Now, I will gather my people and prepare to leave this place, for the sun is not quite ready to go to sleep in its bed far to the west."

"I will speak to my friends about your invitation and give you my answer before you begin your march back to your tribal lands," Rees said to the warrior.

"Good," replied Yellow Knife as he walked away from Rees and headed toward his people, "I will await your reply."

"The Cayugas have invited us to travel with them to their village. What do you say to their invitation? Should we accept it, or should we be on our way to Vincennes?" Rees asked as he approached the others.

"He promised me protection and guides for my return trip to Pittsburgh," Perkins said as he rose to his feet in anger, "my agreement with those savages said nothing about my being taken to their village."

"Perkins," Rees said, without looking at him, "who in their right mind would want you as a companion? You're a hyprocrite, and do not practice what you preach, and I don't know why the good Lord permits people like you to walk this good earth. This evening we will make camp and early in the morning, Yellow Knife has assured me that he will fulfill his promise to you, but please, Perkins, would you be so kind as to refrain from preaching to me for the rest of the time that we are together? I would consider it a personal favor if you would just stay away from me entirely until you leave in the morning."

Perkins' face turned a dull red and he yelled at Rees, "You Papists are agents of the devil; how dare you talk to one of God's messengers as you do? I will pray that he punishes you for your attack on one of his chosen disciples!" Perkins grabbed the reins of one of the horses and stalked away.

"Leave our property here," Rees ordered in a calm voice, "the horses belong to us. Or do you intend to add horse thievery to your other undesirable characteristics?"

Perkins dropped the reins in anger and walked rapidly toward the Cayugas.

"You were kinda rough on him, weren't you, Rees?" Nat turned from watching the preacher leave.

"Leave it be, Nat," Otto said, "we don't need to get involved in the pros and cons of the various church denominations. Perkins has been hostile to Rees from the start, so just let it be."

"You're right, Otto," Nat turned to Rees and said, "I'm sorry, Otto is right, Perkins is the problem, not us. With his own mouth he indicts himself of your accusations."

"We are all God's children and that includes the Indians," Rees said as he slapped Nat on the shoulder. "Each of us pray to Him in different ways, but we all pray to Him as our Heavenly Father."

That night as the darkness encompassed them, Rees, Otto, and Nat sat before their fire eating some of the elk meat which the Indians had given them, while Perkins sat among the Cayugas. It was decided that the three of them would visit the Cayuga village. Rees thought it would be a good

34

education for the two younger men in preparation for their future involvement with both friendly and unfriendly Indians west of the Mississippi River. All three were discussing this and enjoying their supper when Yellow Knife called out, "I want you three to join us." He waved his arm beckoningly.

When the three approached the circle of Cayugas, Yellow Knife rose sternly and motioned for them to be seated at his fire. He glanced at Perkins and said, "this medicine man has been telling us about the history of the Christian religion and he has asked us to forsake our religion and adopt his. What counsel do you wish to give me before I give him his answer?"

"None." Rees seated himself beside the Cayuga leader. "It is your decision to make. I made my decision many years ago and I do not want to speak for you."

Yellow Knife turned from Rees and looked at Perkins and said, "You say that your God was nailed to a wooden cross and left to die. Who did this terrible thing to your God?"

Perkins related the story of the trial of Jesus and His subsequent sentence to be crucified.

"Why didn't the people stop those Romans?" Yellow Knife spoke angrily. "My people would have stopped the Romans from nailing their God to a cross even if they died in the attempt. Why didn't your people do that much for their God?"

"You don't understand," Perkins explained patiently, "His death was predestined. Jesus was sent to earth to die for our sins. God, who is the father of Jesus, planned it that way."

"I cannot understand why a father, even a father who is a God, would willingly wish such a punishment to be inflicted upon His only Son I cannot believe it and I cannot join your religion because if I did, I would be considered a member of a tribe who put their God to death. Surely when I go to meet Manitou, he would punish me for not preventing the crucifixion of His Son!"

"Why do I waste my time trying to save your souls," Perkins said wearily, shaking his head in bafflement. "You probably don't have souls, anyway."

"That's what some of the early Spanish Catholics thought, too," Otto interposed, "but they were proven wrong. The pope and the Spanish crown insisted that the Indians were human beings who possessed souls and so insisted that all of those who served under them proceed as rapidly as possible in converting the Indians to Christianity. Of course, all Spaniards did not agree with their pope or their king and queen, for they considered that the Indians had been put there on earth by God as mere animals to simply labor for the Spaniards.

"There is an interesting story of the last resistance which the Indians in Cuba made against the Spaniards. At the defeat of the Indians, the Spaniards offered to baptize the captives before they were put to death, as this, the Spaniards believed would save some of the pagan souls of the Indians before they died. The Indian chief asked the Spaniards if they went to Heaven, would they find the Spaniards there. The Spaniard replied that of course they would. Upon hearing this answer, the Indian chief said that he did not want to be baptized and sent to a place where he would only find more cruel Spaniards.

"Perkins," Otto continued, "do you see how much damage ignorance can do? Your kind of ignorance and arrogance? Actions and examples are needed, Perkins. If we act in a manner in which God approves, we set a good example and this example can be a magnet which would encourage non-believers to seek us out. They, themselves, will be the source of willing conversion for they will wish to become Christians. Your example is abominable, because it is narrow, bigoted, and hypocritical, and you have the audacity to slur my friend, Rees, by calling him a Papist. The way you used the word, one would think that Rees was a leper or something. Perkins, we are all of God and we each, in our own private way, attempt to please our Maker. The Cayugas' Manitou is the same God which we worship. God will accept the name the Cayugas give him just as long as we learn to live as brothers, at peace with one another. Heaven knows that we are a long way from that idea, but attacking one another's religious belief will certainly not bring us closer together."

Those around the fire were motionless and very attentive to Otto's words. "Oh, forget it," Otto rose and paced back and forth, "all I want is to be treated as a brother, as an equal, with the consideration, kindness and the dignity which God intended, why is that so difficult?" He walked away from the fire into the shadows, back toward their camp.

Finally Yellow Knife's voice broke the stillness, "That Buckskin speaks with much wisdom. It is sad that all people do not feel as he."

Nat and Rees both got to their feet, and Rees turned to the Cayuga leader and said, "You are so right, my brother." They both turned to look in the direction which Otto had taken, and then walked back to their small fire.

"I've changed my mind about going to visit with Yellow's Knife's people," Otto said as he looked up at Rees and Nat from his seated position near the fire. He waited for Nat and Rees to sit down near him and continued, "I'm going west as we first planned. I do not intend or want to influence you two, but I've made up my mind. I'm going west, alone if it has to be."

Rees looked at Nat and both turned to Otto simultaneously and said, "Do you have room for two more?"

Rees serenely lit his pipe and commented, "The western Indians are quite different from those east of the Mississippi River, anyway. Maybe you two could not learn enough by living with the Cayugas to help you much after we cross the big river."

"Just for the record, Rees," Nat asked, "what are these Indians east of the Mississippi River like?"

"Huh?" Rees shrugged his shoulders. "The Iroquois were the cruelest of them all, I would guess. It is said that they are a branch of the more civilized tribe from the Gulf states, the Caddoan and the Muskogeans, mostly. When they broke away, they used the ancient highway which we call the Mississippi River, to reach the headwaters of the Ohio. Once they were established, they organized themselves into a five nation confederation. The Indian who set up this confederation was supposed to be a man named Deganawidah and the Iroquois to this day believe that he was part god and that he was born of a virgin. Well, the five original tribes were the Mohawks, Cayugas, Senecas, Onodagas, and the Oneidas, and later the Tuscaroras were admitted. All of these tribes took an oath swearing that they would not fight each other. The league, 'The Great Peace', they called it, did not have authority within each tribe for the league only took care of war, treaties, and such.

"Each tribe sent their sachems every summer to meet in Onondaga country and it was then that all policies outside the sphere of the individual tribes were set up. No one tribe could go to war unless all of the others agreed. There was a post buried in the ground in the center of the meeting place. It was called the 'war post', and if one tribe wanted war, one of its bravest warriors would drive his tomahawk into this post, and if other agreed, they, too, would drive a tomahawk into the post. At the conclusion of this action, the council would either approve or disapprove of one or more war parties.

"The Iroquois built stockades around their villages, and some were elaborate. My father told me about one the Onondagas built around the time that the French arrived here in America. It had a double wall stockade around it and a large ditch was dug to form a moat similar to those which the European castles used for defense. The French had a difficult time destroying this fortified village, but it was finally accomplished with the aid of some Indian allies. From that day to this, the Iroquois have always sided with the enemies of the French."

Otto cleared his throat and asked, "Were they notorious for their torture?"

"When it comes to torture, the Iroquois are masters; I doubt if anyone can equal them. When this poor prisoner that Yellow Knife will take back to his village is put through his paces, he will first be forced to run the gauntlet, which consists of two lines of all the people of the village who will be armed with weapons of every kind and use their weapons to strike at the runner. Later, he will be placed in the center of a circle of the villagers where every form of torture will be inflicted upon him to attempt to make him cry out. This would signify his inferiority. He will attempt to prove his courage and superiority by trying to remain silent in the face of the torture. He can be subjected to anything from burning tourches pressed against him to having an ear lopped off, or an eye gouged out. Even pieces of his body could be cut off and eaten in front of him. They are masters at their trade, and I don't envy their prisoner. The torture is a ritual which the Iroquois observe as a form of worship to their god of war, Aireskoi, telling him that they torture this prisoner for him, and asking of him to partake in his flesh. When the victim finally dies, his body is cut into small pieces for each of the villagers to eat a small part of it, in hopes that they will benefit from the flesh of a brave man. That is why the Iroquois are known as the cruelist of all Indians, but, my friends, I've heard that some of the Indians in the West can match them."

"I've heard enough," Nat said, "how about you, Otto?"

"Yes, I agree," answered Otto, "after listening to you, Rees, I guess Perkins isn't as far off base as I thought. Maybe I had better go and apologize to him for my behavior."

"No, I don't think you need to do that," Rees told him, "Perkins is the kind of person who would be as cruel as the Iroquoise, in his own way. Let's get some sleep and start out early in the morning, before sunup."

The buckskin camp was bustling about at least two hours before sun-up and their activity stirred the Cayugas into early rising also. Within a few minutes, the buckskins had eaten a hasty breakfast, saddled their horses and mounted when Yellow Knife came to them and again thanked them for their assistance against the Miami. As they rode out of camp, they saw Perkins escorted by two Cayuga braves riding toward the east.

"All is as planned," Rees commented drily as he took the lead and headed westward. "If it's alright with you two, I suggest the we bypass Barnes altogether. After we gather up our cache, I think we should bypass Vincennes, also."

"No," Nat spoke up hastily, "you want to visit with your parents, don't you? We're not in that much of a rush."

"I'm a frontiersman, laddie, and so are my folks. Some day you'll understand that. With our kind of people, first things come first, and everything else has to wait its turn. Their turn will come, as they well know, so don't fret. It is all part of our ways. My parents and I would not, for all of the gold in the world, change our way of life. As you two will learn, it is the only way of life people like us and once it has ended, many years will pass before such an opportunity will come our way again, if ever." He looked from one to the other to see if his words had struck home. "Seize your once in a life time chance and enjoy it to the fullest. You are about to be among the freest men who ever walked the face of the earth. There's been no equal to it anywhere at any time and from this day onward, your lives are in your own hands and no one else's. What happens to you will depend on you and your God-given sense of smell, taste, sight, hearing and intelligence. You'll have to smell, taste, see, or hear danger and when you do, your intelligence will be your key to survival. You either develop those five senses into full bloom quickly or it is all over as quickly as one blows out a candle. I cannot teach you how to use your senses, but can only help you develop them. Don't worry too much about it, though; I consider myself a good judge of men and I would not have teamed up with you young bucks if I had not thought you had the qualities to become outstanding mountainmen. Gentlemen," Rees continued, "the area which we are in, the Ohio country, is in the flux of change. It is beginning to be a rapid change, with all of the whites moving in to take up the land. What do you suppose will happen to the white man's relations with the Indians? Give me your thoughts on it. You first, laddie."

"I haven't given it much thought, but I guess the Indians will continue to fight to keep their land."

"Do you think they'll succeed?"

"It doesn't seem so, for the whites are too many and too hungry for land. I guess the Indians will have to be assimilated into the American ways of life or else be forced out of the Ohio country."

"Good thinking, laddie; I agree with your conclusions."

He turned to Otto, "Where do you think the Indians will move to, Otto? Those who decide to move, that is."

"In the first place," Otto began, "some Indians will not be moved from their ancestral homes without a struggle and some of them will fight to the death, but in the end, those who survive will either be absorbed in the American mainstream, or they'll have to move, as you both have said. I believe that many of these Indians will move either west or into Canada."

"What will happen to the Indians who choose not to move west or into Canada?" Rees asked.

Nat and Otto both began to answer that question at the same time, but Otto stopped and nodded to Nat and said, "Go ahead, you answer that one, Nat."

"They will disappear from the face of the earth, as we know them, anyway. The tribal organization will be destroyed, and those who resist the Americans will be pushed aside, and those that refuse to go along with the Americans and march to the drum beat of this country will be heard from no more."

"I assume that you agree with me," Rees said, "when I say that those who move west will be heard from again?"

"Of course . . ." Nat hesitated a moment as a smile slowly crossed his face. "Now I'm beginning to see the point you're trying to make, Rees. You're trying to make us understand that we will be dealing with some of these eastern Indians in our adventures in the west. Right?"

"Correct," Rees told him, "give the Indians credit for having some sense. If we can see what the future holds for them, surely some of their leaders can see that too. No, my young friends, the Indian ways will not be destroyed or disappear from the face of the earth. Their ways will flourish anew in the west. Their renewal of life ceremonies will be celebrated again from the plains of Kansas, Nebraska, and Iowa, into the Rocky Mountain strongholds, and the southwest. Wherever the sun will rise in the freshness of the morning and set in the cool of the evening, the Indians will reinact their rituals of life. Fires will be put out here in the east, but they will be rekindled wherever the tribes put down new roots, new houses will be built, and they will adopt new ways to make it easier to adapt to their new environments. During the Indian renewal rituals, all old things are destroyed including pottery, homes, fires, and this signifies a new beginning, a new start, a fresh start, in a new and fresh land. The renewal cycle generally occurs every fifty years, but because of the circumstances, adjustment in the time span will probably be made. Great chiefs will justify to their people why the time span must be shortened this one time. They will convince their people of the reason why Manitou has shortened the time span. This shortened span will be explained to the villagers as a sign, a sign that will be interpreted in many ways, by as many medicine men, but accepted by the Indians because of the persuasiveness of the interpreters of the mysteries of the spirit world."

Rees paused and glanced from one to the other of his companions. "Have you heard me run on long enough for one sitting?" He grinned broadly, "I've always been interested in the ceremonies of the different tribes and forget that everyone might not share my enthusiasm."

Nat spoke first, "Some of what you've told us, I've heard my brother speak of, but much of it is new to me, and probably is to Otto, also." He looked at Otto for confirmation.

"I'm afraid that I've heard very little about the various tribes, and so what you've been telling us is very new to my ears!" Otto confessed.

Rees grinned once more and said, "Well, I tried to give you a break, anyway. I've been thinking that the eastern Indians who will inevitably have to move westward, might meet some formidable foes in the Indians who already claim the land west of the Father of the Waters. The western tribes will not relinquish their claim to their lands without a struggle.

"My father once told me about two of the western tribes which he came into contact with when he and other Frenchmen were out there. They had been sent with instructions from the French king to try to prevent the Spaniards from further encroachment into what was then French Louisiana Territory. He said that the Indians out there were fierce and combative peoples. We'll find that out for ourselves once we have crossed the Mississippi."

"What Indians did your father meet?" asked Nat.

"The Comanches and the Apaches," answered Rees.

After the three had stopped to collect their trade goods, they rode for nearly three days through the forest land along the northern shores of the Ohio River. On the morning of the third day, Rees informed his companions that the Cave-in-the-Rock was only a few miles ahead of them. "We'll stop there for a rest and to learn the latest news," Rees said. "Sometimes mail is left at the Cave for travelers such as me."

The trail which led north from the Cave was reached and the three men followed it southward.

Nat and Otto were surprised to find the cave much larger than they had anticipated. It was perched high on a rock ledge which overlooked the Ohio River. Nothing could pass on the river below without those on the ledge observing it. The ledge was supported by the vertical, sheer face of the cliff. Towering trees grew at the bottom of the cliff and their leafy tops seemed designed to camouflage the cave mouth, but their attempt was futile, for the sheer wall of the cliff was visible for some distance. Within the cave entrance stone walls formed windowless partitions, with individual heavy log doors which could be securely fastened.

Cured, splitlog tables were scattered throughout the open space of the cave and half log benches were placed on both sides of the tables. Along the rock walls were piled animal skins with their fur side facing upward. They were probably bedding for those who were attempting to avoid rain, snow, or the extreme cold during the winter months.

A huge log fire burning in the center of the cave shot its flames upward, causing the ceiling of the cave high above to be blackened by the soot of countless fires. The walls of the cave were also darkened, but not as much as the ceiling.

There appeared to be only three travelers in the cave when the newcomers approached from the east side. The sound of approaching riders caused the three travelers who sat at separate tables to lower their drinking vessels and survey the newcomers. One traveler rose to his feet, for obviously he was expecting someone, friend or foe. Upon seeing Nat,

Otto, and Rees, he slowly sank down and took another swallow of his drink.

Rees and the young men tied their horses where they could see them and entered slowly, sitting themselves at the table nearest the entrance of the cave. They cradled their rifles in their arms but they were encased in the fringed scabbards meant to conceal as well as protect them. At close quarters, they knew they could depend upon the pistols and knives which they always had on them. They were also aware that a sight of the new style rifles would arouse envy in the breast of any man who caught a glimpse of them, and so concealment was wise.

The three travelers resumed their eating and drinking after having given the newcomers the once over.

Now the operator of the cave moved from behind a waist high log partition and came to their table. He was a scroungy looking man who wore Indian moccasins, fringed buckskin trousers and a home spun shirt. His long hair and beard were unkempt. The buckskin trousers had apparently not been his originally, thought Rees, for they were much too large for him and showed all the signs of having belong to a frontiersman who was accustomed to wiping his hunting knife across his leg.

"My name is Maurees Marquette and these are my friends, Nat Cochran and Otto Muller." Nat and Otto both nodded their heads to the fellow as Rees called out their names, as Rees watched him closely for any signs that he might have recognized their names. When he did not, Rees surmised that there were no messages for him.

"We would like a drink of your best whiskey," Rees continued.

"We have nothing but the best," the operator told him. "Would you like some victuals?"

"No," he answered, "just whiskey."

The operator lowered his head slightly toward the men and asked, as his right hand jerked toward the woman who was working behind the log partition, "we have good entertainment for those who haven't seen a white woman for a spell. It comes with the compliments of the house if you decide to eat with us and stay overnight."

Neither Rees nor the others commented at this obvious set-up and the man left to get their drinks.

"We've got company," Otto commented as Rees and Nat also observed that one of the travelers had left his table and was approaching them.

"I could not help but overhear you say that your name is Maurees Marquette. Did I hear right?" The man was also dressed in buckskins and held his rifle in this left hand, his drink in his right.

"Could be," Rees countered, "or maybe not."

"My name is Robert Robatile and I come from Vincennes." He did not say any more, but his eyes watched Rees closely.

"Vincennes on Lake Michigan?" Rees asked.

"No, the only Vincennes I know is on the Wabash," came the other's reply.

"Sit down and join us," Rees told him. "Yes, I am Rees Marquette and these are my friends, Nat Cochran and Otto Muller."

Robert nodded at the other two and sat down. "I've been waiting for you for four days. Your father sent me to ask you to return to Vincennes. He has something that he wants you to do; don't worry, he is allright and so is your mother, but the business he speaks of has kept him in Vincennes, or he'd have come himself. He asked me to give you this." He reached into the inside of his shirt to the innerliner sewn inside the shirt. It was only visible when he loosened the rawhide strings which laced the upper third of the his shirt. From this inner pocket, he pulled out a small wampum belt. The belt was made of white beads, signifying peace. The image of a two-headed eagle, Rees's father's symbol, which had been given to him by a friendly Ottawa chief, was of blue beads.

"That's my father's wampum belt, allright," Rees said as he took it. He looked long at it, then looked up at its deliverer. "I'm grateful for your patience, sir. My father has a good friend in you." He looked from Nat to Otto and said, "Let's finish our drinks and be on our way. I don't want to keep my father waiting."

CHAPTER II

Fort Vincennes had been built on a high strategic bluff, overlooking the Wabash River. It was a typical fort in that it was built of upright logs partially buried in the ground. The upper part of the palisades boasted a walkway on the inside of the logs, and extended guard towers completed the fortifications. From the walkway platform, the inhabitants were well able to defend the fort against most invaders.

President Washington had earlier sent General St. Clair himself to take personal command of the troops who were stationed at Vincennes. It was the intent of the president to try to pacify the Indians of the area, but both men failed in that portion of their duty. Washington finally sent a Revolutionary War hero, "Mad" Anthony Wayne to remedy the situation.

At the Battle of Fallen Timber, the Indians fought a pitched battle against the white men. It was after that battle that the Indians began to realize that resistance to the white man was futile and as a result, they signed the Treaty of Greenville. That treaty cleared the way for a flood of immigrants some of whom made their way to the area around Fort Vincennes. As a result, the fort was soon overflowing with land hungry farmers whose homes and other outbuildings were being constructed of the old stockade.

One of the families who decided to leave the overcrowded fort area and move about a mile downriver was Henri Marquette and his wife, Marie. Shortly after the completion of their cabin, Henri was visited by a friend an old Wyandot chief, and about one hundred and fifty of his heavily armed braves and their families. The Indians built makeshift shelters on Henri's land and settled down to wait for Henri's son, Rees.

It was midday when Rees and his friends rode through the tepees and other shelters and made their way to Henri and Marie's cabin. Upon hearing horses right outside, Henri threw open the door and shouted to wife, "Marie, Rees is back."

Marie ran through the door and like a bird, flew into the arms of her son. Henri shook his son's hand and then gave him a bear hug. "Welcome home, my son," he slapped Rees on the shoulder, "You look well."

"You too, father," Rees answered. "Mother, father, these are my friends, Nat Cochran and Otto Muller."

Henri Marquette shook hands with each of them, and said, "Welcome to our home. As long as you stay with us, consider our home your own."

"I received your wampum belt, father; what seem to be the problem?"

"I have no problem, son, but our friend, High Eagle of the Wyandots does. I have sent for him and when he arrives he . . ." Before Henri could finish, the Wyandot chief knocked on the door of the cabin. Henri called, "Come in, come in, High Eagle; the door is not locked."

After the introductions were made, Henri invited the men to sit at the table and then asked High Eagle to present his proposal to his son and his friends.

The Wyandot chief stood straight as an arrow by his chair and his face was stern as he began, "We were once powerful and rich kinsmen of the mighty Iroquois nation, but because of the successful fur trade which our people developed with the Algonquins to the north, the Iroquois grew envious of us, of our success. Sometimes as many as seventy-five to eighty canoes, loaded with the finest of our furs landed at Montreal in one year. The Iroquois could not permit this continuous erosion of their wealth because of the lack of their own fur trading enterprise, while at the same time seeing our success at it. So the decision was made by the Great Peace League to destroy the Hurons as a tribe. When the League council met, the Pine Trees, the outstanding war leaders of the League, led the argument for our destruction, but they alone could not bring the crushing power of the League down upon us without the approval and assistance of the clan leaders called sachems. These sachems control the final decisions of the League and they willfully permitted the Pine Trees branch of the League to push through its demands for our destruction. This League that I speak of is made up of fourteen sachems from the Onondaga tribe, eight from the Senecas, nine each from the Oneida and Mohawk, and ten from the Cayuga. Later, because of the new method of warfare which the Iroquoise had developed, the Iroquoise could, and often did, put as many as a thousand or more warriors into a field of battle at one time. No one could resist such power, so little by little, the five original members of the Great Peace became six, with the addition of the

Tuscaroras.

Other tribes were forced to become subjugated, tribute-paying sub groups of the Iroquois. About one hundred and fifty years ago, without warning, the Iroquois unleased its powerful war machine against my people. We were completely defeated and the survivors were taken to live with one of the Iroquois tribes. This policy of theirs kept the League strong. Well, one hundred and fifty years have passed since that dreadful March day, and much has changed. For one thing, none of the Huron-Wyandot are pure, for we have intermarried with the other Iroquois and their sub-tribes, thereby destroying the strain that once called itself Wyandot. The British, French, and now the American have also made their culture and presence felt upon our land. These Buckskins will eventually drive us from our ancestral lands, at least that is what the people who have followed me here to the lodge of our friend, believe. They have chosen me as their chief to lead them to a new land across the Father of the Waters. In that way, they can rekindle the sacred fires in a new land, and develop a new life far from the land hungry, inconsiderate Buckskins."

High Eagle paused and extended his hand to Rees, "We have come to ask our friend, Double Eagle, to lead us to this new land."

High Eagle held his right hand, palm up, against his chest and slowly lowered it to the ground, sign language for 'please'. As he stood before his friends for this historic and life-saving meeting, he looked every inch a chief in his Iroquois dress. His head was completely covered by a hat made from bright red cloth, the lower part of which had a narrow yellow band which completely rimmed the hat. An eagle feather was fastened at the very crown and tilted backward. He wore a kilt which extended nearly to his knees and fringed at the bottom. The kilt was of British red and was trimmed in green cloth fastened with variously colored glass beads. He wore a wide blue sash around his waist and bell bottom leggings under the kilt. The leggings were split part way up his instep, and they too, were British red. His moccasins were elaborately decorated with glass beads. His shirt was plain dark brown and around his neck hung a large silver disk. Over his shoulder was thrown a fringed dark orange shawl.

High Eagle now sat down and waited for an answer to his plea from Henri, known to the chief as Double Eagle.

"You have heard my friend, High Eagle speak," Henri Marquette paused to clear his throat, and looked at his son, "It is now left to you to give him an answer. What will it be? My years are too many to take part in this extensive effort. It is my son and his friends who must answer High Eagle."

Rees looked at Nat and Otto who slightly nodded their heads. He then spoke, "Our answer will be given. My friends and I will assist you, High Eagle." A smile creased his face as he spoke and he extended his hand to

High Eagle in friendship as did Nat and Otto.

This meeting would be the first of many in the great push westward by the Indians.

Briskly, Rees got down to business. "Much preparation will be required for such a large undertaking. Trees must be felled and left to season so that rafts can be made to transport the people and their goods down river. Corn and other food will have to be gathered and put into waterproof containers. Clothing, especially winter clothing, will have to be made for everyone. These things and much more will have to be done. Nat and Otto and I will help you to supervise the preparations. All above, I want each brave to own a white man's rifle, plus as many bows and arrows as we can transport. Where we are going, the land is already occupied by others, and they will attempt to drive us back across the Mississippi. They will outnumber us greatly and, as you know, people will fight more fiercely if they are defending their own homes. Our rifles will guarantee our success against their vaster numbers of lances, bows, and arrows."

The Indian community was soon a beehive of industry, with everyone assigned to a group with an overseer. Trees were felled as those in charge of building the rafts carefully selected the best trees for that use. Nat, Otto, and Rees could be seen walking rapidly from one group of workers to another, offering advice or praise, or more rarely, criticism. Several kinds of snowshoes were made by some of the women and children. These were made from small ash saplings. Small fires were constantly being fueled by the children so that the ash limbs could be steamed and bent and the two ends tied at the rear of the roundnosed shoe. The crossbar was split at each end and each splinter was fastened to the outside of the frame with narrow strips of rawhide. The rawhide was cut into strips and was woven across the snowshoes and straps were then made with which to fasten them to the feet of the wearer.

Snowshoes with pointed heels and toes and a more narrow frame were to be used in a moist, crusty snow. The women were assured that, where they were going, snow would come every winter as it did in their home land.

The people from the area of the fort came to watch the Wyandots, and as the individual groups of workers finished their products and put them into storage. How many of the townspeople might be spies for the river bandits, Rees did not know, but his plans also included a defense against such a possibility. He also knew that they might expect more than one attempt against them before it was over.

One group of men was making a supply of bows and arrows, and two of their number asked for and got permission to make the famous Iroquois war club. The club was carved out of a single, strong piece of hard wood.

The round ball at the end of the club had a small piece of deer bone inserted in it. There was not time now to decorate or carve designs in the handle; that could be done later, during leisure time as they floated downriver.

Rees had assigned one group of men to make three-man canoes to patrol up and down the main body of rafts to offer protection against possible hostiles from the shore. Large elm trees were located by the men, who, with familiar skill, peeled the bark from the tree in pieces large enough to make one canoe. The bark was laid out on a grassy area and stones were used to keep the bark pinned to the ground while the canoe frame was being steamed and carefully bent for assembly. Long spruce roots and rawhide were used to sew the bark to the frame and sturdy ribs were later attached to the frame. The cross pieces of cedar had wooden pegs hammered into small holes on the topside frame of the canoe, tied with rawhide for extra strength. These would be used as seats by the occupants. The two men who were assigned to gather pitch, next smeared it on all joints of the newly constructed canoes. The canoes were then slid into the Wabash River and fastened securely to shore.

Some of the women workers made bags of various sizes from the skins which the men brought in. Small holes were punched along the top rim of each bag and a rawhide lace woven through the holes, thus when the rawhide was thightened, the leather bag was closed.

Rees had Nat and Otto exchange the trade goods which they had brought from Pittsburgh for gun powder in Vincennes. As the hours, days, and finally weeks passed, stockpiles of provisions began to accumulate and the goods and provisions were wrapped and bound for shipment. The rafts had small retainer walls built in the center of each one. These walls enclosed a space large enough to hold three or four horses. Around the edge of each raft, was built a wall high enough for shelter from enemy fire. Those logs were also notched so that oars could be placed in them to help in navigation.

Four keelboats were purchased in Vincennes and would be used to house the children, and wounded, if they were attacked. Each of the keelboats had a makeshift board cabin which could serve this purpose. This type keelboat was made especially for traveling against the current, and might prove useful in traveling up the Missouri River.

Finally, all was ready and everything had been loaded for their departure. Nat and Otto each would ride in a patrol canoe, one on either side of the long line of rafts. Rees would take the lead, with two canoes and five of the best Wyandot scouts accompanying him. Extra large canoes would escort the rafts. These canoes would contain fifteen rangers each, who were especially equipped and trained in hand to hand combat, for which the Iroquois were noted. They would furnish much comfort for the group as a whole. As the sun rose on a still morning, the armada of assorted floating vehicles pushed off from the shores of the Wabash River.

Rees waved goodbye to his parents from his middle seat in one of the lead canoes. From the first raft behind Rees, a lone Indian hoisted a stuffed eagle, on a long, thin pole, the symbol of the Iroquois Great Peace. Rees turned to looked in surprise at the raising of the eagle and smiled his approval.

The destination of the Wyandot was the American Fur Company's trading post in what later would become Kansas City, Kansas. Francois Chouteau was the founder of this trading center, and Daniel Morgan Boone, the son of the great pathfinder, was reported to have been the first American to set foot on the spot, for he had trapped beaver in the Blue River region before 1800.

Except for a nicker now and then from one of the horses, the flotilla of rafts, keelboats, and canoes, passed silently down the Wabash toward the Ohio River. Rees, along with the scouts, was a good half mile ahead of the flotilla when he turned to look back at his entourage. The assembly of floating object were in single file, and keeping as close to the center of the river as possible. Indian warriors could be seen seated between the horses and the edge of the rafts and each had his rifle ready, resting across his knees, as he scanned the shoreline. Those Indians who were assigned to the rafts which carried only the bundles of supplies, divided themselves equally on either side of the huge bulk which was located in the center of each raft. They, too, kept their keen eyes on the river's shoreline. Rees could also see two warriors on either side of the rafts beside the log buttress. They had by now developed a unified rhythm to their backbreaking task of steering the rafts with long paddles, each of which rested on a u-shaped wooden swivel. The four keelboats were located in the center of the long, silent, snake-like line. The women had done their jobs well and no sounds issued from them or the children. Safety was uppermost in the minds of all and that was the reason for their location in the middle of the flotilla.

Rees nodded approvingly as he scanned the long procession and then he turned back and resumed paddling. A sharp bend in the river could be seen ahead and Rees spoke softly, "We near the junction of the Ohio."

As they paddled, their eyes constantly watched the shoreline and now Rees sensed that something was not right. "Where are the birds?" He spoke half to himself. "There is no sign of wildlife."

The scouts in the other canoe had sensed something wrong at the same time and looked toward Rees. He rose in the canoe and gave the danger sign to the convoy behind him. The raftsmen immediately began to drag their paddles, thereby slowing gradually. Rees then ordered those in the two lead canoes to move faster toward the bend in the river. As they began to round the bend, he and the others could see twenty to twenty-five canoes resting on a sand bar at a considerable distance downriver.

"River bandits!" Rees muttered half aloud. He raised an arm and the canoes calmly but swiftly turned and made for the western bank of the river, signaling for the convoy to do likewise. The large canoes containing the Indian rangers became doubly alert as they rapidly moved to reach shore before the rafts touched the edge of the riverbank. This prearranged assignment was in order to secure a safe refuge before the Wyandots landed. As their canoes approached the riverbank, some of the warriors leaped waist deep into the water and with ropes pulled their canoes safely upon solid ground. They immediately disappeared into a morass of trees, vines, and undergrowth. Within minutes, they had signaled to the rafts that it was safe to come in. Rees had reached the convoy by now, and his voice could be heard as he gave orders. "Make sure that those rafts are securely fastened. Take the horses ashore! Get the women and children to safety. Nat, get your people and begin to dig your trenches. Make sure that they are deep enough and zigzag the line. Otto, take your scouts and check the area beyond the rangers' perimeter."

When all were ashore, Otto reported to Rees and High Eagle that the canoes downriver did belong to river bandits, and they seemed very confident because they hadn't attempted to conceal their movement. They had boarded their canoes and were moving upriver toward them.

"Here they come!" Nat pointed excitedly to the swarm of canoes that were just appearing around the bend of the river.

"Otto," Rees called to his friend, "be sure that you and your men cover our rear positions. This bunch coming up river may just be a diversion."

Otto turned and left without saying a word.

When the bandits reached the opposite side of the river, they casually tied their canoes along the shore, and Rees pointed out to High Eagle that they must plan to use them again quickly, or else they'd have drydocked them.

"High Eagle, send for the ranger commander; we may need him."

High Eagle disappeared and within minutes he parted the limbs of the thick bushes and returned with his son.

"Invisible One, if we can create a diversion," Rees told the tall young man, "can you take some of your choice warriors and swim underwater to the enemies' canoes and punch small holes in the bottoms of them? Small enough for them not to notice them until they are part way across the river and large enough to sink them midstream? When this is done, remain on the opposite side of the river and go around to the back side of the enemy camp. It is quite possible that some of the leaders will remain behind; do your job quietly . . . without rifles. Use whatever weapons you think best for the job, but I emphasize the word 'quietly'. We do not want the attacking bandits to return to shore to lend aid to their leaders."

Invisible One drew himself up rigidly, "It will be done; I will await your signal before we move."

"After we begin to shoot, make your move," Rees advised him.

Nat returned, and wiping his face with an arm, he told Rees, "All of the trenches are dug and the non-combatants are in them. We've also dug enough trenches for the rest of us if needed."

"Good," Rees slapped Nat on the back, "you're a good man. Now we'll prepare for that diversion so that Invisible One can do his job. Chief, summon fifteen of your best shots."

When the fifteen men presented themselves carrying their rifles, Rees told them to pick their positions and prepare to fire when he gave the signal. They all braced their rifles against the trees, waiting for the command to fire. Rees glanced about for a few seconds and then braced his rifle against a tree and yelled, "Pick your target . . .steady, fire!"

A volley of shots rang out and as the firing began, the select group of swimmers slid quietly into the water upstream, using overhanging limbs as concealment. Within seconds, they had disappeared under the water.

As Rees and the others kept up their firing, the bandits began to return the fire. As the two opposing sides continued to shoot Rees could see some of the swimmers' heads poping up among the canoes, and then submering once more, all the while remaining hidden from the enemy.

After judging that the swimmers had enough time to do their work, Rees passed the word along, "Reduce your fire and be prepared for the attack. Every third one of you continue to fire, but the others will hold their fire until I signal otherwise."

It was as Rees had hoped, the bandits thought that the Indians had reduced their fire becuase of their lack of gunpowder. The bandits rushed to their canoes releasing triumphant yells as they pushed their canoes away from shore. They were rushing headlong for the kills and in their minds must have been visions of the booty they'd share as well as their share of the women. They paddled frantically and some of them continued to fire their rifles and utter high pitched victory yells. The canoes began to reduce their speed and their occupants were finally aware that they were taking in water. Having to bail out the water reduced both the number paddling and the number firing, but the swimmers had done their work well, and one canoe after another sank beneath the water, leaving the bandits struggling to swim back the way they had come.

It was at this point that Rees ordered the other two thirds of his fire power to resume firing. Invisible One and his rangers had found two of the bandit leaders remaining behind and had killed them before firing at the struggling remnant in the water. Thus the bandits were caught in a deadly cross fire which soon destroyed their number, putting an end to the enemy threat.

The Wyandot came to the banks of the river enmass when the firing ceased and watched in silence as the half submerged bodies of their enemy floated downstream. The silence was interrupted by the yells of the swimmers on the opposite bank as they displayed the scalps they had taken from the bandit leaders.

Rees, Nat, and Otto turned from watching the floating bodies and Rees said drily, "I guess they have earned their trophies. You, too, may learn to take your trophies with a yell as they have just done, if you're like a lot of men who've lived with the Indians a long time. It may become a badge of pride with you to be considered more like the Indian than like the white man."

"Never," Otto said in a low convincing tone. His eyes were fixed on the swimmers across the river. "The environment will not turn me into an Indian . . . I will never forsake my heritage; never."

"And you, laddie?" Rees turned to look at Nat.

"Only time and circumstance will dictate what I will become," Nat answered soberly.

"Well," continued Rees, "as long as we're all ashore, we might as well stay the night. We'll get a fresh start in the morning." He turned and walked toward High Eagle to see what he thought.

"Do you think that all those bandits were at old Colonel Fluger's place when we passed there?" Nat asked Otto.

"If they were, they kept themselves well out of our sight," Otto answered. "It is my guess that they all assembled at the location just below the bend in the river. Some may have stopped by the colonel's tavern on their way to the rendezvous."

"It's a wonder that colonel and his wife didn't clean them out before they left," chuckled Nat. "Especially when she turned on her charm."

"I don't think they'd dare do that to the bandits, particularly if they were Murrell's men."

The Wyandot camp was bustling with activity a long time before dawn. Horses were again loaded onto the rafts and tethered, and the supplies were checked again to ensure their safety. Meanwhile, High Eagle, Invisible One, Nat, Otto, and Rees were seated around the only campfire which was still burning. "As we hit the big river, the Mississippi, we must turn north," Rees was saying. "I'm afraid that the current will be too strong for the rafts to go upstream. We could try to move them in the calmer water near the bank, but there will still be some current there. Those who man the oars will soon be tired and this could make them less effective if we should be attacked. I propose that we cross the Mississippi River and land on the Missouri side, unload everything, follow the Mississippi River up to where it joins the Missouri River and then follow the south bank of the river until we reach the American Fur Company's trading post.

"Once we are there, we will explore the area for suitable country for the Wyandots to make their new homes, but remember, from the time we hit the west banks of the Mississippi, we are in enemy territory and thereby subject to attack by unfriendly Indians at any time. They, will not welcome any who threaten their possession of the land."

Rees looked around the circle of men, "Upon reaching the west bank of the Mississippi, we will abandon the rafts and keelboats and the horses will carry the supplies. I had originally considered having the horses pull the rafts upriver, but abandoned that idea because there will be too many trees along the bank to make that feasible. Travois will be just the thing to carry the supplies and a horse can pull a lot more than he can carry."

He noticed the puzzled expressions on the faces of his two young friends and elaborated by drawing a picture on the ground, showing a travois. High Eagle nodded his head in approval.

"What the horses can't transport, the people can. That is what I propose. It is for the rest of you to speak."

Otto and Nat spoke in favor of Rees' plan and after speaking to his son in the Wyandot tongue, High Eagle nodded once more, approvingly.

"Let's move, then," Rees said as he rose and began to kick dirt over the fire.

At about noon the following day the rafts were unloaded and left to float downriver and the horses became their means of transportation for their supplies. Everyone who was able rigged up some sort of pack in order to carry as many supplies as he could.

The caravan moved slowly, paralleling the Mississippi until it reached St. Louis, where the muddy Missouri emptied into it. The Wyandots camped five miles south of that town, while Rees and Otto rode on ahead to inform the inhabitants that the Wyandots came in peace, that their only wish was to skirt the small city and be on their way. Because of the large French population in the city, Rees easily found the support he needed for his permission to travel unmolested west of the town until they could reach the banks of the Missouri. Although there were at first some reservations expressed by the community of Americans concerning such a large group of armed Indians traveling so near them, the more hospitable French convinced them. The French knew and understood the Indians much better than did most Americans, and spread the word that they accepted their countryman's words that the caravan was peaceable and meant no harm.

As Rees and Otto rode out of the city, heading back toward the Wyandot encampment, Otto spoke with surprise in his voice, "I didn't realize there were more French Canadians in St. Louis than there are Americans!"

Rees smiled and answered with pride, "Why not? After all, the Louisiana Territory once belonged to the French and it was us who developed the fur trade out here. As I have already pointed out to you and Nat, we are headed for the American Fur Company's trading post west of here, but I didn't tell you that before Chouteau established the first permanent settlement there for the Americans, another Frenchman by the name of Etienne de Bourgmont built the first fort not too far northeast of here, back in 1723, a little over a hundred years ago. In 1764, or thereabouts, another Frenchman, Pierre Laclede Liguest, built the first building in St. Louis."

"How, in heaven's name," the German American asked in puzzlement, "did the British take all of this away from you?"

"Numbers," Rees answered, "it all came down to numbers, Otto. We French had only fifty thousand men in all of New France, seven thousand of whom occupied and held the Louisiana Territory for the French crown. While the British population in all the thirteen colonies combined was over one million. It really is amazing that we held out as long as we did against such odds, especially when you consider the power of the British Empire."

"How did you hold them off for so many years?" Otto asked.

"I guess it was the superior knowledge of the land," Rees answered. "And our leaders . . . we had Frenchmen who knew the country extremely well, and they combined that knowledge with their skillful management of the Indians. We failed in persuading the Iroquois to join us, however, but that was the only large band of Indians which we did not muster to our cause. And of course the British colonies were divided and could not agree on a unified plan of action, and this helped us. Their flag had a snake on it, and under the snake was printed the words, 'Join or Die'. The snake was divided into eight parts. This division worked to our advantage, too, but not enough, obviously."

"What do you think of the American?" Otto asked.

"Anybody is an improvement over the British," Rees answered with a grin. "The British are greedy, arrogant, money hungry and deceitful. We

French have no use for them."

"Those are pretty strong words." Otto commented.

"Not strong enough." Before Otto could continue, Rees spurred his horse into a trot. "We've got work to do; let's get our caravan on the move. It's still quite a way to the river junction."

"I thought we were taking them to the American Fur Company area," Otto said as they trotted briskly toward their friends.

"The American Fur Company is located at the junction of the river," Rees told him.

The Wyandots moved cautiously along the Missouri River bank for many days before one of the scouts reported that they were being observed at a distance by an Indian with a very distinctive scalp lock. Rees took Nat with him to investigate, but after two hours of searching, they still had not spotted the observer. It was early the following morning before anyone sighted him again. This time it was obvious that he wanted the caravan to know that they were being watched as they trudged westward. The lone Indian sat his horse on a high, treeless knoll to the east of them, silhouetted by the sun. Rees was called and as he pulled in his horse along side the Wyandot scouts', he said, "Pawnee." He nodded toward the motionless figure, "That scalp lock that you see is saturated with animal greese, which is why it is so stiff. We knew that we could not travel undetected and that has been demonstrated."

He turned in his saddle and yelled, "Nat . . . Otto!"

When they had ridden to him, he spoke, all the while studying the lone Indian. "That, my friends, is a Pawnee. They were the allies of the French many years ago, and we worked together, the French and the Pawnees, to thwart the Spaniards in their unquenchable thirst for gold and conquest. The Spaniards did not know it at the time and for many years after that, that it was the French trappers, with the help of the plains Indians who stopped Coronado in his search for the seven cities of Cibola. It was Coronado's first defeat by the Indians." Rees chuckled, "During the battle between the Spaniards and the Indians, the French concealed their presence, letting the Indians do the fighting. We just contented ourselves with advising the Indians as to the proper tractics to use with the Spaniards."

"Do you think that these Pawnees will remember the alliance which they had with your ancestors?" Nat questioned.

"They are trained from birth to remember. Their memory is one thing which most Indians develop early in their youth, for the memory is extremely important for survival. The are taught to remember everything. They are instructed to do so down to the most minute detail. If their memories weren't so accurate, many could suffer for that lapse, perhaps pay with their lives. Tribal history is passed on through memory also, as you know. Yes, they'll remember."

From that day onward, the Wyandots could always depend on their lone observer to be nearby. Rees ordered that security be reinforced even further and arms were to be kept always ready and scouts as well as the sentries were doubled.

Finally one day, Rees and Chief High Eagle sat on a bluff overlooking the junction of the Kansas and Missouri rivers.

"This is where your new home will be. The bottom land down there is rich and you'll be able to grow whatever you want."

The chief grunted his approval as he surveyed the wide panorama.

"We'll settle across there on the west side of the river. That way we'll have our village facing eastward across the rivers. We'll not have our houses too near the river, for rivers this large must flood in the springtime."

"You're thinking is good," Rees told him, "for the Missouri extends many many miles to the northwest till it reaches its headwaters high in the mountains. The Missouri and her tributaries can and will make the bottom lands part of the river itself during the spring runoff."

The chief called a council meeting to make plans for the establishment of the village and its location, and while the Indians were making their plans, Rees, Nat, and Otto rode to the American Fur Company's trading post to inform the agent there of the plan proposed by the Wyandots. The agent was not there, but his assistant greeted them, and had many things to tell them, which would influence the new frontiers.

As the frontiers were pushed farther west, St. Louis would no longer be the foremost western frontier. Mexico had declared and won her independence from Spain and a trader by the name of William Becknell, while on a wild horse expedition, was invited by the Mexican residents of Santa Fe to trade with them. He had hastily put together a wagon train and had made the trip to Santa Fe, reaping large profits as a result. Others were also organizing wagons to transport the goods so welcomed by the people in the west.

It was obvious to the most obvious of the traders that the Indians wouldn't welcome a constant incursion of intruders; the federal government had ordered that a fort be built by Colonel Henry Leavenworth perhaps twenty-five miles, up the Missouri. The fort would have a dual role, that of protecting the traders and also to furnish some kind of protection to the immigrants who were sure to follow.

"Even now, our trading post is being expanded to benefit from the boom which is sure to come. You know furs are not the only things we handle. Our warehouses will be expanded to store the goods which will eventually reach Santa Fe. We'll stock items such as hardware, clothing, silks, and velvet yardgoods."

As the young assistant waxed eloquent over the future prospects of his company, Otto took more of an interest in what he said than did Rees and Nat.

Nothing much escaped Rees and it was then that he realized that the threesome which had begun back in Pittsburgh was about to be two.

"The opportunities for a gunsmith are astronomical," Otto told Rees and Nat excitedly. "My rifles could be in demand from here to Mexico, even into California and throughout the Northwest territories. There could be no end to the possibilities!"

Rees glanced at Nat and said, "Well, laddie, I guess that day has come."

"Yes," Nat said glumly, "It's the day I hoped would never get here."

Otto awakened from his excited planning to hear what his friends were saying. "Aw . . . you know I'm not cut out to be a mountainman. I don't much care what lies over the next rise, or mountain, or river. Rees, you and Nat are two of a kind, but I'm the kind of person who wants to put his roots down in one place and call it home. I want to grow with one community and prosper with it. No one could ever have better friends than you two have been to me, and I will always cherish that friendship. We'll see each other sometime. You have to come out of the mountains at some point; when you do, I'll be here at the junction of the Kansas and Missouri rivers."

"True friendship is forever," Rees told them, "it is a continuous, living union that no words from friend or foe will ever destroy. We three have that kind of friendship and it will continue. Our parting is not by choice, but by necessity. There will be no goodbyes, but only the thoughts of reunion." Rees clapped Otto on the back and went on, "You'll be wanting to do some planning, and Nat and I will ride out to visit the Pawnees. Maybe we can explain to their satisfaction why the Wyandots are here, and possibly prevent a clash between the two. When you ride back to the camp, tell Chief High Eagle what we plan to do."

Otto nodded, "I'll tell him. You be careful."

Rees laughed, "Don't worry about us, my friend, the French and Pawnees have a long history of friendship."

Nat and Rees waved as they turned westward and Otto returned the wave before he reined his horse in the opposite direction.

The following day, about midmorning, Rees turned to Nat as they rode in silence and asked, "Can you smell the smoke, Laddie?"

"Just a little," replied Nat.

"Turn up your sense of smell!" Rees grinned as he continued, "What are the fires burning?"

"I don't know," Nat answered, after a short pause. He continued to sniff the air. "I don't believe I've ever smelled that odor before."

"Buffalo chips," Rees told him, "The Pawnees are burning buffalo chips and the village is probably just over that rise a few miles ahead of us. Now, laddie, don't make any hostile or otherwise unfriendly moves once we get to their camp. Let me do the talking. Do as I and nothing else."

"Did you spot the Pawnees who have been following us?" Rees asked a little later.

"No, where are they?" Nat turned in his saddle to scan the area.

"They are riding downwind of us, laddie, and they've been with us since sun-up."

"Then how did you know they were out there, Rees? I sure didn't see or smell them."

"You can't smell them if they're downwind of you, laddie, but you should have been more observant of your horse. He has told you more than once that we had company."

"How?"

"By pricking his ears and glancing in that direction repeatedly. Can you see the smoke now?"

They had topped the knoll and the two men could see smoke curling up from a fringe of trees. As they studied the smoke, they could now see a tepee here and there which stood out. "There must be thirty or thirty-five tepees." Rees said finally.

They rode on slowly and as they approached the village, dogs began to bark and women stopped the work they were doing and looked up at the approaching strangers. Children ran to their mothers, as the braves reached for their weapons. There were five long rows of tepees in the village and each row contained fifteen dwellings. They all faced eastward, and in the center of the first row, Rees and Nat saw activity which convinced them that the chief must be in residence. As they entered the perimeter of the village, older boys began to follow behind at a distance of perhaps forty paces. Braves with weapons in their hands converged upon the two riders, and in a few seconds they were engulfed in a mass of Indian warriors. Now the flap of the chief's tepee was flung back and a tall, well-dressed, handsome Indian stepped forth. At his side came his sub-chiefs. Rees and Nat continued to walk their horses in that direction until they dismounted in front of the impressive Indian leader. "We come in peace and to renew old friendships. I come to honor the memory of your great chief, Iron Horse."

Upon hearing the name of their departed chief, the Pawnees began to whisper to one another as they continued to move in closer to their chief's tepee. Now the chief raised his right hand abruptly as he kept his eyes fixed on the two intruders, and his people moved no closer.

Rees continued, "Henri Marquette, a blood brother of the Pawnees, is my father. He and Iron Horse fought many battles together against the enemies of the Pawnees. My father spoke many times of the greatness of your people and he has asked me to come to you and bring his wishes that Manitou looks with favor upon the great Pawnee nation."

The Pawnee chief whispered something to one of the aides who then walked away.

"I am Chief White Cloud," the leader of the Pawnees said proudly. "You are welcome to our village. Please join me in my lodge."

Rees and Nat dropped their reins to the ground and followed White Cloud into the lodge. White Cloud lowered himself to the ground near the fire and beckoned to his guests to join him. A beautiful pipe was handed to the chief by one of his aides and now other Pawnees entered the lodge and seated themselves around the fire. They did not speak. When all were seated, the chief took a small piece of smoldering wood from the fire and lit the pipe. Now he extended it in the four directions of the compass and upward to the heavens. He repeated the gestures as he puffed on the pipe.

"Oh mighty one, hear our words and accept our humble offering of tobacco as a small token of our respect for your wisdom, insight, and generosity."

The chief passed the pipe to the warrior seated next to him and watched as each of the others puffed on it reverently. When all had smoked the pipe, the chief spoke once more. "Your father is remembered by my people and he is spoken of with great respect and gratitude around the campfires when our storytellers speak. We welcome his son in his place and we extend the honor we feel for the father to his son."

"Your honor is great, White Cloud." Rees spoke with humility, "I will cherish it as life itself."

It was quiet for several minutes until White Cloud turned from the fire and looked straight at Rees asking in a calm voice, "Why does the son of our brother bring so many others with him?"

"The Indians whom I have brought are called Wyandots. They once belonged to a powerful and proud people. Their ways were true and strong as yours are and their homelands defended successfully by their best and bravest warriors for many generations. They, as do you, talk with pride at their campfires about the glories of their people. But that time is no more . . . it is gone as the smokes rise from the camp fire, as the dust rises from your ponies' feet."

Rees looked gravely around at the faces colored by the glow of the fire. "A new nation called America which moves as swiftly as the wind and is as strong as the ocean, is taking the lands of the Wyandot, along with the land belonging to many other Indian nations. Indian nations which you may not have heard of yet, but their names will be learned quickly by every Pawnee child. Names such as the Delaware, Kickapoo, Mohegan, Fox, Cayuga, Illinois, Miami, Seneca, Mohawk, and many more. The Americans are hungry for land. Land is like a medicine to them, and it seems there is no end to their numbers. The Indians are as a blade of grass in a forest of Americans, and the Wyandots are only the beginning of a mass movement of Indians who will be forced from their lands by the oncoming Americans. The Indian nations who attempt to stop this flood of Americans only postpone their fate and in the process, many of their best and bravest warriors will be killed. The chief of the Wyandots is called High Eagle and he has learned that it is hopeless to try to stop the Americans. He knows it is as hopeless as trying to catch the raindrops which fall from the heavens before they touch the ground. He is being wise by moving west. He lived many years among the Americans. He knows their ways and he and his people have, and use, the white man's weapon. These weapons are big medicine, bigger than that of the plains Indians.

"In the many moons ahead, the Pawnees will face new people, new nations, some large, some small, who have no choice but to invade your homeland and the homeland of other plains Indians. It is not a matter of choice, but a matter of survival, for them it a simple matter of move west or die. We Frenchmen were faced with the same decision a few years ago, but we had no place to move to; for us there was one only decision to make and that was to become Americans. We have accepted our fate. You, too, White Cloud, will be faced with the same decision that we French have had to make. Someday there will be no place for you to move to, and you will be forced to become Americans or perish as if you were in quicksand. I bring you not Wyandots, but what the future holds for you and your people. I bring you time, time to find a way to survive, time to convince your people and the other nations of the west what the future is for your people. I bring you time to think and plan, time to convince others that it is hopeless to resist the Americans. You can no more catch all of the raindrops than the Wyandots could.

"My heart is heavy with sadness because of the words which I speak, but my heart speaks with truth, my heart speaks for the interest of the Pawnees. The Americans are many and are becoming more as each sun rises and sets. The time is very short." Rees ceased speaking and turned to gaze into each face around the campfire. The faces of the Indian showed no emotion as they all finally turned to look at their chief.

White Cloud finally spoke, "You bring us sad news, but we do not blame you for the words which you have spoken." He hesitated, then continued, "We thank you for your counsel. You, the son of your father, have lived among the Indians for most of your life, so you know us, as well as we know ourselves. Our enemies are many and hated, and we have fought each other since we were placed on this earth by Buffalo Woman. I do not believe that there is one among our many tribes who has the wisdom to unite all of the tribes as one. We seem destined to fight each other, and if they invade our nation, we will fight the Americans also, until we return to where we came from. Those of us who are alive at the final council with the Americans will remember us, as will their children, and their children's children, but they will see us through the eyes of the Americans. It is then, and only then, that we will live as one. It is then that the killing will stop; it is then that the suffering will stop. Hard lessons will be learned, but all good things come from hard lessons." He turned to Rees and continued, "You and your friends are as us, Pawnee. You will forever be safe among my people."

The council meeting broke up and Rees and Nat were escorted to a tepee which had been prepared for them.

"You didn't paint a very pretty picture of us Americans," Nat said ruefully as they seated themselves upon a pile of buffalo robes.

"The truth sometimes hurts, laddie, but it must be told, especially to the Indians."

"You mean the truth as you see it, from the standpoint of another nationality," Nat retorted.

"Let me tell you the story of Sir William Johnson, a man with vision, a man of much wisdom, a man who could see into the future. He could foresee a future where the white men and the Indians would live together in peace and harmony, as White Cloud has just foretold a future for the Indians and Americans.

"As long as Johnson lived, his vision was beginning to take shape. Before the French and English fought each other in the French and Indian War, Johnson had been sent to America by the English to supervise the Iroquois and he did a bang-up job of it, too. He lived among the Iroquois and treated them as equals, and the Indians loved and respected him for his evenhandedness. He learned their language and married one of them, a Mohawk by the name of Molly Brant. Her brother, Joseph Brant, and Johnson got along very well, also. During his stewardship, the Iroquois were becoming less and less Iroquois and more and more a mixture of many different Indian tribes. The more the Iroquois moved to the Mohawk Valley at Johnson's request, and lived under his protection, the more they gave up, little by little, their Indian ways and habits and began to dress as Englishmen and live in log homes, as did the English.

"But when the American Revolution began, the Five Nations of the Iroquois League broke up for the first time in their history. It proved to be the destruction of the League. When Sir William died, his wife Molly, and her brother, Joseph, convinced part of the Iroquois to continue to support their old faithful ally, the English, but two of the Iroquois tribes, the Tuscaroras and the Oneidas, chose to fight on the side of the Americans. Today, these two tribes and some individual Indians can hardly be distinguished from any other American. But, as we know very well, some Indians refused to become part of the melting pot and chose to move instead. The Wyandots have chosen this path, but they can't run forever. When they stop running, they will become as American as you and me."

"Let's get some sleep . . . tomorrow we'll go back to the American Fur Company's trading post and get the supplies we'll need for our trapping in the Rockies," Rees said as he spread out the buffalo robes.

Before dawn, Nat was awakened by the steady shaking of Rees's hand. "What's wrong?"

"Something is about to happen which we will not enjoy," Rees replied soberly.

Nat sat up abruptly, "What's about to happen?"

Rees pushed back the flap of their tepee and beckoned for Nat to join him. "There she is." Rees pointed at a young Indian girl whose body was painted from head to toe. A group of Pawnees was escorting her toward an elevated earth platform.

"What's going on?" Nat looked bewildered.

"She is to be sacrificed," Rees replied.

"What?" Nat's shocked voice asked, "What do you mean, sacrificed?"

"The Pawnee are the only Indians other than those who live along the coastline from Virginia to Texas who still practice human sacrifice. Because the Pawnees sacrifice a human every now and then, most mountainmen believe that they may be related to one of the coastal tribes."

"We've got to stop them," Nat said as he turned to look angrily at Rees.

"Laddie," his partner said grimly, "if you try to stop them, you will probably be sacrificed along with her."

"What are they going to do with her?"

"Come with me," Rees told him as he passed through the opening of the tepee. When they were outside their lodge, Rees pointed to an earth-covered platform about thirty feet in front of the row of tepees. "That pile of rocks covered with dirt is the sacrificial bier and the young girl will be put to death there to appease their sun god."

The two men watched as the drums beat louder and louder and the chanting increased in volume. The young victim walked slowly toward the sacrificial platform with the strong encouragement of her escorts. Now she stopped in front of the log ladder which leaned against the platform. She seemed completely puzzled at what was happening. She looked about her and then back at the ladder leading up to the floor of the platform. Her eyes rose to the religious leader who waited for her on the earthen mound. When she took her first step up the ladder, the chanting cheered her onward. She hesitated for a moment, then continued.

"Who is she?" Nat glanced at Rees.

"She is probably a captive who knows nothing at all of what is about to happen to her. For as long as she was held captive, she was seen and treated as a goddess, and that is why she is puzzled at what is happening to her now. She was probably selected as a candidate to be sacrificed from the beginning and everyone knew this but her. If they followed the regular procedure, three days ago, her clothing was taken from her and her body painted as you see it."

"What is the Indian doing on the pile of dirt? He acts as though he is fighting an invisible foe."

"He is showing the tortures which he will perform on the victim. The Pawnees are very happy about the willingness of the girl to climb the steps without being forced to do so."

"Why?" Nat was shocked.

"It is supposed to be a good sign," Rees answered, "Now, laddie, in a few minutes some brave who has been selected for the purpose, will shoot an arrow through her heart and the priest who is mimicking on the platform, will strike her in the head at about the same time that the arrow pierces her heart and she will die instantly. Her death will come the very second the sun first appears over the horizon. This is the beginning of the fourth day of her initiation, and when she is dead, each of the men in the tribe will shoot an arrow into her body. Laddie, I suggest we go back into the tepee. What is about to happen will not be pretty to look at."

As the two men were about to reenter the tepee, a Pawnee war cry was heard, and a Pawnee brave raced his pony toward the young victim who stood on the sacrificial mound. Rees and Nat whirled to see what was happening and within seconds, the Pawnee brave had jumped his horse upon the platform, grabbed up the young maiden, jumped off and galloped away, leaving the scene as quickly as he had entered it.

"What on earth was that all about?" Nat turned to Rees in his bewilderment and relief.

"Whatever it was, my friend, it wasn't supposed to happen. Look at the faces of the people, especially the head religious leader." Rees looked in the direction which the rider had taken. "I hope he makes it," he said softly.

No one seemed anxious to pursue the young warrior. Was it possible that they had felt sympathy for the young maiden and had hoped that something would prevent her sacrifice? Perhaps they didn't all approve of the ceremony. Rees and Nat hoped that was the case as they made ready to ride back to the junction of the Missouri and Kansas rivers.

CHAPTER III

"Hello, Chouteau." Rees greeted him in French as he and Nat entered the long, double log building.

Chouteau looked up from inspecting some pelts and studied the two strangers for a few seconds before he said, "Hello to you, too, What can I do for you?"

"My name is Maurees Marquette and this young fellow goes by the name of Nat Cochran. We were here a few days back and met your assistant."

"Yes, my assistant told me about you. How is Canada?"

"It's still there," Rees answered in English.

"I knew a Marquette once," the trader remarked as he stopped checking the furs and gave his full attention to the strangers. "He was one of the best trappers that I have ever seen. Could he have been any relation to you?"

"If his first name was Henri, then I am related, because he is my father."

Chouteau came out from behind the counter which separated him from Nat and Rees and with a broad smile extended his hand to Rees. "Welcome to my post; it's a real pleasure to meet the son of a great trapper and fellow Canadian. Would you care for a drink?"

"I thought you kept the liquor for the Indians," Rees said with a grin. "You wouldn't put four fingers in the cup as you fill it, would you?"

"You're not drunk yet, my friends . . . we only do that to the drunken Indians."

"Thanks for the offer, Chouteau, but we're here strictly on business. We need supplies," Rees told him, "and then we must be on our way. We're a little late as it is."

"Do you want to work for my boss, or do you wish to be free trappers?" Chouteau asked with a sober face.

Rees smiled at Chouteau and answered, "John Jacob Astor is not going to own us, we're going to be free trappers. The money we get for our pelts is going to be ours, it will not go to one of the richest men in America. I know all about your boss and I want no part of him. The only dealing we want with that one is for his agent to sell us some supplies."

"But Rees," Chouteau interrupted, "John Astor is a fair and respectable businessman and I'm sure he would be happy to have the son of Henri Marquette trap for him."

"I'm sure he would," Rees answered, "and after facing the hostile Indians and grizzlies for a year, I would turn over my pelts for a wage of four hundred dollars . . . right?"

"That is a lot of money, Rees," protested Chouteau.

"Not for the amount of furs we will take in one season," Rees replied calmly.

"I see that you're not a greenhorn, but Astor understands your problem. He's a selfmade man himself, you know."

"We have no problem, Chouteau," Rees replied, "but I think you do."

"And what makes you think that I have a problem?"

"Is it that difficult to recruit good trappers, Chouteau? Or are you and Astor trying to flood the Rockies with your men?"

Chouteau smiled, but did not reply.

"As I said," Rees continues, "I know all about your boss. He came to America as a young boy and a few years later, went into the musical instrument and fur business. You probably know more about his life than I do. But don't forget, Chouteau, that I know the fur business as well as the next man and probably better than most, and from what I've heard, Astor had many problems with the Montreal traders, too many for me to want to work for him. I respect Astor's astute business ability, and I know he is no fool, but neither am I, so don't insult me by treating me like some greenhorn. I also know that your boss has become so powerful that he has been able to get some United States senators and governors to do his bidding for him. Through them, he has been able to get the government to give up its fur trading business so he will not have to compete with them. He thereby controls all of it. The government's policy was a good one, for you know as well as I do that the sole reason why the government went into the non-profit fur business was to help develop a good relationship between the whites and Indians. It was working, too, but your boss could not stand to let things be. He convinced the Indians to fight the government but for no reward for the Indians as the governors and senators got their thirty pieces of silver, but what did the Indians get?"

Warming to his subject, Rees rose and paced back and forth as he shot fierce looks at Chouteau. He paused to light his pipe and took several violent puffs on it before resuming. "I'll tell you what they got, Chouteau. They were cheated of the fair prices which the government had been paying for their furs through its factory system. And to make it even easier, the Indians have been sold cheap, rotgut whiskey to keep them satisfied."

Rees whirled at the end of the long room and stared at Chouteau accusingly, "Is that what you do, too, Chouteau? Do you get the Indians drunk first and then practically steal their furs? Now that the United States government's factory system is no more, thanks to your boss, as he controls all of it. Do you want me to continue, my Canadian compatriot? Because if you do, I could stay here a week talking about it. I'm sure you don't want that and neither do I, for it would be a waste of time telling you something you already know."

Chouteau looked at Rees uneasily and finally spoke, "What supplies do you need? Do you have a list or will you just tell me what you want?" His manner was brisk and indicated that the sooner he was rid of Rees and his young partner, the happier he would be.

"We will need some things for our 'possibles sack'. We'll need some soap and sugar to make salve if we should have wounds which fester, some needles and thread, throw in a pipe for each of us, and tobacco. For our trapsack, we'll need some castoreum and ten traps for each of us. We'll also need around sixty pounds of powder, four skinning knives, two tomahawks, two butcher knives, two pistols, and two fusees (short-barreled guns for hunting buffalo) and the usual amount of coffee."

"Don't you need some flints and lead?" Chouteau asked.

"No," Rees answered, "we have our own factory."

Chouteau looked surprised as he glanced from Rees to Nat, then shrugged and turned to fill their order.

It was late September when Rees and Nat reached the junction of the Kansas and Republican rivers. "Do you know where we are, now, laddie?" Rees turned in his saddle to glance back at their two pack horses, then over at Nat.

"From where the sun is right now, I'd guess we're headed almost due west," Nat replied.

"You're right about that, laddie, but what I meant was, does any of this country look familiar to you?"

"Are we close to White Cloud's village?"

"Yes, the village is only a couple of days' ride north of here, but the important thing for you to remember is that we are still in Pawnee country and therefore safe from their harassment, thanks to White Cloud. In a few days that will change, and we'll be entering Cheyenne country. From then on, we'll have to be more watchful. North of the Cheyennes lies the country of the Arapaho and south lie the Kiowa, Comanche, and Apache nations. We'll keep that fact in mind as we follow the Kansas River for three or four more days until we reach its source in the foothills of the Rockies. Then, we'll head due west once more until we reach the upper end of the South Platte River. Once we reach there, we'll begin to watch for a good location to trap."

"The Rockies are not to be believed until you actually see them, laddie, and live in them. There, God created some of His best, and it's undisturbed by man. The mountains reach their pure, snowcapped peaks majestically upward, through the silent air, until they can no longer be seen through the clouds which linger over them. Wall after wall of their blue-green and white, sometimes impenetrable, surfaces unfold before you. The air seems God's breath, itself, so pure it is. The very sound of the rushing water sooths and caresses your nerves until your body relaxes into complete peace and serenity. The gentle breezes rustle through the leaves and they whisper soft sounds of their own.

"The hundreds of species of birds sing their constant blending of choirlike music throughout the mountains. The owl hoots from his night perch and the pigmy owls join in. The mountain quail takes flight as you approach, and the bald eagle screeches his warning from high in the sky as he glides effortlessly through the heavens. The red tailed hawk looks down on you from his perch, with his fearless, piercing eyes. The constant hammering of the woodpeckers, the chirping of the gray-cheeked thrush, blackpoll warbler, bobolink, goldfinch, bluejay, and many other feathered friends of the mountain people, combine to provide a music the like of which you'll never forget."

Rees glanced sideways at Nat, somewhat abashed at revealing so thoroughly his love of the mountains and their creatures. He assumed a more stern expression as he continued, "But danger stalks the mountains also and don't ever forget it. The most dangerous of our foes will be the Indians, but the grizzly come next. A grizzly can weigh better than a ton, and they range everywhere, even to the southwest country. It was not uncommon, in earlier times, to come across fifty or sixty of them in a day's time, and some of the earliest of the mountainmen have told of seeing as many as two hundred in a day. I don't know about that, for my compadres have been known to exaggerate in order to be frightening, but it may not be far off. A grizzly is not afraid of anything and when he stands on his hind legs, he's eight or nine feet tall. Their razor sharp claws can tear a quarry into shreds. What they lack in good eyesight, they make up for with their keen sense of smell. They've been known to retreat when they smell gunpowder, but I wouldn't want to count on it.

"Now the cougar is something different, for he seldom bothers you. He'll see you a lot more often than you'll see him.

"Wolves travel in packs and some of these packs can number as much as a hundred, especially when around buffalo. I guess what I mean to say, laddie, is that old mother nature always has a few surprises waiting for you and not only in animal form. Cold, wind, lightning storms, tornadoes, hunger, and last but not least, even mosquitoes. I guess I hate mosquitoes most of all and the snow mosquitoes can almost drive you mad in their intensity." Rees grinned as he glanced at Nat, "Now, laddie, you can't say that I didn't warn you, and after this, you'll feel lucky if you meet only half of what I've been talking about!

"Sounds like back home," Nat joked ruefully as he rode along beside Rees.

"Yes," Rees answered with a smile, "it sounds just like Pittsburgh, doesn't it?"

"I'll take the dangers in the wild any time to the wildlife to be found in the cities and towns," Nat replied.

"That place up there looks like a good spot to put up for the night. What do you say, laddie?"

"Looks good to me; plenty of good grass and water."

When the two men reached the proposed camp site, they unsaddled their horses and removed the packs from the other horses. Then all of them were hobbled and turned loose to graze.

"Although we're still in Pawnee country, we're close enough to the Cheyennes and Kiowas to keep us on our toes, laddie." Rees scanned the landscape continually as they made camp. "There's always the likelihood that we could run into a war party or hunting party, so be alert, take nothing for granted and suspect any strange movement. What do you say to pheasant or partridge for supper? I saw something move through the tall grass over there in the trees by the river. Why don't you take a crack at the one of the fattest ones? That would make pretty good eating. But don't use your rifle; throw your knife at them . . . it would be good practice for you."

"We'll starve to death if we wait until I can hit one of those birds with a knife," Nat replied with grin, "What's wrong with the rifle anyway? Don't answer that, for I know without you telling me."

"There's probably nothing wrong with using a rifle for chances are that there are no Indians within earshot, but we don't know that for sure, besides, someday you won't have the luxury of using a rifle and then what will you do? Get our supper with your knife, laddie, you're getting pretty good with your knife throwing, so get. I'm powerful hungry."

Nat laid his rifle against his saddle and drawing his knife, headed toward the edge of the trees.

"Laddie!" Rees spoke in a pained voice.

"What's wrong?" Nat turned to face Rees.

"Ain't you going to take that?" Rees's glance turned from Nat to where his rifle leaned, abandoned without a thought. "You won't go wrong if you consider your rifle as one of your arms or legs. You wouldn't leave one of them behind, would you?"

"Sorry." Nat flushed in embarrassment.

"Being sorry won't save your life, laddie, look alive or you won't stay that way for long."

When Nat returned, he had one pheasant and one turkey. He said apologetically, "I couldn't get close enough to get more than one try at the pheasants, but managed to call a turkey."

"Nothing wrong with turkey," Rees said drily.

Nat then noticed some round objects which looked like lily bulbs at Rees's feet.

"What are those?"

"Pomme blanche, we French call them, but you English call them turnips. The Indians call them psoralea lanceolata. I found a few chokecherries, too, laddie. We should have a good meal."

Rees added a few small pieces of dry wood to the little fire as he went on, "I've got some strong saplings peeled so when you finish cleaning the birds, we'll impale them and lay them across these forked sticks either side of the fire. I hope you noticed, laddie, that I've used only dry wood on the fire and I hope you've also noticed that I do not just throw wood on just any old way; lay the dry wood onto the fire so it doesn't smother the flames. That way, there's a minimum of smoke, for smoke can be seen for miles and if not seen, can be smelled by the Cheyennes who are noted for their keen sense of smell."

As the two men sat crosslegged on opposite sides of the fire, eating their meal, Rees began to talk. "Laddie, the French have been allies of the Pawnees for many years and the Cheyennes are bitter enemies of the Pawnees. My father and other Frenchmen fought many battles along side the Pawnees against the Cheyennes, so it goes without saying that we have better steer clear of the Cheyennes if we can, and of their allies, the Hidatas, Arihara, and the Mandans. Just being French is enough of a reason for the Cheyennes to come looking for us. The French knew of the Cheyennes when they lived east of the Mississippi; before they moved into the Dakotas. They were called Chariena then, and they were planters in those days. The Sioux, themselves displaced from their lands east of the Mississippi, drove the Cheyennes southward from the Dakotas. The

Cheyennes are believed to speak a language akin to the Algonquins, whereas the Sioux and the Iroquois speak a language which is similar. I think it is safe to say that if the Iroquois and Algonquins were enemies way back then their offshoots are now enemies as well."

Rees leaned foward to pour himself more coffee and looked inquiringly at Nat who nodded and held out his cup. "Are you tired of hearing me run on, laddie?"

"I'm never tired of learning about the Indians, Rees. I guess one man could never learn all about them, but whatever you can tell me, I'm eager to learn."

"I don't need much encouragement, I guess," Rees grinned, "but to get back to what I started to say, Lewis and Clark reported that they saw the Cheyennes in South Dakota when they were headed west to explore the newly purchased Louisiana Territory, in 1804. Since that time the Cheyennes were driven still farther south and west by other eastern Indians who, with their white man's weapons, had little trouble taking the land of the Cheyennes from them. In order to help stave off attacks from the more powerful eastern Indians, they formed a loose confederation with the Arapahoes, in which they are still involved now. And we, my friend, are about to enter their lands on our way westward.' Rees reached for another piece of turkey.

"When will we leave the river and head for the mountains, Rees?"

"We'll follow the river until we come to the South Platte, than we'll stay with the south bank of it until we reach its source in the Rockies."

"How far is it until we get to the Rockies?"

"About two hundred and fifty to three hundred miles, if we follow the river and to anticipate your next question, laddie, it would be closer if we left the river and headed due west, but it is more dangerous in many ways. First, you have to remember that you are not in Virginia now and there are fewer trees out here, as you have seen. Most trees grow only along the river banks, and once you leave the river, you see nothing but miles of rolling country covered with only grass. Water is scarce out here, laddie, for it doesn't rain as predictably as it does back east. But, when it does rain, mostly in the early spring and summer, it comes up quickly and is usually accompanied by a tremendous thunderstorm, with lightning crashing across the sky like lines in an ancient, dried up lake bed. It can light up the night sky as if it were day, and almost as rapidly as it hits the earth, it disappears into the dry ground. Then come the mosquitoes, gnats, and the like."

"Your lips can crack from the hot wind, and your eyelids burn from the steady, scorching heat. The grass turns brown from the sun and little rain. then, if we were really unlucky, we could meet a tornado or something about as bad, and the hordes of grasshoppers which seem to arrive when things look too good. If that's not enough to worry you, laddie, a prairie fire, hot as it is, can chill your blood, if you ever have the misfortune to see one."

Rees grinned as he filled his pipe. "I'm telling it pretty scary, laddie, but earlier I told you the wonders of the country and thought I'd better prepare you for what can also happen."

He lit his pipe and leaned back against his saddle and went on, "Speaking of chilling your blood, laddie, in the late fall and during the winter, a northern can sometimes catch you. It's a blizzard peculiar to the plains country and can come up so suddenly that in one minute you can hardly find your way through the blinding snow. It seems to be a black cloud with a mixture of snow and sand and it's about as cold as you'll ever want to get. It hits so fast the temperature can drop twenty or thirty degres in a matter of minutes and you and your horse will have to keep moving to keep from freezing."

Nat glanced at Rees and grinned, "You didn't tell me about the boogy men. Tell me about the boogy man, Rees. Tell me that the mosquitoes are so big that the boogy men ride them and make darting dives at you from every direction. Don't stop there, Rees!"

Rees grabbed a piece of turkey and threw it at Nat as they both burst into laughter. "As I said before, I guess I have told it pretty scary, laddie, but it's better to be aware of what we face than not know anything of what to expect. Let's check the horses and scout around a little and then get some sleep." Rees took up his rifle and started toward their grazing horses.

It was two days later, at a location where the river had narrowed to a distance of perhaps one hundred yards and there were very few trees, when, as the men rode in silence, Rees suddenly froze in his saddle. Nat had learned his lesson well and he too, froze, waiting for Rees to enlighten him. It was Rees who spoke first as the ground began to shake under their feet. Their horses had to be checked as they jumped in alarm. "Buffalo stampede," shouted Rees. "Could be a hunting party or a prairie fire!"

Nat pointed off toward the southeast at the dust stirred up by the oncoming herd. Were it not for the trembling of the earth, it might have been just an approaching thunder storm. "It's a big herd, Rees. There must be thousands in that herd!"

Rees was surveying the terrain for a safe shelter and yelled to Nat, "Follow me."

On the same side of the river from which the buffalo were coming, was a high bluff overlooking the river bank. On the bluff grew the only trees in that area. They quickly led their pack horses into the river and followed the line of the shore until they were beneath the trees. The horses were nearly belly deep in the clear, river water. Some of the tree roots were exposed from previous floods which had washed away part of the river bank.

"Tie the horses to the roots . . . hurry" Rees yelled to be heard above the thunderous sound of the approaching herd. Dust filled the air as Rees motioned for Nat to follow him. Rees twisted his body this way and that as he penetrated the thick mass of exposed roots until he was completely concealed in a small enclave beneath the trees. Nat joined him and they watched as the first of the herd set foot in the water. Hundreds of buffalo hit the water running and swam the river not many feet from where the horses and men waited. Many minutes passed before the bulk of the herd had passed and as the herd thinned, more of the bulls spotted the horses and gave them angry glances as they entered the river.

Rees motioned to Nat to ready his rifle as he was doing to be prepared to defend the horses. None of the bulls charged, however, for they were eager to catch up with the herd which was still hightailing it in a north-westerly direction. Rees placed his fingers to his lips to caution Nat to remain quiet and then raised his left hand with the palm down and rubbed his right hand from the fingertips to his wrist over his left hand, warning Nat that Indians could be following the buffalo. Nat nodded his head in understanding and listened intently. Now the distant sounds of the horses' hooves could be heard. Nat nodded at Rees to show that he, too, heard the sounds that they hoped not to hear. The hoofbeats came closer and then voices could be hear.

Rees touched his nose gently with the index finger of his right hand three or four times, then he sniffed, indicating to Nat that the odor he picked up was that of Cheyenne warriors.

Suddenly, the voices became war cries and the hoof beats dashed away. Rees slowly began to extricate himself from the tree roots until he was once again in the water beside the horses. He looked up and down the river several times and then climbed the bank until he could crawl over the edge under a low growing bush. Now he parted the limbs carefully and looked in the direction the warriors had ridden. What had distracted the warriors from their buffalo hunt? He grinned as he saw seven Pawnee braves charging down the slope of a small hill north of the four Cheyenne buffalo hunters. The Pawnees were in full dress war regalia and war paint. The Cheyennes did not hesitate to take up the challenge which was being thrown at them, and raced toward the intruders, brandishing their weapons.

"The Cheyennes were surprised by the Pawnee war party," Rees muttered to Nat who was now at his side. "Watch the Cheyenne warrior with the long lance curved into a semicircle at the upper end. He is one of the bravest men of the Elk Society. Only two braves in that society are permitted such lances and they are the two bravest."

Nat saw that the lance was highly decorated. The entire shaft was wrapped with rawhide and at the end of the curved shaft dangled eagle feathers with colorful bead work above the feathers. Further down the shaft, the hide was dyed with bright green and yellow dye. The owner of this symbol of bravery had a round buffalo hide shield tied to his saddle just behind his left side and an arrow quiver across his back, with the bow atached to the upper side.

Both Pawnees and Cheyennes wore only breech cloths with colorful designs woven into them. The Pawnees wore war paint on their faces as well as on their bodies. Their legs were painted with various colors in a straight line, some vertical and some horizontal. The Cheyennes, however, wore no war paint decorating their bodies because they had been on a buffalo hunt.

As the two parties charged at each other, yelling their war cries, all held their shields close to their bodies, and brandished long handled tomahawks. The Cheyennes held their decorated shields, also. They did not wave tomahawks, but displayed the lances they used for hunting. Nat took the advice of his partner and kept his eyes glued to the Cheyenne warrior with the curved lance. This warrior selected one of the Pawnees as his target and headed straight for him. The Pawnee brave responded with a war cry as he adjusted his shield and charged his adversary. Nat noticed that the Cheyenne slipped his feet from his stirrups as he drew close to the Pawnee and when within ten feet of his quarry, he released his lance with great speed and prepared to spring at his enemy from his charging horse. His shield crashed into the unsuspecting Pawnee's face with such force that the Pawnee was thrown to the ground. Before the Pawnee warrior had a chance to respond, the Cheyenne was on him. Nat could hear the victory yell of the Cheyenne as he withdrew his knife. It was at that point that the remaining Pawnees turned and fled in the direction from which they had come. The Elk Society warrior stood over the body of his dead enemy as he gazed after the retreating Pawnees in bewilderment. One of his fellow braves enlightened him as he pointed to the dust being stirred up by the approaching Cheyenne buffalo hunting party.

The Elk warrior then reached down and grabbed the Pawnee scalplock and with two swift swipes with his knife, held the bloody, dripping scalp high over his head.

"Let's hope that the Cheyennes did not spot us before they were diverted by the Pawnees," Rees muttered as he glanced sideways at Nat and turned back to watch the Cheyennes. The two mountainmen watched in concealment as the two parties of buffalo hunters were joined. Distant voices could be heard as the two groups mingled. The apparent leader of the Cheyennes looked in the direction which the buffalo had taken. Now he extended his arm in the direction of the disappearing herd. He then turned his head in the opposite direction and motioned for the party to return to the main body.

"Luck is sure with us this day, laddie," Rees said as he slid down the riverbank toward the horses. "Let's be on our way before the Cheyennes have a change of heart."

They followed the river thereafter until Rees decided it was time to head for the South Platte, and after days of riding, the men reached the big bend of the South Platte River.

"Now," Rees said eagerly, "we begin to look for beaver. We'll leave our belongings under that huge fur tree over there. It's tall enough and the limbs are bowed enough to serve as a tent."

"Why don't we build a lean-to or a small cabin?" Nat asked.

"For a number of reasons; in the first place we'll have to do some scouting to see if this area is rich in beaver and secondly, no mountain-man worth his salt builds shelter such as you mentioned, exceptin' in the winter. These trees will do just fine. The area is sheltered enough against the wind and it is open enough for our camp smoke to dissipate quickly. We'll hold off on the cabin till winter, laddie, that is if the beaver warrant it."

Their pack horses were unloaded, hobbled, and turned loose to graze in the high grass which grew along the banks of the river. All of their goods were stacked around the trunk of the tree for protection from rain. Then the two men took a few traps and castorum and put them into their trap-sacks and tied them behind their saddles. Each slid a tomahawk under his belt, and checked to see if they had enough of Otto's shells in their am-munition sack to last them through any emergency, a normal precaution.

"I guess we're ready, laddie. Let's look for beaver."

It wasn't too long before Rees said, "There's beaver along the river bed down there. See them?" Rees pointed and continued. "The river here is not running very swiftly so the chances are they've built some dams far-ther upstream. They build them of small branches and twigs and small trees as a rule, and of mud and anything else the beaver thinks will make his home snug." He pointed farther up the river, "There . . . I'll bet the beavers have felled those fallen trees."

When they reached the trees, it was obvious they had been felled to be used in a dam which was nearby. The small limbs, bark, and twigs were so intricately and masterfully woven together that the dam had backed water for quite a way upstream. It had widened and made a good size pond. The spring runoff had flooded the pond and stagnant water contributed to swampy conditions on either side of the pond. Trees of various sizes were partially submerged in the morass which resulted and a good many of them were dead, killed by the sharp teeth of the beaver.

"These are what we call 'lodge beavers' laddie, because they build their homes in quiet water. Those who build near swift water, tunnel their homes into the soft dirt along the river banks just above water level. Those are called bank beaver."

Rees sat in his saddle surveying the area as he searched for sign. His nostrils twitched as they did their work. Every now and then he cocked his head so he could hear unusual sounds. Finally he spoke, "What do you think, laddie are we safe? Can you sense any danger about?"

Nat said nothing as he too, tested his senses. A slight breeze came up as Nat sniffed an additional time. "I think I smell blood, Rees can you?"

Rees nodded, "Animal blood, laddie." He slowly swung from his saddle. He checked his rifle as he cautiously headed away from the river. "Elk . . . over here." He pushed some brush aside with his free hand. Nat joined him and they looked down at what was left of an elk cow. Rees began to search the area again as he said, "Why would they leave their lunch? Us, I reckon." His eyes were fixed on the thick underbrush upwind of them. His eyes returned to the partially devoured elk and he walked closer to it, and got down on one knee to check for prints. "Grizzly!" He quickly rose to his feet. "The varmint smelled us coming and hightailed it that way."

He pointed into the densest part of the forest. He'll be back once he knows we're going to stay. He'll think that we will take his food." The horses began to nicker and show signs of fright as they looked upwind. Their ears were pricked and they were skittish, looking for the slightest excuse to bolt.

"We'd better get back to the pack horses and get across the river before the grizzly get back. I figure he's not too near yet, but he's probably not very far off either, for the horses sure scent him."

They started back to the camp. A strong breeze blew in from the opposite direction and Rees turned his head slightly as he said, "I got a whiff of him then, didn't you?"

"I think so," Nat said as he tried to quiet his horse. "It's a good thing we're heading away from him or old Boots wouldn't be going so willingly!"

"He may be a quarter of a mile away. That's one of our big advantages, laddie, when some danger is upwind of us, it's easier to spot it. I should have caught it sooner, though. I've been out of this country too long, I guess, and my senses are weakened, but they will be back at full strength shortly!"

"They better be," grinned Nat.

They reached the pack horses who raised their heads and watched them as they rode into camp. Nat rode for the horses and drove them toward Rees who quickly haltered them and removed their hobbles. Nat threw the packs back on, as quickly as he could, making sure they wouldn't lose them as they made tracks. They were on their way shortly as Rees chuckled, "Nothing like a grizzly to let a man know how fast he can move."

They loped toward the river and were midstream when the grizzly came out of the underbrush and reared up, pawing the air and sniffing in their direction. If the pack horses had been somewhat reluctant to leave the good grass and had hung back a little as they were led into the river, they now picked up enthusiasm and instead of being dragged along behind the riders, they ran to out-distance them. Horses have very little in common with bears and do their best to avoid them if at all possible.

Rees shook his head as he tried to fathom why the horses hadn't picked up the scent of the bear before this. He must have craftily kept downwind of them, or they'd have stampeded before they ever got back to camp. Even a hobbled horse could travel pretty fast if he had such incentive.

Once they had reached dry land, stumbling up the steep river bank in haste, Rees yelled to Nat to get the horses out of sight in the trees beyond. "Tie them securely and come back to give me a hand." Rees swung from his saddle, rifle in hand. He knelt and took careful aim. Nat had disappeared into the trees as Rees took his first shot. The grizzly let out an agonized roar and again reared to his hind legs, then fell forward on all fours as it lunged into the water. Rees took careful aim for his second shot as the bear reached midstream. The bullet cracked through his skull and the grizzly raised both front legs in a desperate attempt to show his hatred for the intruders, and then, with the sound of death rattling in his throat, sank motionless into the water. Nat was now at Rees's side watching the grizzly as the water turned him slowly downstream.

"That was a close call," Nat breathed as he began to relax. His relaxation was shortlived for he was interrupted by a scream of anger and revenge which broke the silence as the she bear came crashing through the underbush where they had first seen the male. In her angry rush to reach the two men, small trees and bush were uprooted by her powerful claws. She reached the riverbank at the speed of a horse, and her powerful hindquarters propelled her bulk through the air until she splashed into the water at least fifteen feet from shore. Two bullets hit her as she hit the water, but her powerful legs were propelling her body with great speed toward Nat and Rees. The two men fired a second round, hitting her again, but the shots did not stop her forward movement.

"My God," Rees yelled as he reloaded his rifle, "how can she keep coming? She should be dead!"

Their third salvo hit her as she lumbered up the bank of the river toward her targets. She rose on her hind feet as Nat and Rees were about to fire for the fourth time, connecting each time. With all the strength left at her command, she roared her final roar. It was deafening. She slowly slid to the ground and in one last desperate effort to reach her prey, she extended her right front leg with its razor sharp claw extended. The leg slid back towards her body, digging up the grass as it went.

Nat and Rees moved slowly toward the bear with their rifles aimed at her head. When they reached the grizzly, Rees nudged her with the barrel of his rifle. As he did so, the bear's claws extended and retracted, and she sighed as her eyes opened for the last time.

"Look at those eyes, laddie. Did you ever see such a fierce expression? They're formidable enemies and they've killed many a mountainman and Indian." He tapped his rifle stock and went on, "Even with these rifles, they're not easy to bring down. Why don't you go after the horses, if they've not managed to leave the country, that is. I'll skin her out, for we can sure use her hide and grease, though I'm not partial to bearmeat."

They moved back across the river before dark and made camp in the same place they'd chosen earlier.

The following morning the two mountainmen began to set out their traps. When the location was found for the first trap, Rees said, "Let me explain something about trapping as I set one. First, we wade out into the water and find a spot where the water is between three and six inches deep. We then pound a strong stake into the river bed and attach the chain of the trap to the stake." As he talked, Rees extended a small stick from the bank of the river until it reached out over the trap. It shouldn't be over six inches above the water." He reached for the castorum, "Then we spread a little of this on the stick. This is what brings the beaver to the trap. When the beaver reaches the area under the stick, he tries to reach the castorum and to do that he has to put one of his feet on the ground under the water. When he does this, he steps into the trap. Once his foot is in the trap, he tries to get away, and after a struggle, he drowns, for the trap is in deep water. That's all there is to it, laddie. Now, why don't you take your traps and go up the left side of the river, and I'll set mine on the right side, and remember, make sure that your stake is secure because sometimes these beavers can reach ninety to a hundred pounds, even though the average is twenty to forty pounds. If this area hasn't been trapped before or for quite a spell, we could get quite a few of those big fellows." As Nat rode off, he called, "And always watch for sign . . . we don't want any surprises by man or beast."

Rees was standing in shallow water and, as he worked, he could hear Nat pounding in one of his stakes. From time to time he looked up and over at Nat to make sure that he was doing his job right. Rees smiled his approval and returned to his own work.

Early the following morning, the two men were out checking their traps and Nat found a small beaver in his first trap. He waded into the water until he reached the stake and then reached down into the water and got a good grip on the five foot long chain and pulled the drowned beaver to him. After he opened the trap, he pulled the dead beaver to the surface, threw it on the bank and then reset the trap. He then waded back to dry land and slid his skinning knife from its sheath. He turned the beaver onto its back and streched its four legs back as far as he could. In a few seconds, his knife had slit the beaver from head to tail and down to the ends of its legs. He quickly forced the hide from the carcass with his fist. When this was completed, he cut a small branch and made a rack upon which he stretched the pelt. Upon completion of this task, he wiped the blade of his knife by sliding it across his pant leg. He then returned it to its case and leaned the stretched beaver pelt against a tree trunk. His eyes examined the pelt as he reminded himself to clean it later when he returned to camp. He continued along the river toward his next trap, where he was surprised to find that the stake which held his second trap had been torn loose and it and the trap were gone. He stiffened as his eyes surveyed the area. He listened and sniffed the air for any sign of a thief, but could find no indication that any such thing had taken place. He now realized what had happened. Somehow the beaver had pulled the stake loose from its secured position in the river bottom and had dragged it upon dry land as it attempted to escape into the brush. Nat followed the clear trail let by the beaver as it headed into the patch of scrub oak brush. The leaves of the oak were quivering and Nat realized that the beaver with his trap and stake chain were tangled in the brush. He approached cautiously and to his surprise he saw a huge beaver, maybe seventy-five to eighty pounds in weight. It was in the process of bitting off its trapped foot in order to free itself. Nat slid his tomahawk from his belt and before the animal realized he was near, the trapper struck the beaver on the head, killing it instantly. Nat then cut off the beaver's tail for their supper that night. Rees would be surprised at the size of this one, he thought to himself.

"What kind of luck did you come up with, laddie?"

Nat leaned his racks against a tree and dropped down by the fire where

Rees sat smoking his pipe. "Looks like you did fine; how many did you find?"

Nat rose and walked back to the tree and selected the largest pelt and walked back to the fire. "I got quite a few, along with this big one."

"That's good news," Rees said as he inspected the pelt. "Finding this fellow means that this area probably hasn't been trapped in quite a spell. We'd better prepare the pelts." He rose and walked to get his scraper.

The two men laid out their racks of pelts and using some fresh manure mixed with some of the red clay found nearby, they rubbed the mixture into the freshy side of each pelt.

"We'll keep these watered down for a few days, laddie, and then gather some animal brains and mix it with wild berries and ashes and rub that into the pelts to keep them from getting stiff. We will scrape off whatever flesh is still on them, and then the softening process is complete. I don't like to smoke my pelts; it's too dangerous, for the smoke could draw Indians."

The two men trapped progressively farther up the river until they judged that the beaver population was thinned out. "I think it's time to bundle up our pelts and move on up the river, laddie."

The next morning they saw that snow had fallen on the top third of the mountains during the night.

"Winter is approaching," Rees commented as he studied the snow covered peaks.

"Looks like . . . " Nat did not finish his sentence as a sense of danger vibrated through his body. He turned toward Rees and saw that Rees had sensed it before he did.

"Put out the fire," Rees whispered, but Nat did not have to be told. He had the fire nearly out as Rees finished whispering.

The two men caught up their rifles, checked their ammunition, and felt for their knives and tomahawks to be sure they were in place.

"Get the horses and tie them under the tall fir trees, laddie. Pick trees where the limbs come close enough to the ground to conceal the horses. I'll be right back."

"Right," Nat muttered as the two men went their separate directions. Nat had the horses concealed when Rees returned.

"Arapaho," Rees whispered to Nat. "Five of them, less than a mile up the river. They must have crossed the river east of here before the river turned west. They have a Cheyenne woman with them, evidently a captive. Their camp is unguarded, which means that they don't know we're here. Farther to the east, I spotted a lone Cheyenne brave on horseback. He must be a relative of the captive. Apparently, the Arapahos do not know that the Cheyenne is following them. He may have just caught up with them after trailing them for many days. The Cheyenne brave has painted his whole head black and his horse's also."

80

"What does that mean?"

"He will fight to the death against those who have dishonored him and his woman. He expects to die trying to rescue her, but laddie, I think we ought to even the odds a little, and give the Cheyenne a fighting chance. What do you say?"

"What do you have up your sleeve, Rees?" Nat grinned.

"Get me that she-bear skin. The head and legs are still on it. I'll wrap it around me so that the Arapahos will think that I am a real bear."

"Then what will you do?"

"You'll see," Rees answered as he led one of the horses from under a fir tree. "You come with me and hide yourself close to the Arapaho camp just in case my plan doesn't work."

In a short while, Nat was settled in his hiding place downwind from the Arapaho camp. He lay stretched out in a prone position, with his rifle ready. From his vantage point, he could see the Arapahos, seated around their campfire a few feet from the river's edge but he could not spot the Cheyenne brave. None of them suspected that they were being watched. Nat caught a movement about fifty feet from the Arapahos, and he slowly turned his head to see what it was. He saw the Cheyenne warrior walking his horse slowly through an area thick with pine trees. On his left shoulder hung a round leather shield which had painted designs and eagle feathers on it. On his head he wore the hollow hide and horns of a buffalo. He wore nothing else except a breech cloth and moccasins. He carried a lance which curved to a semi-circle at the top, and had a tomahawk wedged into his belt.

"He must be a member of the Cheyenne Buffalo Society, and one of the two bravest, at that," Nat muttered softly.

The Cheyenne never took his eyes from the Arapahos as his pony moved slowly over the thick layer of pine needles upon the forest floor. He finally stopped his horse and sat motionlessly, never taking his eyes from his enemy.

Nat heard some light laughter coming from the Arapaho camp, and he turned his attention from the Cheyenne brave to see what had caused the laughter. It appeared that the Arapahos were shaking buffalo bones in some kind of gambling game, maybe to see who would have the captive next. The winner got to his feet and began to stalk his prize when he spotted the Cheyenne warrior. He rushed for his bow and arrows as he yelled to the others. In a few seconds, all five Arapahos were on their feet, bows in their hands and arrow quivers slung over their shoulders. At first, they seemed puzzled by what they saw and stood there as if hypnotized. Finally, one of them moved toward the Cheyenne as he reached for an arrow. The Cheyenne didn't move as the other four spread out and reached for arrows from their quivers. Then very swiftly, the Cheyenne flung his lance into the ground a few feet in front of his horse and grabbed his tomahawk in the same motion. He was challenging the Arapahos to single combat. None of them seemed disposed to accept his challenge, but instead were preparing to shoot their arrows at him.

"Cowards," Nat whispered to himself, "the Cheyenne does not have a chance." He braced his rifle to his shoulder, to even the odds when he noticed the Arapahos lower their bows and begin to back as they watched the intruder.

Nat was puzzled until he glimpsed what appeared to be a grizzly bear riding a horse through the trees behind the Cheyenne brave.

Nat chuckled to himself for Rees had done a good job of wrapping himself in the hide. It really did look genuine.

Now the Cheyenne was puzzled by the actions of his enemies, but he raised his tomahawk and rushed toward them. But before he could reach them, the Arapahos had sprung on their ponies and beaten a hasty retreat across the river. The warrior did not give pursuit, but leaped from his horse and with one swift blow cut the bounds which held the captive woman. She spoke to him excitedly and pointed to Rees. The Cheyenne whirled just as Rees began to shed the skin of the grizzly.

Nat rose from his hiding place and cradled his rifle in his left arm as he watched the Cheyenne spring into his saddle and help the woman up behind him. He rode toward Rees and then saw Nat off to his right. He pulled his horse to a stop and gave each of the mountain men a long searching stare. Then he trotted off into the forest until the trees shielded him from view.

"That one will never forget us," Rees chuckled as he rode over to Nat. "He burned our faces into his brain. I think we have just made a friend."

The two men had been so preoccupied that neither had realized that it was beginning to snow.

"Now laddie, before long we'll have to begin looking for a good spot to build our winter shelter. Let's go back to our camp and gather our belongings and look for a good location."

The remainder of that day was spent searching for a spot where they could build their cabin. When it was found, they set to work immediately, felling tall straight trees and notching the ends. The cabin would protect them from the cold, howling winds which swept the eastern slopes of the Rockies during the long winter months. Days passed before they completed their task. Rawhide was used to make hinges for the door and leather also held the shutters in place. They built the fireplace of mud, sticks, stones, and grass, and the dirt floor was leveled and spread thickly with grass, leaves, and pine needles. Under their bedding of robes, more of the same was heaped up to make their beds more comfortable. A large bottle shaped hole was dug about a hundred yards up river and into this they placed the pelts which they had tanned so far. Rees carefully used all of his skill to conceal the entrance to the cache and then turned to Nat. "Now laddie, we are nearly ready for winter. We will make some pemmican by mixing wild berries and honey with jerky and grease.

For the next few days the two men turned their energies to hunting game, gathering wild berries and raiding a bee hive. The deer and elk meat was cut into thin strips and laid over small, straight limbs which were held in place by forked sticks. A small, low fire was kept constantly burning under the strips of meat, and between the heat from the fire and the dry air and sun, the meat dried rather quickly. When it was dried, Nat and Rees hammered some of it into a pulp, added fat, berries, and honey and then stored it in the leather bags which the Indians called parfleches.

The hides from the deer and elk were treated and tanned into soft leather which they would later make into shirts and pants. Each man took the choice leather and made himself a long shirt which extended almost to his knees. When the shirts were complete, they took them to the river and let them soak in the water for a few hours. They were then hung from tree limbs in such a way that when they were dry, they were stiff and rigid, so much so that arrows would be deflected from them.

The sun was directly overhead one day when Nat hurriedly returned to the cabin with an armful of kindling. He found Rees inside making lunch. "Rees, listen, you can barely hear them, but I think I heard shots."

Rees stepped outside quickly and listened, "I believe you're right, laddie. We had better see what the shootin' is about. It's my guess that Indians have some trappers in a pinch. We'd better hurry or we'll be too late."

The shooting was not far away now as the two men tied their horses to trees just a few feet from the top of a ridge. They approached the ridge in a crouched position, hurrying through the knee-deep snow until they could see what was happening below. As they gazed down from their vantage point, they could see at least twenty Comanche warriors attempting to conceal themselves behind trees which covered the lower levels of the mountain ridge opposite. From their elevated position, they were able to make out at least three mountainmen behind a fallen log which lay a few feet from a narrow stream.

"I think the man on the right has an arrow in his left shoulder," said Rees.

"I don't see it," Nat answered.

"He broke off the shaft, no doubt," Rees whispered. "Watch him closely and you will see that his left arm is useless. He loads his rifle with only his right hand as he holds it between his knees."

"What are Comanches doing this far north?" Nat speculated. "I thought their stomping grounds were farther south."

"They are," Rees replied absently as he studied the situation below them, "There doesn't seem to be any easy way, so I guess we had better join the three men. We can circle this ridge and hit the river which runs by them. We'll be out of sight of the Comanches until the last few yards."

They were wading the stream on a high lope when the mountainmen saw them and one of them let out a whoop, "Looks like we have reinforcement, and none too soon!"

Nat and Rees reached dry land and made a rush for the protection of the fallen tree as the others gave them a covering fire as well as they were able. As they adjusted themselves for the best possible view of their assailants, the leader of the mountainmen said, "Welcome to our party! I'm called Nelson; the ugly one there," he pointed with his rifle butt, "answers to the name of Mc Dermitt, and our patient goes by the name of Happy . . . right now his name don't suit him too good."

"I'm Rees and my sidekick here is Nat." Rees continued to peer over the tree trunk. "Look like you fellows got yourselves into a bit of a fix."

"Seven to one is a fair fight," Happy said as he got off another shot, "but with you two, it gives us the clear advantage."

"What kind of thundersticks are you two toting?" asked Mc Dermitt.

"They're called 'Mullers'," Rees answered. He took careful aim and pulled the trigger. "They were especially made for us by a friend."

Large snow flakes began to drift down lazily and an eastern wind began to blow. "The worst storms always seem to come from the east," Happy grunted as they watched the sun disappear behind the mountain peak in front of them. "I guess we're safe until morning; the Comanches don't fight at night."

"But we don't have that superstition to hinder us, do we?" asked Rees.

"By golly, I think you've hit on something," Nelson exclaimed. "are you thinkin' what I'm thinkin'?"

The mountainmen looked at one another and grinned cheerfully.

"Happy can stay here while the rest of us slip out in the darkness; the snow and the wind should help us, too."

The air became bitterly cold as darkness settled over the area. Snow blown by the increasing strength of the easterly wind made visibility almost zero. The four men moved out from behind the fallen tree one at a time to rendezvous in the secrecy of a thick stand of pines which grew along the stream and up the sides of the canyon. Nelson, with a motion of his left arm, led the crouched men into the snow and wind toward where the Indians were waiting.

84

"Always downwind, laddie," Rees whispered, "always downwind."

Nelson raised his arm and all of the men froze. Nelson looked toward Mc Dermitt and pointed a little to his left as he motioned with his hand across his throat. Mc Dermitt slid silently into the wall of heavy snow flakes as Nelson motioned for Rees to do the same to his right side. Rees took his hunting knife from its sheath and disappeared into the blinding snow. Nelson and Nat each chose a tree and concealed themselves behind it. Within four or five minutes, Rees returned with blood all over his right arm and chest. He nodded to Nelson who grimly nodded in return. Nearly ten minutes passed before Mc Dermitt returned. He looked at Nelson and nodded. Nelson waved the men forward. They chose their steps carefully as they glided through the snow in a single file, behind Nelson. Now they could smell the fragrance of burning cedar and a muffled voice could be heard occasionally. They could also smell the odor which was distinctly Comanche.

Nelson motioned for the men to spread out and await his signal. Eighteen Comanches sat around a blazing fire. They wore blankets around their shoulders while buffalo robes provided a cushion from the cold ground. Both Nelson and Mc Dermitt showed surprise at seeing that many Comanches and Mc Dermitt tried to hide his chagrin at not having disposed of more of the enemy in a solid day of returning their fire. Nelson glanced at each man in turn and waited for his nod, each raised his rifle and chose a target. Nelson fired first and his shot was followed by three more roars. One Comanche fell forward into the fire and three others fell away from it. The unique mountainman yell filled the heavy, snowladen air as the men closed in for the kill. The Comanches sprang to their feet, but before they could prepare to repell the attack, the mountainmen were on them like mountain lions springing on their prey. Rees plunged his knife into the stomach of his opponent and with great swiftness forced it upward until it could go no higher. A sound of escaping air could be heard as Nelson held a Comanche by the scalp lock, tight against his chest and slid his knife blade across the throat of the Indian. The blood curdling yell of the mountainmen was released continuously during the fight. Mc Dermitt struggled with his antagonist as did Nat, and Nelson continued the fray, uttering his own version of the yell and brandishing a tomahawk which he sank into the skull of Mc Dermitt's adversary. The blood-covered snow was kicked about by the scuffling feet of the contestants. Within a few minutes, a silence fell upon the little clearing and the mountainmen took stock of themselves and their work.

The silence was broken as Rees yelled, "Laddie . . . laddie!" He turned this way and that as his eyes searched the ground. "They've got Nat." His eyes narrowed with rage, "Those bastards have Nat!" He turned quickly as he heard the sound of hoofbeats and as swiftly as a rattlesnake strikes, he dashed toward the horses of the other mountainmen. Rees did not take time to put his foot in the stirrup, but sprang into the saddle in one bound. The startled horse kicked up snow as Rees yelled and dug his heels into its sides. Rees and the horse disappeared into the darkness as Nelson yelled to his men, "We'd better give him a hand."

Mc Dermitt caught an Indian pony as it shied out of the way of Rees's headlong charge, and Nelson caught up another, and they raced after Rees trying to catch up with him, trailing the dark prints in the snow. Suddenly they pulled up their horses in amazement. They could not believe what was before them. A band of Cheyennes led by a warrior wearing a buffalo headdress formed a semi-circle around Nat and the remaining Comanches. The Comanches looked for an escape route, but before they could make a move, the Cheyenne leader raised his lance with its decorated curved top and immediately thirty or forty Cheyennes fitted arrows into their bow strings. The warrior with the curved lance pointed at Nat until a Comanche brave released the lead rope with which he held Nat's horse. Rees watched the entire episode from his position a good distance behind the Comanches. He saw Nat ride away from his captors toward the Cheyennes. A Cheyenne came forward and cut the leather thong which bound Nat's hand. The Cheyenne chief next pointed his lance southward, the Comanches trotted off in that direction as Rees and the others rode out toward Nat.

The chief of the Cheyennes looked long at Rees and then turned his horse slowly and he and his fellow Cheyennes disappeared into the heavy, blowing snow. Rees watched the Cheyennes until they vanished and then continued to look into the direction in which they had ridden. "Thank you," he said, in a low voice. Then he turned his horse and yelled, "Let's get to the cabin before we freeze to death!"

When he had reached the cabin, Nat took care of the horses while the others went inside to prepare for surgery on Happy's shoulder. As Nat entered the cabin, he heard Nelson say, "Are you ready, Happy?"

"Get it over with," came Happy's gruff reply.

Nelson nodded to Mc Dermitt who was heating his knife to red hot. Mc Dermitt nodded and Nelson passed his knife over the flames a few times in an attempt to cleanse it. He knelt down over Happy, lying on a bear skin in front of the fireplace, and started to make a incision. As he watched, Nat realized that this wasn't the first time Nelson had done such work. Happy closed his eyes as Nelson dug for the arrowhead, mumbling all the while he fished for it. Happy didn't utter a sound, although he grimaced from time to time.

After what seemed like ages, Nelson looked up triumphantly. "Got the blasted thing!" He held the arrow point in his hand with the short shaft which was still attached to it. Happy opened his eyes, but Mc Dermitt said, "We're not done yet, my friend."

Happy closed his eyes again once more as Mc Dermitt moved his knife from the flames and pressed it against the bleeding wound. Smoke rose as the hot steel cauterized the wound. From Happy's throat came three separate deep moans and the odor of burning flesh filled the small cabin. Happy finally opened his eyes once more and muttered, "Is that it?"

"That's it," Nelson and Mc Dermitt replied almost simultaneously.

"Good," Happy tried for a smile, "for a minute there I thought you two were beginning to enjoy yourselves."

"I think I left something in there," Nelson grinned as he pretended to do some more digging.

"In a pig's eye," Happy grinned painfully.

"Don't make any sudden moves, Happy," Nelson said seriously, "not until the wound has begun to heal."

"Hand me my Bible," Happy said as he began to relax.

The Bible was duly handed to him and he began to read it.

Later that night, after they had partaken of supper, the men sat near the fire and Mc Dermitt began to read his worn copy of Skakespeare's works.

Nelson saw the glances of surprises which Nat and Rees exchanged and told them, "He's an ex-college professor." Nelson jerked a thumb in Mc Dermitt's direction. "He taught at the University of New Hampshire at Durham for years."

"If you want, you are welcome to read some of those old magazines in my bag over there," Nelson said as he knelt to check on Happy's wound, "or if you prefer poetry, I'm sure Mc Dermitt won't mind if you want to borrow one of his books."

Nat chuckled as he answered, "I'm not sure I can still read even a primer, let alone poetry."

"Time will change that," Happy told him as he glanced up from his Bible.

"I never thought . . . " Nat stopped just in time to keep from uttering an embarrassing remark. "Never mind," he said as he returned to the cleaning of his rifle. After busying himself at this task for awhile, he asked anyone at large, "How high is Pikes Peak?"

Mc Dermitt took his eyes from his book and studied Nat for a moment before he asked, "Don't tell me that you believe that cock and bull story about a mountainman called the 'Macedonian'?"

"The 'Macedonian'?" Nat questioned, "Who in hell is he? All I asked was how high is Pikes Peak and you give me an answer about a mystery man called the 'Macedonian'. I've never even heard of him. Have you, Rees?"

Rees shook his head while Nelson and Happy exchanged glances and looked toward Mc Dermitt.

"Well, since you haven't heard of him," Mc Dermitt began, 'I'll tell you . . . there is a story that has spread throughout the Rockies these last few years about a strange mountainman called the 'Macedonian'. His base is supposed to be on or near Pikes Peak, but no one I have met has ever seen his base, much less the man himself."

Rees chuckled as he looked at Nat and said, "They're pulling your leg, laddie. Fellows, laddie here doesn't need any of your yarns, a la Jim Bridger. Nat here isn't green: he has been in and seen as many battles with the Indians as many youngsters his age, and a lot more than some of them."

"Who's kidding?" Mc Dermitt spoke seriously. "It's true, at least the stories which we have heard about this fellow are true, but we cannot vouch for the accuracy of them. Either he exists or someone else has done such things. You're right about Jim Bridger; he can really tell it scary when a greenhorn is around. They seem to inspire him to new heights each time he trots out his tales. But then I guess we're all tempted along the same lines," he grinned as he thought of some of the tales he'd told in his time. "You know, Rees, old Jim may have invented this 'Macedonian' and spread his reputation among us as well as among the Indians, just to see where it will lead."

"The Indians?" asked Rees.

"Yes, the Indians," Mc Dermitt continued. "There's hardly an Indian in the Rockies who hasn't heard about the 'Macedonian'. To many, the stories told about him and the mystery surrounding him are big medicine. Some even believe he is from the spirit world."

"You've heard of him surely, Rees." Nelson took up the story, "Surely his story has reached east of the Mississippi and into Canada? He is spoken of as far south as Santa Fe."

Rees finally realized that they were not kidding and said, "Tell us the stories about this fellow."

Mc Dermitt looked at Happy and Nelson in turn and Nelson spoke for them both, "You're the scholar, you tell them."

"It is said that he came from the Pindus Mountains of Macedonia, in the Balkans. His father was supposed to have been the town headman of a small village called Valonia. The Moslem Turks ravaged his village and raped and killed his mother and sister. His father was tortured before being impaled upon a stake. The boy escaped somehow, and found his way by ship to California. It is said by those who claim to have talked with him that the Rockies remind him of the Macedonian mountains. His name is difficult to pronounce and so he has been dubbed the 'Macedonian'. He is said to carry a homemade wooden flute and there are some who say that they have heard the sound of Macedonian music floating through the mountain air." Mc Dermitt paused, thinking, and then continued, "I should like to hear such music."

"Have you heard his name?" asked Nat with interest.

"No, but I did hear once that when translated it means rosebud."

"The few people who have claimed to have laid eyes on him say that he always wears a skunk cap of black and silver. Now in my studies, I have read that the national colors of ancient Macedonia during the time of Alexander the Great, who was himself Macedonian, were black and silver. We have also heard that he is a loner, but gives all men, white men and Indians alike, the same treatment. He is said to be fair, honest, and impeccably nondiscriminatory. To him, a man is a man, be he Mexican, Indian, or American. He treats all alike. He has supposedly saved many Indian lives as well as helped many mountainmen when they found themselves in a tight spot."

Mc Dermitt paused to fill and light his pipe and after having taken several puffs continued, "We three think, that the Comanches, were searching for him, hoping perhaps to gain an insight into his powerful medicine. Rumors have it that he can throw a knife at a gold piece and hit it ten times out of ten at fifteen paces. He is said to carry four knives on each side of his vest as well as a knife sheathed on either hip."

"I think we've heard enough of this fairy tale," grinned Rees. He rose and started for the door. "I need some fresh air. Want to come along, laddie? We need to check the horses, anyway."

They walked out into a moonlight night and to the edge of the meadow where they had hobbled the horses. The storm which had come up so quickly had passed, and they could see their dark shapes as they grazed on the tall grass. It was a horse's paradise, a clear, sparkling stream ran through the meadow and the towering peaks surrounding them protected the valley floor from the deep snows. With any luck at all, they would have plenty of grass for the horses until spring.

"What do you think, Rees?" Nat stared up toward Pikes Peak, to their south. "Do you think they're just telling us 'windies'?"

"Only time will answer that question, and if the stories they told us are true, we'll hear them again as we meet up with others here in the mountains. I know one thing, though, when the thaw begins, we'll not continue our trapping up river. Those three in the cabin have probably trapped it out. We'll need to move on and look for a virgin area where there is plenty of beaver."

"Where do you plan on headin'?"

"We can give the White, Green, and the source of the North Platte area a try. I've always had good luck in that area, and once we trap that region for a season, we'll gather our furs, head back and pay Otto a visit. How's that sound to you?"

"It will be good to see Otto again," Nat said.

"I reckon it will be time to hang up my spurs, too, laddie. My folks aren't getting any younger and it's time for me to think of taking care of them, or at least stay nearby to be ready to take over when my father needs me. I'll admit, my bones are beginning to wear out and why not? Goodness knows, they've been put through a lot in the last thirty years! I hate to see the changes that are coming, the immigrants will be filling up the country in a few more years. The poor Indians are the ones who will suffer most. Their entire way of life will have to change. They'll have to bend or be broken. It's a shame, too, for the Indian has much to offer the white man's civilization."

CHAPTER IV

The end of March was near as the men prepared for their departure from their winter home. Nelson, Happy, and Mc Dermitt were heading south and west.

"Watch your topknot!" They waved as they rode off up the valley floor toward the cut which would take them out.

"You, too!" Rees and Nat returned, and they, too, swung into their saddles. "I'd like to visit Mexico some day," Nat said. "From what I've heard, the area around Santa Fe is beautiful and the winters are mild."

"You're right there, laddie, it is beautiful. If it were part of the United States, I would suggest that we have a look there before we head east, but since it's not, I figure I'll stay out of there."

They had ridden single file through a narrow pass for most of the morning before they came out on a little mountain parkland where they could ride abreast. Rees continued with his earlier thoughts. "You know the corruption in Mexico is a way of life. Most accept it as such and make the best they can of it. It's said that even the Catholic Church is involved in it. I've heard that there is a priest who is supposed to serve the people in a town called Mora, but instead of helping the people, he dominates them like a dictator. The whole area is a feudal kindom, with himself as the patron and all the people his serfs. No, laddie, I don't believe I could live in such a place. Maybe some day things there will change, too. Nothing ever remains the same . . . change is inevitable, just as sure as the sun rises every day. When the time is ripe for change, nothing in the world can prevent it from happening. No one, not even the pope can hold back the tide. Some day change will come to Mexico just as it is coming to this country. Nature has a way of letting things run their course, but in due time that course changes just as rivers change their courses. When the warm spring sun melts the snow, it can, and does turn a small and mild looking river into a raging torrent which can carry everything in its path before it. And when the water subsides, the river's course has changed in many locations."

"Speaking of change," Nat said as he shifted in his saddle, "Look at those clouds building up north of us. Maybe we're in for some more snow. Maybe we should have stayed in the cabin for a few more weeks.?"

"It sure does look like we're in for a snowstorm allright," Rees agreed as he studied the clouds. "We'd better look for some shelter."

"We'd better hurry," Nat answered, "the snow is beginning to fall."

In no time at all the ground was covered by three or four inches and the large flakes came down so heavily that it was difficult for Nat and Rees to see each other.

"Stay close," Rees shouted, "we don't want to get separated. But if we do, fire a shot now and then until we locate each other again."

The wind picked up as it blew snow into their faces and within a few minutes its whistle could be heard as it began to bend the limbs on the pine trees.

"It might be too late to find shelter," Rees yelled. "This storm is moving at breakneck speed."

The wind was now so strong that neither man could hear the other even when they yelled at the tops of their lungs. Suddenly, Nat's pack horses panicked at something and they bolted. His horse bucked and threw him as he turned to look after his pack animals. Soon that horse, too, vanished as he galloped after the pack horses. Nat stumbled to his feet and looked for Rees. He yelled a number of times, and when he got no response, he fired one shot, then another, and then a third shot. If Rees had fired in answer, Nat did not hear them, for the wind was blowing at hurricane force, and any chance of being heard was remote. He held one hand in front of his face as he stumbled along in the direction Rees had taken. He watched anxiously for anything which could provide some sort of shelter and when he accidently walked into a thick bush, he fell to his knees and crawled beneath the lower limbs. He realized that this was probably going to be the best he could do in the way of shelter under the circumstances. He leaned back against the base of the bush, his knees drawn up and his head resting on them. How long he remained in that position, he did not know, but when the wind began to die down, he raised his head to look around. The snow had stopped falling and the wind was now reduced to a strong breeze. Everything was blanketed with the purest whitest snow he had ever seen. The limbs of the trees around him were bent almost to capacity with the weight of the heavy wet snow. He crawled out from his shelter and yelled for Rees. Hearing no reply, he fired his rifle and waited; still no answer. Had Rees fallen from a ledge or could his horse have thrown and dragged him? These thoughts went through Nat's mind as he looked about him. As the clouds moved southward, the sun's bright rays reflected on the pure white snow. Nat took the direction he thought they had been going, plunging through drifts and bare ground, swept clear of the snow during the fierce wind. Now he began to find it hard to distinguish the shapes of the trees around him and he belatedly realized that the snow glare was blinding him. He stopped and yelled again, still with no response. He fired his rifle and then fired again with no success. For the first time since the storm had begun, Nat became frightened. He tried to calm himself, telling himself that nothing would be accomplished if he panicked, then, he thought that his mind was playing tricks on him. He stopped and listened intently, "I do hear it, I hear the flute of the 'Macedonia'." He turned this way and that to attempt to locate the direction of the faint sound.

"Over here! I'm over here!" He waited, but the sound of the flute came no closer and he moved in that direction, slowly, cautiously, feeling his way. The music still seemed no nearer and Nat yelled in exasperation, "Stand still, I need your help!"

He could feel pine needles under his feet now as he continued to move toward the sweet, floating music of the flute. It seemed to him that, after what seemed ages, his sight was improving ever so little, and he gave thanks. He realized that he had been led beneath a gigantic ledge at the base of a sheer cliff which had sheltered the area from the blinding storm. Nat realized too that the flute player had saved him and now he had time to worry about Rees and whether he had also survived the storm. He felt that he had, for he was so experienced in the wilds that surely he was all right. He also knew that he had better start a fire and get warm. Maybe the smoke might lead Rees to him. He walked about breaking dead limbs from the evergreens nearby and knelt to try to coax a small flame to strength. In that sheltered spot, the fire warmed him quickly and he tried to decide whether to start out to look for Rees or stay here and wait to see if Rees could have spotted the smoke. But if Rees was hurt, helpless, he should be looking for him now. "He could be dead by morning if he is hurt," Nat muttered to himself as he rose from the fire.

When he stepped out from the protection of the cliff, he was once more in deep snow. "Where should I look first?" He paused and continue to think aloud. "I think we came from that direction, so I'll go on this way. Dear God in heaven, please lead me to my friend."

Nat trudged through the snow as he wove between the trees, huge boulders, and underbrush. His eyes searched for any sign and he listened for sounds. Welcome as the sun's warmth would have been, he was grateful that at least there was no glare to bring back his snowblindness. More and more heavy clouds were beginning to return, and the wind picked up. He knew that if he did not find Rees in the next few hours his friend, if injured, would be dead by morning. If he wasn't hurt, then he was doing the same thing Nat was doing, searching for his friend.

He had walked for what seemed hours when he came to what looked like partly filled hoofprints. He studied them and the direction they were going. They were barely visible and could have been made by some other animal, but he decided it would be wise to follow the tracks. He followed the dim tracks for perhaps an hour until he came upon another sheltered area provided by a high, rocky wall. The sheer wall climbed for at least two hunderd feet before it was broken by an occasional shrub or boulder. The tracks led along the base of the cliff and in spots were more clearcut. He stooped to study one print deciding it was probably not made by an Indian pony. It could be tracks which Rees had made, but where were the other horses? Nat rose and began to trot along as he followed the tracks. Suddenly, the tracks reached a drop of about thirty feet. He stood at the edge, looking down, searching for any sign of movement or anything which might be Rees buried in the snow. Suddenly he thought he saw something, the form of a man covered with snow. "Rees!" He yelled as he slid down the hill, catching at the limbs of bushes as he slid. He rushed to the prone form and dropped to his knees, frantically brushing the snow away. "Rees!" He choked off a cry as he grabbed Rees by the shoulder and began to shake him. "Rees, speak to me . . . Rees!" Nat continued to shake him until his eyes blinked and then slowly opened. A small smile creased Rees's face as he recognized Nat. "Thank God you're alive," Nat said. He examined Rees for any broken bones, and found the left leg was broken, but that appeared to be the extent of the injuries except for a possible case of frostbite. He bent to drag Rees to a more sheltered spot near the bank he had slid down. "You must have hit your head on a rock when you fell," Nat told him. "I thought your head was harder than that." He chuckled as he pulled the fallen man along. Propping Rees against the bank, he began to gather the driest wood he could find and soon had a fire blazing. Then he inspected the broken leg, which seemed to a clean, simple break. "Do your fingers and toes have much feeling in them?"

"No, and neither does my leg as far as that goes."

"Then I want to get it set before any more feeling comes back to it. I don't know too much about setting broken bones . . . maybe you can tell me how?"

"I don't have much choice, do I?" Rees grinned. "The sooner you do it the better, laddie."

Nat left and in a few minutes returned with some limbs he considered suitable for splints. "Can you stand the pain as I pull the leg until the bones are in place?"

"Get on with it." Rees grabbed hold of the trunk of a small tree which grew nearby and braced himself, "Go to it, laddie!"

Nat took a firm grip of the leg and gave a steady pull on it until he felt the broken bone slid into place. Then he took the scarf from his neck and tied it around the injured leg. He fitted the splints tightly to the leg with long fringes cut from his jacket bottom. Several of them tied together served to hold the splints in place. "I think I've got it," he finally grunted as he rose and looked down at his friend.

"Thanks, laddie, you've saved my life, such as it is," grinned Rees wryly.

"You would have done the same for me," Nat told him, "or would you?" He smiled. "I'm going to find a limb of the right shape to make a crutch for you and then we'll head for my shelter."

"Before you do that, laddie, get my rifle, it should be right where I fell."

When the two men had reached the ledge overlooking Nat's shelter, they discussed the probability of finding the horses. The ledge hung over enough to give them shelter from the snow which was falling once more, this time looking as though it would continue for some time.

Rees thought the horses probaby were just down past where Nat had found him. "They may not have wandered far after I fell, Nat. Why don't you have a look before dark?"

Nat checked his rifle and rose to leave.

"Laddie, look for any bark which has been chewed from the trees past where I fell. If they are hungry enough, they'll chew bark as do other animals like elk and deer. It might help you."

Rees looked up from his position by the fire and watched the heavy gray clouds roll in from the north. The high, tree covered mountain towering over him kept him from seeing them until they were directly overhead. He could hear the wind increase its velocity as it whistled through the tree tops. Darkness was falling swiftly when Rees sensed the presence of a human. "I hope that's laddie," he muttered, as he sniffed the air. "I know it isn't an Indian." Now he could smell horses, too.

"It's me, Rees," called Nat as he came into view. "I found my saddle horse and my pack horses, but couldn't find yours."

"Good boy, laddie," Rees murmured, "at least we'll have the jerky and pemmican. And the other horses may come back by morning."

Nat unsaddled his horse, removed the packs from the others. and hobbled them. The packs were slightly loose, but luckily the horses hadn't lost them. When the saddle and supplies were stacked by the cliff wall in the shelter, Nat concentrated on getting them some nourishment. It took a lot of melting snow to obtain enough water for coffee, but this was finally accomplished, and the jerky and pemmican took the edge off their hunger.

"We could use better shelter if this storm keeps on," Rees suggested. "A ditch shelter would be the easiest and best," he told Nat.

"A what?"

"Dig a ditch wide enough for us both to lie down in feet to feet and make it about a foot deep. When you have finished, cover it with enough fir limbs to make an arch. Then dig a small pit in the upper end for a fire. That should protect us from the storm. Tomorrow, if my horses don't show up by themselves, maybe you'll have more good luck and find them."

Nat began immediately on the shelter, feeling grateful that luck had placed the shovel in his pack and not Rees'. By the time the two men had crawled into the ditch and were settled for the night, the storm had picked up in intensity. High over their heads, the wind whistled and whined, but snug in their shelter, they slept undisturbed, too weary to hear the storm as it blew itself out.

Nat was the first to awaken as a drop of water landed on his nose. His eyes opened, but he did not move. Another drop hit him and he slowly turned his head and looked down toward Rees, who was still asleep. "Time to get up, Rees."

Rees opened his eyes drowsily, "It's pitch dark out. It must be the middle of the night."

"I don't think so," Nat answered. "It's dark because the wind has blown the snow up against our shelter." He raised himself on one elbow and looked toward the entrance. "See, the snow has covered it."

He slid down toward the opening on his back and when he reached the end, he kicked with both feet until he had cleared the opening, daylight breaking through. He backed out of the ditch and rose, surveying the beauty of the quiet, sunny morning. He called back to Rees, "It must have snowed all night, for the snow is up to my knees."

In a few minutes Rees pushed painfully out of their shelter and joined him. He got to his feet with Nat's help and leaned on the crutch. "I'll never get used to this damned thing. I've never been an invalid before and I don't much like it. You had better check the horses, laddie. Let's hope they haven't run off again."

When Nat returned, he wore a smile on his face. "You'll never guess what I found with my horses! Or you probably would, since you mentioned the possibility last night."

"My horses have come back, right?"

"Yes."

"Well, I'm not surprised, kinda figured they might be looking for their partners. Or could it have been . . . ?"

Neither man said anything for a few moments, but they both considered the possibility of the Macedonian's having helped them. Nat had related to Rees what he thought he had heard that day before, the faint, lilting strains of a flute. Or had he merely imagined it?

The warm sun was melting the snow quickly in the Crow Village beside the Tongue River. The river was beginning to swell as the water trickled from the wet snow and found its way to the rushing water.

Black Moccasin, a young Crow brave, pushed aside the flap of his tepee and emerged into the clear, cloudless day. His appearence was every bit the brave. Around his shoulders was slung a buffalo robe decorated in beautifully designed beadwork. A necklace of bearclaws hung from his neck and above that was tied a smaller neckpiece made entirely of enemy ears. On his scalplock, he wore three eagle feathers, one of which was split down the center, indicating that he had been wounded in battle. The second feather had a notch cut from its right side, showing that he had killed and scalped an enemy, and the third had a leather band attached along its center from top to bottom, painted with three red dots, which proved that he had killed three enemies.

He was on his way to the chief's lodge to give an account of a five man coup. He stalked proudly and self consciously, and upon reaching his destination, pushed aside the tepee flat and entered the dwelling.

The bravest men of the tribe were seated around the fire, waiting for him to present himself. Among the warriors were three younger men who were present to confirm Black Moccasin's claim. The Crow brave found a vacant spot near the fire and sat down. Now the chief arose and adjusted his blanket, lowering it below his arm. Black Moccasin knew that the lowering of the blanket to this possition meant that the chief was about to speak.

"It has been reported," the chief said, "that you, Black Moccasin have performed five coups simultaneously. If this is confirmed, you will indeed be one of our bravest warriors. Let us hear your story."

Black Moccasin rose and drew himself up proudly; he looked first at his chief and then at the others. "The raiding party which I led into the land of the Pawnee ran across a small band of Pawnee braves, apparently searching for the winter buffalo herd. It was snowing heavily at the time, with visibility next to nothing, and the Pawnee did not know that we were near.

"I instructed Small Bow to shoot an arrow at the nearest enemy, which he did, and when the arrow hit the enemy, he fell from his horse, causing four of his companions to dismount to see what had happened to their friend. I then drew my weapon and made a dash for the dead Pawnee and the four braves who were kneeling around him. When I reached them, my horse was running at full speed and when they saw me approaching, they rose to confront me with their lances ready. When they released their weapons, I jumped from my horse and the lances passed over my head. I hit the ground running and before they could draw their knives, I hit all four with my fist and kicked the dead warrior and then jumped to the back of one of the Pawnee horses and galloped back to my raiding party. That is my deed." He once more sat down in the circle of men, looking at no one.

"Is this accurate?" the chief looked at Small Bow.

"It is as Black Moccasin has said. What he has told you, I saw with my own eyes."

The chief spoke once more, "The greatest of all coups is that of touching a dead enemy while he is being protected by his people. This you have done. You are a brave warrior." The chief now turned to Buffalo Hair, Right Hand, and Fast Legs who all nodded their approval of Small Bow's report.

"Let it be told around the campfires of our people of the great coups which you, Black Moccasin, have made. From this day forward, you may wear five more eagle feathers, signifying your five simultaneous coups. Wear them with the pride and honor befitting a great Crow warrior."

The chief continued after a pause, "The Crow warriors are born to bring pride and honor to their people, Black Moccasin is continuing this tradition. He will, in no way, bring disrespect or disgrace to his people or nation. Death would be preferable to dishonor. This is the code of all great Crow warriors."

Now Black Moccasin spoke, "This is the code which I have respected with deep pride and I have dedicated my life to its preservation."

The group dispersed and as Black Moccasin left the tepee of the chief, he was joined by his friend, Small Bow.

"Where are you going now, my friend?"

"To see the interpreter of dreams," Black Moccasin answered. "I had a dream last night and I am not sure of its meaning. I want it explained to me. I think it was about the white man who travels through many nations doing only good and blowing air into his wooden stick. I must find this man, for it is said that he is not a man but a god. I want to ask for some of his medicine."

When Black Moccasin reached the tepee of the interpreter of dreams, he called out, "Interpreter of dreams, I ask for a council with you. May I enter your dwelling?"

"Enter," a voice answered from within.

When the Crow warrior entered the tepee, he saw its occupant crouched over his fire. He was wrapped in a blanket tucked securely beneath his chin. His hands could not be seen for they held the blanket from within. One eagle feather could be seen standing vertically at the back of his head.

Black Moccasin sat down crosslegged by the fire and said respectfully, "I wish for you to interpret the dream which I had last night."

"Tell me of your dream," the old warrior said as he slowly added three more pieces of wood to the fire.

"I saw in my dream a white man sitting on a cloud in front of a campfire. In his hands he held a peace pipe which was beautifully decorated. He was dressed in buckskin and many knives were placed in sheaths across his chest. He wore a skunkskin cap and lying by his side was a piece of hollowed wood with holes bored into it."

Black Moccasin looked up at the interpreter, trying to see what effect the relating of his dream was having, but the old man's face was emotionless as he listened. Black Moccasin continued, "Around the fire also sat an eagle, a badger, a fox, and a rattlesnake. I was there, but the man and the animals couldn't see me. They spoke to each other in the white man's language, but when I tried to speak, no one heard me. They all appeared to be deaf to what I tried to say and blind to my presence. What could my dream mean? What is it trying to tell me?"

The old man clutched his blanket closer to himself and spoke, "The location of the meeting between the animals and white man, high in the sky on a cloud means that the white man is close to the gods in his behavior. He is a messenger of the gods. His ways are that of the gods and his words are also those of the gods, for his behavior reflects those he represents. The eagle has given the white man his eyesight as well as his dangerous claws which were represented by the knives which he wore encased across his chest. Everyone knows that the badger is the bravest creature on mother earth and he was giving the white man his courage. The fox was telling the man how to be cunning and the rattlesnake was showing him how to strike swiftly and accurately. Black Moccasin, the man you saw in your dream is none other than the mysterious, mythical man who is called the 'Macedonian'."

"Is that all my dream means?" Black Moccasin demanded.

"That is all," the interpreter replied, "but, my brave young warrior, if the Macedonian really exists and you can find him, I'm very sure that he will impart some of his power to you."

Black Moccasin left his village that day in his lonely search for the man who made sounds with his wooden stick, the man called the Macedonian by the people of the Rocky Mountains.

Rees was knee-deep in White River resetting his trap. He had just placed some castoreum on the tip of the stick extending from his trap, and he was in the process of lowing the stick closer to the water when he noticed the sudden stillness all around. The air was misty, damp and close, although he could hear the sound of a slight breeze in the tree tops. He froze and tried to detect with all of his senses where the danger lay. How far away was it? Had Nat picked up any indication? When he had satisfied himself that whatever he sensed was not too near, he slowly turned to look downstream. The river bed was wide as it twisted its way down from the mountains, but for a good two miles along its banks only green grass grew, so he could see a long way.

Rees focused on an object beside the river. It was a good distance away, but now he saw that it was a lone Indian who sat on his pony as it drank from the water at the river's edge. So far the Indian had not spotted him, but as Rees continuted to watch him, the Indian suddenly jerked his head up and scanned the landscape swiftly.

"He knows he is being watched," Rees chuckled to himself. As he said this, he slowly reached for his rifle with eyes fixed on the Indian.

Black Moccasin displayed no hostility as he walked his pony slowly toward Rees. When he was about one hundred and fifty yards away, he reined in his pony and gave the sign of peace as he raised his hand to his lips, fingers extended, and blew from his mouth.

Rees repeated the sign as he walked up the bank of the river toward the Crow. Now the Indian raised one finger signifying that he was alone. He then circled his ear with right hand.

"He wants me to listen," Rees muttered.

The Crow next raised his right hand with his palm turned toward his mouth and then he moved it toward his mouth, he did this several times. "Tell me," he was saying . . . "are you the Macedonian?"

Now the Crow raised his hand opposite his face and separated his middle and index fingers, the palm of his hand turned toward the sky. He then moved his hand in a clock wise motion and pointed his right hand toward the heavens, asking "Are you a god?"

Rees shook his head as it dawned on him that this brave was looking for the Macedonian. Using sign language. Rees told the Crow warrior that he was not the Macedonian, but that he heard other talk about him.

Now Nat came down the south bank of the river, slipping from one hiding place to another as he advanced.

"Come on in, laddie!" his partner called.

Nat strode up swiftly and as he approached, Rees told him, "This is Black Moccasin, a Crow warrior of high standing and he's looking for the Macedonian."

"The Macedonian?" Nat's excitement was in his voice.

"It seems that this mythical being's reputation has spread throughout the Rockies," Rees replied.

"Have you seen him?" Nat asked, using sign language.

"No, I have only heard of him, but I have set out to find him. If I find him, I will ask him if he will bestow some of his powers upon me."

"Do you and the Crow nation believe that such a man exists?" Nat asked, signing as best he could.

"All signs show that there is such a man, but no one in the Crow nation has ever seen him; we have only heard of his deeds."

Rees raised a hand and spoke in signs, "We have heard that he is supposed to frequent the Pikes Peak area; you might go there."

Black Moccasin drew himself up and signed one more time, "If you are not this man, I'll continue my search." He raise his right hand chest high and extended his index finger and the finger next to it and held the other two fingers down with his right thumb. "Friendship," he was signing. He rode away down the south side of the river.

When he had gone, Rees turned to Nat and said, "Look at his footprint carefully, laddie. It is good to know what a Crow print looks like."

They both knelt beside the prints which Black Moccasin had made when he swung off his pony to talk with them. "Notice that from the big toe to the heel on the right side of his foot, the print is almost a perfect semi-circle. Also notice that his instep on the left side curves in a little. A Sioux is the same on the right side, but on the instep side, it is straight from the big toe to the heel. A Cheyenne print is also like that of a Crow, but it curves on the instep. It takes training to distinguish between a Sioux and a Crow print. The Arapahos' prints look just like snowshoe prints. They're round at the top and come to a point at the heel. The Pawnee's print favors that of the Crow except that the curve on the instep is closer to the heel. Now the Kiowa's print resemble that of the Sioux, with one exception; the print looks as if the Indian does not have his two little toes. Do you think you can remember this, laddie? It can come in handy sometime."

"I'll try," Nat replied as he rose. "The beaver are not too plentiful around here, Rees, what do you say about movin' on to a better location?"

"I think we have about enough already. Why don't we pack up in a day or two, head for our other cache and then go by and see old Otto?"

"Sounds good to me," Nat answered. "When do you want to head east?"

"As soon as we have ready what our traps yield, laddie."

Nat looked to see if Black Moccasin was still in sight. "I hope he finds the Macedonian, if he really exists, that is. Do you suppose I really heard a flute during that storm, Rees?"

"We may never know, laddie. Dreams are what men are made of, someone once said," Rees answered as he, too, looked in the direction that the warrior had gone. "Dreams give purpose to life, a sense of usefulness and fulfillment, a sense of adventure. Whether he succeeds or not, he'll at least have some stories to tell around the campfire on a cold winter's night."

They picked up their furs from their first cache at the foot of Pikes Peak and after five weeks of traveling and trapping along the south bank of the South Platte River, they reached the Pawnee village of Chief White Cloud. They were welcomed by the chief as they rode into the village. They entered the lodge of the chief and sat down to smoke the pipe and talk.

"It has been over two years since you kindly extended your gracious hospitality to us, Chief White Cloud. We have caught many beavers since that time and we are now returning to sell the furs at the American Fur Trading Company. Have you any news of that post and of our friend, Otto Muller?"

"You mean the Wyandot post," the chief said without looking at Nat or Rees. "Since you left, the Wyandots moved in closer to that American Post, so close it is difficult to see the trading post because of the Indian lodges. And some more of your people have settled there. Your friend, Otto is still there and he is busy making and selling his big medicine rifles. His lodge is big now, and he has four white men who help him. He once got into trouble with his people because he repaired some big medicine rifles for some of my braves. Huh! Would you believe it, the Wyandot came to his rescue. Otto defended my braves and their right to seek his help, and the Wyandot chief and his people protected Otto and my braves from the whites. Some day, maybe, I make a treaty with your friends, the Wyandots. Some day, maybe, the Pawnee and the Wyandots will be as one on the war path against our enemies. My scouts also said that some Padoucas came to trade with your friend, Otto, but they left empty-handed, so my scouts reported. Why Otto did not trade with the Padoucas, I do not know."

"Who are the Padoucas?" Nat asked Rees.

"The Comanches were once called Padoucas, laddie," Rees told him, "but most white people call them Comanches now and so do some Indians."

White Cloud looked at Nat and said, "Comanche is a Ute word which means 'enemy'. The Utes have always been the enemy of the Padoucas, even when they lived along the Snake River with their kinsmen, the Shoshones, but for some unknown reason, some of the Padoucas moved south, where they and the Apache and Ute nations became bitter enemies. It was the white man who began to call the Padoucas by the Ute word and this word, Comanche, little by little replaced their real ancestral name. Now, many, maybe most people, call them Comanche, as they themselves do."

"You look intrigued with these Comanches, laddie. Do I read you correctly? Are your feet itching as once mine did? Are you thinking what I think you are thinking?"

Nat laughed a low laugh as he glanced at Rees. "Maybe so, my friend. They do have a strong appeal for some reason and so does all of northern Mexico. I can almost hear the strum of the caballeros' guitars as they serenade the senoritas! It is the land of the conquistadors and the seven cities of Cibola, the home of the Pueblo Indians and the Apaches, and the long, blackrobed Spanish priests as they care for their converts. Sleepy adobe towns which bask in the hot, southwestern sun."

"Yes, and don't forget, laddie, the corrupt dictatorial government which can have you arrested and shot without the slightest bit of conscience."

White Cloud looked at Rees and said, "You will travel to the Wyandot village alone, my friend. Your friend has other ideas, the ideas and dreams of young men, dreams which you and I once had. The pull is too strong for him to resist. In spirit, he is where he someday wants to walk. He is vigorous and has a brave heart with a desire to explore. Ah, they will be good days ahead for this young warrior! No mountain is too high for him to cross, no river is too deep or wide for him to ford, no desert is too hot, or dry for him to conquer. Only he can cool the adventurous streak which is unleased in him. Let him run his course, my friend, let him run his course. He was made by the Great Spirit to do what he is about to do and who can deny the will of the Great Spirit?"

Rees looked soberly at Nat, "Is what Chief White Cloud just said correct, laddie? Are we about to go our separate ways?"

"Please try to understand, Rees. Ever since I left Virginia, I had as my goal to see all of the land west of the Mississippi and that goal is as yet, incomplete. You were young once, you know the feeling. You have taught me well and with that knowledge and God looking after the fool that I am, I'll come back to you and Otto in a few years. How can I ever thank you for all that you have done for me? Wherever I go and whatever I see, you too, will be there. No man could be better prepared for my undertaking than I am, thanks to you."

Nat spoke eagerly and earnestly as he looked at Rees and as Rees listened, he studied the young man. He was strong, sturdy, and his deeply tanned face was keen and confident, and with good cause, for he had mastered the life of a mountainman with ease. He grinned, finally and asked, "What shall I do with your share of the furs?"

"Keep the money until I return, or if you do not plan to stay in Missouri, leave it with Otto."

CHAPTER V

The nickering of his horse woke Nat and when he opened his eyes, he could smell the odor of burning grass. With his left hand, he quickly threw back his blanket and with his right hand took up his rifle as he rose. He was facing westward when he got to his feet, and it was still dark in that direction although as he turned he could see a faint glow in the eastern sky. Even as he stared in that direction he was able to discern a long line of orange flames moving rapidly.

He ran to his horses and led them back to his camp where he saddled and packed them in record time. As he put his foot in the stirrup, he caught a glimpse of movement a short distance in front of the line of flames, He mounted but did not take his eyes off the spot where he had detected movement. "It was probably just an antelope or some other animal running from the fire," he muttered, even as his eyes searched for any further movement. "No, it's a man, and he's on foot. Not the best place to be afoot."

He looked once more toward the man and estimated how far behind him the fire was. He couldn't leave him to perish in the fire and smoke. He quickly turned toward where he'd last seen the figure and leading his pack horse, he galloped in that direction. His horses were reluctant to gallop at all into the strong scent of smoke, but he urged them forward as he watched for the sight of a man on foot. The roar of the wind and the fire grew stronger as he raced toward it. He tried to yell, but his voice was muted by the roaring of the burning prairie grass and the wind which whipped it. Once in a while bits of black, partially burned grass blew into his face, hitting his clothing, and he brushed them away, impatiently.

"Where are you?" He yelled at the top of his lungs and at the same time reined his horse to the south so that he paralleled the fire line. The increasing smoke made Nat cough intermittently as he rode nearer and nearer to the fire. He raised his rifle and fired it and after placing it back in his scabbard, he fired his pistols, attempting to get the man's attention. He had almost decided that whoever it was had been consumed by the fire. "God," he muttered to himself, "if my horse should step into a prairie dog hole, we'd be gonners, too."

Suddenly he caught a movement to one side and he quickly looked in that direction and saw an Indian running toward him. "Over here!"

The Indian ran with both hands extended in front of his face. Nat caught him up behind his saddle and as the Indian landed behind him, lightning lit up the sky. Nat then realized that the lightning had probably started the fire. If the weather started it, it can also put it out, he reasoned and galloped his horse in that direction. After a few minutes of hard riding, they began to feel a few drops of rain on their faces. Within a few more minutes, a heavy rain dumped its water over the two men and continued eastward, toward the fire. Nat reined in his horse and the Indian slid to the ground, the rain continuing as the two men stood side by side, soaked to the skin. They could see the flames diminish and sink toward the ground as the rain soaked that area. The rain appeared to be concentrated in this particular region, and as the fire died down, darkness returned. When the lightning streaked across the sky, the two men could see one another during each flash and Nat could see that the Indian was a young Comanche warrior.

"You saved my life," the young Comanche turned from looking toward the fire. "Why?"

"You speak good English," Nat said as he glanced at the dim figure standing beside him.

"You haven't answered my question," the Comanche retorted, "why did you save my life?"

"Wouldn't you have done the same thing if the circumstances were reversed?" countered Nat.

After a short silence, the Comanche answered him, "I guess we are cut from the same cloth, you and me yes, I could have saved you if the circumstances had been reversed. I am a Comanche of the Antelope band and my name is Three Tongues. What is your name?"

"Nat Cochran," Nat replied as he gave the sign of friendship. "What other tongues do you speak beside English?"

"Comanche and Spanish," replied Three Tongues. "I learned the English and Spanish language from my mother who is a white American, my father was a Comanche warrior."

"Was?"

"He has gone to the Spirit World. He was killed trying to count coup against the Apache two years ago."

"What do you say we camp somewhere and talk in the morning?" Nat suggested. "You are familiar with the area, Three Tongues, do you know of a good campsite?"

"The Canadian River is not far from here, maybe three or four miles. It would provide us with safety if the fire should start up again. The fire would never have been a threat to me if my horse hadn't stepped in a hole and broken his leg," Three Tongues went on. "He was a good pony, too," he said softly.

The two men went southward, Three Tongues trotting beside Nat's horse, holding to his stirrup until they reached the Canadian, where they quickly made camp and slept for the remainder of the night.

The early morning sun awoke Three Tongues as he lay rolled in his blanket. He slowly opened his eyes and saw that Nat still slept with his back to the east. Three Tongues rose to one knee evoking a quick response from Nat, who grabbed his rifle and rolled to his feet in one motion. "Oh, it's you!" Nat lowered his rifle, grinning.

"I don't believe anyone could sneak up on you." Three Tongues grinned back as he stood with his blanket crumpled at his feet. "To kill you, one would have to shoot from a distance."

"Well, as my friend, Rees, once said, 'Sleep with one eye open and one ear cocked, and you'll live longer.'"

"Your friend was right and you do sleep with one eye open and one ear alert," the Indian commented drily.

"What do you say we hunt up some breakfast, unless you would like some of my jerky or pemmican?"

"My village isn't over ten miles downriver; why don't we wait until we get there? My mother will cook us a good Comanche breakfast."

"OK, I'm tired of my cooking, anyway," Nat replied. "Let's break camp and be on our way."

They divided the packs and tied part of the supplies behind Nat's saddle, Three Tongues riding the pack horse bareback and carrying the remainder of the supplies.

Three Tongues' village was not very large, maybe forty to fifty tepees. The people, upon seeing the two riders, called to one another and then seeing that their young brave was not dead as they had feared, called to one another with the news. His mother and sister rushed from their lodge near the center of a line of tepeees as they heard Three Tongues' name called out. A happy smile replaced the sad expression on Spirit Woman's face as she glanced at her daughter quickly and rushed from their tepee. Snow Skin followed her closely, also wearing a broad smile.

Three Tongues slid from his horse and caught his running mother in his arms. They embraced for a few seconds as he swept her off her feet and whirled her in a circle three times. When he released his mother, he hugged his sister and with an arm about each of them, he looked at Nat. "My people, this is my friend, the man who saved my life. With his permission, I would like to call him Vlach, because he is my shepherd."

"Vlach?" echoed Spirit Woman, "my son, is he the Macedonian, or possibly a friend of his?"

"Well, Vlach," Three Tongues asked as he smiled at Nat, "are you the Macedonian or a friend of his?"

"I have heard of the Macedonian, but I have not see him, nor have I met him or anyone who has, but I might have heard his flute!" Nat scanned their faces from the vantage point of his saddle. "Have any of you seen him?"

No one answered.

"Just as I thought, no one has ever seen him. No, I am not the Macedonian and I do not have a flute in my saddle bags," Nat said with a smile, "but thanks for the flattery, anyway. And by the way what does Vlach mean?" He looked at Three Tongues inquiringly.

Spirit Woman answered for her son, "I have been to the white man's school and I have learned that the Macedonians call their sheepherders Vlachs, and this I have taught to my son and daughter. My son, because you have saved his life, has decided to bestow upon you the ancient Macedonian name of Vlach for shepherd. Shepherd, we welcome you to our village and we feel honored by your presence."

"I add my words to that of Spirit Woman," the chief of the band of Comanches spoke gravely as his people parted to make a path for him to reach the two men.

Crazy Wolf and Brave Head stood at either side of Chief Dull Knife. "We are pleased that the spirits have seen fit to return you to us, Three Tongues, and they must also be pleased with your friend, Vlach, for through him they have protected you. Vlach has received the spirit powers and so he carried with him big medicine. We welcome your medicine to our village and lodges. May it protect and help us with our enterprises."

The chief turned with dignity and walked back to his lodge, but Crazy Wolf and Brave Head approached Three Tongues. Crazy Wolf said, "We are happy to see that you are alive and well, my friend. We nearly lost our lives in that fire also, but Brave Head was able to catch one of the horses as he ran by him and later he ran into me, and thanks to him I am alive today. We looked for you, but when we couldn't find you, we gave you up for lost."

"I guess we are all lucky," Three Tongues answered, "but I am the luckiest of all because I have added a friend to my list of friends."

"You are right there," answered Crazy Wolf gravely.

Nat now slid from his horse and asked the question which had been bothering him as the men talked. "What are those leather gadgets which are tied to your backs?"

The three Comanches laughed and Three Tongues answered. "When you put these leather gadgets, as you called them, over your head, like this, they keep the sun from your head."

"Oh," said the enlightened Nat, "sounds like a good idea."

"If you want one, I'm sure Snow Skin will be more than happy to make one for you," Three Tongues glanced toward his sister who quickly withdrew her head into her mother's tepee when she saw the men looking her way.

"But be careful, for Three Braves won't like it. He has his eye on her."

"Who is Snow Skin?" asked Nat.

"My sister," replied Three Tongues, "and it is true that Three Braves has his eye on her, but Snow Skin does not encourage him."

"Come, it is time to eat. I know that my mother and my sister will have prepared a feast for us to show their appreciation for your having saved my life. Wait until you have tasted their food! There is no better cooking in all the Comanche nation."

They quickly unsaddled and unpacked Nat's horses and hobbled them to graze with the Indian herd before entering the lodge.

The aroma of cooking food drifted through the air as both women prepared to serve the food. The two men seated themselves crosslegged on the buffalo robes which were spread on the floor near the back of the lodge. Nat glanced at the two women and saw Spirit Woman nudge her daughter with her shoulder. Snow Skin gave Nat a smile before she turned her eyes from him.

"Why is your sister called Snow Skin?" Nat asked Three Tongues.

"Because the pigmentation of her skin is almost as white as snow," her brother told him, "and it should be as she is half white."

"Your skin is not as white as hers," Nat pointed out, "and neither is your mother's."

You're right, Vlach, my sister's skin color must be a throwback to someone on my mother's side of the family, but her hair coloring is close to that of my mother's brown hair, don't you think?"

Three Tongues knew that Nat wanted to look at his sister so he was giving him that chance.

"Yes," Nat replied as he looked at Snow Skin. "She is a pretty girl."

"She is two years younger than me," Three Tongues said.

"And how old are you?" Nat asked.

"Nineteen," came the reply.

The two women turned from the preparation of the food and brought it to the men. "I hope you don't mind eating beef instead of buffalo. I understand that mountainmen, as do the Comanche, prefer buffalo meat to all other meats, but I had already cooked the beef prior to your arrival. I hope it is to your liking."

"Beef!" Where did you get the beef?" Nat looked embarrassed at his question. "That was an inexcusable question, forgive me."

"This is Mexican beef, Vlach, and there are still quite a few more head grazing on our grass. We prefer buffalo, but we do eat other meats. We are not called the Antelope People because we look like that animal. We are called that because out here on the plains, where there are few trees, antelope are plentiful, and over the years we have developed certain skills in hunting them. Some of our people go to the Apache country west of here on occasion and hunt elk. The elk, at times, are also found in the tree covered areas along the rivers. Out here in the open prairie, we usually jerk the meat or smoke it before we return to camp, and when we are back in camp, the women make pemmican out of some of it. My mother's pemmican is the best made anywhere. She says she has a special secret recipe and will not share that secret, with anyone except my sister."

"This secret is not in the ingredients, but in the amount," Spirit Woman interrupted, as she placed a platter of dried pumpkins in front of the two men. Snow Skin placed a platter of sunflower seeds next to her mother's platter as she brushed Nat's shoulder.

"I use all of the same ingredients which the other women use," Spirit Woman continued, "and I grind them into a meal or powder as the other women do, and the quatity of powdered walnuts, berries, honey, plums, pinon nuts and the right amount of dried meat are the same, but it is at that point that I differ with the others. I will not tell them what I do to the meat, how much of it is elk, deer, antelope, buffalo, or beef, and I will not tell them what I use to flavor the meat. Some of them think it is my white mother's seasoning which they do not know about, but I am careful not to be tricked into divulging my secret. I will bring some if you wish to try it."

"Please, if it isn't too much trouble," Nat answered.

Snow Skin rushed to the leather pemmican bag which hung from one of the tepee poles and her mother smiled at her haste. She placed some of it on Nat's platter and said shyly, "I helped mother make this batch, and we believe it is one of our best. Try it and see if you like it."

Nat took some of the pemmican in his fingers and ate it, saying "It is outstanding, it is unique and it's a lot better than what I make, but that's not saying much, for all pemmican is better than I make." He laughed. "But seriously, and all joking aside, this is delicious pemmican. You are to be complimented, Spirit Woman on such a fine serving." Nat quickly added, "You also, Snow Skin, for I pay the same compliment to you."

When the food had all been placed on the buffalo robe, Spirit Woman and Snow Skin sat down facing the men to join in the festivities.

"One meat that we do not eat," Three Tongues said after his mother and sister were seated and began to eat, "is dog. The Sioux and some of the other nations north of us love to eat dog, especially a fat young dog, but to us dog is forbidden, as well as the meat of a wolf or coyote."

"Why?"

"The dog and other animals which belong to the dog family eat humans, and we do not eat humans or any animal that does. We are not Tonkawas," he said scornfully. "We and most of the other nations consider the human eaters south of us subhuman because they feast on other people. The Comanche hate them more than any other people. It is our wish that someday we might kill them all."

"I have never heard of them," Nat told him, "how far south of here do they live?"

"They live near the open water and the water that has no end," Three Tongues answered. "Sometimes they are stupid enough to enter the Comanche territory, but we are not foolish enough to allow them to trespass. Someday a Comanche chief will unite all Comanches for the purpose of exterminating these human eaters."

Commotion was heard outside the tepee as voices became louder and more numerous. Three Tongues glanced at his mother, and then quickly rose to his feet and walked to the entrance of the tepee. He stooped and pushed aside the flap and stepped outside. In a few seconds, Nat joined him, asking, "What's all the commotion about?"

They saw four Comanche braves walking their horses toward the lodge of the civil chief. As they walked they were completely surrounded by women and children.

"The hunters are back and they will report to Chief Dull Knife and tell him that they have found the buffalo herd," Three Tongues said. He looked sideways at his new friend, "Would you like to go on a buffalo hunt, Vlach?"

"As we say back in Virginia, I'll be glad to help bring in the bacon," Nat grinned.

"Where is Virginia?"

"Many, many miles east of here, where it's eastern part borders on the big ocean, an ocean so big that it would take months of traveling before you could reach land again."

"Listen," Three Tongues said as he raised his right hand. "The scouts who were sent out to find the buffalo herd are about to report to Chief

Dull Knife. Let's see if we can hear what they tell him."

Many people had gathered around the buffalo scouts by the time the chief stepped outside his lodge. He stood very straight as he questioned the scouts, "What do you have to report?"

The one who appeared to be the head scout replied, "The herd is about twenty miles northeast of here and it is a big one. We could not see the end of the herd, it was so far away, but its width must be at least five miles or more."

"A job well done," commented the chief, "now ride through the village and tell our people that a buffalo hunt will be undertaken in three days."

The scouts reined their ponies away from the chief and the people and loped them through the village, telling their people what the chief had said.

Three Tongues turned to Nat and said, "We must return to our tepee to the meal which my mother and sister prepared for us. Then, we'll begin to get ready for the hunt. I'll let you borrow one of my buffalo horses, one which is well trained in the way of the hunt. The one I have in mind is quick on her feet. She is small but she makes up for her small size by her quickness. After we eat, we'll walk to the herd and I'll show her to you."

Later, as they walked toward the grazing ponies, Nat asked his friend how many were in the herd.

"Two thousand, maybe more," Three Tongues told him. "My father accumulated most of ours and we have a few mules also which we use for pulling the travois. One of the mules has such a nice gait that you hardly know it is moving. Snow Skin likes to ride her.

He walked close to a small sorrel mare and petted her on the neck. "This is the mare I want you to ride on the hunt; she'll put you right where you'll need to be to get your buffalo."

"I though you only used geldings on hunts," Nat remarked.

"That is true, but as in everything, there are exceptions, and this is a rare exception . . . you'll be pleased with her."

"I'll take your word for it." He liked the alert way the mare moved, with her ears pricked forward inquiringly. Three Tongues grabbed a handful of mane and swung up on her. Using his knees to guide her, he rode her in a figure eight on a fast lope and after she had swung through those effortlessly, he brought her to a sliding stop in front of Nat. "What do you think of her, Vlach, do you like her?"

"She's a beauty" Nat told him admiringly. "I'am honored that you'll let me use her."

"You'll need your hands for killing buffalo," Three Tongues told him, "I'll show you how to signal her with your knees and she'll do the rest." He was obviously proud of the little mare.

"Will you ride the gelding which is tied to front of your tepee?"

"You are right, my friend." Three Tongues walked the mare beside Nat as they moved toward Spirit Woman's tepee. He motioned to the roan standing by the next tepee. "He is my pride and joy. He is my best buffalo pony. All Comanches keep their favorite horse at their lodge and he is my favorite."

"I can see why with his short back and broad chest. I like his build, good legs, everything about him spells speed and endurance." Nat said.

His comments pleased Three Tongues immensely as he slid from the back of the mare and sent her back to graze. The sound of hoofbeats caused Nat to turn his head quickly toward the center of the village. What is that all about?"

"We're about to have a buffalo dance; we always do before we go on a hunt. Whey don't you join us tonight? My people will be flattered if you choose to do so."

"I have never danced in a buffalo dance," objected Nat. "I don't know the first thing about it."

"There's nothing to it," Three Tongues replied. "All you do is go through the same motions that you would make on a buffalo hunt. Why don't you give it a try?"

Nat glanced at Three Tongues doubtfully, then grinned, "All right, I'll give it a try!"

"Good, I know you'll enjoy it."

When the two men entered the tepee of Spirit Woman, they found that she and her daughter were already preparing for the hunt, wrapping knives and scraping tools and tying the stakes which would be used to secure the buffalo hides tightly to the ground so that the fleshy side could be scraped. They would need leather containers to carry these and all of the other paraphernalia needed to work the hides. Some of the mixtures they would obtain on the site of the hunt, things such as grease, liver, brains, roots of various kinds, and tree bark.

"I am going to the buffalo dance tonight and my friend here says he will dance also."

"If you don't watch your step, Vlach, you too, will get the fever and become a Comanche as I did years ago," Spirit Woman told him as she stopped her work to smile from one to the other of them.

"He has also agreed to go on the hunt," Three Tongues told his mother in boastful fashion. "He will ride my sorrel mare, Quick Feet. With her speed and his rifle, the hunt should be very profitable, don't you agree, mother?"

"How can it fail?" Spirit Woman asked with an approving smile, "but, before the dance, let's all of us ask the buffalo spirits for their favor and blessing for a successful hunt, with no injuries to anyone. We will also ask the spirits to convey to the buffalo who are about to be killed, our sorrow in killing them."

Spirit Woman turned from the two men and took a few steps toward the buffalo skull which rested on a small, low earth platform inside the tepee. She knelt in front of it and the others joined her. All were quiet until she spoke. "Oh, spirit of the buffalo, hear my words." There was a short pause before she continued, a pause as if to give the spirit time to hear her voice and give his attention to what she was about to say. "We are once again making ready to journey to your sanctuary, your world in which you and the buffalo communicate. Please tell the buffalo who are about to die that we give our solemn promise that their remains will be treated in the way that is proscribed by Buffalo Woman. We will kill as quickly and with as little pain as possible, and we will show respect for what the buffalo give us; the same respect will be shown and given to those few parts which are not of value to us. This we ask of you, Buffalo Spirit, in true sincerity."

Spirit Woman touched the buffalo skull and then rose to her feet and returned to her packing. Snow Skin, as did her brother, touched the buffalo skull and then rose. Nat, out of respect for his new Comanche friends, did the same, as Spirit Woman watched out of the corner of her eye.

"Before the dancing begins, mother, Vlach and I will ready the travois for travel. Then all we'll have to do later is strap the packages on the travois and harness the mules when we are ready to leave."

"I hope you realize, Vlach, that on this hunt the buffalo hides won't be of as high quality as during the winter hunts. It is then that mother nature provides the buffalo with the finest wool."

"Yes," Nat responded, "so my friend Rees told me."

"That friend of yours must be very adept at the ways of the Indian as well as those of nature. Did he have any experience with my people?"

"No, I don't think he ever came this far south. He is a Frenchman, Canadian, now, an American, as he proudly calls himself."

"If the Great Spirit permits us to live long enough and if your friend Rees ever comes this far south, be sure to bring him to visit us. We would like to meet him."

"I doubt that he will ever come south, Three Tongues, he is getting too old, at least that's what he says. I think he's just using that for an excuse to stay near his old mother and father who live near a village called Vincennes, in Ohio, across the Father of Waters. They are the ones who are getting old, and he feels he must watch over them, provide for them. He is a good man and friend, they come no better than Rees."

"Loyalty is good," Three Tongues said, "Rees is lucky, too, for having such a loyal friend as you and he should be complimented for having such devotion to his parents."

"Yeah, I guess we were both pretty lucky. Good friends are hard to find and even harder to keep." Nat said as his mind seemed miles away.

"Enough of looking back," Three Tongues told him, "let us look to the present and our hunt."

That evening they walked toward the fires and the dark figures moving around them. "Is there any religious significance to this dancing? If there is, I'll sit it out, because I wouldn't want to offend anyone by doing something which might seem to be sacrilegious."

"No," Three Tongues told him with a laugh. "This dance is for fun and fun only; there's no religious significance to it at all."

The two men danced with the others and moved about the circle, going through motions similar to those the others made as they simulated the hunt gestures. Nat was glad when Three Tongues finally said, "Let's get some sleep before we leave."

Two hours before sunup, Spirit Woman woke the others to give them instructions. "We eat as we move toward the buffalo and not before," she told Nat. "And we must have everything packed so that when Chief Dull Knife orders us to move, we are ready."

The two young men went for the mules and their mounts while the women prepared to leave the lodge.

The whole camp was humming with activity as men, women, and children went about their duties. Dogs ran about barking and were scolded for being in the way or trying to play. Horses were being brought in by the warriors while others were already tied by the tepees. Some of the warriors were placing their handmade saddles on the horses that they would ride on the trek. Others were packing the travois which would be pulled by horses or mules. Some of the saddles were especially made for the horses which would pull the travois. Each of the saddles were equipped with a tall saddle horn as well as a high cantle. Some long, thin travois poles were decorated with colorful beadwork. Others were covered with beautifully braided leather, but some had only designs painted on them. It was obvious that the owners were proud of the many long hours which had been spent in their construction. Leather loops had been attached near the upper end of the poles. These had been soaked in water and had dried hard upon the poles, making them fit tightly, so they would not slide. Some women had even notched the travois poles at that location as an added strength. Later the men would cross the ends of the poles as they looped the rawhide straps over the horn of the saddle. Heavy, thick shoes especially made to prevent the end of the poles from wearing out as they dragged on the ground, were fastened securely in place. These shoes were made from the thickest parts of the buffalo bull's hide and to make them more durable, the women made three or four sets of them, each of them slightly smaller than the one before so that the pole could fit snugly inside it.

The wide leather baggage platforms that would carry the baggage were checked to see if the rawhide laces were in good condition. Some of the women tucked extra strands of rawhide strips into a small leather bag which was tied to the bottom of the platform.

Men were tying additional arrow quivers filled with arrows behind their saddles. Leather saddle bags would carry spare parts such as extra lance and arrow heads, knives, and medicine in case of injury from a fall or by a wounded buffalo.

Three Tongues, Nat, Snow Skin, and Spirit Woman had their mules, horses, and provisions and were standing at their horses' heads when Three Tongues said excitedly, "The chief has just left his tepee, we had better get mounted."

Spirit Woman and her daughter each rode a horse which also pulled a travois, and behind them several pack mules would follow.

All could hear Chief Dull Knife as he ordered four scouts to proceed before the main body of the hunting party. Nat could not understand enough of the Comanche language to know why the four left early, but he surmised the reason.

"Yes, they are the advance scouts. Their job is to make sure that no enemy comes near our temporary camp once it is set up. In a few moments, two other scouts will leave and they will locate a good place for our camp, a location which has plenty of water, grass, and shade, preferably along the Canadian River. You can see the chief giving them instructions now, see them on either side of him? They are the two who are now being assigned the task of finding the location for our camp."

After the two men left camp, Chief Dull Knife rode to the head of the column, accompanied by two of the bravest warriors of the Antelope band. He turned his horse and faced the hunters and their families, and ordered, "Keep as close together as possible, and all of you keep your eyes and ears alert for any danger. The success of this hunt depends upon the cooperation of every single one of you." He then moved his horse to face the open country ahead and yelled. "Let's move out at a slow walk."

Three Tongues and Nat followed behind Spirit Woman and Snow Skin to make sure that the mules kept pace. The terrain was open, rolling country, empty of any discernible life, with many deep and wide arroyos to be crossed, some of them so deep that the whole hunting party could hide if necessary. The riders kept constant surveillance as they walked their horses slowly. At times some of the men dismounted to lead their horses as they watched for any prints not made by their people.

Dogs and young colts chased each other in every direction. Some of the women who rode carried their papooses strapped to their backs, snug in their cradleboards. Others were content to wrap their papooses in a blanket and tie the corners of the blanket around their shoulders.

Spirit Woman suddenly thought she detected a movement in the brush at the bottom of one of the ravines, and she stood in her stirrups to have a better view.

"What is it, mother?" Three Tongues rode along the line and looked in the direction she faced.

"I thought I saw movement in the brush down there," she replied absently, "but I don't see anything now."

"Let's have a look, Vlach." Three Tongues called to Nat who loped his horse foward and together the two rode down the sloping hillside. When they reached the floor of the ravine, they rode through the brushy vegetation searching for anything that might be hidden. Suddenly they caught the flit of a deer's tail and three deer bounded up the side of the ravine and on up to the rise above it. The two men grinned and rode back toward the column. "Your mother has keen eyesight," Nat said.

"Yes, and her sense of smell is just as keen. She may not have been born a Comanche, but the Antelopes say that she has made one hell of a Comanche!"

When they trotted their horses back to Spirit Women, she said, "Did you notice the two scouts sitting on the ridge up ahead? They wait for us. The herd is east of here, for we always keep downwind of them."

Late in the day, when camp was made, Chief Dull Knife called everyone to him and said, "We will all rise an hour before the sun comes to lighten the day and the men will make a huge, semicircle around the part of the herd which we plan to separate from the main herd. We will remain in the canyons and ravines downwind of the herd until I give the signal for the two ends of the semicircle to cut their way through the herd and enclose the part which we will hunt." "While we know that the buffalo has poor eyesight and can't hear very well, we also know that he has a very sensitive, keen sense of smell, so I will remind you to be aware of these facts as we begin to move into the herd. Prepare your weapons before you lie down to sleep tonight, because you'll have no time for preparation in the morning. That is all I have to say. Is there anyone who wishes to speak?"

No one wished to add anything, and the people went about their tasks, the women to prepare the evening meal and the men to ready their weapons.

Anticipation ensured that all were awake well before the sun appeared, and the men rode away from the encampment to make their semicircle while the women placed their tools ready to begin work.

When the men were in their places, Chief Dull Knife raised his right hand straight above his head. He looked out over his men to ensure that everyone appeared to be in his place and then dropped his arm to signal the men to ride out.

Within minutes, Nat was racing his mare through the buffalo herd some of whom sprang to their feet as the men rode by them. They were running as they got to their feet. Cows bellowed to their calves and tried to lead them to safety. The bulls forced the cows and the calves into the inner circle as they attempted to protect them and the Comanches kept the smaller herd milling in a circle as they began to bring down a bull here and another bull there. The noise of the galloping hoofs and the dust raised by the frightened, stampeding animals made it impossible to communicate, so each man was on his own.

Nat raced the sorrel mare toward a huge bull and as he reached its side, he brought his rifle up and fired into the region of the heart. When the bull felt the bullet, he quickly veered toward the horse and rider. It was then that Nat realized why Three Tongues had spoken so admiringly of the quickness of the mare. Even though Nat had dropped the reins on her neck as he shot, she turned quickly to evade the bull and kept running, putting Nat beside another huge beast which was lumbering along ahead of them. Nat was loosened in the saddle as the mare was so quick, but he told himself he'd be better prepared the next time. He fired a shot into the bull, which was close beside him now, and was prepared this time as the mare lunged out of the bull's way as he dropped in his tracks. Nat turned back now to see if the other bull had fallen and saw him lying still on the ground not far behind him. The tireless little mare put him beside another bull even as he turned to look ahead, giving him little time to reload. This one, also, he dropped with one shot, but the next bull almost got the mare for he didn't wait until he was hit to charge her. She was ready for him and evaded him as he made a swipe at them and then charged them. Nat caught a glimpse of the rage in the bull's eyes as he made his first feint but could not see anymore as he tried to stay with the mare as she veered away from the bull. When they had evaded the bull, the mare wheeled, giving Nat a good shot at him. He took careful aim and dropped him, kicking and bellowing. As he waited to be sure the bull was dead, he saw a Comanche's horse go down before a bull's charge. Nat galloped toward the fallen Comanche and then, as several buffalo galloped between the warrior and himself, he thought he was too late. But then through the haze he saw the brave dodging as the buffalo rushed heedlessly past him. Nat galloped between the buffalo and reached out arm to the fallen warrior. The warrior leaped up behind Nat's saddle as they galloped out of the circle to safety. Chief Dull Knife gave a Comanche war cry of approval as he saw what Nat had done.

By this time, enough buffalo had been killed and the rest of the herd had been scattered in all directions or had rejoined the main herd, so the hunt was discontinued for the day.

Now the women raced onto the field and looked at the arrows or lances which were embedded in the sides of the buffalo. If the arrow or lance did not have her bushand's or son's mark on it, she moved on to another fallen animal. When she found one which was hers, she gutted it quickly and cut the liver or kidney loose and with the blood still dripping from the organ, she sank her teeth into this most delicious of all delicacies.

Spirit Woman and Snow Skin knew Three Tongues' mark and they also were on the lookout for any dead buffalo with no arrow or lance protruding, for they would be the ones which Nat had shot. The whole area was a beehive of activity as the women went about the process of skinning and carving of the carcasses. The men facilitated the process by slitting the dead buffalo from head to stern and down each leg and peeling the hides off. A few of them were skinning their kill in a different way. They staked the buffalo to the ground by driving a long, heavy stake through the nose and tied one end of the rope to the end of the hide and the other end to the horn of the their saddle. When they made a quick run, the speed of their horse peeled the hide from the buffalo.

Others rejected this process because as they pointed out, the hide didn't always come off in one piece that way, but in two or more pieces as it tore, so, most of the Comanches preferred the slower, but more efficient method.

That evening, tripods with cooking pots slung from them were to be seen and smelled as they simmered over the fires. Men with their share of the work finished sat not far from the fires, talking of the day's hunting, talking of how many they had killed and how surefooted their ponies had been. One of them bragged of how one of his arrows had gone clear through one buffalo and into another running beside it, thereby killing two buffalos with one arrow.

The women, meanwhile, were engaged in staking the hides to the ground, the flesh side up. Afterward, they would scrape the remaining flesh from the hide. Young girls were helping their mothers do this and in families where enough girls were available, the scraping process could go on simultaneously with the cutting of the meat into strips to dry on racks over low fires.

Spirit Woman and Snow Skin were scraping their hides while Three Tongues sat and talked with some of the men, but when Nat pulled his knife from its sheath and began to help them by slicing the meat for drying, many of the women looked up in surprise and glanced from Nat to their menfolk before resuming their tedious tasks. The men refrained from taunting Nat because he had rescued one of them from being trampled. They accepted what he did because he was white, and so could be forgiven for having such strange ideas, but no Comanche could follow such an example.

When the sun had set and it became too dark to see to work, Chief Dull Knife assembled his people and said, "Three Tongues' friend, Vlach, has done a great thing this day. He put his own life in jeopardy to save Yellow Hawk. For this heroic deed, he will be permitted to wear an eagle feather in his hair or hat, whichever he chooses, and from this day forward, as is our tradition he may remind our people of the deed which he performed, during all war party dances. And if he should choose to go on a raiding party, he can ride out with an extra rider behind his saddle for a short distance before the rider returns for his own horse."

The chief turned to Nat and said, "We welcome you to our band as a blood brother. You will never be forgotten, but will be recorded in the history of our people by our storytellers around the campfires. May the Great Spirit protect you and guide you in the future."

Before Nat could respond to the chief, one of the Comanche scouts rode into camp and told his chief that while the Antelope people were killing the buffalo, another Comanche band, the Yap band, was also killing buffalo a few miles north of them. One of the Yappies was spotted by the Antelope scout and invited to bring his people to his camp. The Yap band was waiting not far from the camp for the chief to give permission for them to enter.

"Show them to our fires," Chief Dull Knife told the scout, and a few minutes later, the members of the Yap band walked their ponies into the camp of the Antelope people. Even as this occurred, three Antelope braves raced their ponies into camp and told the chief that a party of Apaches had been spotted two days ride from the main camp beside the Canadian River.

White Eagle, the war chief, jumped to his feet and looked at Dull Knife who nodded to him. White Eagle turned to his warriors and issued orders quickly, and the warriors trotted for their horses.

The Yap chief walked to White Eagle's side with dignity and asked if he and his braves could be of any help in the fight against their hated enemy.

White Eagle smiled politely and quietly replied that since there were only twenty Apaches, he and his warriors could take care of them with no trouble. "But we thank you for the offer and we ask you to stay in this camp to protect our women and child until we return."

Nat and Three Tongues were among the warriors who rode to meet the Apache war party.

"This time I will get an Apache scalp," Three Tongues yelled to Nat as they rode abreast. "I've been waiting for this opportunity for a long time, but now I will not have to wait much longer. Who knows? Maybe I'll be lucky and get two scalps. When we get back to our main village, Vlach, we'll have a victory scalp dance and one or more of the scalps that will hang on the scalp pole will be mine. My mother and my sister will be proud of me, proud that I have avenged the death of my father. I will take many Apache scalps in the future, too, and the Apache will know and fear me as they did my father."

"Do you think the Apaches may have set up an ambush? Or is it possible that this is a trap to entice us away from the village and the hunting camp, too, so that they can strike at one or the other?" Nat looked at Three Tongues questioningly.

"It is possible," Three Tongues admitted after a pause during which he considered that idea.

They rode along for several minutes and then Three Tongues spoke again, "I think I'll ride up and tell White Eagle what you have said." He kicked his pony in the side and loped toward the front of the file. Nat watched as Three Tongues pulled his horse in beside White Eagle and rode along taking to him. Now Three Tongues reined out of his place beside the chief and waited for Nat to join him. "White Eagle does not think that it is a trap or trick to get us away from the two camps. He thinks that the Apaches do not have enough braves to risk an attack on our main camp during daylight. It could cost them too many braves and they are not known for doing stupid things. He says that the Apaches while brave, are crafty and cunning . . . and that they'd never risk the loss of even one brave, not even one, unless the benefits of the raid would bring a very large booty. I remember my father saying the same words, and as for the Apaches attacking at night, it will never happen, for they believe if they are killed at night, they will travel forever in darkness in the next world. But, on the other hand, if they die in battle during the daylight hours, they will receive good treatment in the next world.

"We Comanches believe that we must preserve our scalps at all cost. I would gladly risk my life to save a fallen brave from losing his scalp because, if this should happen, all that he has accomplished here on earth would be destroyed and forgotten. Any of our warriors would do the same for me.

"The Apaches seldom take scalps, so fighting Apaches removes that fear from us. Although occasionally an Apache might take one scalp in order to have a victory dance when they return home. The Apache, Vlach, is our traditional enemy and they will continue to be until the end. They feel toward us as we do toward them, but I have to give them credit, they are a formidable enemy. They are most difficult to see if they do not want to be seen, for they are the masters of illusion."

"Do you think they wanted your scouts to spot them, then?"

Before Three Tongues could answer, White Eagle held up his band and the war party halted. The chief dropped from his horse and studied some hoofsprints. Finally he straightened and said to those nearest him, "They were here yesterday and the Apaches are not looking for battle because they have women with them. It is my guess that they, too, are on a buffalo hunt, but they have invaded our territory and, for this they will pay."

"The Apaches have many sub-tribes or bands as do the Comanches," Three Tongues told Nat softly. "These Apaches are probably from either the Mescalero or Jicarilla tribes."

"How many bands of Apaches are there?"

"I'm not sure, Vlach, but I have heard of the Mescaleros, Jicarilla, Lipan, and the Chiricahua all of my life and I have fought against all of these except the Chiricahua. I have heard that more of them live farther west and are called the White Mountain, Tonto, San Carlos, Cibecue. As I said before, we Comanches have respect for the Apaches because they are a tough breed, but the Comanches are tougher and much better warriors, and when they invade our nation, we are always successful in driving them back to their land west of the Pecos River, but we have difficulty in fighting them in the mountains of their own country. To be honest, Vlach, they usually chase us from their mountains. You see, the Apaches makes much of his living from stealing. They make it their business to steal and they are experts at it; while we Comanches will make raids on our enemies for glory and fame, this is not true of the Apache. He raids not for glory and fame, but for what he can take away from others. He is respected by his people if he can bring much booty back; it does not matter what kind of method he uses to gain that booty. He may kill for it, use cunning, deceit, trickery, or whatever is necessary to get what he wants."

"But these ways are not the ways of the Comanche, and are not accepted by the Comanche. We fight with dignity and honor, and we fight face to face, with no deception. When we meet an enemy, he knows we will try to kill him, but an Apache may try to convince you that he wishes to be your friend and if you accept his overture of friendship and welcome him, he may kill you at the first opportunity. My friend, the Apache is treacherous, he cannot be trusted, and if you are foolish enough to trust him, you are as good as dead."

"You make the Apache sound equal to the Evil Spirit." commented

Nat wryly.

"No, Vlach, he's not equal to the Evil Spirit, he is the Evil Spirit or worse, if that can be possible."

"I had better remember what you have told me about the Apaches," Nat said.

"If you don't, and you meet up with an Apache and are fooled by him, I'll meet you in the spirit world. Remember, Vlach, the Apaches do not raise any food, they leave that for others to do and after the hard work of planting, irrigating, and harvesting is done, the Apaches move in to take it. They are smart all right, and don't forget it. If you do, it's at your own peril."

"How many bands of Comanches are there in your nations?"

"There are many bands, some are small, maybe just one family or two or three families who have joined to form a band. Sometimes maybe a group splits off from a larger band and this splinter group may not be of any one particular family, just friends. There are as many bands as there are groups who wish to form another band. There are three main bands, though, the Southern, Central, and Northern, and all of the smaller bands have broken away from one of these. The small bands are identified by something they do, such as Corn Eaters, or like my band, the Antelope, or there are the Liver Eaters and the Yap which eat lots of yap, which you call a potato. Then there are the Quick Singers, Honey Eaters, Wanderers, and many more."

White Eagle now called a halt which interrupted Three Tongues' discussion with Nat, and motioned for everyone to gather around him. When they had assembled, he said, "I think the Apaches have returned west of the Pecos River. Their scouts probably spotted us and warned the main party because we have more braves than they have and, as they also have their women with them, they probably thought it foolish to stand and fight. They are not fools and they never act as fools. We had better return to our people and bring them back to the main camp. Does anyone wish to speak?"

The warriors agreed with White Eagle and turned to ride back to the buffalo country. When they reached the camp, White Eagle rode to join Dull Knife and the Yap Comanches while Nat and Three Tongues rode to Spirit Woman and Snow Skin. While the men had been gone, Spirit Women and Snow Skin had jerked and smoked the buffalo meat and had it packaged and ready to transport. The buffalo robes were tied in bundles and ready to be packed on the travois for the trip back to the main camp.

"We could not find the Apaches," Three Tongues said as he slid from his horse.

"There will be other times," his mother answered. "Your sister and I have the bull buffalo hides in a separate bundle for you so that when we are back in the main camp you will be able to make your shields."

Chief Dull Knife gathered his people and they began the trek back to their encampment. When they reached it, Spirit Woman and her family unpacked their belongings and she instructed her son and Nat to go about the camp, and share some of their meat with the old and disabled as well as with those women who lived alone because they had lost their husbands.

When evening came, Three Tongues began to cut leather for a shield in front of his mother's tepee, and explained to Nat the procedure he would follow. "Before I begin to work on my shield, I want to tell you what designs I will put on it and why. You see, Vlach, most Comanche braves have older, more experienced men to make their shields for them, and as a result, because of the older men's experience in making shields, the shield is of excellent construction and quality, but I have decided to make my own shield out of respect for my father's memory. It was he who taught me how to make one and he learned his skills from his father, who was considered to be the best maker of shields this band has ever had.

"Most of the design which I will put on the cover of my shield will include some of what was on that of my father, but on the remainder of my shield, I will paint what came to me in a dream not long ago. You see, Vlach, I have asked the spirits to answer my questions, the question of my future and what it holds for me. The answer came to me in the form of a dream, but I am not sure what that dream meant and neither does anyone else, including the interpreter of dreams. It is one of the few dreams which he does not understand, and he told me that the spirits will, in time, let me know what it means. He further told me that I had been chosen by the spirits for some special mission, which is why the dream is uninterpretable by man and can be interpreted only by the spirits themselves."

"What was your dream? Or would you rather not say?"

"In my dream," Three Tongues told him, "I was sitting by the campfire in front of my tepee and I was alone. The fire burned brightly and as time passed the fire grew brighter and brighter, until a pack of wild dogs approached me from out of the darkness with their fangs showing under their curled lips. In place of their eyes I could see dead Comanche warriors. By this time the dogs seemed ready to attack me, but just before that occurred, one of them assumed human form and that human dog raised a tomahawk high above his head and advanced upon me. He wore such a fiendish smile on his face! I tried to rise to defend myself, but I could not move, and just as he was about to drive his tomahawk into my skull, I heard a loud noise. It appeared that the noise had some destructive power because the human dog fell dead at my feet. My dream ended at that point."

"I can see why no one can interpret your dream, for it sound crazy," Nat told his friend.

"It is not a crazy dream," The Comanche answered with dignity. "It is the spirits' way of telling what the future holds for me and it is for me to figure out what the message means."

"What will you paint on your shield?" Nat asked, thinking to switch to a safer subject.

"At the top of the shield, I will paint two dead Comanches and I will paint a circle around them, indicating the eyes and in the center of the shield, I will paint an orange fire surrounded by dogs. On the left side of the shield, I will paint a black circle which will represent the unknown area from which the noise in my dream came, and at the far right side of my shield, I will paint a large elk. This is the design my father had painted on his shield and under the elk's front feet, I will paint the trampled body of the dead human dog. Will you help me in making the shield?"

"I don't know a single thing about it," Nat told him, "so if you want me to help you, you'll have to show me what to do."

"Fair enough. I'll cut three pieces of the toughest bullhide which we have and place one on top of the other to give me the proper thickness. While I'm doing this, you can build a small fire so we can smoke the hides dry and after you do that, build a small round mound of wet dirt. We will then stake the hides over it tightly, thereby making the hides convex. They will retain this shape after they are dried. This curvature helps to deflect arrows."

The two young men labored two days constructing the shield and when it was finished, Three Tongues told Nat that now they had to make a cover for it, of soft deer skin.

"Why do you need a cover for something so tough?"

"The cover will protect the medicine which the spirits have given me and the cover will keep the medicine from escaping. I will remove the cover just before going into battle. In that way, the medicine will be at its strongest."

As Three Tongues was drawing the cover over his shield, a Comanche brave rode into the camp. Three Tongues told Nat that he was from the Southern Comanches.

They found that the representative of the Southern Comanches was asking for a council of all the bands for the purpose of deciding what to do about the Tonkawas. During the ensuing meeting the various bands could come to no united decision, and so decided to wait and think about a possible solution.

The seasons passed swiftly for Nat as he continued to live with the Comanches, taking part in their ceremonies wholeheartedly. It was during the second year of his time with them that he and Snow Skin were united in the Comanche marriage ceremony to their great joy and the quiet satisfaction of Spirit Woman and Three Tongues.

It was during the third year of Nat's life with the Comanches that another movement began among the branches of the Comanche nation to consider once again the increasing problem with the Tonkawas. A council was to be called once more and would be held on the bluffs which overlooked the bottomless lakes near the Pecos River. This would be a two day's ride from the Apache stronghold in the mountains to the west and perhaps that far from the cave of the bats. The meeting would be convened just after the snows had stopped falling.

For the next few days the Antelope camp talked of nothing but the approaching war which the whole Comanche nation would wage against the man eating Tonkawas.

"This council should have more support than the first one," Three Tongues said to Nat in excitement. "They have committed more outrages against our smaller bands and it's time we set aside our differences and joined together in a common effort to destroy the hated Tonkawas once and for all."

"Are you going to the council meeting?" Nat asked.

"Yes," answered Three Tongues, "and I'm sure Chief Dull Knife and Chief White Eagle will consider it an honor if you were part of our delegation. Will you come with us?"

"I'd be highly honored to be a member of the Antelope delegation," Nat told him.

"I'm sure they would welcome any ideas which you might contribute on how to deal with the Tonkawas. We have about six months before we meet, which should give the Antelope Band enough time to come up with a plan which we could present to the council," Three Tongues replied.

A number of meetings were called by Chief Dull Knife and Chief White Eagle for the sole purpose of trying to formulate a single plan which the Antelope people could present to the grand council. Nat attended each meeting with Three Tongues, but he listened and was silent while the others put forth their contributions. At the final meeting, Chief Dull Knife turned to him and said, "Vlach, you have not said what is on your mind. Would you like to speak?"

"I don't know the Tonkawas as well as do the Comanches, and I do not feel it is my place to speak unless asked to do so. You have asked, however, and so I will give my counsel. I have a friend many days ride east of here who is a maker of rifles such as the one I own. I believe that he would make us as many of these thunder sticks as you want or can afford, but he will need time. So my counsel is that we hunt buffalo from this winter's herd and gather all of the robes that we can and when they are cured and packed, we should take them to the Taos Fair and trade them for gold or silver. Then we can use this payment to purchase as many rifles as possible. After we have done this and have enough ammunition for our needs, we should train as many Comanche warriors as we can to use the rifles as well as possible. We should do our utmost to prevent the Tonkawas from knowing that we have this trained unit of highly skilled thunderstick experts, and when the crucial time arrives in the battle with the Tonkawas, we should bring this special unit of fighters into action. The surprise which this unit should have on the enemy, plus the added strength of the Comanche forces armed with their usual weapons, should give us a clear, decisive victory.

"I know that most of the Indian traders who visit the Taos Fair do not have silver or gold, but many of the Indians who come to the Fair can trade their goods with the Mexicans. We all know that they have gold and silver, but we must have fine buffalo robes to trade. I would also like to ask some of you who have been to the Fair if perhaps we should bring some horses to sell, as well as the robes? If wild horses won't sell and gentle horses will, let us start now to capture them and gentle them." He turned to the others at the council meeting and waited for the answers to his plan.

"Vlach has some sound advice," Little Raven said, after everyone had remained silent for a long time. "I say we follow his plan and take both buffalo robes and broken ponies to the Fair. Broken ponies will bring more gold than wild ones."

"Anyone else wish to speak?" Chief Dull Knife asked.

Three Tongues spoke, "I agree with Little Raven, but I wish to add that Vlach should be the trainer and leader of the special unit which he described, and I also say that he alone should select who and how many men should be in this unit."

"Anyone else wish to give counsel?" Chief Dull Knife again asked. When no one spoke. Chief Dull Knife added, "It will be done; we will follow Vlach's plan. Once we are ready to move south to join our brothers against the Tonkawas, White Eagle will be your chief, but in the preparation of our mission, we will work together. Is that acceptable to you, White Eagle?"

White Eagle looked at the chief with dignity and replied, "That is how it will be."

"If anyone disagrees with White Eagle or me, speak now."

No one spoke and after a pause, Chief Dull Knife continued, "Our council at the lakes will be as Vlach has said. Let us hope that they will heed our words. Preparation is vital for the success of this venture, and time is needed to make the proper preparations.

"Let us prepare for the winter hunt and the gathering and gentling of the wild horses, and if our counsel is not heeded at the meeting place, we can trade the horses and robes for what our band needs."

The wild horses were to be gathered before the winter migration of the buffalo, and White Eagle was given the task of overseeing the capture of the horses by Dull Knife. When he had chosen the warriors he wanted on the hunt, he issued these instructions. "We will divide ourselves into two parties, not far from the waterhole where they come to drink. When they come in, they will be tired and full of grass. We will let them add water to their bellies and our horses will have the advantage as we close in on them. Try to rope only the younger horses."

Their tactics worked and fifty horses were caught and brought in to their village grazing lands. Now those men assigned to the task of gentling them began to work with them, moving around them talking softly and getting them accustomed to a human's presence.

The hunters meanwhile rode toward a more distant waterhole, prepared to be gone until they were successful.

The men who stayed behind to work with the skittish horses were gentle with them, moving about them quietly and surely and, as the days, passed their calm, patient treatment was successful. They were taught to lead with the aid of a gentle horse and when this lesson had been learned, his Comanche trainer would rub his back, belly, and neck and finally put a little weight on his back. When the brave judged the horse was used to him, he would ease himself onto the back of the horse, riding him bareback. This sometimes passed without incident but sometimes the puzzled pony would buck, trying to rid himself of his rider. Gradually, the young horses became accustomed to the weight of their riders and then the additional burden of a blanket and saddle were added as their education continued. Using these methods, bunch after bunch of wild eyed mustangs were brought in and gentled until their count reached over two hundred. During the winter their education went on as the men tried to handle each of the green horses frequently, keeping them gentle and used to being handled and ridden.

The women spent the coldest part of the winter preparing buffalo hides and preserving the meat. All were looking forward to the trip to Taos which would be during the fall of the year. At last the time arrived when those chosen to make the journey began to prepare for the trip, and it was the middle of the summer when the Comanche braves left their encampent for Taos, leaving behind a little more than half of the men and all of the women and children.

White Eagle rode in the lead, with some of his braves following as they guarded the travois which carried the buffalo robes. The robes were of the highest quality and their prime condition would be eagerly sought by the traders in Taos.

Three Tongues and Nat rode some distance in the front, keeping a sharp eye out for danger. Other scouts rode approximately the same distance to each side and the remainder of the braves drove the horse herd. Everyone was well aware of what could happen to the hoped for war against the Tonkaws if the horses and buffalo robes were stolen from them.

They followed the south bank of the Canadian River westward until they reached the point where the river made an almost forty-five degree bend northward. They then would ride toward Canon Largo and on to Valmora. Somewhere along the Mora, at a good location, they would hold the horseherd while the rest went on into Taos with the robes. Any prospective buyer could view the herd there, or if he didn't want to come for them, arrangements could be made for their delivery wherever they were wanted.

The column of Comanches moved slowly westward across country which had few or no trees, but the topography of the region varied from long stretches of rolling country to deep arroyos and canons. Each one that they encountered had to be scouted before the main party drove through.

"What are those trails we see along the river?" Nat asked Three Tongues.

"Those are Comanchero trails."

"The Mexican or part Mexican and part Indian traders you told me about?"

"Yes," grinned Three Tongues. "We trade with the Comancheros for whatever we need, such as guns. They are the middlemen in our trade relations with the people of New Mexico. The cattle and horses which we take from Texas and Chihuahua are traded to the Comancheros, who in turn sell them cheaply to the peons of northern New Mexico. In fact, much of the beef, alive or dead, that the people of this region get, carry brands of the large haciendas of Mexico, far south of here. Years ago we took only the amount of cattle we needed at one time, but later we began to take an amount above that for use in trading. Since the coming of the Comancheros, we take whole horse herds, anywhere we find them. We have taken so many cattle and horses in recent years, and also captives, that a large part of Texas which used to be the home of many Mexican frontiersmen has become a wasteland of abandoned rancheros and haciendas. Adobe ruins can be seen everywhere and buffalo have returned to their old grazing grounds again. We like to see the buffalo back where they belong."

"You mentioned captives; what do the Comancheros do with captives?"

"The young Mexican boys and girls whom we capture are raised as Comanches, but the men and women whom we used to kill are now traded to the Comancheros who hold them for ransom."

"What if no one pays the ransom?"

"Then they are sold as slaves to whomever will pay the price, and if no one pays the price, the men are killed, and the women, if they are pretty enough, become wives of the Comancheros. Sometimes the leaders of the Comancheros will not permit their men to keep the captive women, because it causes too much dissension among them."

"What happens to the women who aren't considered pretty enough?"

"They are traded or sold to other bands of Comancheros."

In reaching the vicinity of Valmora, they had been fortunate in not encountering any difficulty. Because the braves were not wearing warpaint the villagers would realize they were a trading party, not a war party. Indian movement was expected at this time of year as the bands headed for the Fair, especially if it was evident that they carried trade goods. No one wanted to be guilty of breaking the long established unwritten law of safe passage for those attending the Fair, whether they be Mexican, Indian, or an occasional American trapper. Although exuberant braves had been known to break the custom, as a rule it was honored by almost all.

As they drew near Valmora, they met an occasional Mexican, who watched guardedly as they passed. The Mexicans whom they saw did not linger long to observe the Comanches, but moved rapidly toward the comparative safety of the village, so fearful were they of their traditonal enemies.

"Brave people, deprived of weapons, are made to appear as cowards," Three Tongues observed to Nat.

"I don't understand," Nat said, "you say the officials who rule over these people are cruel and unfeeling and treat them as animals? That the Mexicans are used to make life easier for the owners of the land and the officials of the corrupt government in Mexico City? If that is how these proverty stricken peons are looked upon by much of their ruling class, why don't they revolt?"

"My friend, have you not noticed that the Mexicans whom we have seen so far have no weapons? Their government will not permit them to own guns. Only the soldiers have guns and of course that way it is easier to control them. Defenseless people are easy to bully, and to add to that the lack of education which the authorities maintain and the people are cowed. And to make sure that they keep their place, the church scares them into being docile. You know, Vlach, after years of living in such an environment, people, any people, will accept their lot. That is the status of the peon today. We have made many raids on Mexican villages and when we do, the people do not resist, but run and hide and let us take what we want; only occasionally do the soldiers fight. They will usually leave town if they have enough notice that we are coming. From such raids, we gather horses, mules, cattle, sheep, goats, and captive women, whom we train to be good Comanches. Most of them make good Comanches and we believe this is true because they have a better life with us than they did living under the heels of their lords and patrons. Sometimes we ask the women if they would like to return to their villages and almost all of them prefer to stay with us."

"Who are the patrons?"

"The patrons are the ranchers and the peons are the beasts of burden who do the work on the ranches, which are called haciendas. That is the easiest way I can explain what a patron is, but I should add that patrons fall into two catagories. Many of the patrons in northern New Mexico genuinely seem to care for their peons, appearing to consider them as an extended part of their family. Their needs are provided for and this care even extends to those peons not attached to a hacienda, but who wander in, asking for help. I've heard that this type of patron has even gone as far as helping some of his own peons to begin ranching on their own.

"The second kind of patron is one who cares little for the welfare of his peons. To him, the peon is to be used with no regard for the conditions under which the peon lives. The peons unfortunate enough to live under such a patron are worked to the breaking point. You will find many of this type living south of here."

"Why do these people become peons to the patrons? Why don't they work for themselves?" Nat asked indignantly.

"For two reasons, my friend," Three Tongues answered. "One reason is for safety and security. If a person lives by himself, he must defend himself from the bandits and marauding Indians, especially the Apaches, Utes, and my people. This is impossible for him to do when he is not permitted by his government to own weapons to defend himself. We Indians usually possess much better weapons than he does. The Indians would fall upon such isolated farmers and ranchers like wolves upon a wounded buffalo, and kill him and carry off his women and children. His chances of survival at living alone and undefended are almost none, so, for protection, he becomes a peon on a hacienda, seeking the safety of larger numbers of people.

"Others become peons because they have become indebted to a patron and because they have no money or material goods to pay off this debt; they must work it off. Sometimes this debt can keep one generation after another working to pay it. A patron so inclined, can keep his peons on such low wages that they will never be able to break their bondage. In fact, the reverse can be true and they will, in fact, go deeper into debt. Such a system is intolerable to me, Vlach, for it's just another word for slavery, as far as I am concerned.

"Some day the peons will fall upon the corrupt government in Mexico as rain falls upon the dry plain and free themselves of the terrible yoke which they have carried for so many years. No, my friend, do not make the mistake of thinking that the Mexican is a coward. He is as brave as any other people, and one day we'll see evidence of that."

They rode in silence for a long while as Nat mulled over in his mind what his friend had told him. Things were often so much different than they seemed on the surface. He vowed to himself that he would see that Snow Skin and the child which was coming would never live under such hardships.

Three Tongues broke into his reverie, pointing to a high peak which loomed ahead of them. "The peak up there with its snow cap is called Truchas Peak. There is a valley north of it between Cerro Vista Peak and Truchas. The Mora river winds between the two and that is the way White Eagle will lead us. We will probably ride through snow before we reach Taos, but before that we will leave the horses on good grass beside the Mora."

"What is Taos like?"

"Taos is a typical adobe Mexican town and has an Indian pueblo near-by. The houses are flat roofed and usually only one story high, and are constructed of bricks made of mud and straw. The floors are mostly of dirt and the furniture is homemade with brightly colored designs painted on them. Of course I haven't seen inside the houses of the ricos, the richer Mexicans. Religious paintings and the crucifix and crosses are prominently displayed in the houses.

"The Catholic church is located at the most convenient and prominent place in the village, thereby giving everyone easy access to it. Robed priests can be seen everywhere, including the pueblo northeast of the village. The pueblo is built of adobe also, some of its buildings several stories high. The pueblo church is also of adobe, and on either side of the main structure you will see two belfrey towers which are higher than the main part of the church and in the towers can be seen crosses. A huge cross can be seen at the highest peak of the church itself. I'm not sure if the adobe wall still stands around the church yard. The last time I came to Taos I was with my father and I was small, but the adobe walls were there then. All of the walls, including the walls surrounding the church, were very thick. No arrow or even a bullet from that rifle of yours could pass through such a thickness.

"If you've noticed," Three Tongues motioned to their surroundings, "we've been climbing ever since we left Canon Largo. It's been a slow climb so far, but once we leave Valmora and head up the Mora River, the terrain will change quickly. The trees, pinons, juniper and cedar will be seen as they cling like patches of green grass to the sides of the hills which will gradually elevate into the mountains which are covered with Ponderosa pines as well as a variety of hardwoods. These trees grow so densely that we'll have trouble pulling our travois through them, which is why we'll leave the horse herd below. Because if we meet a grizzly in such timber, we could lose the whole herd."

They soon reached a parklike valley beside the Mora which would provide the open country necessary to graze and hold the herd. As they climbed, they left the herd behind them.

Three Tongues and Nat turned in their saddles as they rode to look back at the long double line of horse drawn travois. Braves rode most of the horses which pulled the travois, but, occasionally, a rider could be seen walking beside his horse. Indians did not abuse their horses and so the braves who were walking were either giving their horses a rest or they themselves needed to stretch their legs.

"We are approaching Valmora," Three Tongues said. "Watch the Mexican women and children head for cover once they see us. White Eagle has decided to skirt the village instead of going through its main section."

When the village had been reached, faces could be seen peeping from behind the windows of the houses as the Comanches passed. Those were the faces of a new breed of people. Hundreds of years of Spanish and Indian marriages had developed this new, hardy, hardworking people; people who had learned over the years to adapt to almost every kind of economic hardship and oppression, and still they went on.

"How these people survive is hard to understand," Three Tongues commented to Nat, "they have suffered every kind of hardship known to man and nature and still they look to the future with hope and assurance that better times must be just around the corner. Some Indian people despise them, but others, especially those from the nineteen pueblo tribes along the Rio Grande River and the old Coronado Trail, have learned to live with and among them. I think it makes it easier for both peoples to seek peace with each other when they remember that they have intermarried for so many years that it becomes difficult to fight against one's own kind. It wasn't that way at first, though. The early Spaniards and Indians fought many a fierce and bloody battle. We still fight them and so do the Apaches."

Many of the men of Valmora, some in groups and some alone, stopped what they had been doing to watch the Comanche column as it moved past their village. A few Mexicans even called friendly greetings with words, "Buenos dias, amigos," (good morning, friends). Or "Como estas usted," (how are you?)

"Muy bien, gracias, y usted." (very well, thank you and you?) Three Tongues responded.

However, most of the Mexicans did not say anything, but watched the feared Comanches with guarded caution. A few showed tentative smiles and still a smaller number spoke in soft voices, barely audible, "Bien venido," (welcome) as if by habit.

"Sounds like friendly and likable people," commented Nat.

"Some people would agree with you, especially the Americans," Three Tongues replied. He started to say something further, but stopped himself.

"What were you going to say?"

"I'll let you make your own judgement about the Mexican people, my friend. I do not want to cloud your mind with all of the prejudices which the Mexican and Comanche peoples have for each other and the fewer of our prejudices you know, the better it will be for all. New, clean blood, unexposed to the Mexican and Indian environment, is what it will take for all of us to learn to live together in peace and treat each other as equals."

"The air is sure getting thinner and cooler," Nat said as he looked about them and realized that he had paid very little attention to the scenery while they had been talking. Beautiful green meadows spotted the mountains ahead and below, resembling a patchwork quilt as they scattered over the mountainside; long stretches and grassy valley extended upward like fingers of a human hand.

"Dark Canyon is just ahead," Three Tongues said, "and once we get through it, we will head downward until we ride into the wide, fertile Rio Grande valley which is the home of Taos."

"Why do you call it Dark Canyon?"

"We Comanches call it Dark Canyon because the river valley becomes very narrow at that point, and the mountains on both sides looks as if someone had cut them off abruptly with a huge knife. The mountain walls are sheer rock and are as verticle as one could make them. Very little sun can reach the valley floor; the only sun rays which reach the lower canyon floor do so when the sun is directly overhead."

"How far does the Dark Canyon extend?"

"Perhaps half an hour's ride or better," Three Tongues answered, "but I'm not sure if the Mexicans and the Pueblo Indians call this canyon by the same name we do."

The canyon seemed dark and damp to Nat as they slowly walked their horses along the dry part of the river bed. The riverbed itself was wide, but the water in the river was only ten or fifteen feet wide now. It was obvious that when the snowmelt began, the water level could rise considerably until the water in the river could extend from bank to bank. The air was moist and very close because the sun was no longer visible and the trees and underbrush became thicker as the valley slowly widened. Now a cool breeze sprang up as the wind blew its fresh breath through the gorge. Heavy, thick, green grass grew plentifully where openings appeared beneath dead, fallen timber. It wasn't very long after the valley widened out before the caravan sighted Taos lying below. They rode until they found a good camping place not far from the little river where the grass was abundant. A space was claimed between the Pojoaque and Cochiti Indian booths where they would display their buffalo robes, although the chief told his braves confidently that no booth was really needed to display the robes for they would be stacked on the ground, and if they were fortunate, a buyer might take them off their hands that same day. They were to take turns staying by the robes until they were sold.

Three Tongues and Nat used their free time to roam through the fair grounds to see what else was for sale. They saw that most of the Pueblo booths displayed pottery and foods stuffs, such as dried fruit, honey, cornmeal, beans, Indian bread and the like.

"The Pueblo people are farmers," Three Tongues told Nat. "These are the kind of people the Apache watch closely, because when they begin to gather their crops, the Apaches do the harvesting instead.

"You saw the Taos Pueblo as we came down out of the mountains. Their houses of adobe are built one on top of another. You can count five stories in some of them. The way they are built makes them merge together in one large building. Each can be entered from an outside door and each individual home also opens into one beside it through an inside door. In this way, if attacked, their defence is much stronger. The wooden ladders which they lean against the walls are used for climbing to the upper level of rooms. The lower floor is used for storage only and if attacked, they draw up the ladders, and, since the lower floors have no doors or windows, they are impregnable.

"If you noticed as we rode by the Pueblo Indians booths, the women were using an horno to bake their bread. It is just like the ones they use every day in their pueblos. When their bread is ready, they push it into the horno with long poles with a flat board attached to each one. Some of their ovens or hornos are six or seven feet across and that high. They are constructed of the same material as the pueblo, adobe brick. Their Indian bread is delicious; I like it better than the Mexican tortilla."

"I see all of the Pueblo booths are together this year," Three Tongues said. "They are all over there to our right. The Tesuque, Pojoaque, Nambe, Picuris, Taos, San Juan, Santa Clara, San Ildefonso, Cochiti, and the Santo Domingo pueblos in that order. Some of them, like the Acoma, aren't here yet, or maybe they aren't coming this year for some reason."

"Where do the Acomas live?"

"Acoma is called the Sky City because it sits on top of a four hundred foot mesa and the mesa walls are so vertical that no one can climb to the top except where small toehold steps have been cut into the walls. This one access makes the pueblo very easy to defend."

"What happens if an Indian tribe should lay seige to it? How would they get their food and water?"

"They always keep much food stored in their storage rooms and they have a large cistern which never goes dry and a number of smaller cisterns, all of which are on top of the mesa."

The two men walked beside the Indian booths as they talked. The booths all seemed to be facing toward the east as did the tepees behind the booths. "The Indians just ahead of us," Three Tongues told Nat in a low voice, "are Jicarilla Apaches. Their tribal lands are west of Taos. The Mescalero Apaches have their booth set up just to the other side of the Jicarillas. The Mescaleros come from the Sierra Blanca Mountains several days ride south of here. They are the ones who killed my father and someday I will have many of their scalps.

"The Navajos are here and so are the Zuni, Laguna, Hopi, Kiowa, Arapaho, Cheyenne, Wichita, and even a few Osage and some Utes. I'm surprised to see the Lipan Apaches so far from home, but they are here, too."

The various booths displayed many different kinds of goods which their occupants had ridden many miles to trade. They saw smoked buffalo tongue, buckskin clothing, sea shells, pipestone, beaver pelts, knives, axes, beads, tobacco, sugar, salt, eagle feathers, vermilion, bear claws and a few white bear robes, saddles, blankets, pottery, baskets, mirrors, wooden bowls, and turquoise. All of this and much more was available as the two men walked from booth to booth.

In the Mexican and American booths, a trader could find tortillas, frijoles, chili con carne, dulce, which was a brown sugar candy, and pinonate, which was a pinon nut candy. They could also find metal spears, arrow points, tin for the use of making arrow heads, corn, beans, rebozos or shawls, crucifixes, crosses, combs, cosmetics, knives of every length and width with colorful handles, kettles, bread, tobacco, sugar, castor, saddles, boots, bridles, spurs, bits, mirrors, trinkets, red cloth, paint, brass wire with which to make rings, ribbons, coffee, calico, and much more.

Whiskey and guns were not allowed to be sold although some guns were sold secretly. Mounted Mexican soldiers, with their long, steel pointed lances, patrolled the Fair to keep order and to try to prevent the sale of guns or whiskey. Soldiers on foot also walked freely among the traders. Of course if one knew the right soldier or officer, he might not notice an illegal trade if the fee was enough.

"Do you have horses for sale?" A Mexican near them spoke to a party of Osage braves.

"Some," answered an Osage. "How many do you want?" the brave spoke in broken Spanish.

"How many do you have?" The Mexican spoke in a loud and agressive voice, and it was obvious that he had no fear of the Osage braves or any other at the Fair.

"We have maybe fifteen," came the reply.

"Not enough," the Mexican scoffed, and stalked away.

Nat looked at Three Tongues and the two hurried after the Mexican. "Excuse me, sir," Nat said as they caught up with the horse buyer. "Do you speak English?"

The Mexican halted and wheeled to face Nat and after looking him over, he turned to scrutinize Three Tongues. The Mexican had only one eye; the other eye socket was closed and a long scar extended from the middle of his forehead, across his blind eye and halfway down his cheek. He wore a trimmed beard and mustache and his weathered skin showed clearly that he was an outdoorsman. "Si, a little," he replied. He looked once more from Nat to Three Tongues and back.

"We could not help but overhear you back there at the Osage booth when you inquired about horses. We have some," Nat told him.

"How many?" The Mexican spoke sharply.

"How many do you want?"

The Mexican looked up at the sky, shook his head slowly from side to side and answered in a sarcastic voice, "For the love of God, what are we playing here, a game? I want horses, plenty of horses, at least two hundred. Do you have that many broken horses?"

"I think we can do business, mister. What did you say your name was?" Nat asked.

"I didn't say."

"My name is Nat, but the Comanches call me Vlach. This fellow to my right is called Three Tongues."

"Three Tongues?" The Mexican echoed in an arrogant tone as he turned once more to stare at Three Tongues. He said in Spanish, "Do you speak Spanish?"

"Si."

"Do you speak English?"

"Yes," Three Tongues answered again.

"Do you speak Comanche?" again questioned the Mexican.

Three Tongues smiled but said nothing.

"That's a good name for anyone who can speak three languages," the Mexican conceded. "My name," he continued, "is Sancho and that is all you need to know, so don't ask me any more questions. I want to see your horses."

"They are not here; we left them at another location," Nat told him.

"At another location? I won't buy horses sight unseen!"

"We can deliver them for your inspection not far from Valmora after we sell our buffalo robes here at the Fair, but we want gold and silver for the horses. We are not interested in trade goods."

"Huh," Sancho ejaculated. "So you won't take trade goods, but only gold and silver? Do you intend to buy rifles with the gold and silver you'll get from me?"

"You said no questions," Three Tongues grinned.

"So I did," conceded Sancho. He glanced beyond them toward the Mexican soldiers, then continued, "How much do you want for the horses?"

"We'll sell you the lot, two hundred and thirty-two broken horses, for five thousand pesos in gold or silver."

Sancho rubbed his chin for a few seconds and said, "That's kinda steep, wouldn't you say?"

"Not for these horses," Nat answered.

"You look like an honest man, or should I say, you'd better be," Sancho said with a hard look. "I'll take your word for it that the horses are sound and well broken and I'll give you four thousand pecos for them upon deliver in six days. If you are not there in six days, the deal is off, fair enough?"

"We're not horse trading, my friend, we want just what we said we wanted, five thousand. Good horses are not hard to sell," Nat told him grimly.

"If they're as good as you say, I'll pay it," said Sancho after deep thought. He shook their hands and said, "Don't try to cheat me, my friends, because if you do, you will see hell on earth and that's not just a threat, but the plain truth."

"You have my word," Nat told him.

"I'll have something other than your word if you try to trip me up," Sancho answered arrogantly as he looked Nat straight in the eye. He turned on his heel and stalked away into the crowd.

"Who the hell is he?" Nat asked Three Tongues.

"He is a Comanchero and one of the best; no one has ever cheated him and lived to tell of it."

"Is he one of the Comancheros who uses the trail we saw back along the Canadian River?"

"He is the leader of one of the bands who roams throughout New Mexico. There are many bands."

"Will he keep his word?"

"That Comanchero will," Three Tongues answered as he looked in the direction which Sancho had taken. "And we will keep our word if we value our hides. White Eagle will welcome our good news; let's go tell him."

When White Eagle heard about Sancho he said, "We are old friends, Sancho and I, we go back a long way. He is a fair trader and can be trusted. I will take most of the braves with me and ride back to start the horses this way. I'll leave five braves here with you and Vlach until the robes are sold. We'll meet you along the way, or if it takes longer to sell the robes, we'll see you back at the Antelope Camp."

White Eagle hastily assembled his braves and they were soon on the trail once more.

After they watched them ride out of sight, Nat turned to Three Tongues. "Why don't we go into town to see if we can't scare up a buyer? the others can watch the robes."

As they rode toward the outskirts of Taos, winding along the narrow, dusty road toward the plaza, they could hear the faint sound of music.

"Baile," Three Tongues said, "or a fandango." Seeing his friend's puzzled expression, he continued, "There's a dance in the plaza."

"At this time of day?"

"Why not? Apparently some trappers are in town and they like to eat, drink and dance with the women when they come in. Is there a special time for that?"

When they reached the plaza, they saw Mexican women dressed in their finest and prettiest dresses dancing in the dusty street in front of one of the cantinas. Their partners were buckskinned mountainmen. Nat and Three Tongues reined in their horses on the edge of the crowd and watched a couple as they whirled in circles. The mountainman had a bottle of whiskey in one hand and a woman in the other. He stomped the ground and waved the bottle, yelling like a wounded bear. His partner held the corner of her skirt in one hand, lifting it slightly as she whirled, showing the men a glimpse of her pretty legs. The mountainmen who were not dancing yelled at those who were. "Spin them faster!"

"It is fleesing time," Three Tongues commented drily.

"What do you mean?"

"Fleesing time, the trappers have a lots of money to spend and the girls, traders, musicians, gamblers and the owners of the cantinas are all here to get their share."

"Those musicians aren't much," Nat said as he looked at the men who stood near the wall of the cantina.

"They're good enough for the mountainmen, all they need and want is some kind of music which has a rhythm to it. The guitar, or heaca, the mandolin and the Indian drum fill that need. The women will furnish the more important needs and when they have spent all of their money, they'll head back to the mountains again to trap for more furs. Those that are lucky will return again for another sample of what they're enjoying right now."

The two men continued to sit on their horses outside the circle and watch the commotion until a voice interrupted their enjoyment.

"Forgive the intrusion, mi amigos," the stranger said. "I am Fernando Filipi Castillo from San Antonio, Texas. I understand that the buffalo robes back there at the fairground belong to you. Am I correct?"

Three Tongues and Nat turned from the spectacle and looked at Castillo. "Yes, that is correct," Nat answered. "My name is Nat Cochran and this is my Comanche friend, Three Tongues."

"Como esta usted?" Three Tongues greeted the Mexican caballero. He extended his hand for the customary handshake.

"Muy bien, gracias, y usted." Castillo answered as he shook their hands. "If the price is right, I would like to purchase your buffalo robes," Castillo told them. "What is your price?"

Nat studied Castillo for a moment and then said, "You have an honest face so I'll quote you our rock bottom price from the start. We'll take two and a half pesos in gold or silver for each of the robes. They are prime hides; we'll guarantee them."

"I know," Castillo assured him, "I've looked at them and they are prime. It's a deal," he said as he extended his hand to consumate the trade. "I'll have my men come by with my carretas within the hour to pick them up. I will have the money then. May I buy you a drink, gentlemen?"

"Indians are not served whiskey," Three Tongues said, "You two go and I'll go back to my people and tell them we have sold the robes."

"Bueño, mi amigo," Castillo answered with a slight nod of his head.

Three Tongues reined his horse away from Nat and Castillo and trotted back toward the fair grounds as Nat tied his horse to a hitching rack and joined Castillo to enter a cantina. Castillo pointed to a table at the back of the cantina and Nat nodded and followed him to it. As they sat down, Castillo called to the bartender, "Dos whiskey, por favor, señor."

The whiskey was brought and after the bartender had returned to the bar, Nat said, "It's the first time I've ever been in a cantina. This one isn't much is it?"

"No, mi amigo, but most frontier village cantinas are like this one, with little or no ventilation and plenty of flies, smoke and dust from the dirt floor and street outside. And then there are the rough, unkempt workers who patronize them. But enough talk about our environment. Let's enjoy our drink. Salud." Castillo raised his glass to Nat. Nat raised his glass in return and repeated, "Salud."

The two men downed their drinks and when their glasses were empty, Castillo leaned toward Nat across the table and said softly, "Señor, I need a favor of you. You are a friend of the Comanches and I need a third party such as you to contact the Comancheros. You see, mi amigo, my wife was captured three weeks ago in a Comanche raid on San Antonio. That is the reason for my presence here in Taos, and as I walked among the booths at the Fairgrounds, I was hoping I might see my wife among the Indians, but I did not. And then I saw the Comanche booth. I observed them closely for I knew that they would be the key to locating my wife, because of their dealing with the Comancheros. I decided to purchase the buffalo robes from the Comanches as a good will gesture in hopes that in return, you would help me to find my wife. Will you help me, señor? Please? I will be indebted to you for the rest of my life if you could help me in securing her release."

"We are going to meet some Comancheros soon. I cannot tell you when or where, but when we do meet," Nat told him, "I will ask them about your wife. But I don't know your wife or what she looks like and if they do have her or know of her, they too, will not know if she is your wife."

Castillo reached into the inner pocket of his jacket and pulled from it a folded piece of painted canvas. "Here," he whispered as he passed the painting to Nat. "This is a portrait of my wife, Ursala. You keep it; it will help you in your search for her and in identifying her. Please señor, please find her. I will pay you handsomely for her release. You name the price. If I went to the Comancheros myself, they would ask more than I have or could ever borrow. You see, the Comancheros dislike my social class deeply. They may have even killed my wife by now if they have found out her social class, or she may have already experienced such personal indignaties that she will not want to live. I hope for the best, for I have no other choice if I want to keep my sanity . . . I must hope for the best."

"Señor Castillo," Nat said, Castillo interrupted, "Please señor, I would consider it a personal favor if you would call me Fernando."

"All right, Fernando, I will meet you in Las Vegas in a week or so. Wait until I get there. I hope that I'll have some word of your wife by then."

"Bless you, my friend," Fernando replied as he rose from the table. "I must join my men now before any Comancheros see us together, for that will not help matters. I will go for the buffalo robes now. Vaya con Dios."

Nat watched Castillo and tried to imagine how he would feel if the circumstances were reversed and Snow Skin was being held captive.

"Hey, you," a half drunken trapper yelled at Nat. "I want to see if you can answer my question . . . none of these damn Mexicans can." He flourished his arm to take in the people sitting at his table. "If you can answer my question, I'll give you what I have promised these people if they answered my question. They don't know the answer, so why don't you try?" The gurrulous trapper reached into his catchall sack and tossed some gold coins on the table. "What do you say, sport?"

"What's the question?" Nat asked as he rose to leave.

"What is the name of the man who wears a skunkskin cap, plays a wooden flute, and is considered the keeper of all mankind?"

"The Macedonian," Nat answered.

"Well, I'll be damned!" The trapper rose excitedly to his feet and almost fell backward. "You're right, the Macedonian is the right answer. Here, take the five hundred pesos."

"I don't want your money," Nat answered politely. He started to walk by the trapper.

"Hey, mister," the trapper slurred, "a bet is a bet and you won so it is only fair that you take the wager. Beside if you don't take it, within a half hour from now, I'll be in the alley, passed out and these vultures at my table will pick my pocket of the gold pieces. It would be better for you to have it . . . you've earned it anyway."

"Oh, I'll take it," Nat said, "if you put it that way."

The trio of surly looking Mexicans showed their displeasure when Nat picked up the five hundred pesos worth of gold.

"Thank you, my friend," Nat said to the trapper. He then turned to the Mexicans and said, "Adios, mi amigos." He raised his hand in salute, smiled, and left the cantina.

Three Tongues stood leaning against the hitching rack as Nat stepped out of the cantina into the street. Nat laughed as he told his friend about what had happened with the trapper.

"No one in there ever heard of the Macedonian?" Three Tongues asked in surprise.

"I guess not," Nat replied, "or they would have picked up some easy money."

"Where do those Mexicans live, anyhow, in a monastery?"

"Not by the look of them," Nat chuckled, "forget them, Three Tongues. What do you think of our chances at doubling the five hundred pesos at the gambling table?"

"It's a fifty, fifty chance," Three Tongues said optimistically. But he quickly added, "If it's an honest game, that is, which I'm sure it isn't so that makes the odds a lot worse doesn't it?"

"Let's try it anyway," Nat said recklessly. "If I'm lucky, we can buy at least twenty more rifles. You can sit nearby and watch the dealer. If you are watching him, maybe he'll not try to cheat."

"I'm game!" The Comanche grinned. "Let's give it our best shot."

The two walked to the gambling house up the street and Nat moved over to a table where a professional gambler was dealing cards to two men seated at his table. Nat asked if he could join the game.

"The more the merrier." The well dressed gambler looked up and nodded to an empty chair.

Three Tongues pulled an empty chair from a nearby table and sat down next to Nat.

"Is the Comanche going to play?"

"No," Nat replied, "just me."

"All newcomers have the choice of what game we play," the gambler told Nat. "What will it be, stranger? Monte, poker, or brag, euchre, or seven-up?"

"Five card draw." Nat placed the gold pieces in front of him on the table.

The gambler's eyes brightened as he shuffled the cards. Three Tongues eyes were bright too as he kept them glued not on the gold pieces, but on the gambler's hands.

The gambler saw that Three Tongues was eyeing him closely as he dealt out the hands. Nat picked up his hand slowly and watched the faces of the other players as he did so. He played his cards close to his chest, spreading his cards just enough to see them. He had drawn two aces, a king, a nine and a seven. He glanced around the table once more, than at Three Tongues and finally at the gambler's hands and the deck of cards. He threw down two cards as he heard the player to his right open. "I'll open for five pesos," the other player said.

Nat threw his pesos into the center of the table and drew two cards when his turn came. He watched the other men as he reached for the two cards. The first card was a king. Nat looked around the circle as he slid the last card to the edge of the table and then held it with the other against his chest. He could hardly believe his eyes when he looked at the last card and saw that it was an ace.

"What'll you bet?" The gambler looked across at the player who had opened. While the man to his right considered the bet, Nat still glanced around the table, judging what the others were thinking. Finally the man to his right hesitantly pushed two more gold pieces into the pot.

"I'm pressed for time so I think I'll go for broke." Nat slid all of his gold into the center of the table with his right hand. "There's four hundred and ninety five pesos there," he said with a grin.

The gambler looked at his cards again and then looked at the other two men, then back at Nat. Nat returned his stare and saw his eyes turn to Three Tongues. The Comanche's eyes had never for a second left the gambler's hands and that deck of cards. One of the other players threw his card face down on the table, but said nothing. The gambler looked at the other player who after a few seconds of hesitation also dropped out.

"Do you call me?" Nat asked, softly.

The gambler did not reply, but continued to study his cards. He then counted out his pesos, dropping them one piece at a time on to the discarded cards. "I call."

"A full house aces high." Nat spread his cards out in front of him, but kept his eyes steadily on the gambler.

The gambler looked at Nat's cards and said in a chilly voice, "I guess that beats my flush. The pot is yours, stranger."

"Thank you gentlemen." Nat gathered the gold pieces from the table under the cold stares of the three men.

Three Tongues spoke for the first time as he rose from his chair, "Muchas gracias, caballeros."

Nat and Three Tongues walked from the building and Three Tongues said softly, "We had better not linger long in town, that gambler back there is not a happy hombre."

"Our business in Taos is completed and I don't see any reason to hang around. Let's get the others and ride to join Chief White Eagle," Nat said with a grin.

When the two men caught up with White Eagle, he had moved the horses farther up the Mora River and had met with the Comanchero leader, Sancho, who was in the process of paying him.

As they joined the others, Sancho jibed, "Ah, the buffalo hide merchants are back." His grin faded as he noticed Nat staring at one of the women with his Comanchero band. Sancho looked from the woman to Nat and asked sarcastically, "Didn't you see enough women in Taos?"

"I guess not," Nat said as he turned back to Sancho.

"Do you like her?" Sancho asked with a smile

"She is a striking woman," Nat answered, "she has beautiful features and her skin is of an olive tone I've never seen before."

"Do you want her?" Sancho wore a wide smile as he slapped his leg and then laughed aloud.

Nat did not answer immediately, but looked at the woman searchingly.

"She is yours, mi Americano amigo. You can call it a gesture, a gesture showing my appreciation for your honesty in selling me these fine horse. If I throw her into the deal, maybe it will make it a more even trade." He laughed heartily, "I, too, want to be perceived as an honest trader!"

"I'll take her," Nat answered, "and many thanks, Señor Sancho."

"So it's Señor, now," the Comanchero leader replied, "I'd better be going; if I stay any longer, you will be addressing me as a caballero, no?"

"Si!" Nat grinned.

Sancho wheeled his horse and rode toward where his men held the horse herd.

After he was out of earshot, Chief White Eagle looked from the woman to Nat and said sternly, "What do you want her for? You have one who lives back in the Antelope camp."

Three Tongues also showed his displeasure by walking away, leading his horse.

"Wait a minute, Three Tongues, I have something to tell you."

Three Tongues walked back, but didn't try to hide his feelings as he waited for Nat to speak.

"Remember the caballero we talked to in Taos? The one who bought the robes? When I had a drink with him, he told me his wife had been stolen and asked for our help. He gave me this painting of her to use for identification and thought maybe, since you deal with the Comancheros, they might be cooperative." Nat pulled the painted canvas from beneath his shirt and opened it for Chief White Eagle and Three Tongues to see. "Now do you see why I accepted Sancho's gift?"

Nat next turned to Ursala and said, "Señora Castillo, your husband is waiting in Las Vegas for you. He has been hoping and praying that I would be successful in obtaining your release from the Comancheros."

When Ursala heard Nat's words, she burst into tears, but after she had wept her tears of rejoicing, she composed herself and said, "How can I ever thank you, señor, for the wonderful thing which you have done this day. Only the Holy Mother can know what joy you have brought to me!"

"Your reunion with your husband will be thanks enough, senora," Nat told her, embarrassed at her overwhelming gratitude.

She spoke again eagerly, "When will we go to this Las Vegas place, señor, if you will excuse my anxiety?"

Nat looked at Chief White Eagle who nodded his approval. "We can leave right now if you are up to it."

"Up to it?" Ursala fairly screamed. "Up to it? Lead the way and I'll follow, but please señor, do not ride too slowly."

"Do you want to come?" Nat asked Three Tongues.

"No," said his friend, "I think you can handle this mission all by yourself."

"Do you wish for us to wait for you, Vlach, or shall we meet you farther on?" Chief White Eagle spoke.

"You had better go on," Nat said, "I'll meet you back at the Antelope camp."

Nothing else was said as the Comanches rode eastward and Nat and the señora turned due south. They rode for several hours and then Nat made an early camp as he saw how tired Ursala was. Her spirit was willing, but she was drooping in the saddle from exhaustion. As soon as they stopped, Nat gave her some of the pemmican from his saddlebags, she dipped up water from the stream nearby and within minutes she was sound asleep, with her saddle blanket wrapped around her. Nat grinned as he thought how happy her husband would be when they reached Las Vegas, and how surprised that it had happend so quickly.

The next day as they pulled their horses in after trotting for quite a while, Nat asked Ursala what it had been like being a prisoner.

"I suppose I had three things to sustain me," she replied thoughtfully. "First of all of course was my faith, which gave me the courage to endure. And then I had hope that my husband would find a way to rescue me by paying a ransom or whatever, and I kept telling myself that it didn't matter what happened to me as long as I didn't let it reach the inner me, as long as I didn't let it touch me inside. Not that it wasn't important what happened, but that I didn't let it break me." She rode looking straight ahead as she spoke, but now she looked aside at Nat and asked, "Do you know what I'm trying to say?"

"I know you're a very brave lady," Nat said, "but I think I do know what you mean . . . that whatever life hands us, the way we deal with it, with courage and fortitude, is very important."

"Of the highest importance, I think," Ursula told him. "And I hope I can live by that creed now that I'm safe once more."

They crossed the Gallinas River just on the outskirts of the village of Las Vegas and walked their horses up the gradual slope past the flatroofed adobe houses which lined the street leading to the plaza. Some people were afoot and others on horseback and still others rode small burros or drove carretas.

Most of the benches on the plaza lawn were occupied by people sunning themselves or talking with friends. A few people sought the shade provided by the tall trees which were scattered throughout the little parklike plaza.

Nat spotted four carretas drawn up to one corner of the plaza. Their freight, Nat observed, was the buffalo robes which they had sold to Señor Castillo.

"Your husband is here," Nat told the señora, "those are his carretas with the buffalo robes I told you about."

Ursala straightened in her saddle for the day had been long and tiring and looked quickly around. "I don't see him," she said excitedly. "Where is he? Do you see him?"

They trotted their horses toward the carretas and as they approached, the señora called, "Porfidio!"

One of the men whom Señor Castillo had left to guard the carretas turned quickly as he heard his name called. "Señora Castillo!" Porfidio wore a broad grin, "We were afraid we'd never see you again." He shook her hand with enthusiasm as he removed his sombrero and bowed. "It is so good to see you again. God has answered our prayers. Wait here and I'll summon the señor. He is eating over there in the cafe." Porfidio ran toward the little restaruant and in a few seconds, Señor Castillo and his men came running out of the cafe and toward them. Their faces beamed with happiness as they raced toward her. Upon seeing her husband, the señora slid to the ground and ran to meet him. when they came togehter, they embraced and whispered to one another as tears rolled down their faces. They hugged each other for long moments as everyone in the area cheered and yelled in support of the happy reunion.

When Castillo finally released his wife, he walked over to Nat and shook his hand vigorously, saying, "Thank you señor, thank you from the bottom of my heart. You have made life livable once again. God bless you and may the angels forever watch over you."

"It has been my pleasure," Nat replied. "You are a lucky man to have such a beautiful, gracious, and courageous wife, señor."

"Thank you again, Señor Nat, I cannot argue with you on that point. I agree with you totally and more, if that is possible." He hugged his wife closely to his side.

"Well, I had better be going; I have a long way to go."

"Before you go, señor," Castillo said, "Please permit me the honor and privilege of returning the favor which you have done for us. I would like to pay you for returning my Ursala to me."

"It was my pleasure, Señor Castillo; I'm sure you'd have done the same for me if the circumstance were reversed," Nat protested.

"If you will not accept pay, then permit me to give you the buffalo robes. I really have no use for them; as a matter of fact they would be a burden to me on our return journey to San Antonio de Bexar."

"But I," Nat did not get a chance to finish for the Mexican interrupted, "Please señor.'

Ursala added, "It would make our hearts much lighter to express our gratitude in such a way."

"I would recommended Miranda's store if you want to sell them, señor," went on Señor Castillo.

"All right," Nat answered in hesitation, "could you have your men drive the carretas there? I'll see if he wants to buy that many."

"It will be done at once," Castillo answered, and he turned to issue orders to that effect.

"Good luck and good bye." Nat told him as he reined his horse to follow the carretas.

"Vaya con Dios, Señor," Castillo called.

"Please, Señor, come to visit us," Señora Castillo said and as she fought to hold her tears back.

Nat waved to them once more as he rode away.

He had no trouble selling his robes at the Miranda Trading Post and as he headed east to join the Antelope Comanches, he thought often of his own wife and the child they would soon have. He smiled to himself as he thought how lucky a man he was to have found Snow Skin. As he thought of his loving wife, he broke into a trot, eager to be back in their tepee, eager to see her smiling, upturned face once more. He felt as though he'd been gone much too long.

Now he began to worry, wondering if she were all right, had she perhaps had the baby while he was not there? Thinking these long thoughts, he covered mile after mile, stopping only long enough for his horse to rest and graze and for him to catch a few hours of sleep. When he finally rode into the Antelope encampment, he first saw Three Tongues who strode toward him with a broad grin on his tanned face. "What kind of a daddy is it who is not there when his son is born?"

He grasped Nat's hand in congratulation as his friend jumped off his horse and ran past him. "She's fine . . . she's fine," he reassured him as Nat disappeared into his tepee. He shook his head as he walked over to his buffalo horse and laid an arm across his neck. "Will I be like that, some day?" He muttered to his favorite.

CHAPTER VI

It was some weeks later when Chief Dull Knife called a council for the purpose of selecting and sending a delegation to the lakes for the meeting with all the bands. Nat and Three Tongues, as expected, were among the delegation as it left camp under the leadership of Chief White Eagle.

When the Antelopes reached the bluffs overlooking the bottomless lakes, many of the delegations were already present and had their tepees erected. A huge semi-circle of perhaps forty tepees faced east, the direction in which the sun spirit rose early each morning.

As the eight Antelope delegates, led by their war chief, White Eagle, rode into the camp, other warriors who knew White Eagle, Three Tongues, and the rest, dropped what they were doing and came to greet their fellow braves. All eyed Nat with surprise and suspicion until White Eagle, upon seeing their skepticism, said to them as he dismounted, "The white man who accompanies us is an Antelope warrior, proven and tested to be a Comanche in spirit as well as in his heart. He is to be trusted as much as any Antelope brave here. If he is not accepted as such, we will return to our village. He is also the principal architect of the battle plan which we Antelopes will present to the Grand Council."

A loud voice from the front of the one of the tepees could be heard clearly as it said, "Your word, White Eagle, is as true as an arrow. I welcome the white man as one of us."

White Eagle turned in his saddle to look in the direction from which the voice had come and recognized his old friend, Running Bear.

"Welcome to my tepee, White Eagle," Running Bear said. "It has been too long since we rode together, way too long; come, get down and let us talk."

White Eagle dismounted and handed his reins to one of the delegates and said, "Three Tongues, find a location for our tepees and unload the travois. I'll return after I have talked with my old friend from the Quick Singer's Band, Running Bear."

It was eight days from the time the Antelope delegation arrived at the lakes before the last contingent arrived for the Grand Council. When the Honey Eaters had had a day to rest, the Grand Council was convened in the large lodge erected in the center of the large, semi-circle of Comanche tepees. The braves assembled dressed in their best regalia and sat around the fire. Food was prepared and served by the younger braves, and as Nat ate, Three Tongues said to him, "We have no religious society, clubs, or organizations, and we have no priests. Each of us is his own priest and interprets the way of the spirits for himself. Each of us communicates with the spirits in his own way, using whatever methods work for him. For myself, dreams work best, others see visions, but from these dreams and visions we all ask for puhua or medicine from the Great Father."

"I thought that your main god was called the Great Spirit," Nat said.

"Some call him the Great Spirit and some call him Great Father, and still others call him the Father of us All. Others call him by similar titles, but all of these names refer to the same Spirit, just as your people, according to my mother's teaching, anyway, sometimes refer to your God as Christ, and sometimes He is called the Lord, and at other times he is called Jesus, the Savior, Son of God."

"What is your belief as far as death is concerned?" asked Nat with interest.

"When we die," Three Tongues said, "we all go to meet the Great Spirit in a land which he has prepared for us. In this land of his, all sadness, sickness, suffering, disease, and other evil things that we find here on earth will not exist. All Comanches will be the same age and they will enjoy a climate that is forever beautiful and pleasant."

"Where is this Happy Hunting Ground?" Nat asked.

"In the land where the sun goes to sleep for the night, west of here," Three Tongues answered. "But now let us listen, because Running Bear is about to speak."

"I smoke the pipe of peace with my fellow Comanche warriors on this important day. May the Spirit world hear our words and bestow strong puhua on our venture and give us the wisdom necessary to create a plan which will give us victory." Running Bear blew smoke in the traditional directions and then passed the pipe to the warrior on his left. The pipe circled the group in a clockwise fashion, until the last warrior had smoked it.

Running Bear now spoke again, "The Comanches need a chief to lead us against the Tonkawas. This chief must have been proven in battle and must be one who has shown that he has strategic ability and must also be the bravest of the brave. Most important of all, he must have leadership qualities, for we need such a man to unite us all as one. We need such a man, a man that we all follow and obey without question. Such a man I believe is White Eagle. I have spoken."

Silence filled the tepee as the warriors waited for any other nominations, but none came. "Do I take this silence as a unanimous vote for the war chief of the Antelope band?"

All present grunted their approval of Running Bear's selection. Now White Eagle rose to his feet and told the council, "I am honored to be selected as your chief in our common war against the man-eating dogs, the Tonkawas. The white man who is among us today is called Vlach by the Antelope band of which he is a member. I would like now for him to present, for your consideration, his plan for victory over the enemy."

Nat rose and described the plan that he had presented to the Antelope band a few months earlier, and when he had finished, all of the council members asked questions concerning the plan. After the questions had been answered to their satisfaction, White Eagle told the Grand Council that it would take perhaps as much as two years to prepare for the Tonkawa War and that Vlach and Three Tongues would travel throughout the Comanche nation, selecting men for the special unit. Upon the selection of these braves, they would move to the Antelope camp and begin their training. In the meantime, everyone else would make their own preparations by making arrows, bows, lances, shields, and whatever else was needed. The time and place of the gathering of all warriors for the attack on the Tonkawas would be brought by an Antelope messenger. "Until then," White Eagle told them, "we will break camp here and go back to our villages and begin our work."

The pipe was smoked once more before anyone left and then the warriors rose and were leaving the tepee when Nat said, "I would like for the Timber Band to wait for a few minutes because I have some special instructions for them."

When all had left the tepee except the Timber delegation, Nat turned to them and said, "I have a very important mission for your band." He then knelt on one knee in front of them and cleared the ground with his hand until the area was free of all grass, weeds, and pebbles. He looked over his shoulder and told Three Tongues to pay close attention to what he was about to describe because he would be his right hand in the venture. He then drew a large square on the ground and proceeded to draw four more boxes within the large one, each one small enough to fit within the next larger. When he finished, he had five boxes fitting inside each other.

He then placed a number of pebbles on each of the lines. "These pebbles represent warriors," he said as he looked up at the Timber warriors. "Each one of these warriors will be armed with a long lance made of oak. The first line of men will have lances which are five feet long. The second line will have lances six feet long, and so on. The last line will have lances nine feet long. The men who carry these must be of exceptional strength, both in arms and legs. The other details of this formation will be explained once I have chosen and trained the men who will form this phalanx. I want you band to select enough oak poles and peel and smooth them for their use in this phalanx. Can you do this for me?"

The Timber Band was honored to be selected for this important mission and they assured Nat that they would find enough oak poles in the forests of their mountains for his needs.

"They will have to be strong enough to stop a charging horse. They cannot have a flaw in them or they will snap on contact with such force," Nat told them. "When the Tonkawas charge our phalanx on horseback, just before they reach it I will give the order from the center of this formation for the warriors to brace their oak lances into the ground, the poles will receive all of the oncoming weight of the horses. The warriors of the phalanx will then drop their lances and charge the unhorsed Tonkawas with their tomahawks and knives and at this time, White Eagle will bring the main forces of the Comanches into battle."

The chief of the Timber Band now spoke, "We will have all of the poles which you will need for the battle, and we will have the straightest and strongest ones that grow in the forest. They will be ready when you need them."

"I will send for them one year from now. Will that give you enough time?"

"Yes, more than enough," the chief answered.

"Good," Nat answered, "then I guess we are finished here. I will see you in one year."

The Timber Band rose and left the tepee and when Nat and Three Tongues walked out, they saw that most of the Comanches had already departed or were in the process of disassembling their tepees in preparation for departure.

"This phalanx thing should surprise the Tonkawas," Three Tongues said.

"If we don't keep it a secret, it won't," Nat told him.

"The secret will be kept," Three Tongues assured him.

"I certainly hope so," Nat replied, "we had better join our delegation before they leave us here."

When the Antelope warriors returned to their main camp on the Canadian River, Dull Knife called a council meeting and Chief White Eagle reported on what had transpired at the meeting by the lakes.

"Good, everything is as we hoped," Chief Dull Knife said with satisfaction. He turned to Nat and Three Tongues, "Now you two must make your journey to the camp of the white man to order the rifles. You will leave as the sun rises."

"We will be ready," Nat replied.

As the sun threw its first rays over the prairie, Nat and Three Tongues had already said their goodbyes and were a good fifteen miles northeast of their Comanche village.

Their journey to the junction of the Missouri and Kansas Rivers was uneventful, but Nat immediately recognized the changes which had taken place at that location since he had last seen it. The American Fur Company Trading Post which Francois Chouteau had established was called Westport Landing now and there was another settlement four miles south of Chouteau's post which was called Westport. All of the cargo which came up the Missouri River which was destined for Westport was unloaded at Chauteau's and then hauled overland. The people had begun to call the American Fur Company's Trading Post, Westport Landing, because it was there that all of the supplies for Westport had to be unloaded.

When Nat and Three Tongues reached Westport Landing, Nat said, "There it is, he must have a good business. The sign on that large building to the left reads, Muller's Gun Manufacturing, that's our man!" The two men rode to the hitching rack which stretched along the front of the building in question and tied their horses.

"What a hodge podge of people," Nat commented, as people of many nationalities bustled past them. Wyandot, Osage, and Pawnee went about their business and the German language was heard as well as French and others that Nat did not recognize. Mountainmen, river boat men, business men and half breeds were there, all intent upon their business. When Nat and Three Tongues entered Otto's establishment, they saw Otto behind a counter talking with a customer. Otto did not look up when they entered, but continued to listen as his customer complained, "That runny nose kid did it again and Dave would have made a good saddle maker of him if the kid had just stayed put." As he finished speaking he withdrew a copy of the Missouri Intelligencer, a newspaper. "See here, Otto," the man continued, pointing to the paper, "it says right here that David Workman has posted a one cent reward for anyone who will bring Kit Carson back to finish his indenture. The West just had too much of a pull on the kid, I guess."

"Yeah, I know how Kit feels. I have a friend who couldn't stay put either; he went West too." Some sixth sense caused him to look up just then and he let out a yell and rushed around the counter, "Nat! Speaking of the devil! Boy, is it good to see you."

The two men grasped hands and then Nat said, "This Comanche answers to the name of Three Tongues. He is also my brother-in-law."

Otto shook the Indian's hand and glanced around, "Where is she?"

"Where is who?" Nat grinned happily.

"Your wife of course."

"She's back at the village, taking care of our little son," Nat told him proudly. "Is Rees hereabouts?"

"No," responded Otto. "He went back to Vincennes after he sold the pelts, but he left your share of the trappin's with me. It's a sizable amount, too."

"We'll talk about that later," Nat told him, "but right now, let's go somewhere where we can talk in private."

"Lets's go into my office. I'll see you later, Sam," he called to his friend who waved a hand in farewell.

After they were seated in Otto's office, Nat said, "Otto, we need about two hundred of your rifles and we'll pay for them in gold. Can you make them for us?"

"Gold?" Otto spoke in excitement. "There's little or none of that around here. Yes, of course I can make them. When will you need them?"

"As soon as possible," Nat answered. "What will they cost per rifle?"

"I'll let you have them for twenty-five dollars apiece."

"I don't want you to lose money on this sale, Otto, so please don't mix friendship with business on this transaction."

"I'll break even on thirty dollars apiece, or I could even make a little," Otto assured him.

"I'll pay you the going price; we've got the money," Nat urged.

"No," Otto replied, "Thirty dollars is what I want to charge."

"We'll need two or three factories and plenty of ammunition to go along with the order. Will there be any problem with that?"

"I've got seven men working for me, Nat, and they're all good, reliable men. It will take me nearly six months to fill your order, though. Is that too long? If it is, we could try to shave some time off by working longer hours."

"No, six months will suit our purpose just fine," Nat said.

"Good. I'll start some of my men on them tomorrow. I have other orders to fill, but some of the men can continue with them."

Nat poured Mexican gold coins out on Otto's desk and began to count out the eight thousand pesos. "Six thousand for the rifles and two thousand for the factories and ammunition. Do you think that will cover it?"

"It should," Otto replied.

"If it doesn't let me know, or better still, take what else you need out of my trappins' money."

"Sounds fair enough."

"I think it's only fair that you know why we want the rifles."

"I'm sure you have a good motive," Otto said, "if you'd rather not tell me for any reason, I'll understand."

"Otto," Nat said, "there are some Indians in south Texas called Tonkawas who are cannibals."

"Cannibals?"

"Yes, cannibals, and the Comanches think it is high time that they put a stop to their eating of Comanches. Otto, the success of our plan depends, in part, on secrecy, so keep what I have just told you under your hat."

"Your plan is safe with me," Otto assured him.

"I'll be back for the rifles in about six months," Nat told his friend as he rose.

"Why don't I sent them to you by way of the Santa Fe Trail? You could begin to watch the wagon trains in about six months just in case the rifles are ready sooner. Or better still, you could have some of your Comanche scouts watch the wagon trains from about five and a half months on. I'll inform the wagon master that you will pick up your goods before he reaches Santa Fe. I'll have to list them as something else on the manifest, though. What do you say we label the freight as mining equipment?"

"Fine, but how will I know which wagon train will be carrying the 'mining equipment'?"

"That will be easy," Otto said. "I'll paint a big white 'M' on each side of the wagons, and just in case you can't see that, I'll also have a big, black 'M' painted on the canvas."

"Sounds like a good idea, Otto. Let's do it that way. Now, let's talk about you, Otto. It seems you're doing all right." Nat glanced around the office.

"Why don't you look around Westport Landing for a little while and meet me at the hotel up the street in about an hour? We can eat and I'll fill you in on what's going on here."

"Sounds good, we'll see you later."

A little later the three men sat down in the dining room of the hotel where Otto lodged. As they ate, they continued to reminisce and then Nat brought Otto up to date as to what he'd been doing.

"It sounds like just the life for a wanderer like you, Nat, and in a way I envy you but, in my own way, I'm doing all right, too, and hope to do better. Nat, what do you say about investing some of your trappins' money in with mine and make some money on the Santa Fe trade? We can't miss; you'll make more money than you can spend in a lifetime. The Mexicans are buying up everything that reaches Santa Fe. Sometimes even before the wagons are unloaded. I'm thinking of going into boat transportation, too, and I'd like to have you join me in that. I have a river boat pilot who wants some capital to build a fleet of boats to go up the Missouri River. We could form a three way partnership. The source of the river is around two thousand miles upriver, Nat. Think of all of the business we could get hauling cargo alone, not counting passenger fares. The military posts, trappers, Indians, and miners will all ship their freight by boat because it will be faster and cheaper than shipping by pack mule. What do you say? Let's be partners!"

"I'm not a businessman, Otto; I'll be gone from here, and it wouldn't be fair to let you do all the work."

"Nat, it would be a pleasure to take care of your end of the business. I'll have to take care of mine, anyway, so wha't a few more figures to put in a ledger?"

"Well . . ." Nat began, but was interrupted.

"Good, that's settled." Otto grinned at his old friend. "Can you stay for a few days . . . perhaps watch as we get started on your rifles?"

"I hate to mention it, partner, but Three Tongues and I have a long way to travel and these towns don't agree with us, so we'll be heading west." Nat rose from his chair as he spoke.

"It's been good to see you Nat and I wish old Rees were here to see you and meet Three Tongues. From what you've told me, you two have had your share of adventures! It was nice meeting you, Three Tongues. Give my congratulations to your sister. Bring her with you next time you come."

"I will," Three Tongues answered, "You'll have to come out to visit Vlach and my people sometime, too."

"Vlach? How did you get that name?"

"I'll tell you about it on another trip, Otto."

"Next time you can stay with me and my wife."

"You didn't say you were married, Otto!"

"Well, I'm not, yet, but by the time you get back this way, I hope to be."

"Well, when you do, congratulate the bride for me, for I think she'll be a lucky woman, too." Nat shook Otto's hand once more as did Three Tongues and they headed for the freedom of the western plains.

———————————

When Nat and Three Tongues were back in the Antelope Village, they met with the two chiefs and told them when they could expect the rifles to be ready.

"It is time now to make our plans for the gathering of our forces and the training of our warriors," Dull Knife said. "The warriors who are selected must report to Palo Duro Canyon instead of here as we planned at first. The canyon will give us added secrecy during our training."

"How long will it take to gather the warriors?" ask Nat.

"Several months." Chief White Eagle replied.

"Good, that will give us time to prepare lodges for them. It is time to let the Timber Band know where we will train and when we expect them to be there. Chief White Eagle, it will be for you to select the warriors for the phalanx when we are all assembled. Remember, they must be strong men who will obey orders, for discipline is the key to our success; without it we shall surely fail, but with it we will be victorious."

"I will select the riflemen, too, when we are all assembled," the chief said gravely. "The war chief of the other bands will help in this selection for they will know their warriors best and can choose the best qualified."

The riflemen must be as disciplined as the men of the phalanx," Nat observed, "but they must have an added quality; they must be calm and be good shots with the bow. Let's hope they can make the crossover from the bow to the rifle without too much difficulty."

Chief Dull Knife sent messengers in all directions the following morning as the first fingers of light tinged the eastern sky with color. Next, the chief selected the men and women to ride to Palo Duro Canyon to make preparations for the arrival of the warriors of the different tribes. The men would hunt for food and protect the women who would put up the tepees and dry and jerk the meat. Nat, Snow Skin, and their child would be among those to make the journey to the canyon, as would Spirit Woman.

Sentries were posted along the canyon rim day and night and when the first warriors began to arrive, they were assigned living quarters. When the warriors had ridden in from each of the bands which had taken part in the council at the lakes, a general meeting was called. White Eagle spoke in welcome and then told Nat to explain the training program.

"Everyone who belongs to the phalanx will make a new shield, the design of which Chief White Eagle, Three Tongues, and I have decided upon. When this meeting is over, you will report to one of two groups. The phalanx warriors and the riflemen will stay here with Three Tongues and me. The rest of you will go with Chief White Eagle.

The first stage of the training consisted of physical fitness training for everyone. Running, jumping, and lifting were done and if anything, the lifting was emphasized the most, for as Nat explained, "The lifting is very important for the phalanx warriors, as you know."

Chief White Eagle continually inpressed upon all of the warriors the importance of the campaign they had undertaken and urged each of them

157

to put everything they had into it.

Each morning, they exercised vigorously, performing the toughening exercises and then partook of a hearty meal at noon. An hour of relaxation was allowed and the remainder of the afternoon was occupied with making shields for the phalanx. These shields would be long enough to conceal the pole carriers once they knelt and braced their poles into the ground to catch the brunt of a charge of the enemy. Smaller shields were also made for the charge which would then be made against the Tonkawas at the same time that the Tonkawas and their horses ran into the wall of pointed poles. Straps were fitted to both kinds of shields so they could be carried easily.

The quivers were modified so that bows could be attached to them and each warrior would carry a tomahawk in his belt.

Long drums were made in such a way that they emitted a deep roar suitable for the phalanx warrirors to march in step.

Until the rifles arrived, the prospective riflemen practiced daily with their bows. At the end of a month of vigorous training, Nat and Three Tongues asked permission of Chief White Eagle to take three warriors and go for the rifles. This permission was granted and they rode away from the canyon the following morning.

White Eagle ordered that now that the shields were finished, the scabbards for the rifles were to be made, scabbards which would disguise the weapons which they carried. He also ordered that a special chant be developed to sing with the cadence of the drum beat. This would add a little psychological warfare to the prebattle conditions, perhaps causing confusion for the Tonkawas.

CHAPTER VII

Otto instructed his employees to be extra careful when the rifles were crated in strong boxes, and to make sure that each box was labeled with a painted sign which said mining tools.

"Toby!" Otto yelled through the door which separated the store from his factory.

"Yeah?"

"Watch the store. I'm going over to Burkhardt's to make arrangements for the shipment to Santa Fe."

"Go ahead, boss, I'll be right there," Toby yelled back.

As Otto left his store and walked up the street toward Burkhardt's he observed anew the changes that had occured in Westport Landing in the short time that he had been there. Westport Landing's businesses bordered the river, but new businessmen who came to the area either had to go up or down river if they wished to build their businesses adjoining the river. This was necessary if their warehouses were going to comfortably accommodate the river trade.

Saloons of every size and shape had been built at locations that would make it easy for the customers to reach them, although in truth their customers would have found them wherever they were.

Behind the business district, high up on the bluffs overlooking the river, the people had built their homes.

Westport Landing had a newspaper too, as did all the other little towns which were springing up along both the Missouri and the Kansas rivers. But the newspapers seemed to carry very little news of an importance, but had a tendency to fill their pages with attacks on neighboring towns and many advertisements.

"Otto," someone called, "come here!"

Otto turned and saw George Harvey and Jim Riley lounging aginst the wall of a warehouse. He walked over to them and asked, "What's your problem, boys?"

"Tell this thickskulled bullwhacker that mules are best suited for the Santa Fe trade, and not those mangy oxen!" Jim chortled.

"Otto," George told him, "tell your mule skinner friend, here, that oxen are cheaper to buy and they don't need all the harness that you need for mules. All the oxen needs is a yoke and a chain."

"Those varmints you call oxen are slower than a mule and they stampede a mite easier than my mules too, and besides they are scared to death of snakes," Jim retorted.

Otto grinned, "I don't have time to settle your arguments right now, boys. I've got urgent business with Burkhardt." He continued on up the street. "I'll be more than glad to discuss the pros and cons of the oxen versus the mule in a little while."

When he entered the Burkhardt warehouse, Glen was talking to one of his wagon masters.

"Hello, Glen." Otto pulled the door shut behind him.

"Otto, come in. Nice to see you, you know Dan Weber, my wagon master, don't you?"

"Yes, how are you doing, Dan?"

"Fine, and yourself?"

"Just fine," Otto answered. "Are you going to be the wagon master of the train which takes my wagons toward Santa Fe?"

Dan looked at Glen Burkhardt and said, "You'll have to ask Glen that question, I just work here, I don't make assignments."

"He's the one, Otto," Burkhardt answered. "We have just now finished discussing the details of the wagon train."

"How many wagons will be in your train this time?"

"Forty-five, in addition to your three," Glen replied.

"You want me to send my wagons on to Council Grove?" Otto asked.

"Yes sir, that's where I officially take charge it's your responsibility to get your wagons there and you'll also have to get your papers from Glen here, if you want your wagons to head west. Without papers, I can't take them."

"I'll have them there, Dan. That's why I'm here," Otto assured him. "Incidently, my drivers were told that the wagons will be under your direct control. They will have no authority over the wagon or their contents. All they are being paid to do is drive the wagons until my friend Nat comes for them. At that point, they are unemployed. That's the understanding that they and I have agreed upon."

"Is that agreeable with you, Glen?" Dan looked at his boss.

160

"I'll pay extra," Otto interrupted, "but I want my wagons handed as if they were yours, Dan, and I would like for them to be the last three wagons in the train."

"It's agreeable to me, Dan, if it does not put an undue burden on you," Burkhardt said.

"Well, I guess that's how it will be then, Otto," Dan said. "If you have any more instructions, Glen, I'll be heading for Council Grove in the morning."

"Dan, wait a minute," Burkhardt called after him, "why don't you take Otto's wagons with the others from here? You have everything ready, don't you Otto?"

"I can have them ready, I'd feel better if Dan took them all the way," Otto admitted.

Burkhardt and Otto made the final arrangement for Otto's three wagons and Otto paid him in gold coins.

Dan called all of the drivers together on the evening before they were to leave Council Grove. "Circle around me, men, and sit." Dan was an imposing presence as his thirty-year-old, tall, lean figure stood in the center of the circle of men. His face was the color of tanned leather. He wore the regulation blue company shirt as did the others, but his trousers were of his own choice, homespun, and his boot tops reached halfway to his knees. At the left side of his belt, he wore a knife and on his right hip a pistol. For protection from the heat, he wore a broadbrimmed hat.

"Just in case some of you have just begun to drive for Mr. Burkhardt, there are some things that you need to know. I know that most of you have made at least one trip to Santa Fe, either with or for Mr. Burkhardt. Some of you may have made more trips to Santa Fe than I have, but seniority does not count on this trip. Once we stretch the wagons out and are on the trail, my orders are to be followed without question. My orders are law. My orders are the only law, and I have the privilege to change them as I please, without consulting anyone.

"A wagon master is also the enforcer of the law. There is no trial by jury once we are on the move. The only authority out on the prairie will be me. I especially want you greenhorns to understand that, because if that does not suit you, I suggest that you leave.

"There are forty-eight wagons in this caravan and I have placed my two lieutenants in charge of twenty-four wagons each. Lieutenant Hoffman will command the first division and the second division will be under the command of Lieutenant Holliday. The two men will answer to me and take orders from me only. They will select a sargeant of the guard for each unit of eight men. These men, two at a time, will stand guard for a quarter of the night. All will take their turn at guard duty unless expressly excused by me.

The sargeant will also divide you into eating groups and you will always eat with your assigned group. Each eating group will select its own cook and this cook will be relieved of all other duties which includes guard duty, but he will still have to drive his own wagon, of course. The others in the eating group will provide the cook with wood for the fire and if there is no wood available as, much of the time there won't be, they must provide him with buffalo chips. Water will be furnished by you to your cook as well as meat for the pot.

"The sargeants will also assign day and night herders to care for the stock. As you have noticed, the lower half of each wagon is painted blue, the upper half painted red. The canvas is white and that makes up our national colors. Let's treat them accordingly. Most of you, if not all of you, have chosen a name for your wagon and have painted these names on the wagons, which is your prerogative. I prefer this because it will make it easier for me to call your wagon by name if we are under attack. I see that the wagon named the Constitituion is with us on this trip. It lives up to its namesake, Old Ironsides' reputation. It has come under attack more than once and has survived more than one emergency. Other wagon names that I have seen are the Ohio, The Liberty, Freedom, Nellie, The Golden Goose, Independence, Pinkerton Academy, and White Church.

"The last three wagons in our train are especially built to carry a heavy load of mining equipment. Barrels of gun powder will be in these wagons, also, which is why they will bring up the rear. When we form our circular wagon corrals at night for protection, these wagons will be left out of the circle for obvious reasons.

"We will begin each day at sunup and continue to roll the wagons until ten o'clock in the morning. At that time we will rest, eat, repair broken equipment and whatever else needs to be done. At two o'clock we will stretch them out again and continue until six at night. We will have one day a week for rest for everyone, especially for the animals. I am responsible for the twenty-two thousands dollars worth of wagons and for the one hundred and twenty-five thousand dollars worth of trade goods. We carry every kind of trading goods on this trip that you can imagine, from shoes to dresses, mirrors, tobacco, spices, to pianos, so gentlemen, let's earn your twenty-five dollars a month wages, the lieutenant's their seventy-five and me my hundred.

"We have only mules pulling our conestoga wagons because the bull whackers and mule skinners argue too much, which is not good for anyone, especially me! Besides, I prefer mules to horses or oxen. They can pull more over a longer haul than horses and they do not get sick as often, either. They do not need a measure of grain at night and their

162

working lifespan is longer. About the time a horse has given his best years, the mule has just reached his peak. I know some of you will give me an argument on this and so I'll add that this is just my opinion. But I'm the wagon master!

"Each of the two wagons has two canvas tops for better protection against the elements, especially the large hail stones which we'll run into no doubt. There are also two water barrels, a tote sack to gather buffalo chips, a container of tar, and some odds and ends. I will have two scouts riding ahead of us, two on either side of the train and two in the rear. If they report danger, listen for my order before you circle the wagons. OK, men, get some sleep and we'll leave tomorrow morning!"

Early the following morning, the men were eagerly waiting on their wagons, each hoping that he would be the first driver to yell, "All set!" It was a matter of pride to attempt to be the first to answer Dan's call of "Ready?" when Dan did yell the word which the drivers were waiting to hear, a quick reply could be heard as an old timer yelled, loud and clear, and with obvious pride in his voice at being the first, "All set!"

In seconds, his voice seemed to echo as the words, "All set," rippled throughout the train. The drivers were now waiting for Dan's order to move out. When Dan did give the order, he rode to the front of the wagon train flanked by his two lieutenants, looked back at the wagons, asked his lieutenants if they were ready, and then in his loud, crisp voice, yelled, "Stretch out! Stretch out!"

Dan then turned to his lieutenants and told them, "It is about a hundred and thirty miles to the great bend in the Arkansas River. Between here and there we will have plenty of water and grass along the many streams and creeks. After that, water will become scarce so be sure that everyone fills their water barrels to the brim. When we leave the bend, the grass will become shorter and not so green. Remember what I have just told you. Now I think you'd better get back and check your divisions, to make sure that everyone got started all right."

"Hey, pilgrim," Dan yelled at a lone rider who rode towards him. "Get back to the wagon train and stay there. No one is supposed to be up here unless I specifically order it. I don't want any trouble from you or anyone else. I have enough on my mind without worrying about you and your erroneous Eastern ideas about the West."

"But Weber," the man protested, "how can I get the correct information for my book if I am not free to check out everything?"

"To the devil with your book, Barrett, my concern and my only concern is the safety of this wagon train, and if you get in the way of that, I'll leave you at Bent's Fort. Now get back to the wagon train and stay there."

"But, Weber," Barrett said again, "aren't you going to circle the wagons? There are Indians ahead on the trail."

"Those are Wyandots and they are friendly Indians. It is obvious that you can't tell the difference. You are more dangerous to us than they are. Otto helped them resettle near Westport Landing years ago. The Wyandots are from back east somewhere. Their women are with them also, so that means that they are not a war party and if you'll open your eyes you can see that the travois are loaded with buffalo meat and hides, showing that they are returning from a buffalo hunt."

A lone Wyandot brave broke from the long line and started toward them. He raised his right hand when he neared Dan, with two fingers extended and the others held back with his thumb. Dan returned this sign of friendship as the Wyandot rode up to him.

"There are many signs out there, Dan Weber," Straight Tongue said, "and they are all war party signs."

"What tribe?"

"Kiowa, maybe twenty-five to thirty warriors. I think they may be waiting for you."

"Thank you, Straight Tongue. I appreciate the information; we'll be on the alert for them."

"I have told your advance scouts what I have told you, so they know also." Straight Tongue saluted as he reined his horse away and trotted back toward his people.

Dan turned back toward the wagon train and Hoffman and Holiday rode to meet him.

"Kiowa, somewhere ahead. Tell the men," Dan ordered.

"Right away," the two lieutenants turned and rode toward their respective divisions.

When six o'clock came, Dan ordered the wagons to circle. The lead wagon, the Constitution, swung to the right, the second wagon the Liberty, swung to the left, the third wagon followed the Constitution, and the fourth followed the Liberty. This method was followed by all the other wagons until the Constitiution and the Liberty met and halted. Each wagon pulled up along side the one just in front of it until the wagon's front wheels were opposite the rear wheels of the wagon just ahead. All of the movement took place in a calm, methodical way as was to be expected of seasoned drivers. When the wagons were all in place, the mules were unharnessed and turned out to graze. The teamsters then chained their wagon wheels together. The tongues of the wagons were turned inward as was the case if danger was afoot. In this way, the animals had the protection of the wagons and could not be driven off easily by the Indians. When no danger was imminent, the tongues were turned outward so it would be easier to water and feed the mules.

Dan ordered the guard to be especially alert that night and to report anything which looked or sounded suspicious immediately.

That night went by without incident, however, and early the next morning the mules were driven inside the wagon circle and the teamsters caught their teams and harnessed them. After breakfast, Dan rode out in the lead and yelled, "Stretch out!" The wagons slowly uncoiled and the Constitution took the lead.

It was not more than an hour after they had begun to roll that the scouts came galloping toward Dan. "Kiowa war party!" they yelled as they came into earshot.

Dan reined in his horse and galloped toward the wagons, repeatedly shouting the order, "Circle the wagons!" At the same time he made a circular motion with his hand over his head. His lieutenants got the message and began to gallop along the train, telling the teamsters to circle the wagons. When the circle had been complete once more, the mules were unharnessed and turned into the wagon corral and the other animals were also driven in with them.

The men picked shielded places, checked their rifles, and waited. The three drivers of Otto's wagons unharnessed their mules and turned them into the corral, but left their wagons at some distance from the others. In less than half an hour, the Kiowa war party could be sighted north of the wagons. They were trotting their horses toward the train and were stretched out in a single line, the leader in the center with his war bonnet flourishing in the brisk breeze.

War cries could be heard as they readied themselves to circle the train, then for no reason that the men of the wagon train could fathom, the Kiowa chief gave the order to break off the attack and retreat. Within a few minutes the Kiowas were out of sight.

"What are they up to?" Dan glanced at his scouts, puzzled. "I have never seen such behavior. Check it out, boys, but be careful, they may want to eliminate you so we would have eight fewer men to fight with later."

Within an hour the scouts reported back to tell Dan that the Kiowas were nowhere to be seen. "Do you think when they rode to where they could see the three separate wagons for Nat they decided to leave us alone?" The head scout scratched his head as he speculated.

"So that was it," Dan agreed. "Nat and the Comanches have told the Kiowas not to attack any train with three wagons with the 'M' painted on them."

"Who's this Nat fellow?"

"He's the fellow who will claim the three Muller wagons," Dan said.

"Is he a Comanche?" One of the others looked interested.

"No, he's a mountainman and frontiersman who came west with Otto, but while Otto stayed at Westport Landing, Nat went on with another friend, an old mountainman named Rees. Boys, keep your eyes peeled for the owners of the supplies in Otto's wagons. I've got a feeling they'll be showing up before long. Well, I guess we'd better be moving on as soon as you scouts get on out ahead."

The lieutenants rode away from Dan back toward the wagons where they could see the driver of the Constitution watching for the signal to move out. Even as they watched, Dan raised his hand and yelled, "Stretch out!"

The whips of the mule skinners could be heard cracking and the sound woke the mules from their drowsiness and they leaned into their harness.

"When we get to Pawnee Rock, we'll stop for a day's rest," Dan told his lieutenants later that day.

"When did you carve your name on Pawnee Rock?" Hoffman asked Dan.

"On my first trip to Santa Fe," Dan answered. "I was a youngster then and youngsters do things that they don't do when they're older. I was teamster and I named my first Conestoga wagon, Sandra, after my girlfriend. I was eighteen at the time and when I returned from Santa Fe, Sandra had run off with another fellow." He chuckled, "I guess it was not to be, at least that's what she thought, I suppose. I drove one of the first Conestogas that Mr. Burkhardt purchased. It sure was a funny looking thing, for those of us who were used to driving a regular freight wagon. I couldn't figure out why the floor of the wagon was higher in the front than it was in the back, and so I asked my wagon master. He said that the load wouldn't slip forward when going down a slope that way and the load wouldn't slip backward when pulling up a hill. That made sense to me. He didn't want me to call the 'Sandra' a wagon, either, but called it a schooner. I remember very clearly how he ordered me to stand in front of 'Sandra' and look at her, and pointed out how she looked like a boat or a ship, rather than a wagon. He showed me how the walls of the schooner slanted out at the top. While many of the teamsters called the Conestogas wagons and some of them referred to them as road wagons, some of them did call them schooners, prairie schooners. Maybe they called them schooners just to please the wagon master . . . I don't know. I just called mine 'Sandra' and that way I didn't get into an argument about it. I sure loved that Conestoga, though! If I remember right, she was about twelve feet long, maybe three feet or so wide and about three feet high from the floor, that is the wooden part of her. My first load weighed nine hundred pounds."

Holliday interrupted Dan's reminiscing by asking, "Captain, are you going through Raton Pass, or the Cimarron Cut-off?"

"We'll take the Cimarron Cut-off," Dan told him, "I don't like the Raton route. It's too rough and dangerous and it slows you down too much because the mountains are so steep; so steep that in some places we'd have to lower the wagons down the mountainside by rope. It can cause a train to lose as much as a month going that way. Sometimes a wagon can fall and drag its mules to the bottom, destroying them, too. No, I'll take the less rough Cimarron Cut-off. I know there's a lack of water on that route, so we'll rest the stock for a day where the Cut-off joins the Arkansas River; that should give the stock plenty of time to soak up all the water they will need. Most of these mules have traveled on the Cut-off and I'll bet they'll remember that there is a lack of water up ahead. It's your job to make sure that the greenhorns fill their canteens and waterbarrels before we leave the Arkansas. The old timers know better and you won't have to be concerned with them. Now remember that the Arkansas is treacherous; it has quicksand in some places and in addition, it has a narrow flow of water. That narrow channel can be pretty deep in some spots. Let's hope the river is low, but if it is running high, we will have to hitch many pairs of mules to each wagon so that the current won't carry it and the mules downstream when we cross. We don't want to lose any of our freight or mules. I know it takes time to unhitch and rehitch the mules in such an operation, but we must be sure that we get each wagon across safely. We need to have that long string of mules so that there will always be some with their feet on dry ground because others will be in the deepest part of the river where their feet can't touch the bottom. If the river is high, we have to warn the teamsters that all of the freight which might be damaged by water will have to be stacked high. Most will remember, especially when they see the others are shifting their loads."

"We'll miss the new fort that the Bent Brothers have built at the entrance of the Raton route," Hoffman said.

"That's right," Dan answered, "I understand that the Bents have built quite an imposing fort there, as well as a pleasant environment for the travelers and an excellent repair facility. If we don't need to take advantage of that by the time we reach the Cut-off, we'll take the Cut-off."

CHAPTER VIII

"**H**ere's the Santa Fe Trail," Nat said. He reined in his horse. "It must be nearly three hundred feet wide at this location. Let's look to see if there are any signs that a wagon train has passed by this way lately."

When no recent signs were found, Three Tongues asked, "What are we going to do now?"

"I say we follow the trail back toward Pawnee Rock. I'm sure the train has not passed by here yet."

"Look here," Pasquel called. He knelt on one knee and examined something by the trial.

"What have you found, Pasquel?"

"Unshod horse tracks, many of them, and here is a moccasin print, a Kiowa print."

"Surely you don't think that the Kiowas would attack the wagon train with our wagons in it?" Nat looked at Three Tongues.

"No I don't," Three Tongues answered positively.

"Then what are they doing here?"

"It's a Kiowa war party all right, but I know they would never attack a wagon train which had our wagons in it," Three Tongues insisted.

"I guess the only way to find out for sure is to backtrack until we find the wagon train or what's left of it," Nat said grimly.

"We'll find the wagon train and it will be unmolested," Three Tongues said, "I know that the Kiowas keep their word."

"Could some renegade braves slip out of camp and attack a wagon train without their chief knowing it?"

"No," Three Tongues answered quickly, with hurt in his voice. "No renegade could get the number of warriors that would be needed to attack a large wagon train, and if he did, they surely would be found out and exiled from their band. Exile is worse than death to an Indian because he is left out in the open with no tribe to give him protection. Every Pawnee and Cheyenne brave for hundreds of miles would be after him and when he was captured, as surely he would be, the warriors who captured him would enjoy many hours of fun torturing him. Before lifting his scalp. Not a very strong incentive for disobeying tribal law, would you say?"

"I guess not," Nat conceded, "but how do you explain the Kiowa pony tracks then?"

"My guess," Three Tongues said, "is that a Kiowa war party came to attack a wagon train and when they saw that our wagons were in the train, they withdrew."

"Well, as soon as we meet the wagon train, we'll find out. I just hope that the first train we meet has our wagons in it. How far do you think Pawnee Rock is from here?"

"I don't know, but there are advance scouts over there on the horizon!" Three Tongues pointed behind Nat.

Nat jerked his head in that direction and said. "Let me ride out to meet them alone; the rest of you follow me at a good distance. We don't want them to think we're unfriendly."

When the scouts spotted the five strangers, they halted and watched them. They saw Nat ride toward them alone and when he came within yelling distance, he shouted, "American! My name is Nat Cochran. I'm looking for three wagons that belong to me!"

"What is he yelling?" One of the scouts looked puzzled as he checked his rifle.

"That he is an American, and he said something about his wagons," the other scout answered.

"Could be that he is the owner of the Muller wagons and he's come to fetch them. We'll know soon; you keep your eyes on those four Comanches behind him and be ready for any tricks. If you see any signs of a trap, we'll hightail it back to the wagons."

"Right," came the reply.

When Nat rode up to them, he said. "We've come for our three wagons with the 'M's painted on them. That is, if they are among your wagons."

"We have three such wagons in our train, but you'll have to talk to our wagon master about them."

"Thanks. I'll go back for my companions and then we'll head for the train. It wouldn't hurt if one of you rode back ahead to tell them who we are." He spurred his horse and trotted back toward Three Tongues and the others.

"This is the right train," Nat told Three Tongues. "Let's go see the wagon master and get our wagons."

The five men trotted their horses eastward until they reached Dan.

"Howdy," Nat said as he and the four Comanches reined in their horses. "I understand that you have the three wagons which my friend, Otto Muller has sent to me."

"Could be," Dan replied and he continued to walk his horse westward. He studied Nat for a few minutes and then looked at the four Comanches. He then looked back at Three Tongues and said, "So you're Three Tongues."

The Comanche looked from Weber to Nat, but said nothing in response.

"He is Three Tongues, isn't he?" Weber looked at Nat.

"Yes."

"Can he speak, or is he mute?"

"What do you think with a name like mine?" Three Tongues grinned. He had spoken in English.

"Bueño, Quién es el?" Weber asked Three Tongues as he looked at the brave sitting beside him.

"He's a Comanche brave whose name is Pasquel." Three Tongues answered.

"You're the ones Muller told me to give the wagons to," Dan said. "He told me that a Comanche rode with Nat Cochran and that the Comanche spoke three languages. I'm satisfied that you are Nat Cochran and that your sidekick here is Three Tongues. Let's go back to the train. The last three wagons are yours."

They reined their horses and walked them back toward the train.

"It appears that great changes are about to happen out here west of the Mississippi," Dan commented.

"What do you mean?" Nat looked interested.

"The Secretary of War presented to Congress a new Indian policy concerning all of the Indian tribes east of the Mississippi River. This new policy states that all Indian tribes are to be resettled west of the Mississippi River, and that those who refuse to move will be driven out by the army. Most of the people think that the president will go along with the Congress."

"You can't be serious," Nat exclaimed with concern. He glanced at Three Tongues with a troubled look.

"That's what I heard just before I left Westport Landing," Dan replied. "Treaties are being made with many of the tribes right now, this very day. Many other treaties have already been made. There will be a whole lot of them moving out here, so you had better brace yourselves for some real trouble, Three Tongues."

"If what you say is true," Nat said, "then the whole west will become one big battlefield, with Indians killing Indians. There'll be more Indians killed in this struggle than have been killed by the white man up to now."

"I'm afraid you've got it about right," Dan said, "but there is a silver lining in this if you want to look for one."

"And what might that be?"

"The treaties which are being made with the tribes all state that the United States will forever secure and guarantee to them, and their heirs or successors, a country so exchanged with them. In other words, for those who survive the wars out here, the land west of the Mother of Waters will be theirs forever."

"If you believe that, you're crazy," Nat said in anger.

"Don't blame me," Dan replied. "Most of them are resisting, but I believe that they are foolish. They can't win. The army will win in the end and the Indians will have fewer warriors to defend their people once they settle out here."

"Wouldn't you defend your country from those to came to steal it?" Three Tongues interrupted the two way converstaion. "You can't expect honorable men to leave their sacred tribal grounds without a fight, can you?"

"I understand what you're saying, Three Tongues," Dan told him. "I was just stating what I believe would be the wisest course to follow. I may be wrong, but I guess we'll have to wait and see. Every man must decide what he must do for himself in circumstances like these, and then sit back and wait and when it is all over he must abide by the consequences."

"The Wyandots chose to move rather than fight," Nat said in a voice just above a murmur. "I wonder if they now wish they had stayed and fought."

"What did you say?" asked Dan.

"Never mind," Nat replied. "I was just thinking out loud."

"The Black Hawk War," Dan went on, "was the result of two tribes, the Sauk and Fox who refused to be moved. Their main chief, Keokuk wanted to move west, but an old chief by the name of Black Hawk, with encouragement from the British, decided that they would not move, but fight. When the army came, however, the Indians fled their villages and crossed the Mississippi River, but some came back with Black Hawk, which prompted the government to send a large army, some of whom were West Point students. A number of battles were fought, but in the end the army won and only a little over a hundred of the original one-thousand warriors were captured alive. More than once, I am told, Black Hawk wanted to surrender or at least talk, but the volunteers and the army did not stop their fighting and killing even when the white flag was raised. Can you imagine our army firing on a white flag of truce? They did, mind you, and they then fired on the defenseless women and children who were put on rafts in the Wisconsin River so that they could float down to the Mississippi, cross it and join their people. All of the women and children on the rafts were either killed, wounded, or captured. The troopers shot those poor defenseless women and children as if they were turkeys or deer. It makes you ashamed to think that they are our countrymen. After hearing that story, Three Tongues, I thought it would be the better part of valor if other Indians remembered the lesson which the Sauk and Fox had to learn, to their everlasting sorrow and to the shame of the Americans.';

"I understand now what you meant," Three Tongues said. "I may have spoken too quickly."

"A man has to do what he has to do at a given time and under a certain set of circumstances," Nat said.

"Yes, I guess you're right there," Dan admitted. "It is difficult to say what you would do under a certain set of circumstances until the time comes. I guess if I were mad enough, I would stand my ground and die for my beliefs and my loved ones, just as millions of people all over the world have done before me. Well, there are your wagons."

They had passed the entire wagon train as they talked.

The Comanches replaced the wagon drivers and the three wagons turned southward. Three Tongues rode in silence for many miles until Nat became concerned. "What's on your mind, Three Tongues?" Nat rode up beside his brother-in-law.

"Do you think what the wagon master said back there about all of the eastern tribes being forced to move west of the Mississippi River is true?"

"I'm afraid so, my friend," Nat told him, "I don't see why Dan would lie to us."

"Maybe all of the tribes will learn to live in peace. No, we won't do that because the tribes have different languages and customs."

"There are too many inherent animosities toward one another and along with those, deep distrust. The future does not look good for the Indians. I guess that we'll have to wait and see what the future brings, and hope that it won't be as dark as it appears to me right now."

It seems to me that's all we can do." Nat answered.

When they reached Palo Duro Canyon with the three wagons, they wasted no time in continuing with their preparations. The riflemen were issued their rifles and Nat selected ten warriors and instructed them in how to use the factory. When the warriors understood how to make the bullets, Nat left them alone until they had manufactured the amount that he thought each rifleman should have. In the meantime, he instructed the riflemen in how to handle their rifles. They were taught how to brace them against their shoulders and how to use the sights. He was surprised when he learned that some of them were so ignorant of the rifle that they believed it had so much medicine that they didn't have to aim it at all. They thought that you just had to point it in the general direction of the enemy and the enemy would fall dead.

It took Nat a week to teach the warriors the rudiments of being riflemen, and then it would require much practice to hone their skills. Most of them became very proficient in their marksmanship. Now that the riflemen were familiar with their arms, Nat turned his full attention to the phalanx, letting the riflemen practice on their own.

The phalanx warriors practiced without their poles at first. They were taught to concentrate on keeping in step to the beat of the drum. Everytime the warriors' left feet hit the ground, the drummer would beat the drum. On the third step, the dummer hit three beats, one for the left step and a quick added beat for the right feet and the third for the left feet again. The drill continued until the phalanx moved as a machine, the warriors taking great pride in the smooth movement of their mass as a whole. When Nat thought they could move as he wished, he gave them their poles. The poles were to be carried upright until the command was given to lower them. When all of the men had their poles and were in formation, he placed himself, in the phalanx square with the drummers. The riflemen would be added later. Nat ordered the warriors to attention and when they became motionless, they resembled wooden soldiers. He then ordered the drummers to begin the beat and the phalanx moved in perfect unison. Pride was evident on the warriors' faces as they stepped smartly forward. A smaller drum would give the signal to lower their poles into place. Nat now signaled for the smaller drum to be beaten in a rapid cadence. The warriors, upon hearing the signal, lowered their poles in unison. Their long shields were then slid in front of them. This drill was done continuously until the phalanx worked perfectly. When the poles were in place, all that anyone would see were the warriors' faces and feet. The signal for the pole carriers to stop and brace their poles in the ground was a combination of the drummers of both small and large to beat their respective drums rapidly, in unison. This routine was followed until Nat, with Three Tongues assisting him, was satisfied that it was done properly.

"Tomorrow," Nat told the phalanx warriors, "the entire procedure will be done, from the beginning until the faked contact with the enemy, as if it were the day of the battle. It will be a dress rehearsal."

The next morning, Chief White Eagle and the non-phalanx warriors gathered two hundred yards in front of the phalanx. They wanted to see what the phalanx would look like from the Tonkawas' position. Chief White Eagle and the others could now hear Nat issuing orders and the phalanx warriors took their positions in the square. The drummers gathered near Nat in the center and the riflemen got into their formation within the square also. Chief White Eagle and the others heard Nat call his men to attention. It was an impressive sight to see all of the warriors in the square become motionless, remaining that way until the drums began to beat. The square then moved foward as smoothly as anyone could expect and on command they began to sing their special war chant. When the chant stopped, the warriors braced their poles in the ground and each fell to his left knee. The upper half of the riflemen's bodies could now be seen above the heads of the kneeling warriors.

Nat gave another order and all of the riflemen raised their rifles to their shoulders as one. To the surprise of the onlookers, another order was given which they had not heard previously; the whole square dropped their poles and large shields about thirty yards away from them and sliding their small shields into position on their left arms, pulled their tomahawks from their belts and made a fake charge on the observers who at first stepped back a few feet before they halted in embarrassment.

"When my men make that charge," Nat told Chief White Eagle, "that is when you and your mounted men who will be stationed behind us to our left and right, will charge the Tonkawas."

It was a cool morning when the Comanches left Palo Dura Canyon and headed southward toward the land of the Tonkawas. Travios carried the food, phalanx poles, and all of the other necessities of war. Two thousand Comanches moved slowly across the plains as their scouts rode far and wide searching for any enemy scouts who might report on their activity. After three weeks of moving southward, Chief White Eagle warned that they could expect to make contact with the Tonkawas at any time, because they had entered Tonkawa territory. The scouts reported at least once a day and the Comanches no longer tried to conceal their movement, but on the contrary, they hoped that the Tonkawas would spot them and gather their forces to give battle. White Eagle hoped that he and his warriors would be seen early enough, so that the Tonkawas would have enough time to summon a large force to throw against them. In this way a decisive battle would be fought and many Tonkawas killed. This would end, once and for all, their future invasion and depredations in Comanche territory.

For the past three days, the Comanche scouts had reported that Tonkawa scouts were watching them. "Good," Chief White Eagle said with satisfaction. "That means that they are gathering their warriors and

174

preparing for war. Sleep well, eat well, and look to your weapons. You'll be facing Tonkawa braves any day now."

The next morning all of the scouts came racing back to the main body of Comanches and told Chief White Eagle that a large Tonkawa force was about five miles ahead of them.

"How many of them are there?"

"As many as ours," was the reply.

Chief White Eagle, Three Tongues, and Nat held a council to decide on their next move. "I think we ought to give the men a full day's rest and at the same time, make the Tonkawas think that we are about to attack, thereby keeping them on the alert. In that way our men will be fresh when the battle begins and theirs will be fatigued. This will give us added advantage," Nat suggested.

Chief White Eagle and Three Tongues thought that Nat's idea was good strategy, and White Eagle ordered the scouts to watch the enemy closely while he ordered the rest of the warriors to assume their battle positions. When that was done, he told them to sit down and eat, rest, and apply their war paint.

During the day, the Tonkawas moved to within sight of the Comanches and waited for them to attack as they sat on their war ponies. But the Comanches did not attack. Just before darkness arrived, however, a few Comanches were seen building small fires, using buffalo chips as fuel and the Tonkawas continued their vigil, anticipating an attack momentarily. The Tonkawas watched as the Comanche warriors gathered around the fires and seemed to be relaxing and eating and preparing for sleep. The Tonkawas, as Nat had hoped, thought that this was some kind of trick, and that when nightfall came they could expect an attack under cover of darkness; that the Comanches might abandon their religious belief against fighting at night.

Nat could see the Tonkawa subchiefs riding their horses among their warriors, apparently expecting and hoping for such a night attack. When darkness came, dead silence settled over the area, the only sounds which broke the stillness were the occasional nicker of a horse or the muffled voice of a Tonkawa warning his braves to be alert. What the Tonkawas did not know, however, as they waited for an attack was that the Comanches were all asleep, except for a few who were seated on the ground about fifty yards ahead of their camp, making sure they were not attacked during the night.

The Tonkawas sat their horses all night waiting for the Comanches, and when the sun rose in the morning, they perceived to their surprise the Comanches rising from their beds and preparing to eat their breakfasts. When they had finished their breakfast, they leisurely fell into their battle positions.

The phalanx, with its poles raised in a vertical position, had moved to a position one hundred yards in front of the two mounted groups of Comanche warriors which were stationed on each side and to the rear of the phalanx.

Three Tongues and his braves had moved during the night around the right flank of the Tonkawas and were positioned in concealment behind them, ready to cut off a retreat.

The Tonkawas watched in puzzlement the movements of the Comanches in front of them, probably wishing they had attacked the Comanches the day before.

When the Comanche drums began to beat and the phalanx began to move forward, as did the mounted warriors, the Tonkawas looked at one another in awe. Their chief yelled an order and his braves spread out into a single line.

Nat's voice could be heard as he yelled a single order and the Comanches began to chant. This too, startled the Tonkawas, some of whom began to retreat, but these were haltred by a sharp command from their chief. The Tonkawas could not see the rifles of the riflemen in the center of the phalanx because they kept them below chest level. The Tonkawa chief yelled an order, held up his right arm, and in a few seconds, the entire left side of the line of braves dashed forward as their chief lowered his arm.

Upon seeing the Tonkawas charging and screaming war cries as they came toward his phalanx, Nat gave orders to the drummers. Upon hearing the drum signal, the phalanx halted, lowered their poles into position facing the oncoming horses, braced the butts of the poles securely into the ground, swung their long shields off their left shoulders, placed them in front of them and dropped to their left knees. It was all done with much precision.

Some of the Tonkawas stopped yelling while others turned and glanced backward at their chief as if to ask what was happening. In the next few seconds, the oncoming Tonkawas saw the phalanx riflemen raise their rifles to their shoulders and aim them directly into their faces, and when the Tonkawas drew nearer, the riflemen opened fire. Horses screamed and twisted in agony as they stumbled and fell to the ground. The Comanches riflemen's aim was much better than Nat had dared to hope. He saw over a hundred Tonkawa warriors slide from their horses and fall to the ground, but the rest of the charging braves continued to race toward the phalanx. Nat now saw the Tonkawa chief raise his right hand high and in lowering it, release his right flank to support the first charge. The phalanx riflemen reloaded quickly. Each had two bullets in his teeth and when the remainder of the first charge of the Tonkawas were still perhaps fifty yards away, they fired their second volley, toppling most of the remaining riders. The ones who were not hit crashed their horses into the walls of lances, knocking their riders to the ground, and by this time, the Comanche riflemen had reloaded for the third time and were taking aim at the second wave of charging Tonkawas. A roar from their rifles proved that their aim had been much improved over their first two volleys, and nearly two hundred of the oncoming Tonkawas fell from their horses.

The phalanx now dropped their poles, threw down their shields, slid their round combat shields into their left hands, pulled out their tomahawks and charged their unhorsed enemies amidst bloodcurdling Comanche war cries. It was at this point that Chief White Eagle waved the two blocks of Comanches light cavalry forward to join in the battle. By the time that he and his braves had reached the battlefield, Nat and his warriors had taken a heavy toll of the completely demoralized and confused Tonkawas braves. A few of the Tonkawas who were still mounted turned and fled back toward their chief while the Tonkawas who were on foot tried their best to disengage themselves and retreat also. Three Tongues and his braves were waving their lances and screaming the Comanche battle cry as they charged down on the remaining Tonkawas from their rear. Less than thirty of the enemy were able to escape, while the rest died at the hands of the swift and well organized Comanche braves. Nat pulled his tomahawk from a Tonkawa brave and rose to his feet, seeing Comanches everywhere scalping their dead enemies and screaming their delight in the complete defeat of the Tonkawas. Some even gave a short war dance as they moved to another fallen warrior and removed his scalp in one or two swift swings of their knives.

When all was quiet, they counted only seventeen Comanche dead while the Tonkawas had lost nearly two thousand warriors. The few Comanche dead were buried with great honors and reverence and Chief White Eagle ordered his warriors to mount their horses for the return trip to their respective villages to celebrate the great victory with the scalp dance.

Of the Antelope band, only one warrior had died in battle. As the Antelope band approached to within a few miles of their village, Chief White Eagle halted his warriors and told them, "We are nearing our village and, as is our custom after a raid by a war party, we may not enter the village until early morning, so we will camp here for the night and just before the sun rises tomorrow morning, I will send our youngest warrior, Red Arrow, to ride to tell our people that we have returned."

Thus a single horseman left the Comanche camp before the sun rose the following morning and rode for the Antelope village. While he was riding to give the good news to the villagers, the warriors behind him were preparing themselves for a victorious entrance into their village by donning war paint and dressing in their finest war clothing. They adjusted the feathers on their heads and painted their war ponies with symbols which befitted their station as warriors, and rubbed them with grasses to make them shine in the bright sunlight.

They could hear the sounds of rejoicing in the distance as the Comanches who had been left behind celebrated with even more joy than usual, so great had been the victory over the Tonkawas.

Meanwhile, back in the war party camp, the warriors were finishing up their preparations before entering their village in triumph.

Now some of the braves were attaching Tonkawa scalps to their lances, others were tying them to the handles of their tomahawks, and the riflemen were tying them to the barrels of their rifles. Those who had taken many scalps even tied some of them to the lower jaw of their war ponies, signifying their great hatred for the Tonkawas. When all were ready, Chief White Eagle, with a war bonnet of many eagle feathers sitting firmly on his head, walked his horse to the head of his warriros, raised his head proudly, then lifted his colorfully decorated lance and motioned for his men to follow him.

On approaching the village, Nat looked for his wife, Snow Skin, in the crowd of waving, jumping, yelling and screaming women, and finally he saw her run toward him with a child raised high in the air and wrapped in a beautiful Navajo blanket. She, too, was shouting something which Nat could not understand, but just before she finally reached him, he leaped from his saddle and caught her as she ran into his arms. Tears streaked her face as she kissed her husband and told him, "We have another son, a big healthy boy!"

Nat held Snow Skin with one arm as she turned the blanket back from the baby's face so Nat could look at him for the first time.

Nat looked long at his son and then hugged them both closely as he murmured into his wife's ear.

The other returning warriors had been engulfed by their familes also and the rejoicing people now moved slowly toward their lodges.

The remainder of that day was spent in preparation for the victory dance which would be held after dark.

The medicine men went directly to a small lodge which was five feet high and five feet in width. They would purify themselves in the small lodge before the victory dance began. The small curved roof lodge was called the sweat lodge. In its center, a three foot hole had been dug into the ground. In this hole, large, hot stones were placed. Water was poured over the stones, causing steam to rise and fill the small building. In a short time the medicine men would begin to perspire and after they had perspired enough to cleanse themselves of all the evil spirits that could have followed them home, they left the sweat lodge and jumped into the nearby river.

A large pole was erected in the center of the village so that the warriors could attach their Tonkawa scalps to it during the dance. Wood, dry grasses, and brush were piled near the pole so that when lit, the fire would furnish the light by which the villagers could dance.

When darkness fell, and the fire was lit, the drummers began to beat their rhythms and singers joined in. All were dressed in their finest. Two long lines were formed with men in one line and the women in another. The two lines faced each other and as the drums beat, everyone began to sing, and the lines moved toward each other. Nat reached out and touched Snow Skin's hands as the lines met. He gave her a broad smile and she wrinkled her nose at him in return as the lines began to move back. Next to Nat, Three Tongues was paired with his mother who danced beside Snow Skin. After the two lines had met and danced away from each other several times, they formed a circle around the scalp pole, fire, and drummers, and began to move in a clock-wise fashion, all the while singing the victory chants.

Now the whip holder rose from his seated position near the fire and stopped the dance, his privilege according to custom. He told how he had counted coup on the enemy and when he had finished he asked the sun to punish him if he were not telling the truth. And then the dancing resumed once more.

Those celebrations were several years behind them when Nat and Snow Skin retired to the tepee one night; Nat was silent for so long that she became concerned and asked what was wrong.

"Snow Skin, I am not a Comanche by birth as you are, and I cannot live the rest of my life raiding and killing the enemies of the Comanche nation. I am weary of it and want to go somewhere and settle down. I have been a wanderer long enough."

"Where would you like to go?" Snow Skin asked with a smile.

"First," Nat continued, "I need to go to my friend, Otto, and see what is happening with him before making future plans."

"It will be difficult to leave my brother and my mother, but I also know that I must be with you, so I'll let you make the decision and I will accept that decision and go wherever you go," Snow Skin whispered as she walked into the shelter of his arms.

Nat kissed her forehead and asked tenderly, "Do you think that your mother and brother would come with us?"

Snow Skin leaned back to look up into her husband's face and exclaimed, "Do you mean it?" She wrapped her arms once more around her husband's waist, put her head against his chest and hugged him.

"Yes, I mean it," Nat told her, "that is, if they would like to come with us."

"Let's go to mother's tepee and ask her right now!"

"Let's go," Nat said as he hugged his wife once more.

When they entered Spirit Woman's tepee, they saw Three Tongues seated near the fire cleaning his rifle while his mother sat nearby, sewing on a new shirt for her son.

"Mother," Snow Skin said with excitement, "my husband has something he wishes to say to you both!"

"What is it?" Spirit Woman smiled as she motioned for them to sit by the fire. She stopped sewing and looked from her daughter to Nat.

"Well," Nat began, "I don't know how to say this but I guess the best way is to say it straight out. Snow Skin and I are leaving, and we would like for you both to come with us."

"Leaving?" Three Tongues looked up in astonishment as he stopped rubbing his rifle and looked quickly at his mother. "Where are you going?"

"To see Otto in Westport Landing first and after that, I don't know," his friend told him gravely.

"But we're Comanches," Three Tongues protested, "we cannot live in a large village surrounded by the white man."

"Have you forgotten, my son, that you are half white?" Spirit Woman calmly began to sew once again.

"But I have been raised as a Comanche," Three Tongues replied with pride. "That makes me all Comanche."

Spirit Woman continued to sew without looking up and finally spoke, "How much longer will the Comanche be able to live as they do now before the white man builds his villages all over the land?"

"What are you trying to say, mother?"

"What I am trying to say, son, is that the Comanche way of life is coming to an end, and you know that very well. You have visited the white men's villages when you went with Vlach to order the rifles. You have seen their power and their numbers and you, my son, have seen only the point of the lance. There are many more whites than what you have seen, more than the Comanches can imagine." She stopped sewing and looked up at her family and continued, "The time is now, it is time to make a new beginning. Maybe the spirits have sent Vlach to us as a sign, a sign which has been on my mind for a long time now."

Her face was sad as she gazed into the fire, "Nothing lasts forever and those who do not change with the times are destined to be destroyed; the time for change is at hand." Now she looked at Nat. "I want a straight answer from you, my new son, before I speak more." For long moments she stared into Nat's eyes and then she continued, "Do you really want us to join you when you leave the Antelope camp, or are you asking us only to make Snow Skin happy?"

"Both," Nat said without hesitation. "Don't ask me how or why, but I have this feeling which comes from deep down in the pit of my stomach that we should all stay together."

"But, we are Comanches, we can't leave our village!" Three Tongues interposed.

"Before you go on," Spirit Woman spoke to Three Tongues, "let me ask you what the Southern Comanches told you about the Americans under the leadership of Austin, who now, this very day, is moving into Texas. Do they think the Americans will stop coming? Or will the Mexicans stop coming?"

"We can handle the Mexicans," Three Tongues replied calmly, "we have for hundreds of years."

"Go on!" Spirit Woman said, when her son paused.

"What do you mean, go on?"

"You didn't mention how you are going to handle the Americans," she reminded. "They are a different breed from the Mexicans. They are a breed apart, a new breed, and you are a part of that new breed whether you like it or not, a new breed made up of many nationalities and races. Remember also, my son, this new breed is just beginning, many more will follow, maybe enough will follow to set a whole new standard of behavior for the world. No, my son, we should not fight the future because the future cannot be defeated, it conquers all. We should join it and the reason why I believe this is very clear to me. You and your sister are part of that new breed of people which call itself American, for you are as much American as you are Comanche."

Spirit Woman paused for a moment and when she continued, she had a smile on her face. "You know, if you think about it, the Comanches are Americans, also. Yes, we Comanches are Americans." A tear rolled down her cheek as she looked down at the shirt she was sewing. She attempted to speak again, but her emotions forbade it. Snow Skin rose swiftly and went to kneel by her mother's side. She kissed her cheek and whispered, "Thank you mother, I love you very much."

Her son looked fondly at her across the fire and said, "You speak strong words mother, you would make a great chief."

Spirit Woman wiped her tears and said, "Thank you, my son."

CHAPTER IX

When the little party of two women, two small children, and two men were two days ride from Council Bluffs, they spotted two wagons on the Santa Fe Trail. They were some distance away as yet, but they could see that men were working on one of the wagons. As they drew nearer, they saw that a wheel was off and it was being repaired. They halted at a few paces from the working men and Nat asked if they could be of any help.

"You can be of great help!" The canvas of both wagons was thrust aside and over a dozen men pointed their rifles at Nat and his family.

"It would not be wise to make any foolish moves, señor," a Mexican said. "Please drop your weapons on the ground."

When the weapons were gathered by one of the men who had been standing by the wagon wheel, the leader of the Mexican band continued, "Please get down señors, and you señoras, also. My name is Felipe Sandoval and me and my men have just taken you prisoner, but don't worry; no harm will come to any of you if you do as I say. So you're the one the Comanches call Vlach." Sandoval walked up to Nat as he spoke.

"What's all this about?" Nat spoke angrily.

"Ransom, I believe you gringos call it." Sandoval spoke in a slow, calm voice as a hideous smile crossed his face. "Don't you think Señor Muller would be more than happy to pay for your safe return? I think he will."

"What do you want?" Nat gave Sandoval a furious glare.

"Now, now, Señor Vlach, such behavior is not called for. I believe I said that no harm will come to you and your amigos if Señor Muller will contribute a little to the Sandoval fund."

"What do you consider a little?" Nat asked.

"I think thirty wagons loaded with items of my choice will be adequate, don't you think, mi amigo?" Sandoval asked with a contemptuous smile. "Don't you think that Señor Otto would be willing to pay such a small price for your safety? We think so. Now, let's get down to business, shall we? Your Indian friend will carry my list of demands to Señor Muller and he will then send the wagon train toward Santa Fe. My men and I will meet the train somewhere between here and Santa Fe, and will drive the wagons from that point forward. You, mi amigo, and your wife, children, and mother-in-law will then be set free, unmolested and uninjured. I will keep my end of the bargain if Señor Muller will do the same."

Sandoval smiled in anticipation and continued, "You see, Señor Vlach, it is a simple plan, but if any tricks are tried, or Señor Muller does not cooperate, well, let's just not think of such things at this point."

Sandoval now handed Three Tongues a leather pouch and told him, "In this pouch, Comanche, are my demands to Señor Muller. The life of your family depends on your getting through to Westport Landing and convincing Señor Muller that he must meet my demands. Is that clear?"

Three Tongues nodded as Sandoval turned his head and yelled for a fresh horse. Three Tongues swung into his saddle on the horse which had been brought as Sandoval yelled, "Maybe the Macedonian will be waiting out there, somewhere, Comanche," Three Tongues could hear the jeering laughter of the bandit leader as he galloped toward Westport Landing.

"What's happening at Henderson's Saloon?" Otto glanced at his friend as they strode up a street in Westport Landing.

"Don't know," answered John Prichard, "but from the looks of it, I'd guess that a bull whacker and a mule skinner have had another one of those wagers to see which of them can handle a whip best."

John and Otto could see men pouring from the saloon and they could be heard wagering about the outcome of the bet. They formed a large circle in the street with little disregard for halting the traffic. People converged around the circle of men to watch the contest as one of them placed an empty whiskey bottle on the ground in the middle of the street. The bartender who had followed the crowd outside placed a silver coin on top of the bottle.

"Be my guest," the bull whacker told his opponent with a magnanimous wave of his hand.

"If I cut the coin from the top of the bottle without touching the bottle, it will be mine, plus twenty-five dollars. That's the wager, right?"

"You are correct, my friend," the bull whacker replied with a grin on his face. "But don't you worry none about spending the money, because you can't cut it loose."

"I can't huh? Just watch this!" The mule skinner stepped into the circle and laid his whip out on the ground behind him. He held the handle firmly in his hand.

"Quiet, everybody," the bartender roared in his role of arbiter.

"The rules of this contest are as follows: The mule skinner will use his customary ten foot whip and the bull whacker will use his eighteen foot whip. Neither man may step across the line which I've drawn on the ground, although they may stand as far back as they wish. They cannot put as much as a toe on the line. Each man will have only one chance at removing the coin from the top of the bottle in the first go-around and if the first man removed the coin on his first try, the coin will be replaced on top of the bottle so that the second contestant can have his chance at removing it also. If the second contestant fails to remove it, the first contestant will be declared the winner, but if neither is able to remove the coin without toppling the bottle, the first contestant will try again; if he succeeds on his second try, he will be declared the winner. If neither succeeds on the second go-around, the contest will continue until one of the contestants succeeds in removing the coin. He will then be declared the winner. If they both remove the coin on the first go-around, the contest will begin anew. Is this clear to the contestants?"

Both of the contestants nodded their agreement. The mule skinner stepped up to the line once more and with an easy flip of his wrist, he again laid out his ten foot whip behind him. He braced his feet firmly on the ground, twisting each foot a few times so as to guarantee solid footing. He eyed the coin for a few seconds and glanced back to see that his whip was stretched out as he wanted it to be. He turned his eyes back to the coin and bent his knees slightly twice. Then leaning forward a little, he let his left arm hang loosely at his side. He gave one more glance at his whip and returned his attention to the shiny coin. In a flash, his wrist moved the whip forward and as it cracked, the coin flew across the street. The crowd cheered his dexterity and he gave a mock bow as he drew his whip back and extended his hand toward his competitor.

"I'll bet that the mule skinner will prevail," Otto heard the man next to him remark. He turned to Otto, "Do you have an opinion?"

Otto glanced at the stranger who wore a skunkskin cap and an odd looking buckskin shirt, in which he had several knives sheathed.

"I have not really thought about it," Otto answered. "I was just enjoying the contest with no pressure. I always enjoy watching professionals at work."

"Nat does, also," the stranger continued. He watched the bull whacker who was preparing to take his turn.

Otto jerked his head back to the stranger and asked, "Do you know Nat?"

"Not really . . . we have not actually met, but I know of him," the stranger replied calmly.

The loud crack of the whip sounded and Otto turned quickly at the sound. The bull whacker had removed the coin without touching the bottle. He quickly stretched out his whip behind him and all could hear the swift second crack as it hit the silver coin in flight. The crowd roared its approval as the bull whacker turned to the mule skinner with a smile.

"I can't beat that," the mule skinner said, "the coin is yours and here is my twenty-five dollar wager."

The two men shook hands and started back toward the saloon followed by the crowd. "The drinks are on me!" The bull whacker yelled as he disappeared into the dimness of the tavern.

Otto turned toward the stranger again and said, "Let's go to my office. I think you have some information for me."

"Yes," replied the Macedonian, "and I'm afraid it's not very good."

When they were seated comfortably in Otto's office, Otto asked, "What is your news."

"Your friend Nat who is called Vlach by the Comanches, his wife, children, his friend Three Tongues and mother-in-law are being held for ransom by a Mexican bandit who calls himself Felipe Sandoval. Three Tongues should be here shortly with the ransom note."

"How do you know all of this?"

"I'm not with the bandits, Mr. Muller, believe me. As Three Tongues will verify when he arrives. If you have misgivings about my loyalty, maybe we should wait until he gets here."

"No offence, but I think that might be a good idea," Otto said.

"No offence taken," the Macedonian replied, "It is the prudent thing to do."

The door to Otto's office opened and Three Tongues entered. Otto rose to his feet quickly, "Three Tongues! Am I glad to see you! This stranger and I were just talking about you."

Three Tongues' eyes turned from Otto to the stranger who was seated near Otto's desk. He took in the skunkskin cap and the handles of the knives which were sheathed in his buckskin shirt.

"Forgive me for not introducing you to the stranger," Otto said and then hesitated, "I guess I can't introduce you after all, because I don't know his name myself."

"That's all right, Otto," Three Tongues said, "I don't know the stranger, but I've heard of him. You're the Macedonian, right?"

"That is correct," the Macedonian said as he rose to shake Three Tongues' hand.

"So you're real," Three Tongues grinned, "I was beginning to think the stories that were told about you were imaginary."

"Will someone tell me what is going on here?"

"This man can be trusted as much as any man alive," Three Tongues said as he turned to Otto. "He is a legend out west. When we have more time, we will ask him some questions, but right now we have more urgent business." The Comanche handed Otto the pouch which contained the ransom note. Otto quickly opened the pouch and read the note and then glanced over at the Macedonian. "How did you come to know about this before I did?"

Otto turned to Three Tongues, "You didn't talk to anyone since you left Nat, did you?"

"No," answered the Comanche.

"Well?" Otto looked at the Macedonian once more. "I'm waiting for an answer."

"I have my informants," the Macedonian replied.

"Otto," Three Tongues interrupted, "believe me, this man can be trusted, so why don't we spend our time on Sandoval. He's the culprit, not the Macedonian."

"All right," Otto conceded, "do you know what the note says?"

"Not exactly, but I know that Sandoval expects thirty wagon loads of supplies which he has listed in the note and if you don't comply with his demands, he will kill Nat and my family, which I know he will do if we don't come up with the supplies or a plan to stop him."

"Do you have a plan? You have had some time to think of one."

"I have one," the Macedonian interrupted.

"Let's hear it," Otto said as he sat down and motioned for Three Tongues to pull up a chair.

"Here's what I think we should do," the Macedonian began. "First, we load the wagons with the supplies which Sandoval wants. We can not afford not to because he may have informants here. Just look outside and you'll see almost as many Mexicans walking the streets as you do Americans. It wouldn't be too hard for one of his men to hide himself among them.

"What we should do is have Three Tongues ride out to the northern Comanches, select thirty trusted braves and bring them back here disguised as Mexicans. But before you leave to get your braves, have one of the wagon drivers show you how to handle a team of mules. When you do leave, take a team and the harness with you so you can teach your braves how to handle them. It is not easy to handle wagon mules. You

186

don't use reins as on a buckboard, but instead there is a long single line that is tied to the left of the nigh leader. It comes back through rings which are attached to all of the other mules. To turn left you give a long, steady pull on the line and to go right you give the line a series of short jerks which is why it is called the jerk line. But the mule skinner will tell you all this and more, before you leave." The Macedonian thought for a moment and then continued, "And you'd better disguise yourself so that Sandoval's spy won't see you leave town. While Three Tongues is doing his share, Otto, you have some of your trusted employees build some boxes in such a way that they look nailed shut but actually are not. Inside each box will be a Comanche brave dressed as a Mexican. There will be a box in each wagon and when a brave is inside, he will be able to fasten it securely until the time comes for him to get out. When the wagons are turned over to Sandoval's men and they have driven for awhile, the Comanche in the last wagon will slip out of his box and kill the driver of that wagon, and assume the driver's role. The Comanche in the preceding wagon will observe this through a peep hole in his box and do the same, taking over the team as his fellow brave did."

"But you're forgetting something," Otto interrupted, "what about the rear guards?"

"They will be dead. Two Comanches off the trail will take care of them the first thing with arrows. They will then jump on the horses of the guards, and anyone looking back will notice nothing wrong. After the Comanche in the last wagon sees this has taken place, he will make his move and not before."

"If all goes well then, Otto said, "each driver will be replaced with a Comanche until all of the wagons are driven by Comanches dressed as Mexicans!"

"Yes, and we will need some additional Comanches also, Three Tongues. I'll let you decide on the number. The additional Comanches will shadow the wagons after they have been turned over to Sandoval and Nat and the others are free. They will appear on the horizon just before the rear guards are killed, for their appearance will be timed to keep the full attention of Sandoval and his men, thereby giving the Comanches more safety in making their attacks. When the drivers are all dead and replaced by our people, we will make our last move against Sandoval and the rest of his men, who will probably be riding ahead of the wagon train. that is a plan which I believe will work, if you both agree, of course."

"What do you think, Three Tongues?" Otto asked as he turned to the Comanche.

"It sounds good to me," Three Tongues admitted.

"Me too," Otto told the Macedonian.

"Modifications may be required if things do not turn out as we plan, but I believe the braves can adapt, don't you, Three Tongues?"

"I'll select braves who have proven themselves in this area, and I'm sure they will be able to handle this responsibility. I'll leave here tonight under cover of darkness just in case Sandoval has spies here."

"And I'll begin loading and modifying the wagons right away," Otto said as he rose from his chair.

"Remember, the sooner we are ready to stretch out the wagons, the sooner the hostages will be freed. Otto, you will travel with us, won't you?"

"A team of wild horse could not keep me away! I'll select my best mule skinners and Dan Weber as my wagon master."

It was foggy, early morning as Dan Weber bustled about the wagons organizing the train. As he passed by Otto and the Macedonian, Otto called out, "Are you about ready, Dan?"

"I'm making my last check, boss. Why don't you ride out to the head of the train and I'll meet you there shortly?"

Half an hour later Dan joined Otto and the Macedonian, stood in his stirrups, raised his hand high and yelled, "Stretch out!"

The wagons began their slow movement as the cracks from the whips of the mule skinners could be heard repeatedly. Behind each wagon, a horse was tied. The horse would be the drivers' transportation after they had turned over the wagons to Sandoval's men.

Each driver was more heavily armed than usual, a sign that trouble could develop and they wanted to be prepared.

"I hope your friends Three Tongues and Straight Arrow are as good as scouting as you say, boss." Dan turned once more to look back at his train.

Otto, upon seeing his wagon master looking back also turned in his saddle to see his train as it began to stretch out and replied, "They are the best. You can find no better; after all this is their home turf. They know it like the back of their hands."

Their journey was routine, uneventful, probably the most trouble-free journey which Dan had experienced. "This trip so far, boss," Dan said, "is unbelievable. We haven't even had a wheel to give us trouble." He grinned. "I hope you don't think my previous trips were this free of problems. If you did, you'd want to cut my pay."

Otto laughed as he said, "Dan, these wagons are my latest; they're constructed of the best seasoned lumber around, and all the holes that were bored in building and assembling these wagons were bored with a heated iron rod, instead of the usual auger. The holes, I am told by the men who use this method, were bored just a little smaller than the bolt which goes through them. This method is supposed to prevent the wood around the bolt from rotting or cracking. If you will notice, the tongues of the wagons are no longer stiff and stationary, these new tongues permit the wagons to turn more easily in a shorter space."

"Yes, I have noticed the changes in the construction of these wagons as compared to those on my previous trips. It would be a shame if the bandits got away with them."

"They won't," Otto replied with confidence as he turned to look at the Macedonian. "We have the best strategists alive on this trip and they have planned well."

It was mid-day after the train had left Pawnee Rock that Three Tongues and Straight Arrow came in. "The bandits are four or five miles ahead of us," Three Tongues told them as he reined his horse to ride westward beside the others. "They must be pretty confident because they are all sitting around their campfire and hardly paid any attention when they saw us."

"Are Nat and the others with them?" Otto asked.

"They're there," Three Tongues replied confidently.

"Three Tongues, why don't you ride back and tell the Comanches to get into the boxes, and give him a hand, will you Macedonian? Dan and I and Straight Arrow will keep watch up here."

The train rolled westward for almost an hour before Sandoval and his men appeared ahead of them.

"There's enough of them," Otto commented wryly, "there must be at least forty of them. Does anyone see Nat and the others in that crowd."

"They're in the center," the Macedonian said after a pause.

When the bandits rode up, Sandoval was the first to speak, "Welcome!" He and his men pulled their horses to a halt in front of Otto and the others. Sandoval eyed each of them in silence for a few seconds and then he looked at Otto and resumed. "Señor Muller, you are a wise man." He stood in his stirrups and looked past Otto at the wagons.

"How did you know that I am Otto Muller?" Otto spoke in a cold voice that was anything but cordial.

"Señor," Sandoval wore a smile on his face, "do not take me for a fool, There are five of you here, two Indians, a mountainman, and Dan Weber, your wagon master who is well known in Santa Fe. That leaves only you, my friend." He turned and gave orders to his men some of whom rode past the group toward the wagons.

"With your permission, señor, my men will check the wagons to see if you have brought what I have asked for."

"It's all there," Otto answered calmly as he continued to stare coldly at the bandit.

"With your permission, senor, I think I'll have my men double check. That is, if you have no objections."

"There is no objection."

"Good," replied Sandoval, "we don't want any misunderstandings at this late date, do we?"

"Are you all right?" Otto called to Nat and his family.

Nat nodded but said nothing. He and Spirit Woman had their hands tied to the horns of their saddles. Snow Skin's hands were untied so that she could care for her children.

Sandoval's men rode back and reported that all seemed to be in order. The bandit leader summoned thirty of his men to replace the men presently driving the wagons. "Tell your drivers to step aside and permit my men to replace them if you please, Señor Muller."

"Do as he asks." Otto instructed Dan. Dan rode back toward the and one by one the mule skinners walked back to their saddle horses. They rode ahead to join their boss.

When all of the wagons were in the control of Sandoval's men, Otto said, "I've kept my end of the bargain now turn my people loose."

Sandoval's eyes skirted each of the Americans as they rode in front of him and noticed that they were well armed and he saw anger in their faces. "You wouldn't be foolish enough to try anything, would you?" He asked Otto. "I say this because I want you to know that the women and children would be our first targets if you did try something."

"We are not that stupid," Otto retorted. He glared at Sandoval and continued, "I certainly hope that you are not."

Sandoval smiled and yelled for his men to bring the prisoners to him. "These belong to you now," he said as he cut the ropes on Spirit Woman's and Nat's hands. Take them and be gone."

The Americans turned their mounts and started away although they kept their eyes turned toward the bandits. As they watched, the wagons began to roll.

"I hope you have a plan to even the score and regain the wagons," Nat said as he looked from Otto to Three Tongues and shook their hands.

"We do," Otto replied in a clam voice. "Oh by the way, Nat I don't believe you know this fellow here, he calls himself the Macedonian!"

Nat eyed the lean figure of the Macedonian as he lounged in his saddle and said, "You saved my life once in the mountains of Colorado."

"I remember," the Macedonian replied with a grin.

"I never had the chance to thank you." Nat extended his hands. They both grinned broadly as they shook hands and Nat turned to his family. "This is my wife and our children."

190

The Macedonian nodded and removed his cap and said, "It's my pleasure, ma'am."

"And this is my mother-in-law, Spirit Woman."

The Macedonian nodded and tipped his cap once more and looked into Spirit Woman's eyes searchingly. When their eyes met, he felt an almost uncontrollable urge to take her in his arms. Nat saw the flicker of his eyes as the Macedonian continued to gaze at Spirit Woman, who smiled and nodded.

"It is my pleasure to make your acquaintance, madam." He then turned from her and said to the others. "We had better hurry and join the Comanches."

The wagon train looked like a white snake as it twisted its way slowly westward. Sandoval's men had to yell at the mules to keep them pulling because none of the men had whips, or the proper language to encourage the stubborn beasts to continue at a more rapid pace. What the bandits did not know was that while they were talking with Otto and the others, a few Comanches were digging two shallow trenches just ahead of them and a few feet north of the trail. When they had completed their work, two Comanches lay down in the holes. Each clutched a bow in his left hand and three arrows held thightly in the right. When they had adjusted themselves comfortably, they nodded to the other Comanches who were standing over them, waiting to cover them with a buffalo robe. Dirt and clumps of grass and brush were dumped over the robe until they were completely concealed except for their heads. When that was completed to their satisfaction, the other Comanches surrounded the heads of the buried warriors with tall grass until their head were invisible also. The footprints were wiped out by brushing the ground with grass, leaving the area undisturbed. The Comanches chose their steps carefully as they retreated to their horses, leaving no moccasin prints. When they joined the main body of Comanches, Otto and the others were there. On seeing the returning Comanches, Otto said, "It's time to shadow the train."

Three Tongues looked at his friend, Many Horses, and nodded; Many Horses gestured toward the disappearing train and rode away.

Sandoval turned in his saddle and looked behind at the wagons and smiled with satisfaction. "It was a stroke of genius," the bandit chief said, "all this and the loss of not a single man."

"You speak too quickly," Fernando said as he pointed to the Comanches in the distance.

Sandoval turned quickly to look in the direction and then asked, "Can you see gringos among them?" He looked intently to see if he could discern Otto or the others.

The small group of five men who were riding with the bandit chief looked in vain for any sign of American with the Comanches.

"It appears that the Americanos and the Comanches are not linked," Sandoval concluded as he continued to watch the Indians who were riding in a parallel line with the trail.

"Circle the wagons," Sandoval yelled and his lieutenants reined their horses and dashed at top speed toward the wagons. The wagon train was in a confused state as the amateur drivers tried to guide the mules in a cicular direction. The wagons went in every direction as they made the attempt, for the Mexicans did not know how to use the jerk line. They finally ran to the lead mules and grabbed their headstalls in an effort to get them turned. Finally, after a prolonged struggle, the men succeeded in persuading the mules to make the circle. Then they prepared for the attack which Sandoval anticipated.

These maneuvers were unexpected as far as the Comanches in the boxes were concerned, but they remained silent in their hiding places.

"Why don't they attack?" Sandoval asked of a lieutenant. "They haven't moved one step toward us, but just sit on their horses, watching us. What are they up to?"

"We have a large force," Ramon reminded him as he checked his rifle and continued to eye the distant Comanches. "Maybe thay think we're too strong for them."

"You may be right but then again you may not be, Ramon," Sandoval conceded. "I think I'll play it safe. Maybe we can buy them off with a few presents. Cover me," he said as he stood up and waved at the Comanches. He stepped out from behind one of the wagons and walked toward the Indians. After walking about fifty yards, he placed his rifle on the ground and gave the Indian sign for peace. Many Horses slid from his horse and walked toward Sandoval. Upon seeing this response, Sandoval continued to walk toward them. When the two finally faced each other, Sandoval spoke first, "I bring you presents for the privilege of traveling through your nation." He turned and waved to his men and Santiago led one wagon toward his leader. Many Horses smiled at Sandoval and nodded in approval and beckoned for a Comanche to come and get the wagon.

When the Comanche had reached his chief, he dismounted and sprang upon the back of the lead mule taking the wagon away. Many Horses grabbed the rope bridle of his brave's horse and turned and rode away. The Comanches then disappeared over some rolling hills.

Sandoval turned to Santiago and commented, "That was too easy. Let's get the wagons moving again and tell the men to keep a sharp eye out for the Comanches. I think they may return. What I can't figure out is why they didn't attack during the confusion while we were trying to circle the wagons? We were in a very weak position at that time, weaker then we are now. They're up to something."

He rode back to the wagons and gave an order for his men to move them out. Everyone remained on their toes as they watched for any sign of Comanches. As the last wagons passed by the two hidden Comanches, the Indians slowly rose from their prone position, carefully rolled the buffalo robes to one side and sat up. They eyed one another and nodded as each placed an arrow in his bow and pulled his bow string as far back as possible. Once more they eyed each other, nodded, and released their arrows simultaneously. Each quickly replaced the spent arrow with another, but they were not needed because the two Mexican bandits slid to the ground without a sound. The two Comanches ran toward the horses and vaulted in to the saddles. They quickly calmed the surprised horses by talking to them and rubbing their necks. They continued to walk in a quiet fashion as the bandits had done.

It did not take long for the first Comanche to leave his hiding place when he saw the two braves kill the rear guards. Within seconds, the first Mexican driver fell to the ground with his throat cut from ear to ear. The Comanche took his place, adjusted his sombrero and cradled the rifle in his left arm as the bandit had done.

Wagon by wagon, the Comanches replaced the Mexican drivers, until only Comanches were driving. If Sandoval or any of his aides had changed to look back, they'd have noticed nothing for the Comanches rolled the bodies of the Mexicans off of the trail into the grass as they disposed of them.

"There they are again," Fernando pointed off to the right. The Comanches rode toward them at a trot, this time showing no concern for their safety. "Circle the wagons," Sandoval bawled once more, but upon hearing his order a party of Comanche braves rushed to cut his lieutenant off from reaching the wagons. The bandits, seeing that they wouldn't be able to reach the wagons, turned and rode back to their leader. Otto was among the Comanches and yelled, "It's all over, Sandoval, lay down your arms or we will be forced to kill all of you, and don't expect any help from your drivers for they are all dead."

"You lie!" Sandoval yelled angrily.

"It is true," Otto told him as he drew nearer and beckoned for the Comanche drivers to come closer.

Sandoval could not believe his eyes as he saw the first of the drivers walk toward him. As they walked, they shed their Mexican clothing and when they reached Otto, Sandoval realized that they were not his men, but Comanches. "Where are my men?" He shouted with rage as he looked at the wagons. In a fit of frustration and anger he reached for his pistol but before he could clear it from the holster, Many Horses shot him. As he slid to the ground, the other bandits raised their hands hastily.

"Mexico is that way, I believe," Otto said as he pointed westward.

"I wouldn't come back this way again if I were you. You had better ride now, very quickly, because I cannot guarantee that I can keep these Comanches from taking your scalps for very long."

The bandits glanced at one another and then jabbed their spurs into the sides of their horses, the sudden rush forward of the startled horses creating such a cloud of dust that the bandits were almost invisible as they galloped away.

"They'll have plenty of fighting waiting for them in Mexico," Nat said.

"What do you mean?" Otto looked at Nat in surprise.

"Some of the Mexican states are in revolt agianst President Santa Ana," Nat told him.

"You can't betray people as Santa Ana has done by revoking the Constitution of 1821," The Macedonaian commented.

Everyone looked at the Macedonian and Otto said, "And you knew of this, also?"

The Macedonian smiled but said nothing.

"I know," Otto said with a grin, "you have your informants, but I'm informing everyone here now that you are all invited to the wedding."

"Wedding? What wedding?" Nat asked in surprise.

You may be a good tracker and observer in the wild, my friend," Otto continued, "but you are blind when it comes to matters of the heart. Spirit Woman and the Macedonian, of course!"

Spirit Woman and Macedonian looked at each other and Spirit Woman said, quietly, "Otto, you are imagining things."

"Well, perhaps I'm a little premature, but I'm not far off the mark," Otto said complacently as he looked toward the Macedonian.

"You are a wise man," was the Macedonian's comment.

Otto grinned again and spoke to the Comanches, "Without your help and that of your people, Many Horses, we could not have rescued our friends. To show our appreciation, I would like for you to take the thirty wagons. That is if Nat, my partner, approves."

"I approve of Otto's gift wholeheartedly and I too, want, on behalf of my family and friends, to add my many thanks to you, Many Horses and your Comanche braves. However if it meets with the approval of everyone, I would appreciate it very much if we could have one case of those knives and a few rifles. Rifles, I'm afraid, will be mightly scarce where we're headed; we would also like whatever our women could use from the wagons."

"Your wish is granted, but we would like for you to take more," Many

Horses replied politely.

"No, what we ask for is all we want," Nat answered. "We do not want to be burdened with too much baggage. It would slow us down and provide too much of an enticing prize for scavengers. And if it suits your fancy, Otto, I would like to have about eight of Sandoval's horses."

"What?" Otto turned to look at Nat. "What's in that head of yours now? Aren't you going back to Westport Landing with us?"

Before Nat could reply, Otto went on, "I suppose not. I should know you by now. Where are you going now? I can see that wandering look in your eyes!"

"You're right there, my friend," Nat replied. "I haven't seen enough of Mexico yet, and until I do, I'm afraid I'd be of no use to you."

"All right," Otto replied to Nat's request. "Who are you taking with you?"

Nat hadn't replied when Snow Skin spoke up firmly, "I go where my husband goes and so do my children."

"I'd like to see more of Mexico myself," the Macedonian said softly.

"And of course my son and I will go!" Spirit Woman added.

Otto now looked at Three Tongues, who grinned cheerfully at everybody.

"These are fine wagons," Many Horses said, "we will return them and your mules after we have unloaded them at our village. You would have more use for tham then we would."

"It's a deal," Otto replied with satisfaction.

The last wagon rode slowly over the hill and disappeared from view as a small group of American sat on their horses and watched.

"There goes my past," Three Tongues finally said in a sad voice.

Spirit Woman rode to her son's side and said softly, "The future will be rewarding also, my son. We will not and cannot forget the Comanche nation for they have given us so much, so much to be thankful for. They have given us so many wonderful and unforgettable memories! May the spirit look down upon our people and guide them along the true path of happiness and wisdom as long as the grass shall grow and the wind shall blow. The good is forever, the Great Spirit gave birth to good; surely he will not forget the Comanche people because they are good."

"Bravo!" The Macedonian rode over to where Spirit Woman sat on her horse and looked down at her admiringly.

Spirit Woman looked long into his face and then in a low voice she spoke, "What shall I call you besides Macedonian?"

"I think it's time that everyone stopped calling me the Macedonian and let that man remain a myth. I don't want anyone other than those who are here to know my past. I would like for it to remain a mystery and I will take my real identity and name, James Toli Tirnava."

"I'll keep my Comanche name if there are no objections," Three Tongues said as he looked in the direction the wagons had taken.

To break the short silence, James said as he looked at Spirit Woman, "We are in America, maybe I should take an American name."

"America is made up of all kinds of people from every nation in the world so there is no such thing as a typical American name." Spirit Woman pointed out. "Don't you agree? Tirnava can be just as American as Washington or Jefferson!" She mused for a moment and went on, "But I think I will drop the second half of my name and be known as Spirit only." She smiled up at James with a twinkle in her eyes, "That sounds more American, somehow!"

"Do you mind if I keep my name?" Otto interrupted, laughing.

"Nat, I would like to tag along with you if you don't mind an outsider joining you," Wilbur Ferguson, one of the mule skinners said. "I've always had a hankering to explore northern Mexico and this could be my chance."

"What do you say?" Nat looked around the circle of his family.

"Under one condition," James answered.

"And what might that be?" Wilbur asked.

"That you teach us how to use that whip of yours."

"It's a deal!" Wilbur replied delightedly.

"Well, let's pack the horses and be on our way," Nat said exuberantly. He turned to James and asked, "Do you agree?"

"There can be only one boss if an outfit is to function properly and I suggest you be that boss," James said.

"I don't even get one vote?" Three Tongues jokingly sulked.

Otto and his men rode toward the east as the American Team, as Otto had dubbed them, rode westward.

"The American Team," Spirit mused, breaking the silence. "I like that."

"Why, if I may ask, do we need all of the extra rifles and knives, Vlach, or should I say Nat from now on?" Three Tongues asked.

"I'd like that," Nat told him. "We only had five extra rifles and who knows what could happen in the days and months ahead? We may need them and besides, good rifles are almost impossible to obtain in Mexico."

"What about the knives?" Three Tongues asked.

Nat glanced at James and asked, "You know why I want the knives, don't you, James?"

"Jim sounds better," James replied. "I think I'd like to be called Jim."

"All right, Jim, you can guess why I wanted the knives?"

"I can guess," Jim replied as he continued to gaze straight ahead.

"Tell the others," Nat suggested.

"Nat probably wants me to teach the rest of you how to throw a knife and I don't think that's all he expects of you, either. Tell them what comes after that," Jim told Nat.

"You're right, Jim," Nat replied. "I want all of you to be as good as you can be at throwing knives and I also want all of you to be good with a rifle and whip as well. That includes you women, of course."

Wilbur turned when he heard the word whip and looked at Nat.

"When we reach Bent's Fort, we will make camp and we will not leave the fort until everyone is proficient with the rifle, knife, and whip. Jim, I think it would be best if everyone had their knives attached to their upper backs, about the shoulder level. You can keep yours as they are, Jim, but I believe the rest of us can adapt more easily if we could just reach up to our shoulders for the knives if we needed them in a hurry. What do you think, Jim?

"Let me think about it for awhile, Nat," Jim replied after a pause.

CHAPTER X

When the American Team left Bent's Fort, they headed for Raton Pass and after riding through it they entered the ranch, along the Vermejo River, which belonged to Bent and St. Vrain. All of them except Jim wore their Green River knives in sheaths on their upper shoulders and each also carried a long blacksnake whip tied to the saddle. They cradled rifles in their arms. As they eased their horses down a steep slope of the tree covered mountain, Nat and Jim almost simultaneously raised a hand and stopped. No one spoke for a moment, but it did not take long for the others to smell the smoke.

They dismounted as Nat pointed to a thicket ahead of them down the slope. A small stream of smoke drifted into the air and dissipated once it rose a few inches above the tops of the trees. Nat made a circular motion with his right hand and the others nodded as they moved down the side of the hill, this time on foot, leading their horses. Nat motioned for Snow Skin and the children to stay with the pack horses. She frowned, but obeyed. When Nat reached within twenty yards or so of the fire, he could see the huddled figure of a Mexican leaning over the meager flames. The dejected figure appeared stupified, dazed. He seemed to stare into the fire unblinking.

Nat's eyes searched for his group and spotting them, he began to walk toward the Mexican. "Hello, the camp," He called as he continued to walk toward him. He dodged one tree and then another as he progressed through the thick growth. He noticed that the Mexican did not move. He must have heard my call, Nat thought. He called again, "Hello, the camp!"

By this time he was within a few feet of the stranger. Is he dead?" Nat muttered. "It may be a trick so I'd better be alert to any quick moves by the Mexican." He saw no rifle or pistol and the only weapon which the stranger apparently had lay on the ground to his right. It was a bow with a quiver of arrows lying nearby.

He touched the Mexican's shoulder gently with his left hand, but kept his right trigger finger handy on his rifle.

Upon feeling Nat's touch, the Mexican grunted and jerked to one side. It was then that he became aware of the presence of the stranger. He responded in a low, dejected tone, "I have nothing, but you are welcome to what I do have for I have no need of anything. You might do me the favor of shooting me, also."

Nat motioned for the others to come in and turned to signal to Snow Skin to bring in the horses. As they circled the Mexican, Nat asked, "Are you hurt?"

"More than that, señor," he answered. He continued to stare into the fire for long monents before he resumed wearily, "My hurt cannot be cured. Only death can put an end to the pain."

"What's wrong with him," Spirit asked as she knelt nearby.

Upon hearing a woman's voice, the Mexican rose to his feet quickly and called, "Fidela, is that you?"

"No, my friend," Nat said with pity as he placed his hand on the stranger's shoulder. "She is with us."

It took them nearly twenty minutes to bring the stranger back to awareness and it was then that the Mexican told his story. "It was the Apaches," he said with a tremor in his voice. "They attacked our home, killing three of my friends, and taking my wife, Fidela, and our three children with them."

"Where is your home?" Three Tongues asked.

"Back there a short distance," the Mexican pointed behind them.

Nat motioned with his head and Jim and Wilbur left for the house of the Mexican. When they returned, they told the others that they had buried the three Mexican men and a Apache. They kept the clothing of the Apache, thinking it could come in handy. Nat nodded his approval and said, "Fernando, these two men are Jim and Wilbur."

Fernando shook hands with each of them as he removed his sombrero and thanked them for burying his friends.

"When did it happen?" Jim asked.

"About sunup," Nat replied. "Fernando began to follow the Apaches hoping to retrieve his family somehow and then he remembers nothing."

"Why didn't the Apaches kill him as they did the others?" Wilbur wondered aloud.

"They must have thought evil spirits had possessed him. Indians will steer clear of insane people for they believe that such a sickness is contagious," Three Tongues explained. "Let's go after the Apaches and rescue Fernando family," he suggested urgently.

They glanced at one another and someone else said. "Let's go!"

A rifle was offered to Fernando, but he refused. "I have never used a rifle, especially one such as you have. Besides, I'm pretty good with my bow."

The Apache trail was picked up and the American Team followed it down the bank of the Vermejo River southeastward.

"The Vermejo empties into the Canadian River not long after it leaves the mountains," Jim told them. "It is my guess that the Apaches will stay clear of the open prairies, because of your compadres, Three Tongues, and hug the bottom edge of the mountains. The open country is Comanche territory and I doubt if the Apahes wish to tangle with Comanches when they have prisoners with them."

"I agree," Three Tongues replied, "the Apaches will follow the lower slopes of the mountains and head south towards Mora."

"But they will be taking a big chance," Nat pointed out, "there must be many villages that way. Surely the villages will see them and try to rescue Fernando's family."

No. Señor Nat," Fernando told him. "If my people spot the Apaches, they will go into hiding, for the Apaches are feared by my people. Our weapons are no match for them. My people's only defense against the Apaches has been to flee into hiding."

"Welcome to Mexico, Nat." Jim said softly, "You too, Wilbur. If Fernando's family is to be saved, we're the ones who will have to do it. I doubt if even the soldiers in Las Vegas or Santa Fe would waste their time and effort to save some peasents whom most despise anyway."

"I don't think I'm going to like Mexico," Nat said with disgust.

"It isn't the peons," Three Tongues said, "Most of them are good people, so don't be upset with them. It's their government that is bad. You will never see a more corrupt government than you are about to experience. Blame it and not the poor people."

"I'll remember that," Nat told him grimly.

A strong wing blew into their faces and it was around three in the afternoon when everyone except Wilbur picked up the scent of Apaches. The Apache camp was unguarded, for they apparently believed that no Mexican would dare attack them, but they had not taken into account the possibility of Americans in the area. The American Team developed a plan and then crept up as close as they could, undetected, before they put it into operation.

A tree large enough to conceal a person was selected. Ropes were tied to three small pinon trees to one side of the large tree and to bushes on the other side, making it possible for a person standing behind the large tree to manipulate the small trees and bushes. This was done repeatedly until four of these had been completed in a semicircle at a distance from the Apache camp. When darkness fell over the Apache camp, a stillness accompanied the night. The American Team waited for the right moment and that time came when, the moon shining brightly through the trees, an Apache rose and walked from his place by the fire to check on the prisoners. It was when he turned to retrace his steps that Nat, in a muffled voice said, "Ooosahn, Ooosahn, Ooosahn, Ooosahn." The Apache froze in his tracks and turned his head slowly as his eyes searched the forest behind him. It was at this point that Spirit pulled on one of the ropes, making the small pinon bush move to and fro. After two such tugs, she did the same to each of the other bushes, giving the appearance that a spirit was making its way through the bushes. Snow Skin, Nat, and Three Tongues followed Spirit's example, thereby giving the impression that the spirit seemed to move around the outer permimeter of the Apache camp. Now Fernando, on the opposite side of the camp created a diversion by crashing through the brush. While the rest of the warriors rose, commenting excitedly on the unexpected sound and stared into the darkness, Jim threw his knife, piercing the heart of the first Apache, who slumped to the ground dead. Almost as soon as the knife hit the Apache, Wilbur flicked his wrist and with one quick jerk, his whip snatched the knife from the falling Apache and brought it back to him. The American Team now remained perfectly still.

The Apaches noticed for the first time that one of their number lay dead. After they examined him, they rose from their kneeling positions and with much fright apparent on their faces, looked at the forest which surrounded them, searching for the spirit which had stabbed one of them without a knife. By this time, Nat had crept to the opposite site of the camp and now repeated his Usen act once more. Once more the Apaches looked in superstitutious fear toward the sound of his voice and Wilbur, with a quick snap of his whip, wrapped it around the throat of another Apache. He then jerked it quickly with both hands, breaking the neck of the Apache brave. Again the Apaches rushed to the side of another one of their tribe who lay on the ground and examined him. They found that the spirit had broken the neck of their comrade without being present. They then panicked and began to pray, asking Usen, their god, to please forgive their taking of the prisoners, if that was their crime. After they finished they walked to Fidela and asked her if she could find her way home if they released her and her children. At this moment, an arrow struck the tree trunk just above Fidela's head and she and the Apaches jerked their heads upward to look at the arrow. Fidela recognized the arrow as one belonging to her husband. She remembered painting that very stripe on the shaft of each of his arrows. She knew for the first time what had caused the death of the two Apaches and the mysterious moving of the pinon bushes and the strange disturbances. She turned her eyes slowly to the Apaches. "My children and I will be safe. Usen is out there and he will see to it that we return safely."

The Apaches did not argue with her because they believed that Usen was angry with them for taking her and her children. The leader of the Apache war party politely told her that she was free to go and he further said in broken Spanish that he wished them a safe and comfortable journey back to her loved ones. As an after thought, he asked, "Are you closely enough connected with your god that he could have interceded with Usen and they together caused the bushes to move and the death of my braves?"

"Yes!" Fidela answered in a strong, clear voice. She now realized the extent of the fear which had taken possession of their captors. "I am president of the altar society of my church and my sister is a nun."

Upon hearing Fidela's words, the Apaches looked at one another and realized why Usen was unhappy with them. They mounted their horses and rode away, taking their dead with them and leaving Fidela standing near the campfire with her children clutching her skirts. She made a stirring picture as she picked up her youngest child and gathered the other two close to her. She stood erect, her head held high as she faced the departing Apaches. She uttered no sound nor did she move until the Apaches were out of sight and sound. "You can come out now, Fernando," she said in a clear, confident voice as she continued to look in the direction which the Apaches had taken.

Fernando rushed through the trees and brush and gathered his family into his arms. When their joyous reunion had taken place, Fernando embraced his wife once more, repeating her name over and over, "Fidela, Fidela, Fidela! I never thought I'd see you again! I thought I had lost you forever and would never see you in this world again." He held her tightly and closed his eyes as if in silent prayer.

"Thanks be to God that He has seen fit to unite us again," his wife said as she gave her husband another kiss.

Realizing now that her husband was not alone, she looked at the members of the American Team as they assembled near the fire, grinning with satisfaction, and tried to fix her hair and smooth her skirt. "Why don't you introduce me to your friends, my husband?"

Fernando proudly introduced his wife and children to Nat and his friends. "My new American friends," Fernando said, "this is my wife, Fidela, and my oldest son here," he pulled his son to his side, "is Arturo. My other son is Orlando and my daughter is Sylvia."

Fidela and the children shook hands with each of the Americans and thanked them for coming to their rescue.

After checking to ensure that the Apaches had really left, they made camp. Fidela and the children gathered wood to replenish the fire and a little later all were seated around it when Fernando politely asked where the Americans were going.

"We're not sure yet," Nat replied. "We just want to travel until we find a place that we like and maybe settle down if the Mexican government will give us that privilege. But if it does not, or we can't find a place we like, then we'll head back for the States."

"That's where you're wrong," a voice said downwind of the camp

The members of the American Team jumped to their feet, and whirled with rifles in hand to challenge the stranger.

"Rees!" Nat yelled in a surprised and happy voice. He ran toward Rees who sat his horse some fifty yards down the Vermejo River. He was partly hidden by thickly growing cedars. Rees slid to the ground as Nat reached him and the two gave each other a bear hug. A wide smile creased Nat's face. "You old buzzard, you! You snuck up on me again the same you did when we first met . . . remember? I was by the river with my horse and didn't have my rifle in my hand, but I do now."

"It appears that you have learned the fundamentals of survival," Rees answered as he, too, showed his happiness at being reunited with his friend.

Nat introduced his old friend to the others when they reached the camp fire. "Where are you headed, Rees?" Nat asked.

"Here."

"Here? What do you mean, here?"

"I came to find you because I thought you could use another hand on your cattle drive."

They all stopped eating and glanced at one another and after a few seconds of silence, during which Rees sank his teeth into some venison, Jim asked, "What cattle drive?"

"The one we will make after this territory becomes part of the United States," Rees told him as he continued to chew.

"Is this friend of yours loco?" Three Tongues asked Nat with a grin.

Nat looked from Rees to Three Tongues and said, "After you've had a good meal and good night's rest, you'll feel better," he told Rees.

"I reckon you're right there, laddie," Rees answered.

"Laddie?" Spirit echoed with laughter in her voice. "There's a new one for us."

Nat glanced around the circle and shook his head, signifying that he wanted no one to irritate Rees.

"Let's take a walk, Rees," he said as he rose to his feet and grabbed another piece of venison.

"Why not?" He too, took another piece of venison and rising to his feet, joined Nat as he walked down the bank of the Vermejo.

The American Team watched in silence until Nat and Rees sat down some distance away and began to talk.

"How are your parents?" Nat asked Rees.

"My father died before I reached home after leaving you and Otto, and my mother died six months ago. I had no particular place to go and nothing to keep me in Vincennes any longer, so I decided to look you up."

"I'm sorry to hear about your folks," Nat told him soberly, "but I'm sure glad we're together again."

"Thank you, laddie, I'm glad too," Rees said simply.

"What's all this about a cattle drive, Rees?"

"Laddie, you have been out of touch with what's happening. When I visited Otto to ask about your whereabouts, everyone was talking about how Texas fought and won her independence from Mexico. She has asked to be admitted into the Union and the Mexican goverment has warned the United States that if we do admit Texas as a state, there will be war between the two countries. Mexico feels confident that she can whip the United States. She claims that she has a larger army, her country is larger, and she has the promise of help from some foreign countries, especially England."

"Do you think there's a chance she can whip us?"

"No!" Rees said decisively. "If Mexico takes on the United States, she will lose the war and much of her territory."

"What do you mean losing much of her territory? What territory?"

"New Mexico, for one thing, laddie. That's why I've looked you up. We need to look the area over and find a good location for a ranch and when that location has been found, we should sit on it until it has been taken over by the United States. Then we'll file claim on it and from then on, we'll have our home, a good home, especially for your children."

"Do you really believe what you've just predicted will happen?"

"I'm as sure of it as I am that we're sitting here on the bank of this river!"

"Let's go back to the others and tell them what you've told me, and see what their reaction will be," Nat suggested as he rose.

"Suits me, laddie," Rees rose to his feet and they walked back toward the group.

When they were seated by the fire once more and the moon had disappeared behind the mountain, Rees told them what he predicted, and he elaborated, telling them about what the Americans were beginning to believe about the West. "They call it Manifest Destiny. Many Americans are beginning to believe that it is God's will that the United States extend our system of government, with its freedoms, and justice, to all of the people all the way to the west coast. Some even want to take it farther, into Cuba, Mexico, and farther south. Americans are serious about it, too, it's like a religious calling to them. But many Americans, especially northerners, are beginning to have second thoughts and think that this Manifest Destiny Philosophy is just a cover, so that the people who believe in slavery can spread it into new territory. That's all everyone seems to be talking about. The slave issue comes into every conversation regardless of the subject.

"President Polk wants to bring the Oregon Territory into the union and he says that he'll fight the British if they don't accept the boundary of the fifty-fourth degree of latitude on the north by the forty-second parallel on the south. Below the forty-second parallel is Spanish territory which I believe will become part of the United States in the not too distant future, especially if Mexico is foolish enough to go to war over Texas. The Mexican people are becoming more restless and unhappy with their president, Santa Ana, who has thrown out the Mexican constitution and has assumed dictatorial power. He calls the proclamation under which he seized power, the 'Plan of Cuernavaca'. The Catholic church and the wealthy land owners have joined forces with him in controlling the country. The poor people are very unhappy at these developments."

Here, Fernando interrupted excitedly, "Yes, we heard, even this far away, that the new constitution would have given us the freedom we have dreamed of. Was it true that our constitution was based on yours?"

"Yes, I've heard that it was based upon our Constitution," Rees told him with sympathy. "I didn't realize that this was known this far north; if that is true, the unhappiness with Santa Ana will include unhappiness with the governor of New Mexico, Manuel Armijo, who is said to be one of Santa Ana's cronies.

"This means that we are in unfriendly territory because Armijo hates Americans as much as Santa Ana does."

"When you consider the humiliating defeat Santa Ana suffered at the hands of the Americans," Jim said, "it's not hard to imagine the revenge he must be planning against the United States!"

"Well, the way I see it, when the war with Mexico ends, all of New Mexico and possibly more, will belong to us. This whole fuss with Mexico will decide once and for all if a dictorial system of government will rule this hemisphere, led by Mexico of course, or if a democratic system of government led by the United States will prevail. Personally, I'm placing my bets on the United States," concluded Rees.

When Rees had finished talking, no one spoke for a few minutes until Wilbur cleared his throat and began, "I don't know if you knew I was in the army for a stretch before I went to work for Mr. Muller. I was assigned to the quartermaster corp which is where I first learned how to handle a team of mules. The last half of my stay in the army was with the record keeping office near General Gaines' headquarters. He is the commander of the western department. While I was there, I saw and heard much about our western army. I do not know much of anything about the army east of the Mississippi River, but the army west of the river isn't much, in my opinion. There are maybe eleven thousand men under Gaines' command and, from what I saw of these men, most are immigrants and do not speak English too well. Their weapons were nothing to be proud of and some of the men did not even have uniforms."

"Have you ever hear of Colonel Dodge?" Rees asked of Wilbur.

"No, I don't believe I have."

"Well," Rees went on, "he was put in charge of nearly a quarter of the western army and he has developed it into a topnotch outfit. He also has two crackerjack officers with him by the names of Lieutenant Colonel Stephen Kearny and a youngster who is a good strategist by the name of Jefferson Davis. When war comes with Mexico, as I'm sure it will, I believe we could build an army around this core. Our country has many men from Arkansas, Missouri, Tennessee, Kentucky, and Louisiana who are familiar enough with weapons to fill the ranks of any army which can wipe out whatever the Mexicans can put into the field. People from all over our country went to help Texas win her independence, people like those who made up two companies of cavalry from New Orleans, the New Orleans Braves. When freedom is assaulated, you'll find Americans ready to fight in defence of that freedom, whether it be in the United States or in Mexico.

"Do you have any comments about what Rees has been saying?" Nat asked as he glanced around the circle.

"No country that does not give its people freedom can withstand a country that does. We will win." Jim stated flatly as he puffed on his pipe.

"You have a great team here," Rees commented as he looked around.

"The Macedonian, the mule skinner, the Comanche warrior and his mother and sister, and you, my friend," Rees said as he looked at Nat. "And now Fernando and his family. Quite impressive."

"How did you know that Jim was the Macedonian?" Nat realized even as he spoke that Otto must have filled him in as to who traveled with him.

"Otto told you, right?"

"Right," Rees answered.

"And now we have a French Canadian mountain men who is known throughout the west as one of the cleverest if not the most clever in the mountains," Spirit commented with a smile. "I agree with Rees, we do have a formidable force."

"Señor," Fernando now spoke up politely, "would you permit humble people such as myself and my family to join up with you? We would be no bother. Please señor, give us your permission. We have no home now and no place to go."

"Yes, Fernando," Spirit told him eagerly, "but please, do not feel that you are not the equal to any of the rest of us. You will be an American shortly if our new friend, Rees is correct. That means you must act like an American, you must convince yourself of that fact."

"Thank you, señora," Fernando replied, "we will not disappoint you, we will make good Americans and will prove our loyalty to our very new, as yet unborn, country."

"Well, there you go, Rees," Nat told him confidently. "We will find and develop a great ranch together!"

"Are those pantaloons comfortable?" Wilbur now asked Fernando.

"Si."

"What is the purpose of having the legs split on the sides to the knees and what is the reason for the buttons to either side of the split?" asked Wilbur.

"They are split up the legs so that when unbottoned your legs can enjoy the cool air . . . it can get pretty hot in some parts of New Mexico," Fernando explained.

Wilbur asked no more questions about Fernando's dress but observed the colorful shirt which he wore, and vest which was decorated with one of the most beautiful designs Wilbur had ever seen. He could see the corn shucks in Fernando's pocket with which he rolled his cigarettes. He noticed Fernando carried a flint and steel with which he lit his cigarettes. He thought to himself that it would be a fine thing to have Fernando, Fidela and their children as a part of their team. He would learn much from them.

CHAPTER XI

The years passed uneventfully and the American Team roamed widely over the area encompassed by New Mexico.

They were now a formidable fighting unit, especially after Fernando, his wife and children were added to their number. His son, Arturo, now age fourteen, younger son Orlando who was twelve and their sister who was ten were all taught to use the pistol and rifle. Nat's and Snow Skin's three sons, Clark, named after the famous Indian fighter George Rogers Clark, was ten years old. Henri who was eight, was named after Rees's father and his third son, Comanche, named in honor of Snow Skin's father, was six years of age. Nat gave his three sons almost daily lessons in throwing a knife and using the pistol and rifle.

The three women and Sylvia had shed their women's clothing and wore buckskins as did the men. Each wore a pistol strapped on one hip and knife on the other and all were expert in the use of both weapons.

They had spent the years traveling throughout New Mexico, searching for the right spot in which to begin ranching. Their first winter had been spent on the shores of Eagle Nest Lake between Cimarron and Taos, but when spring came, they moved on farther west. The Eagle Nest area seemed to them to provide too short a summer and too long a winter for it to be good for year around ranching. Chama was a rerun of the Eagle Nest area so they moved into the Animas Valley near Durango, but this too was given up because most of the good large tracts of land were already taken.

They had spent two seasons trapping the Animas River for beaver, and the surrounding area for bear, wolves, fox, and other critters of the high Colorado mountains. Their trapping venture proved to be extremely rewarding and the American Team decided to take their furs into Santa Fe to trade them, then head south toward Apache country. They believed that they would be more successful in finding what they wanted there for others avoided that area because of the Apaches.

Fernando told the others that from what he had heard, the country around the Gallinas and Jicarilla Mountains had few if any settlers. Most of the people preferred the safety of the Rio Grande settlements westward, thereby leaving a good part of that area to the Apaches, coyotes and wolves.

The American Team broke camp in the spring of 1845 and headed for Santa Fe, intending to stop over at the ranch of Fernando's cousin who lived at Abiquiu on the Chama River. As the women cooked their meal over an open fire on their first night out on the trail, they realized, as did the men, that they had been followed since leaving the Durango country.

"When do you think they will strike?" Wilbur asked as he ate some of Fidela's atole.

The other men glanced at one another, but said nothing, some of them dipping their tortillas into chili while others chewed on venison which was cooked in frijoles. Finally Jim said, "Why don't we get it over with by giving Ortega and his band of misfits the opportunity to take our trappins'?"

"Suits me," Rees commented as he took a drink of coffee.

"Let's do it tonight," Three Tongues said. He beckoned to the others to move close to the fire so they could talk together more easily.

They agreed upon a plan of strategy and an hour after sundown, it was put into play. All of the men and Arturo slipped off into the forest while the women and children threw more wood on the fire, making more noise then usual. Some of the bundles of furs were camouflaged to give the appearance that the others had already turned in. After an hour had passed, Ortega stepped out from behind his hiding place and yelled, "I have your camp surrounded and if anyone moves, they will be killed!"

Spirit turned toward Ortega quickly and said, "Who are you and what do you want?"

"Señora, my name is Ortega," the bandit chief said as he aimed his rifle at the ones around the fire, "my men have your camp surrounded."

"I don't believe you," Snow Skin slowly rose to her feet.

"You don't believe me?" Ortega took two steps toward the fire in rage and disbelief and gave the command which was supposed to bring his men from their hiding places which circled the camp. One man stepped forth. Ortega bellowed his command once more but no one else appeared. "Where are the others, Vicente?" Ortega growled. Before Vicente could reply, a knife flew through the air, striking him in the center of the back. The bandit fell forward and was dead before he hit the ground.

"What took you so long, muchacho?' Fernando asked his son as he stepped into the firelight from the darkness behind Ortega.

Ortega whirled to face Fernando as he commanded angrily, "Drop the rifle, señor, Your men are all dead."

"You lie!" Ortega yelled once more for his men to appear, but he called in vain and instead of his men appearing, the men of the American Team stepped from the darkness into the light of the campfire.

Ortega started to raise his rifle at Fernando, but before it reached his waist, Fernando fired and Ortega fell dead. "These bandits have killed and plundered for the last time," he commented grimly as he turned Ortega's body over with his foot. "Everyone in northern New Mexico feared him and his men. He was so feared that many families disciplined their children by saying that if they did not behave Ortega would get them. Now they will have to invent another fear to make their children behave! We will be heros to my people for destroying their scrouge."

"One of them escaped," Arturo interruped.

"No, son," Rees told him, "he was not with the bandits. He is a Mexican army scout and I let him slip away to report what happened here."

When the American Team reached Fernando's cousin's ranch at Abiquiu, they were told that the governor had ordered the army to capture the Americans and bring them in on spy charges. Upon hearing this report, the Americans decided that the best course to follow was not to run, but to evade the Mexican authorities when and where possible as they traveled to the Gallinas area. Once they reached their goal, they would build a fortress which would be sturdy enough to withstand any Mexican or Apache assult. There they could sit tight until that area became part of the United States. The Apaches, the American Team reasoned, would help deter intrusion by the Mexican authorities.

But first, the furs must be sold and a plan was worked out whereby everyone except Rees and Jim would travel to Santa Fe in small parties of two or three persons. Once arrived there, the small groups would disperse and mingle with the people, thereby hindering detection. For self defense they would try to be in the vicinity of the fur buying post, and able to help one another if any were detected.

Jim and Rees would bring in the pack horses laden with the furs to trade. The American Team believed that only two trappers would arouse little suspicion and thus they would avoid trouble with the authorities. Salazar would be looking for the whole little band and separately the American Team hoped to slip through his fingers before they headed south. And, it must be admitted, they enjoyed the prospect of entering Santa Fe and under the noses of the authorities!

The Palace of Governors, or The Royal House as it was once called, occupied the entire north side of the Santa Fe plaza. It was a massive building which housed the governor's living quarters as well as the administrative offices for the state. The entire area was enclosed by an adobe wall within which were the various buildings necessary to support the compound, such as the stables, blacksmith shop, commissary, and others. The parade grounds, barracks, mess halls, and kitchens were included in this walled perimeter. The numerous buildings confined within the space also included the legislative chamber and office space. The entire government complex was located on the same ground where and Indian pueblo had once stood.

Many of the rooms of the Palace of the Governors were small, and were heated by adobe fireplaces set into a corner of each room. They were furnished with crudely built furniture and a smattering of finer pieces which had been imported from Mexico City. Access was from one room to another eliminating the use of hallways. The adobe walls throughout the sprawling complex in the governmental enclosure were massive, perhaps thirty-six inches in width, making it a fortress in itself. One could understand why the Spanish authorities, during the pueblo revolt of 1680, rallied their forces and settlers behind such a barrier. In fact they were dislodged from this impregnable position only after the Indians were able to cut off their water supply.

The Santa Fe Trail entered the city from the east and turned north a few blocks from the oldest church in New Mexico. The wagon trains which were finally ending their long treks from the United States next would cross the Rio de Santa Fe and head for the plaza and other locations where they would dispense their trading goods.

It was on one of those clear, crisp March mornings which were so common in Santa Fe that those in the Palace of Governors were startled to hear the loud, angry voice of Governor Armijo as he bellowed, "Salazar! Salazar!" The governor turned to his aide and bellowed again, "Find Salazar and tell him I wish to speak with him immediately!"

"Yes, your Excellency!" The aide scurried from the office of the irate governor.

When he had departed, the governor looked up from behind his desk at a soldier who stood at attention before him. "Sit down," he barked to Amando Lucero. He returned to the written report which he had been studying. "There cannot be any mistake about the whereabouts of these Americans when this happened. Are you sure that they killed Ortega and his band of cutthroats?"

"It is no mistake, your Excellency, they were the ones. I, myself witnessed the battle from start to finish. I, too, could have been killed if one of the Americanos had wished it to be, but he permitted me to slip away because he knew I was not with Ortega."

"How did he know that?" Armijo scowled at this.

"I do not know, your Excellency."

"These Americans are no fools," Armijo answered as he rose and began to pace the room. "Where is Salazar?"

"Here, your Excellency," Salazar answered as he hurriedly entered the room.

"The Americanos whom we are looking for have killed Ortega and his men," the governor told Salazar.

"Are you sure, your Excellency?"

Armijo stopped pacing abruptly and stared at Salazar, saying in a menacing voice, "Are you calling me a liar?"

"No, your Excellency, but I find it hard to believe that Ortega is dead. We have been trying for years to capture him, without success. He has always been able to evade us."

"One of your scouts," Armijo motioned to Lucero, "says that he saw the whole thing."

"It is true, mi capitan, I saw Ortega and his men killed by the Americanos with my own eyes."

"These Americans have done us a favor, capitan, but I still want them arrested and brought in to me. They are spies of the United States. I know it! For what other reason would they keep traveling all over New Mexico? They are probing for our weaknesses and if we do not capture them soon, they will leave New Mexico and report to their superiors. Salazar, select some men and see if you can overtake the Americanos, they should be in the Abiquiu area. Make sure you take enough men, I don't want those spies to slip away." Armijo waved his hand imperiously at the departing soldiers.

Salazar had been gone two days when one of the palace guards poked his head into the governor's office and said, "Excuse me, your Excellency, Sargeant Lopez wishes to speak with you. He says it is urgent."

The governor was busily writing and did not look up as he absently answered, "Send him in."

"Your Excellency!" Sargeant Lopez came to attention and saluted.

"Yes, yes, what is it? Can't you see that I am busy? What do you want?"

"Your Excellency, I believe that I have spotted some of the Americano spies."

The governor jerked his head up and rose to this feet quickly. "What did you say?"

"I believe I saw two of the Americano spies, your Excellency," came the sargeant's reply.

"Where?"

212

"At Antonio Gutierrez's Fur Company, your Excellency."

"Are you sure?"

"Yes, your Excellency."

"Salazar!"

The orderly entered the office and reminded the governor that Salazar had left two days before for Abiquiu.

"When I need him he is never around," snorted the governor. "Send for Lieutenant Herrera, quickly!"

Within minutes, the lieutenant appeared before the governor and after receiving his orders, left to gather some of his men.

Jim led the pack horses and Rees rode drag as they walked their horses up the dusty streets of Santa Fe. All went well and Jim dismounted in front of the buyer's warehouse, nodding to Rees to tie his horse to a hitching rack and then went into the store. In a few minutes, Jim came back out, accompanied by the owner. The Mexican inspected a few furs and then said, "Bring the horses in, señors, we will unpack the furs so that I can have a closer examination of your merchandise. They looked like top quality, but you can understand that I must inspect each of them before I can offer a price."

A bargain was struck and Jim and Rees had left the compound of the warehouse and entered the street when thirty or more mounted Mexican soldiers, equipped with long steel-tipped lances bearing small flags, confronted them. 'Your names, please, señores?' The officer spoke politely although in a firm voice which was accompanied by an unfriendly stare.

A crowd of people quickly gathered to see why the soldiers were there and Jim and Rees saw the various members of the American team make their way toward the front of the crowd where they watched the soldiers whose attention was fixed upon Jim and Rees.

"What's wrong?" Rees spoke as his eyes moved over the troop of soldiers.

"Your name, señor?" The officer reminded him as he shifted in his saddle.

"My name is Rees and this fellow with me is Jim," Rees told him politely.

The officer's looked at Rees and then turned to look searchingly at Jim. "Are you alone?"

"I don't understand," Rees protested.

"Don't play games with me, gringo," the officer retorted as he stiffened in his saddle. "Where are the rest of your people?"

"We seem to be all there are," Jim said with a slight smile.

The Mexican officer jerked his glare from Rees and stared once more at Jim. "Don't take me for a fool! I know who you are and I also know that you have just come in from the Chama country. Lay down your arms you are under arrest."

At this moment, Rees and Jim raised their rifles and fired, killing the officer and one other and then dove for cover behind a nearby wall. People fled in panic as shots could be heard coming from all directions. Soldiers fell, not knowing where the shots came from. After the American Team had fired their first round, many soldiers lay dead in the street. The team then drew their pistols and fired them again and more soliders fell, either dead or wounded, before they could locate the owners of the guns being used against them. Two Mexican soldiers spurred their horses into a rapid retreat and the American Team quickly mounted their horses and driving their pack horses before them, made a dash up the road toward the open country, amidst screaming and running spectators. They rode eastward, toward Las Vegas, and as they rode, one at a time, they pulled off and hid among trees until only Rees and Jim were left as they drove the pack horses before them.

"Slow down, Jim," Rees called, "we don't want to outrun the soldiers . . . not yet, anyway."

The governor sat down behind his desk, smoothed his hair into place, adjusted the collar of his uniform and bellowed, "Orderly!"

"Yes, your Excellency," the orderly replied as he hurried into the office.

"How do I look? Is everything proper? I want to look my best when these spies are brought before me."

"Everything looks fine, your Excellency," the orderly reported.

The governor waited and drummed his fingers on the desk. "Santa Ana will reward me handsomely for this," he mused in a voice barely audible.

Shots ran out and the governor jumped to his feet and shouted, "I want them alive, Herrera, you fool, I want them alive!" He rushed from behind his desk, through the palace and out onto the portal. He saw people screaming and fleeing in panic as they ran down the street, and saw a cavalryman galloping toward the palace.

"What has happened?" The governor called to one of the sentries, "Go and find out!"

The sentry had taken only a few steps before riderless horses came racing into the plaza. Among them rode two soldiers, who upon seeing the governor in front of the palace, forced their way through the horses and hurried to tell him what had happened.

By this time, soldiers were running on foot from their barracks to the corrals and once saddled, their officers led them to the front of the Palace of the Governors.

"The Americanos were last seen leaving town going east toward Vegas. After them!" The governor was pale with rage and frustration.

"Here they come!" Jim pulled his horse to a walk and glanced behind them once more to look at the cloud of dust which surrounded the Mexican soldiers.

When the long line of soldiers were within the scope of the hidden American Team, they opened fire, completely surprising and dispersing those who were not killed. Those fortunate ones wheeled their mounts and raced back toward the safety of Santa Fe.

Now the American Team mobilized quickly and continued eastward, realizing that their safety lay in Comanche country until they could turn westward again.

After leaving the scene of their latest rout with the Mexican soldiers, they traveled until they reached the Pecos River and followed it southeast, camping beside it that night. Before sunup they were in the saddle again and rode until they had reached the safety of the open plains. When they reached the juncture of the Gallinas and Pecos rivers, they turned south, stopping at Pintada for some much needed rest.

After three days of rest, the group rode to Pinos Wells where they decided to make camp and check out the surrounding countryside as a possible location for a ranch. After two weeks of exploring, during which not a living soul was seen, they found exceptionally good rangeland everywhere.

A high knoll was located which all agreed seemed to be the perfect site for the ranch headquarters. From the top of this mesa, one could see for miles. To the east, the pinons, cedars and juniper grew more and more sparse until nothing lay beyond them but an ocean of gramma grass, belly high to a horse. To the west, the hills rose higher and the trees and brush grew thicker and taller.

Four temporary log cabins were erected, one for Nat and his family, another for Fernando and his family, one for Jim and Spirit, and the fourth for the rest of the men. Their first winter there was spent in the newly built cabins, but when the usual mild weather of February came, Fernando and his son, Orlando were sent to Las Vegas to find out what was happening in the relationship between Mexico and the United States.

Not a single person had passed that way during the winter, not even the Apaches, so if the American Team wished for any news, someone must go some place where civilization existed; they had decided upon Las Vegas. The two Mexicans would be less conspicuous than the others.

The American Team waited patiently for three weeks until Fernando and Orlando returned. "The war is on, and Las Vegas is in the hands of the Americans," Fernando reported. "People of Las Vegas surrendered to an American general by the name of Kearny, the one you told us about, Rees, with hardly a shot being fired. Once the Americans reached the vicinity of the town, apparently the people who had heard what Santa Ana had planned for New Mexico were glad to see the Americans."

"What did Santa Ana have up his sleeve?" asked Rees with interest.

"It seems that he had planned to pay Mexico's debts by selling New Mexico and California to France, Germany, or England, or in fact to any other country who might be interested. When the people in Las Vegas heard these reports they decided that if they could not remain as part of Mexico, they would choose the United States as their adopted country. No one wanted to be a colony of some European power.

"Kearny then marched on toward Santa Fe. The governor spread the word that if the Americans took Santa Fe the people would be sold into slavery. Some of the priests, I understand, helped to spread these rumors. The people built barricades outside of Santa Fe at Apache Pass and waited for the Americans to come. Armijo, however, had all of his gold and other valuables packed and loaded into wagons just in case the Americans breached the defenses.

"Many of the Indians and peons had only lances, and bows and arrows with which to fight. Just before Kearny reached the barricades, Armijo rushed back to Santa Fe, took his wagons, and fled southward. Apparently, he had made the effort he had because he didn't want Santa Ana to think he hadn't put up any resistance. Whatever the reason for his actions, when they heard of it, some of the people fled also.

"Anyway, now Santa Fe is in the hands of the Americans and Kearny has left for California, and other Americans have taken the war into Mexico south of the Rio Grande and are pushing Santa Ana's army before them on every front. It seems that it is only a matter of time before the war is over!" Fernando finished triumphantly.

Nat looked at Rees, smiled and said, "You were right again."

"Now we can go for the cattle," Rees replied, taking Nat's compliment as a matter of course.

"Where are we going for them and how many do you think we should buy?" asked Wilbur.

"I figure our trappins' money should buy about five thousand head," Jim said, "what do you think Nat?"

"It's a figure we can hope for now; we won't know for sure how many we can buy until we get to Texas.

"I think we should buy the cattle somewhere near the Pecos River, and drive them back along the river. In that way, we will eliminate any trouble with the Indians. As you know, that country is Comanche territory. Although the Lipan Apache could give us trouble in the Cave of the Bats area."

"That sounds like good thinking to me," Rees said, "but how far down the Pecos will we have to travel to find cattle?"

"I have never traveled into Texas," Fernando said. "I was born and lived my entire life on the Vermejo Ranch or near it, but I have heard my whole life about the San Antonio de Bexar area. There are many large rancheros there and there seems to me to be a good place to build a herd."

"When do we start?" Arturo spoke eagerly.

"Is in the morning early enough for you, son?" Nat asked with a smile.

CHAPTER XII

During the days after they reached the San Antonio de Bexar country, they were continually adding to their sizable herd. They purchased cows and bulls from many different ranches and when the cattle were purchased at each location, Wilbur's job was to count them. For every hundred which passed through the gates, Wilbur tied a knot in his tally string. Over fifteen hundred head were bought from one ranch alone and part of the deal made with this ranch was that the ranch foreman Travis, an experienced cattleman, would take charge of the drive and deliver them to the ranch of the American Team with their help.

Travis Baxter purchased a chuckwagon and started to hire a cook, but the Americans told him that their women could do both the cooking and drive the wagons. Travis, after some heated discussion, finally conceded that the women could handle it, but only after a display of marksmanship by the three women. "If they can shoot that well, they ought to be able to dish up some grub."

"They're just as good with horses and wagons," Jim said to Travis as the women slid their rifles back into their saddle scabbards.

"God help anyone who messes with this outfit!" Travis said with a grin. He went on more quietly, "Gather around me, everyone, for since the herd moves out in the morning, I'll instruct you now in the daily routine and night duty as well. But for starters, I don't want anyone pushing the cattle. Old Sam, the lead steer, will lead the way and the others will follow. Cattle will balk if they are driven too hard. The secret of moving cattle is to let them move at their own pace just as long as they are moving in the right direction. They will be no problem if they think they're not being rushed. We have a remuda of horses so don't overwork any one of them. A good cowboy takes care of his horses, so if you think the horse you are riding is beginning to tire, change him. I know all of you are familiar with horses, but being familiar with them and using them on a cattle drive is two different things. I don't want any horse overworked.

"Ladies, I want the chuckwagon to take the lead. You'll need to go on ahead to find water and wood or whatever fuel is available, and begin cooking, so that when we get there it will be ready. I also want the chuckwagon open and available to all of us at all times, day or night. I'll leave the assigning of the shifts to you ladies, and I'll leave it to you to choose your own boss. It has been my experience that well fed men are happier on the trail and do not get as irritable as long as their bellies are full.

"We'll have an added worry on this drive and that is the Mexican problem. I don't have to remind you that we are at war with Mexico and they seem to think that the war gives them the license to do as they please and not answer to the law. Most Mexicans are law abiding and will not give us trouble. It's the renegades, both Mexican and Anglo, with whom we will concern ourselves. Many Mexicans in Texas oppose Santa Ana and fought with us to gain our independence. Remember, they are Texans as much as the Anglos are, for their blood was spilled at San Jacinto along side ours. To me, everyone who is a citizen of Texas is a Texan regardless of his heritage. I fought with Sam Houston and many of his soldiers died driving Santa Ana and the likes of him out of Texas, so as far as I am concerned, all Texans are just that. I don't want to hear anyone make the distinction of calling some of us Anglo Texans and other Mexican Texans."

"We go even a little farther than that, Travis. All of us include the Indian in our reference to Americans," Jim told him.

Travis looked at Three Tongues and said, "I stand corrected. It seems that I have fallen in with good, down to earth people. It will be my pleasure to act as your trail boss."

"The pleasure is ours," Spirit said.

"Let's turn in because we will be up way before sunrise," Travis suggested.

A hasty breakfast was eaten the next morning and then the chuckwagon moved out to the front of the herd. Fidela was to drive the chuckwagon on the first shift. Her horse was tied to the tailgate of the wagon as it rolled away from the camp. Snow Skin drove the bed wagon and the others rode beside her. From a distance the women were indistinguisable from the men in their buckskin clothing. Fidela's voice was heard in the calm, crisp, morning air as she yelled encouragement to her mules.

Three Tongues rode well in advance of the herd as scout. The chuckwagon rolled on, searching for the proper place to stop and prepare the next meal.

Wilbur covered the east flank of the herd, the west flank Fernando, and Arturo and Orlando were the point men. Rees, took up his position west of the lead cattle and Spirit came back to ride east of the lead cattle. Their job was to stay back from the lead cattle a short distance and keep them from spreading out too far. Nat and Jim rode drag, keeping the trailers from escaping altogether. Travis oversaw the entire drive, riding here and there continually.

The riders walked their horses as they watched the cattle graze now and then and then move slowly northward. The herd was strung out over a considerable distance. After the herd had been on the trail nearly three hours, Travis rode to each of them and suggested that they change to a fresh horse.

They had covered perhaps twelve miles at the end of their first day on the trail.

"Why quit so early?" Nat asked. "There should be at least another hour before sundown."

"The cattle need time to graze and find a location on which to bed down. Ease up, Nat, give the cattle a little time to rest. They're much easier to handle if they aren't hurried. Let them mosey over to the river to drink and just mill around."

It was a still Texas night with only a very slight breeze when the cattle began to bed down on a little rise. They seemed to appreciate the refreshing breeze just as much as their herders did.

"Ride around the herd slowly," Travis cautioned his riders, "and work them inward gradually until they're pretty much together and then ease off." The cattle were beginning to lie down now in large numbers.

Night herders were assigned for three-hour shifts. The night herders rode slowly around the cattle and either talked to them softly or sang as best they could. The quiet sounds lulled the cattle who lay chewing their cuds or sleeping.

The rest of the crew ate the meal which the women had prepared and then turned in for they would do their turn at night herding later. Each cowboy had at least one blanket and a wagon sheet to protect him from rain. By the end of the second day, all knew their routines, duties, and responsibilities and carried them out faithfully and efficiently.

Heavy clouds began to gather in the east on the morning of their fifteenth day on the trail. By noon, light rain began to fall and Travis gave orders that the drive be halted and the cattle be permitted to graze and rest.

He further instructed that if a lightning storm should spook the cattle into a stampede, they were to try to keep the cattle together as best they could until they began to tire and they could turn them. "The main job you'll have is to try to keep them together and strung out in one line. This is Mesquite country so keep your chaps on at all times. If you should need them in a hurry, you won't have time to put them on."

By this time the rain was pouring down heavily and lightning cracked the sky. The cattle began to move about restlessly, not grazing, and the herders talked to them soothingly as they rode around them. The lightning increased until a bolt hit the ground not far from the herd, who had hardly needed that to start them to run. Snow Skin glanced back and raced the chuckwagon out of the path of the oncoming cattle. Everyone not already in their saddle mounted quickly and rode to try to stay with the herd. Pouring rain, lightning, and the thick mesquite made their job that much harder, but with superb effort they managed to keep most of the cattle together. The sudden storm began to move on, the lightning ceased, and with the reappearance of the sun, the herders begin to push their charges back the way they had come, though at a more respectable pace.

"We'll stop and camp for the rest of the day and begin early tomorrow morning," Travis told them. "It will give the cattle time to settle down and graze and rest, and by morning they should be ready to move again."

Some of the men rode herd while the rest sat near the chuckwagon drinking coffee.

"How far do you think we have come?" Wilbur asked.

"Better than two hundred miles," Travis estimated.

"That means we still have at least four hundred miles or more to cover," Nat observed as he lowered his cup from his lips.

"At least, maybe more," Travis answered. "That translates into a month or more on the trail if we're not held up for any reason."

Hoofbeats could be heard and everyone looked up as Three Tongues rode in. He dismounted, dropped his reins, and walked to the wagon to pour himself a cup of coffee.

"What's out there?" Travis looked up inquiringly.

"Nothing but miles of empty space," Three Tongues told him as he took a sip of the scalding coffee.

"Any creeks or arroyos nearby?" Travis asked.

"There's a creek maybe seven miles or so ahead of us," Three Tongues replied.

"How steep are the banks of the creek?"

"Pretty steep, maybe ten feet."

"Cattle can't climb that steep a bank. How deep is the water?"

"I'd guess three feet deep."

"We'll have to hold the herd here, then, until we cut some of that bank away." Travis took his coffee cup to the wagon and told them, "Let's get to our saddles, someone get the shovels and the pick from the wagons."

"What are we going to do?" Fernando asked.

"Cut a path through the creek bank," Travis replied. "If we don't the cattle won't be able to reach the water or if they do, they'll pile up on one another and some will drown while the others are trampled. We'll have to cut a path for the wagons, anyway. Once we cave in the bank on either side a good distance, we'll funnel the cattle through the gap. Otherwise the lead cattle will be forced by the ones behind them to jump off the steep bank. I don't have to explain all the trouble we could have in that case. When we're ready to drive the cattle across the creek, as I said, we'll form two lines to funnel them across."

The men searched for quite a distance along the creek before they were forced to begin digging out the steep side of the rushing stream. They worked the remainder of the day at the creek and it was after dark when they returned to camp once more.

The next morning the women fed everyone and prepared to move out but not before Fidela fed Old Sam some left over tortillas. She then climbed to the seat of the wagon, adjusted her holster on her hip and moved out, with Old Sam following close behind.

When they neared the creek, the men drove the cattle slowly and all of the others, including the women, helped to form the funnel which would guide the cattle. But as the herd neared the creek, they balked and would not cross. When the men began to push them, they began to scatter. "What do we do now, Travis?"

"Let's rope a few of them and pull them toward the creek and maybe the others will follow."

A few of the men took down their ropes and roping some of the nearest cows, began to pull them toward the creek, but they dug in their feet and had to be dragged. "Slack off, boys," Travis advised, "if we have to drag them bawling across the creek, the rest won't go. Turn them loose."

Spirit broke off from her position as part of the funnel and riding over to Travis, she said, "Why don't you rope a few calves and pull them across the creek? I'll bet their mothers won't hesitate long when they hear their calves bawling. And when they cross, maybe the rest will follow them."

"That sounds like a right good idea," Travis said with a grin. "Let's give it a try."

The calves were roped and as they were pulled from their mothers' sides and away from the herd, the mothers hesitated only briefly before breaking from the herd to catch up with their calves. Some of the cattle in the herd watched the cows for a few seconds and then began to follow them tentatively. More joined in until finally the herd was once more moving slowly. When the last cows had their fill of water and crossed the creek, Travis ordered that the herd be kept moving. It had taken most of the rest of that day to water and move all of them across the little creek, so it wasn't long before the day's drive was called to a halt. The cattle seemed content as they milled around and found some higher ground which was carpeted in thick buffalo grass. This would be good bedding and fodder.

The evening sky was clear and the stars were brilliant. An evening breeze came flowing in from the west and bent the tops of the tall grasses. The cattle seemed to appreciate the cool breeze and began to lie down and chew their cuds.

The drovers could be heard as they walked their horses slowly around the herd, gently pushing them into a relatively compact circle. Some of them talked to the cattle and others used their horses to nudge them inward toward the higher ground where several hundred cattle already lay.

Orlando, Wilbur, and Arturo took the first watch. To calm the cattle, Arturo had developed his whistling skills while the others were content to sing softly as they circled the herd.

The men rode a short distance from the outer perimeter of the cattle riding in oppisite directions so that they met occasionally as they rode around the herd. The women had finished feeding their menfolk and were cleaning up while some of the men still lingered near the fire, drinking coffee. Their bedrolls were scattered on all sides. When they turned in later, they would shed little but their boots for who knew when they would be needed in a hurry, and time was of the essence in times of emergency. The precious time spent dressing could make the difference between the emergency becoming a disaster or being controlled.

When the women had finished their chores, they joined the men by the softly glowing fire. All was peaceful and quiet as some of the men smoked their pipes, sending a pleasant aroma floating through the air. Others still sipped their coffee and others leaned back quietly looking into the flames or staring into the starry heavens. The silence was finally broken by Rees who first chuckled to himself. His low laughter caused everyone to turn to look at him. He shook his head, still laughing softly.

"What's the matter, Reese?" Nat asked as he removed his pipe from his mouth.

"Nothing is the matter," Rees replied, "unless you want to consider our mixture of national origins as a concern. Look around this campfire for a minute. What do you see? I don't know if you see what I see, but I see a Macedonian, a French Canadian, some who are part Comanche, some who are Mexicans and two Americans of English and Scottish descent, and we are all friends, in fact have become a close knit family. No one anywhere could be any closer to one another than we are. We take this union for granted, but it augurs well for the future of this young country. In reality it is a union that is rare and if, in this imperfect world in which we live there were some way to capture this intimate feeling and bottle it, we could put an end to much of the woes of the world. Each of us has locked up in our heads stories of our forefathers that are unimaginable to the rest of us. Stories which each of us are unwilling to share because we imagine that the others would not understand or care to hear. What are the prides, prejudices, and sufferings which we all harbor in the individual secret sactuaries of our brains? We are not Irish-Americans, German-Americans, Mexican-Americans . . . we are Americans, one and all. Such terms only tend to separate Americans from each other." Rees grinned as he began to fill his pipe once more.

Before dawn the following morning, the women had finished with breakfast and had moved the wagons to the front of the herd once more, with Old Sam following eagerly in their wake.

The herd continued to move slowly northward as the sun's rays lit up the clear blue eastern skies and, within a few minutes, the rim of the sun made its quiet entrance as it spread its life spreading warmth over the peaceful landscape. The prairie grasses seemed to bow their heads eastward as though in prayer to the sun who once again honored the earth with its presence. A light gentle breeze now began to strengthen as it fought the sun for the moisture which had accumulated on the grass during the night.

The American Team had now reached the area not far from the cave known as the Cave of the Bats. Not many days ahead, the team would reach the country of the Bottomless Lakes where the Comanches had once held their grand council meeting.

They saw Three Tongues lope his horse toward the east and following him with their eyes saw the three Comanches who sat their ponies on one of the many rolling hills which blanketed the area for many miles. Three Tongues met them and they sat motionless as they talked, and then Three Tongues wheeled his pony and the four rode toward the herd at a brisk trot.

Travis beckoned to Rees, Nat, and Jim to join him and the four of them rode to meet the approaching riders.

"Many Horses!" Nat called a greeting to his old friend.

"We thank the spirits for permitting us to meet once again," Many Horses replied while still at a distance.

Travis was duly introduced to the Comanche warriors after which the Comanches told them, "I guess you know you have visitors west of you."

"What visitors?" Travis asked in surprise.

"Apaches," Many Horses told him, "maybe forty of them. They are surely a raiding party because they are traveling light. My guess is that they are after your cattle and whatever else they can take from you. I have thirty-five warriors hiding three hills east of us. We are ready and anxious to help you to fight the Apaches."

"Do the Apaches know that you are near?" Rees asked.

"I don't think so," came Many Horse's quick reply.

"Let's turn the tables on them and surprise them before they surprise us," Rees suggested as he rested both hands on his saddle horn and leaned forward toward Many Horses.

"What do you mean, exactly?" Nat looked interested.

"I say let's take our American Team and ride to meet the Apaches, leaving the Comanches to watch over the herd," Rees suggested.

"The Apaches may send some of their braves after our cattle once we confront them and are away from the herd," Jim grinned, "they'll be thinking that taking the herd will be as easy as taking candy from a baby. The main body of them will be thinking that they can destroy our small party easily, but when the other Apaches reach the herd, Many Horses and his braves will be waiting for them and will attack and drive them toward the location of the battle which we will, by then, be fighting. Together with our Comanches allies, we should have little trouble in routing the Apaches."

Nat turned to Travis and told him, "I'll take charge now, Travis, I've had more experience then you for what we are now to embark on."

"I agree," Travis said with a grin. "I've never really looked very hard for such experience."

"What Rees and Jim have suggested sounds good to me," Nat went on, "let's put it into action!" He turned now to Many Horses and said, "let's leave the herd, wagons, and children in your care."

Upon hearing this, Many Horses sent one brave to bring back the rest of the Comanches that were waiting for them and Three Tongues rode to the front to bring back the wagons.

When the American Team was assembled, Snow Skin and Spirit sat on their horses as the proud Comanches they had been. Nat rode to their left flank and Jim to their right, next to Spirit. Three Tongues asked Snow Skin and Spirit to let him ride in between them. Fidela and Sylvia rode up to the left of Nat, and Arturo, Orlando, and Fernando joined them to the left. Rees sat to one side watching the formation develop and when all were in line, he motioned for Wilbur to line up on Jim's right and Travis on Fernando's left. He then rode to join Wilbur. Now all were abreast and Nat stood in his stirrups and looked down the line to his left and then to his right. He noticed them checking their weapons.

"Is everyone ready?" The word ready echoed down the line. "Then, let's move out!" Nat yelled.

The horizontal line moved slowly and the riders carried their rifles cradled in their arms.

"Today, my son, we avenge the death of your father," Spirit said although she looked straight ahead. She wore a determined look on her pale face.

Three Tongues answered, "Yes, my mother, this is our day." He glanced now at his sister and she looked back. She exhibited no emotion, but he saw a spirit of revenge in her eyes as they gazed into his.

The men, at different times, glanced at the women and then sat back in their saddles, confident that they would prove to be good fighters. When they saw the Apaches ahead of them, the line halted. The Apaches appeared as frozen statues, sitting their horses quietly and only their hair moved as the westerly breeze blew it into their faces.

"We seek no trouble," Nat called, "let us pass unmolested. We have no quarrel with you or your people."

Not a single Apache moved after Nat's request.

"They're determined to fight us," Rees remarked in a low voice as he continued to watch them closely.

"But why?" was Wilbur's question.

"They believe that they have the upper hand and are convinced that they can win with miminal losses, which is the Apache way," Three Tongues said.

"They came to take our cattle," Spirit said, "and they intend to take them and kill us, regardless of what we do."

"Let's see if mother is right," Three Tongues said as he squeezed his heels into the side of his horse. His horse pranced out perhaps twenty-five steps in front of the American Team and then he reined him in and sat motionless for a moment and then signaled that he wanted to engage in single combat with an Apache. It was then that the first Apache moved and the one who moved raised his hand and then dropped it. Ten Apaches galloped toward the herd as they yelled their battle cry.

"Are they in for a surprise," Nat muttered as he stared straight ahead at the remaining Apaches. "Now let's hope we won't be similarly surprised!"

Three Tongues watched the remainder of the Apaches until one of them reined his horse in Three Tongues' direction and took up a position in front of him. Then he quickly yelled his Apache battle cry, clamped his heels into the sides of his pony and raised his battleaxe, charging the Comanche. Three Tongues didn't move until the Apache was close

226

enough to suit his purpose, then he quickly reached for one of the knives which rested on his shoulders and threw it at the charging Apache. The knife sank, causing the Apache to fall backward off his horse.

Now faint shots could be heard from the direction of the herd. The startled Apaches glanced in that direction and saw that one who had been sent to take charge of the herd retreating, the Comanches hot on their heels, rapidly shortening the distance between them.

"Now!" Nat yelled and the American Team opened fire, dropping thirteen Apaches instantly. The surprise of seeing the Comanches and the rifle fire from the Americans caused the Apaches to retreat in complete disarray as they left their dead behind. That action alone would bring much disgrace to them when they returned to their village.

Nat now ordered his team not to pursue the Apaches. "All good leaders have a plan to cover a retreat if that becomes necessary and because this raid was planned well in advance, no doubt they have such a plan, it would be foolish for us to ride into an ambush. Let's go back to our cattle and permit them to return to their dead. Let's hope that they abandon any plan of taking our cattle after this."

"What kind of Apaches were they?" Wilbur asked.

"Mescaleros," Fernando spoke up before anyone else could answer.

"How do you know that?" Wilbur asked once more.

"Because in this country, one will see only Lipan or Mescalero Apaches and it is a well known fact that the Lipans resemble the Comanches in their style of dress. These Apaches were not dressed like Comanches so that leaves us with only one answer. Although on some occasions, the Jicarilla Apaches hunt this far south, it would be unusual, for they usually hunt in northern New Mexico, the panhandle of Texas and southern Colorado."

Three Tongues heard these comments as he rode up to them and added, "The Chiricahua also hunt here for buffalo or join forces with the Lipans or Mescaleros to hunt Comanches! In the Guadalupe and Sacremento Mountains, though, its a good bet that Mescaleros are the Apaches that you'll see. Those two mountain ranges are part of their stronghold but the White Mountains are their sacred mountains and it is there that their hearts lie."

"It seems then," Wilbur commented, "that we will more than likely have a lot of problems with the Mescalero Apaches. After all, we will be ranching not far from their strongholds."

"You are right about that," Spirit said before her husband could speak.

"We'd better get back to the herd," was Nat's contribution to the exchange.

A silence fell as they rode back toward the herd as each of them contemplated the possibility. "We have a few hours of daylight left and we'll hope to make camp tomorrow night at the junction of the Rio Penasco and Pecos Rivers. Travis will decide where and when we will make camp tonight," Nat offered.

When they were back with the herd, Many Horses spoke, "We'll go now, but if I were you, I'd watch out for Apaches from now on. They are all over this area, and the ones we just fought will try to avenge the fallen braves. Remember, if the Apache does not want to be seen, he will not be seen. He is a master at concealment and illusion and he usually does not attack if he believes that braves will be lost, so keep your weapons at hand at all times and be prepared to use them at a moment's notice. This will be your best defense against Apaches. Do not underestimate their intelligence for, if you do, you will be the loser. They are cunning, swift, deadly with a bow and arrow, and have no morality to hinder their methods of getting what they want." Thus spoke one of the Apaches' deadly and traditional enemies.

"I'll remember all of that," Nat said soberly, "and I want to thank you for your help. I hope some day we'll be able to return the favor."

"It will be many years before we can repay you and Otto for the rifles and other supplies which you gave us back on the Santa Fe Trail. It is for us to thank you. Until we meet again." Many Horses wheeled his pony and galloped away, followed by his war party.

The American Team continued on up the Pecos River, passing the junction of the Hondo and the Pecos and when they reached where the Arroyo del Macho entered the Pecos, they turned northwest and headed toward Pinos Wells. As they moved onward, the terrain became less flat and open and took on a gradual rise which was studded with pinons, cedar, juniper and mesquite. As they continued, the brush gave way to more trees as they rode farther away from the wide Pecos Valley. Herds of deer and elk numbering in the hundreds were spooked by the approaching cattle.

"What are those mountains over to our far left called?" Nat asked Three Tongues.

"The ones nearest us are called La Sierra and the one farther north and west of them are called the Jicarillas."

"What are they like?" Nat asked.

"The further you travel up the slopes of these mountain, the thicker the forest becomes. At first the trees are almost entirely pinon, cedar, and juniper with a few Ponderosa pines scattered among them, but the reverse becomes true as you climb higher, until the trees become huge. If any of our cattle get into those mountains, we may have to give them up for lost, not because of the forest and thick underbrush, but because of some of the treacherous terrain which the mountains conceal from us at this distance. It is murderous with its rocky mountain slides, which are so steep that vegetation will not grow. When the rain and snow falls, the moisture loosens the shale on the surface of the cliffs and permits it to slide downward, cutting the vegetation like a knife and burying it beneath tons of shale rock.

"Mountain lion and bear are plentiful and will prey upon any cows foolish enough to stray into the mountains, and then there are always the Apaches! The many bands of Apaches who scatter themselves throughout the mountains venture out of their strongholds in groups of from two to many more and bring death and destruction to all who attempt to get too close, who try to trespass upon their tribal lands. We will have many visits from them as we build our ranch and we must be eternally vigilant concerning them or we will surely all perish. No one can invade what the Apaches consider their domain and not expect resistance; strong, forthright resistance."

"If we can hold our ground until the United States military arrives and builds their forts, they will furnish protection of a sort and we will survive from that time on. Time will be on our side!" Nat spoke confidently as he turned to look at his friend who rode beside him.

"You are right," Three Tongues answered. "The question, is, however, will we survive until the soldiers arrive?"

"We'll give it our best effort," Jim interrupted. "Who knows, we may even be able to reach some kind of understanding with the Apaches."

"You really don't believe that do you, Jim?" Three Tongues looked at him in surprise.

"Anything is possible, don't you think?"

"Not with the Apaches, I don't. You don't know them as I do. I don't hold any illusions about their letting us alone to prosper unmolested on the fringes of their stronghold. The extreme opposite is more likely in my view."

"Well, only time will tell," Nat commented. "In the meantime, we will heed your counsel and be forever prepared for any eventuality."

In the rolling country north of the Jicarillas, the cattle were allowed to graze and the American Team began to make plans for the construction of the permanent buildings and corrals which they would need on their ranch. They would build on the same small mesa in the sheltered valley where they had built their temporary cabins. The higher location gave them a commanding view for miles around.

Through Fernando's supervision, adobe bricks were made and left to season in the hot, dry sunlight. It was not long before adobe walls were being laid and some semblance of homes began to take shape.

Rees, Nat, and Travis went to the mountains to cut vigas or beams for the ceilings. "I've been with you all for quite a spell now, Travis said as they rode slowly up the lower slopes of the Jicarillas and I've grown attached to you all. I like what you believe in and our closeness to one another. You're like a big family and I like that. Would you have any objection if I stayed on?"

Nat turned in his saddle to look at him and said, "You're our kind of person, too, Travis, and who knows the cattle business better than you? It would be a load off our minds if you climbed aboard and advised us on the cattle ranching business."

CHAPTER XIII

The Apache woman was sitting by the fire with her two small sons when they heard a horse outside their tepee. "He is back!" Evening Star rose to her feet eagerly as she glanced at her sons. "Now we will learn more about the white eyes on the other side of the Jicarillas."

The flap of the tepee was thrust aside and Thunderbolt stooped and entered. He smiled as he looked at each member of his family.

"Sit," Evening Star invited her husband. "I will bring your food."

"What have you found out about the white eyes who are beginning to ranch north of the Jicarillas?" Their oldest son looked up at his father inquiringly.

Thunderbold sank down near the fire and reached for the bowl which his wife held out to him. She sat down once more and said, "The bread and meat are before you. What news do you bring of the white eyes?"

"According to what I could find out in Santa Fe, some people think that the one who is called Jim is in reality the Macedonian."

"The Macedonian?" Evening Star questioned. "Is that name suppose to have some significance?"

Their two sons both tried to answer their mother at once, eager to tell her of what their friends had said, but their father stopped them and then continued. "Little is known about the one they call the Macedonian although there are many stories concerning this man of mystery." Thunderbolt helped himself to another helping of the food before him and took several bites before he began once more, "It is a story which is hard to believe," Thunderbolt said after a hesitation. "That is, if it is true, of course. And if this Jim is really the one called the Macedonian.

"Many Indians believe that he is a god. That is what we have found out about him, but it seem that most of the others with him follow his philosophy, especially the leader of the white eyes and his friend, Rees. Both of them came to the west together from back east, where you come from, my wife.

"The one they call Rees is more Indian than white eyes in appearance and he has taught all he knows to Nat whom he considers as a son. Nat married a woman who is half white eyes as our children are, and she is called Snow Skin. Her mother is with them and it is said that she was captured by the Comanches years ago and also has a son called Three Tongues who is also half Comanche. Her name is Spirit now, but she was called Spirit Woman before she married Jim, who is apparently the Macedonian."

Thunderbolt then went on to relate the history of the others as he learned it and told his family that they were called the American Team. When he had finished, they were quiet, thinking of what they had learned, until Evening Star spoke. "You have just described the future of the United States, my husband. This American Team which you speak of is made up of good people as shown by their actions. If anyone is permitted to settle near us, it should be people like them. But remember, all Americans are not of their thinking, for many will come to kill, cheat, and steal, and they will continue to do this until we cannot resist them any longer. As I have told you many times in the past, our ways are nearing an end.

"I think we should cultivate the friendship of the American Team because they could be very useful in the days ahead and we should counsel the rest of our people to do the same. It is the best thing that we can do if we expect to preserve some form of our culture for the future."

Thunderbolt sat in deep thought and then spoke slowly, "We must ask for a gathering of all Mescalero bands to be held as soon as possible so that I may present your mother's proposal to them."

Even as the Mescalero grand council was in session, a band of renegade Apaches who opposed such action were on their way to attack the three men as they selected and cut the tall pines which were to be used for the vigas in their homes.

Rees stopped swinging his axe and laid it against the trunk of the tree he was chopping. "We have company." He reached for his rifle as he looked downwind. "Ten or fifteen of them, I'd say."

Nat and Travis sensed the danger also, for they too had laid their axes aside and picked up the rifles which lay nearby. They formed a circle as they listened and watched for the Apaches they sensed were drawing nearer.

"There's a buck deer," Travis whispered to Rees. He motioned with his head in the direction of the buck. Rees studied the area for a few seconds and then whispered softly, "That's no deer."

"What is it if isn't a deer?" Travis was indignant, "I guess I know a deer when I see one."

Rees never took his eyes from the form as he answered Travis, "Why would a buck move in our direction and since when does a deer's hind-quarters move a step or two after the front legs have stopped?"

"What?" Travis took a closer look at the object of their attentions. "By golly, you're right, Rees. Three Tongues is right when he says they're good at creating an illusion."

"Those Apaches killed that deer and two of them have taken cover under the hide. I'll get the front end and you get the rear."

The two men raised their rifles and within a second or two, they both fired, dropping the two Apaches. The lead Apache fell first and the one impersonating the hindquarters staggered before he fell. A stillness again fell over the forest until, a few minutes afterward, the Apaches could be heard yelling their war cries as they galloped off with plenty of fanfare.

"I guess we've seen the last of them," Travis lowered his rilfe and look-ed in the direction which the Apaches had taken. He glanced at the others for confirmation.

"When are you going to learn the ways of the Indian, Travis?" Nat softened his remark with a grin as his eyes continued to search for any movement in the trees which surround them.

"You heard them hightail it out of here, didn't you? They turned tail and skidaddled," Travis said with satisfaction.

"They sure wanted you to think that," Nat said quietly. "They made too much commotion in their retreat to suit me. They acted as if they wanted us to think they have given up the fight and fled."

"What are you getting at?"

"Nat is right," Rees interrupted impatiently. "It is my guess there are Apaches still out there just waiting for us to let our guard down and when we do, they'll strike."

"Let's accommodate them, then," Nat suggested.

"Let's, laddie!" Rees turned and gave Nat a smile. "Travis, you and Nat begin to chop again and I'll watch for Apaches!"

The two men began to talk louder now, louder and normal, between chops of their axes, Rees put in a word now and then as he kept a lookout. Finally he muttered, "I've spotted one . . . I'll keep an eye on him and see if I can find any more. Keep chopping, we don't want to tip our hands."

For long moments there was no sound except for the steady chopping as Rees watched the Apache draw nearer. He took careful aim and squeezed the trigger. Once more the other two men took up their rifles and the three watched for any additional movement among the bushes and trees. The silence was broken finally when Nat whispered, "I smell horses. I think the others are back."

"You're right there, laddie," Rees replied slowly. He rested on his right knee and slid another shell into the chamber of his rifle. His eyes probed the forest in all directions for any further sign.

"How many do you think are left?" Travis spoke softly.

"Enough to do us under," Rees answered.

"They sure don't discourage too easily," Travis conceded as he watched the surroundings forest nervously for any sign of movement. "Three Tongues says that Apaches will not fight if they think they cannot win or will have heavy losses."

"We'll see if that applies to this pack of coyotes," Nat muttered. "They have lost three and we've lost none up to now."

"Can any of you smell horsehide any longer?" Rees broke in.

Nat and Travis strained their sense of smell and finally Nat replied, "You're right, Rees. The horses are gone; they may have given up the fight."

Rees slowly rose to his feet and a bowstring hum could be heard as an arrow pierced the air and struck Rees in the chest. Nat turned quickly toward Rees as Rees grasped at the arrow with his left hand and fell backward. Nat rushed to Rees and knelt by his side as a lone horse could be heard galloping away. Nat heard Rees gasp his last words, "Oh, life's been good . . ." Rees then grabbed at Nat's hand weakly and squeezed it as life left his body.

Rees' body was brought back to the ranch headquarters and the other members of the American Team showed their sadness and disbelief at the loss of this unique man. Not a dry eye could be seen as Rees's body was gently lowered from the saddle by Nat, who carried him in his arms to the shade of a cedar tree. He gently laid the body of his friend on the brown cedar needles and adjusted his arms and legs and then stood up. With great effort, as he brushed the tears from his eyes he said, "We will bury this friend and proud American beneath this giant cedar. It is only fitting that one giant should spread it's protective limbs over the body of another giant, and protect Rees from the scorching sun of summer and the cold snows of the winter." As Nat stood up and looked westward from the spot where he had laid his friend, teacher, and companion, he felt a slight breeze and saw the bell-shaped flowers of the yucca plants which studded the mesa before him, bend in the breeze. "No one can hear your bells ring but Rees," Nat murmured as he watched the creamy colored bell shapes of the yuccas swing in the breeze as if they were hanging from a church belfrey. They seemed to symbolize the deep love which Rees had for the great wilderness where he'd spent most of his life.

They took turns at digging Rees' grave and when all was ready, he was wrapped in a blanket and lowered into it. The dirt was slowly and gently shoveled over the body and when the mound was complete, the women smoothed the dirt with their hands and Nat placed a cross at the head of the grave. He then stood, moved over behind the cross, cleared his throat and said, "Rees, you were of the first generation to adopt America as its country. You have served her well. You and men like you have developed and nurtured the West to maturity. Most Americans do not know of your deeds or will never hear your name. My French Canadian, American friend, teacher, and partner, I speak for all Americans, present, past, and future when I say thank you for being an American. Thank you for honoring our soil with your body. Amen."

Now four Apaches were seen as they rode toward them across the prairie. A woman rode in the lead and in her hand she carried a bouquet of wild flowers. An Apache warrior and two small boys followed her. The warrior was unarmed and his face, was well as the faces of the boys, was painted black. When they reached the spot where the Americans were gathered, they halted. No one on either side spoke as the Apaches looked down at the grave. The Apache woman slolwy turned her eyes from the grave and looked at Spirit, but said nothing. Spirit returned the look as they studied one another. It was then that Jim realized that the Apache woman was a white woman, probably having lived through a situation similar to that of Spirit. Now the woman dismounted and slowly walked to the grave and placed the flowers against the wooden cross. She then bowed her head and closed her eyes as if in prayer.

The American Team watched in complete silence and when she opened her eyes again she returned to her horse and mounted. She then turned to the Americans and said, "I am called Evening Star and my husband," she turned her head slightly to her right, "is called Thunderbolt." She then turned her head to her left and said. "These are my sons." Evening Star's pride in her family was evident as she introduced them. Then she continued. "The Apaches who have done this evil thing to you are renegade Apaches, outlaws as you call them. The Mescalero Apaches are not responsible for their behavior. We neither condone this action or sympathize with it. Rather, we deplore such actions. We hope that you will not hold all of our people responsible for the actions of a few who attacked and killed your friend.

"We must always remember that both of our societies have people in them who break the law. You have just seen that kind of Apache. You have them also, and will continue to see them in your own society. Let us hope that you and the law abiding Mescaleros whom I speak for can live in peace, side by side, you here on the plains and we in our mountain strongholds. The Mescalero Grand Council wishes it to be so, for it has spoken."

As she ceased speaking, she looked in turn at her husband and then at her sons and they reined their ponies and rode slowly away.

"Those Apaches knew that Rees was their friend, even though they had never met him," Nat said in a low voice as they watched the four riders disappear in the distance. "They realized that a deep injustice had been done to Rees and they came to try to rectify it as best they could."

As the American Team watched the Apaches ride away, only Spirit noticed her husband as he slipped quietly back to the grave of his friend, Rees. Spirit watched as Jim stood reverently by the grave, and she could see that he was speaking although she could not hear his words. Then slowly Jim reached into his shirt and removed his Macedonian flute. He raised it to his lips and began to play. As the first note floated serenely through the air, the members of the American Team turned their heads in Jim's direction and remained in silence as they listened. The sweet lilting sounds which escaped from Jim's flute were those of a Macedonian sheepherder's tune, that which was played as a last tribute for a relative or friend high in the Pindus Mountains of Macedonia. It was a sad but soothing sound which reached the ears of the listeners they realized that Jim was saying his personal goodbye to his friend Rees in this most ancient and time honored method of the Macedonian people.

Upon hearing the flute, the Apaches halted and they too turned to watch the tall buckskin clad figure silhouetted against the clear blue New Mexico sky. Rees must have been pleased as he looked down upon the gathering of people who were the future of America. His smile of approval would surely insure a bright future for his adopted country.

236

www.ingramcontent.com/pod-product-compliance
Lightning Source LLC
Chambersburg PA
CBHW031946010726
47493CB00007B/2098